"Are you still mad at my daddy?" Tres asked.

Regina and Thomas's eyes met over the boy's head. She silently pleaded with Thomas for help. He held her gaze and waited for her answer, offering no help.

"Well, are you?" Justin, Regina's son, chimed in.

"No, I'm not angry at anyone," Regina answered.

"Well, give him a hug," the very bossy Tres instructed.

"Go ahead, Mama, give him a hug and a kiss," Justin echoed.

Thomas held his arms open wide and Regina stepped into them. He wrapped her in a warm, firm embrace that felt to her like a welcome home. She stood close to him, enjoying the warmth of his body and listening to the rhythm of his heart.

"You've got to kiss and make up," Tres said, giggling.

"Yeah, kiss him," Justin agreed.

Regina rose on tiptoe and moved to plant a kiss on Thomas's cheek at the same time that Thomas lowered his head. Her lips missed their target and their lips met. A thrilling warmth swept through her body.

Slowly and gently, he coaxed her mouth open with his tongue. At first, she was shocked by his boldness, and then she gave in to the burning pleasure, hoping that she would not self-ignite.

Regina gave herself completely to the feel of his lips on hers, his tongue teasing hers. She was in a timeless place until she heard the applause.

She pulled away. Thomas looked as lost as she.

BOOK YOUR PLACE ON OUR WEBSITE AND MAKE THE ARABESQUE ROMANCE CONNECTION!

We've created a customized website just for our very special Arabesque readers, where you can get the inside scoop on everything that's going on with Arabesque romance novels.

When you come online, you'll have the exciting opportunity to:

- View covers of upcoming books

- Learn about our future publishing schedule (listed by publication month and author)

- Find out when your favorite authors will be visiting a city near you

- Search for and order backlist books

- Check out author bios and background information

- Send e-mail to your favorite authors

- Join us in weekly chats with authors, readers and other guests

- Get writing guidelines

- AND MUCH MORE!

Visit our website at
http://www.arabesquebooks.com

SWEET DESIRE

CHRISTINE TOWNSEND

BET Publications, LLC
http://www.bet.com
http://www.arabesquebooks.com

ARABESQUE BOOKS are published by

BET Publications, LLC
c/o BET BOOKS
One BET Plaza
1900 W Place NE
Washington, DC 20018-1211

All Kensington Titles, Imprints, and Distributed Lines are
available at special quantity discounts for bulk purchases for
sales promotions, premiums, fund-raising, and educational
or institutional use. Special book excerpts or customized
printings can also be created to fit specific needs. For details,
write or phone the office of the Kensington special sales
manager: Kensington Publishing Corp., 850 Third Avenue,
New York, NY 10022, attn: Special Sales Department,
Phone: 1-800-221-2647.

First Printing: February 2004
10 9 8 7 6 5 4 3 2 1

Printed in the United States of America

GRATITUDE

First and foremost, I praise God from whom all blessings flow. I thank Him for James, the real-life romance hero to whom I've been married for the past twenty years, and our two wonderful teenage children who have taught me so much. They have been wonderfully supportive and understanding when I hide away each evening to delve into my world of fictional characters.

I am blessed with three fantastic sisters, Lois Shelton, Mary Harris, and Joyce Townsend, who have read my manuscripts and told all their friends that my book was a "must read." I thank God for such wonderful, patient, and encouraging friends as Elveeta Timmons, Gwynn Crutcher, Thelma Osborne, and Dr. Millicent Lownes-Jackson, who allowed me to bounce ideas off of them and ask endless questions, and yet who still love me. I am indebted to my friends in the on-line writing group, FictionFolks, for generously sharing their knowledge and experience.

Finally, but just as importantly, I am truly blessed to have worked with the kind, gentle folks at BET who guided me through my writing debut.

> *"Bless the Lord, O my soul, and forget not His benefits. . . ."*
>
> *Psalm* 103:2

ACKNOWLEDGMENTS

In attempting to write about a subject of which I had little knowledge, I relied on research. To learn more about lupus, I explored the Lupus Site, http://www.uklupus.co.uk/, and the Web site for the Lupus Foundation of America: http://www.lupus.org,

For a greater understanding of the charges of academic fraud against which Thomas had to defend himself, I went to the National Collegiate Athletic Association (NCAA) Web site: http://www.ncaa.org.

While I was writing this manuscript, Otis Blackwell's obituary appeared in my local newspaper. The facts about him were published on-line in the Tennessean.com. I was fascinated with Mr. Blackwell's prolific songwriting career and the hits for which he'd been responsible. To review the article you may go to www.tennessean.com/obits/archives/02/05/17210598.shtml?Element_ID=17210598.

How could I write a book about a black woman in the country music industry without mentioning Frankie Staton? She graced the local airwaves on the *Ralph Emery Show* for many years. When she disappeared from sight, it took a while to realize what was missing from my mornings. I read about her in the *St. Petersburgh Times*, at www.sptimes.com/News/042400/news_pf/Floridian/Belting_It_Out.shtml.

Chapter 1

The doorbell rang a third time before Regina could dry her hands on the kitchen towel. "Hold your horses," she shouted as she ran the short distance down the hall to the front door.

The doorbell rang again as she passed the staircase and entered the foyer. "I'm coming! I'm coming!" she shouted at the still closed door. When she threw the front door open, she stood face-to-face with a tall, stout, middle-aged woman with a broad gray streak in the center of her hair.

"Hi," Regina said in a friendly voice, swallowing her surprise at seeing a stranger at her front door.

"Hello, my name is Nadine Simmons. I think you already know my grandson, Tres," the woman said, indicating the child standing next to her that Regina had not noticed.

"Hello, Tres. We haven't seen you around for a while," Regina said, bending toward the young man and offering her hand for a shake.

"I know. I've been going to work with my dad every day after school," the self-confident young man answered.

"Well, it's good to see you today."

"It's good to see you, too."

Standing again, Regina looked at the older woman.

"How are you today, Mrs. Simmons? I believe I've seen you with Tres at Peabody School a couple of times. Tres and my son, Justin, are in the same class."

"Yes, I am visiting my son. Tres is my grandson. Do you mind if I come in?" she asked.

"Of course you may. Excuse my manners. Please come in," Regina said, opening the door wider and stepping back. She ushered her guests into the large, spacious family room to the right. The cathedral ceiling added volume to the huge room, but peach-colored walls and creamy leather furniture gave it a warm, cozy atmosphere. Every wall featured a colorful oil painting. Shelves on either side of the fireplace displayed brightly colored pieces of ceramic art, along with books and photographs.

Mrs. Simmons looked around the room carefully and, seemingly satisfied, she focused her attention on Regina. "Your artwork is beautiful," she commented.

"I like to support the local arts community," Regina replied. "Please have a seat," she continued, indicating the love seat before she settled onto the big over-stuffed chair.

"Please excuse my intrusion, but I need your help. I, um, need to ask you a favor," Mrs. Simmons finished with less confidence than she'd started.

"What can I do for you?" Regina asked curiously.

"I came to Nashville to take care of Tres for my son. He's on the road recruiting for his basketball team at Renaissance University and I promised that I'd take care of Tres, but I just received word that my husband has been taken to the emergency room back home. He has symptoms of a heart attack and I need to go home right away," she said, twisting a well-worn tissue in her hands.

Regina leaned forward in her chair. "What can I do for you?" she repeated, gently laying her small hand over the older woman's trembling one.

"I don't know who'll take care of Tres. I can't take him home with me because I have no one there to care for him while I'm at the hospital. I've called Tommy, my son, and I can't reach him. The automatic message on his cell phone keeps telling me that he's not available. I don't even know for sure where he is today." Panic was rising in the older woman's voice.

"It's okay," Regina said. "I'll take care of Tres for you. He's been over to play with my son. He'll be safe here with Justin and me. Give me your son's cell phone number and your phone number. I'll try to reach him for you. Justin is upstairs taking a nap."

"Tres told me that he's been over to play with Justin. That's one of the reasons that I thought that you would help us," Mrs. Simmons said, now much calmer. "I hate to impose, but I have no choice under the circumstances. I hope you don't mind."

"I would say no if I minded. You have other things to worry about. I assure you, Tres is in good hands. Don't think any more about his care. Do you need a ride to the airport?"

"No, no. I don't want to put you out any more than I already have. I'll take a taxi," Mrs. Simmons said, obviously anxious to leave. "I'll put some things in a bag for Tres and bring it over. Tommy, that's my son, is not due back until the end of the week, but I'm sure that when we reach him, he'll return right away," she said, rushing toward the front door.

After his grandmother left, Tres spoke up. "May I play with Justin's Mega Blaster?" he asked.

"I'll tell you what," Regina answered, "since Justin is in his room asleep, I'll go up and get it for you. You can play with it down here. Have you had a nap yet?"

"I don't take naps anymore," the child said proudly.

"Oh, you don't? Aren't you a five-year-old?"

"Yes, but kindergarten children don't take naps."

"Don't you ever get tired and want to take a rest?"

"Never," the five-year-old said firmly.

"Well, you sit here and watch *Barney*, while I go get the Mega Blaster."

"I don't watch *Barney* anymore," Tres said.

Regina raised an eyebrow and left the room. The five-year-old sitting on the floor in her living room was a lot older than the five-year-old upstairs taking a nap. If he was going to stay with her, she and Tres were going to have to come to an understanding. Every day after school, Justin took a nap. Nap times gave her a chance to work on her music.

She entered Justin's room and looked at the sleeping child. He had kicked all of the covers to the bottom of the bed and had turned nearly sideways across the mattress. His rough sleeping habits were one of the reasons that she hated sharing a bed with him. She covered her son, grabbed the Mega Blaster, and rushed from the room.

Reentering the family room, Regina was in for a small shock. Her houseguest had taken books off the bottom shelves and used them as a step stool so that he could reach a ceramic firgurine on one of the top shelves. Regina shook her head before speaking. "Tres, I put that statue up high so that little boys can't get to it," she said sternly. "Please put it back and then put the books back on the shelf."

"I don't want to. I want to play with it," Tres said.

"It's not a toy. You may not play with it," Regina said.

"I like it. I'll take it over here and see if it rolls," Tres said, jumping from the stack of books.

"Listen here, young man, that's my statue and I said that you may not play with it. Bring it to me."

Tres looked at the brightly colored object in his hand and then looked at Regina. Sensing that she meant business, he reluctantly placed it in her out-stretched hand. "Thank you so much, Tres. I like it when you obey me. Do you want the Mega Blaster now?"

"No, I want to go play in Justin's room," Tres said, racing toward the stairs.

Regina dashed after him and caught him around his waist. "Justin is still asleep in his room. You may play down here until Justin's nap time is over," she said calmly.

"Okay," he said and headed toward the family room. Before she could breathe a sigh of relief, Tres said, "I'm hungry. Do you have peanut butter and jelly?"

"Sure I do. Would you like me to make you a sandwich?"

"Yes, I would."

"Okay. Come to the kitchen with me," Regina said. She didn't dare leave the child in a room alone again. While she made the sandwich, Tres chatted brightly about a boy named Bryan at school who beat up on everyone.

"Why do you think Bryan fights so much?" Regina asked Tres.

"I don't know."

"Have you ever fought with him?" Regina asked.

"Yes."

"Did he hurt you?"

"Yes."

"What did your teacher say when you told her about his fighting you?"

"She said don't fight. But he likes to fight anyway."

"Did you tell your father?"

"Yes."

"What did he say?"

"He said that I have to be a man and to stop whining," Tres said in a very grown-up voice.

Regina winced. One of her pet peeves was adults who expected children to act like adults. Her firm belief was that a child should act like a child and be treated like a child.

She didn't know Mr. Simmons well, but he'd been pleasant enough when she'd spoken to him on the rare occasions that they were outside at the same time. A few months ago, when Tres had wandered across the street to their house after seeing Justin playing in the yard, she'd been concerned for the child's safety. Without a second thought, she'd looked up his number in the neighborhood directory and called him immediately. The father had been unfazed, asking her to send his son home when she grew tired of his visit.

"I'll talk to your father," she found herself saying, doubting as she spoke that it would do any good. "Someone needs to help Bryan stop fighting. The next time he wants to fight, just tell him that you don't want to fight with him."

"But I like to fight," Tres said.

Regina sighed and spread a layer of jelly on the peanut butter already on the soft bread. The child probably liked to fight because his father expected him to take care of himself. If his father was the custodial parent, his mother's parenting skills must be reprehensible.

After making the sandwich for Tres, she noticed that he was not actually hungry. He nibbled his peanut butter and jelly sandwich, but he did seem to enjoy Regina's company. He devoured her attention and entertained her with story after story so that she would give him her undivided attention.

While Tres was still sitting at the kitchen counter playing with his sandwich, Justin came down from his nap and asked for a PBJ also. He was delighted to see Tres at his house. As soon as he finished his sandwich and a glass of milk, the boys went up to Justin's room to play.

Regina tried the cell phone number for Thomas Simmons a few more times while working in her office. Still no answer. She pulled out the itinerary Mrs. Simmons had left with her and tried the number for the hotel where she'd been told the coaches would spend the night. The front desk told her that they had not checked in yet.

Regina was still in her office trying to finish up a song when the boys rushed in with arms full of Lego blocks. They lay on the floor for assembling Go-Bot action figures when she became distracted by their play. She listened intently and was fascinated by their imaginations. They were making elaborate plans for the invasion of another planet. She had to suppress a smile at their pronunciation of some words, but she was impressed, nonetheless, with their strategies.

Before the invasion was complete, however, Tres was ready to go back into the family room to play a video game. "Wait just a minute, young men," Regina called after them. "Take your toys with you."

"We'll get them later," Tres replied as he led the way from the room.

At the sound of her voice, Justin stopped in his tracks, turned around, and gathered up the blocks. Regina thought of ordering Tres to come back and help him, but reconsidered. With luck, his father would come retrieve him first thing in the morning and his habits would no longer be her problem. She was growing a little vexed with his general air of disobedience.

"I'll get everything, Tres," Justin said, seeing the look of disapproval on his mother's face and not wanting her to do battle with his newly found best friend.

"Thank you very much, precious." Regina rewarded

her son with a smile. "I appreciate you helping keep my music room clean and safe. It would hurt if I stepped on one of those in the dark."

While Justin hurriedly gathered up the blocks and joined Tres in the family room, Thomas and his assistant were meeting with their top prospect for the new recruiting season. They had flown into Newark International Airport the previous evening and had met with prospective players and their families well into the night. That morning the coaches had taken a train into Elizabeth, New Jersey, to attend a basketball showcase where they'd seen more than a hundred dunks in the first few hours of play.

One hundred fifty coaches from as far away as Texas, Kansas, and Florida courted unsigned and uncommitted high school players from New York, New Jersey, Connecticut, and Pennsylvania. Some of the finest basketball players in the northeastern United States had attended the showcase, but Thomas knew that he needed a special kind of player for Renaissance University. He was convinced that Conway Howard was the kind of player that he wanted on his team. Now his job was to convince Conway's parents to let their seventeen-year-old son move to Tennessee.

Thomas and his assistant took the Howards to dinner. While they were finishing dinner, Conway's father caught Thomas off guard when he said, "I know that recruiting my son is a business for you, so let's cut to the chase. What does your small school down South have to offer my son that he can't get at one of the big conference schools that's already put their money on the table?"

Thomas carefully aligned his knife and fork across his plate, gathering his thoughts before speaking. "I know that Syracuse, Villanova, and the University of Connecticut want to sign your son. I have to admit that I was intimidated by the schools that want Conway and I almost passed on talking with him. I figured that a midsized school like mine wouldn't stand a chance," he said, looking Mr. Howard squarely in the eye. "But, after I looked at his academic record, I knew that it would be unfair to your son to pass over him. He deserves the opportunity that we can offer him at Renaissance. He's bright and intelligent. At a big school he'll get lost in the shuffle. At Renaissance he would be a star in both academics and athletics. We'll take pride in developing all of his skills. In fact, I would put our alumni up against the alumni from any school in the nation. Do you know that our goal is to see that ninety-three percent of our players graduate in four years with a degree?"

"That's awfully ambitious," Mrs. Howard, said leaning forward.

"We're on our way to achieving that goal. Since I became head coach, I have sought students who will not only give us a winning team, but those who will benefit from the academic challenges that our institution offers. We do not use the term student athlete loosely. We make certain that our students go to class consistently and that they are prepared when they go," Thomas said, moving into the sales pitch that he'd repeated so many times. He could say it in his sleep, but because of his commitment to his basketball program and to the young men it, he always said it with complete sincerity.

"Tell us about your business school. You know we want Conway to major in business and come back home to help me with my company," Mr. Howard said, prompting Thomas.

The assistant coach spoke up. "I am a business school graduate myself. Our program at Renaissance is fully accredited and corporations all over the country come on campus to hire our students. Since we know that very few of our athletes will go on to play ball professionally, we make sure that they are well prepared for life when they leave our campus."

After hours of intense grilling from the boy's parents, Thomas and his assistant returned to their hotel without a commitment. The Howards said that it was still too early for them to make a firm one and they wanted more time to think. Thomas discreetly reminded them that it was already April and slots for most teams were filling up rapidly.

Thomas sat on the side of his bed in the hotel, exhausted but satisfied. He'd felt a rapport with Conway Howard. While the young man had not said much with his parents present, he'd told Thomas earlier that he was very interested in attending school in Tennessee. He wanted the black college experience and he thought it would be exciting to be so far from home. *We'll see, we'll see*, Thomas thought to himself as he unbuttoned his shirt.

Maybe he'd have time to call Tres. Glancing at his watch, Thomas realized it was too late to call home. Although it would be only ten o'clock in Nashville, he knew that his mother would have a fit. Thank God she had come to take care of Tres. If he had left his son with anyone else he would have called home every hour. With his mother in charge, everything would go as smoothly as if he were there.

Although it was also bedtime in Nashville, Tres was not yet asleep. Regina turned off the lights downstairs, set the security alarm, and headed upstairs with a glass of water and an apple. That's when she noticed Tres

sitting up in the twin bed in Justin's room. She stepped
into the room to see what was wrong.

"Hey, young man, aren't you sleepy?" she asked, trying to keep the concern out of her voice.

"No. My daddy always calls me to say good night and
he hasn't called yet," Tres said, sounding worried.

"Let's call him then. Come to my room with me so
that we won't wake up Justin." Regina helped the child
into his house shoes and led him down the hall to her
room. She sat on the side of her king-sized bed and
lifted the cordless phone from its cradle. Letting the
phone ring longer than her patience normally would
have allowed, she gave up waiting for an automatic
voice mail to click in. She hung up and redialed the
hotel.

When the phone answered on the other end, she
asked the clerk if she was sure that Mr. Thomas Simmons had checked in. The clerk told her she was
certain he had. She assured Regina she was well aware
of who Mr. Simmons was and she knew for certain that
he was still out for the evening. She knew, she assured
Regina, because Mr. Simmons would be hard not to
notice.

While Regina pondered what she meant, the clerk
asked, "Would you like to leave a message for him? I'd
be glad to see that he gets it when he returns."

After a moment of thought, Regina decided that she
did not want to leave a message telling him that his father was in the hospital and a virtual stranger was
caring for his son. She decided she'd try again later.

"Your father is still out," she explained to the child
sitting next to her, who was quickly losing his composure. He no longer looked like the self-assured brat
she'd dealt with all day; he was now a five-year-old in
need of comfort. "Would you like to stay in here and
watch TV with me?"

"What are you going to watch? I can't watch any monsters before I go to sleep," he said, some of his usual self-assurance returning.

"I'd like to watch *Monsters Inc.* Would you?"

"Yes, if there are no monsters in it."

"There are monsters, but they won't scare you. They're nice to children." Five minutes into the movie, Regina's guest was snoring lightly.

Early the next morning the ringing phone awakened Regina. She was fully alert when she heard the strong, energetic voice through the receiver. "Hello, this is Nadine Simmons. I'm sorry to call you so early, but I'm about to leave to go back to the hospital. I wondered if you'd heard from my son yet."

"No, I haven't," Regina answered, trying to control the sleepy sound to her voice. "I tried the numbers that you left yesterday, but I never reached him."

"That is so unlike Tommy," Nadine said with a nervous edge to her voice. "I can't believe he didn't call last night. In the past, I've had to remind him that I raised him and I know how to take care of his son. He picked a fine time to take my advice."

"Yes, I guess he did. But Tres is okay. He was a little lonesome for his dad last night, but otherwise everything is all right here. How is your husband?"

"He gave us a real scare, but he's much better. We believe it was probably indigestion rather than a heart attack. They're going to run some more tests and keep him for a few days," Mrs. Simmons answered. "I have to run now. Do you mind if I call you later?"

"It may be more convenient for me to call you. I have to work in the studio this morning after I take the boys to school. We won't be home before three o'clock. Would you like for me to call you then?"

"No, I'll call you. I'll probably be at the hospital still,

but I sure do need to let Tommy know that his father is in the hospital."

"I know," Regina answered sympathetically.

"I'd better let you get moving. Give Tres my love, please," Mrs. Simmons said, ending the conversation.

Thomas decided to let his assistant coach, Isaac Mathews, go on to Texas without him. He felt a need to spend a day at home with Tres. Besides, his mother probably could use a break from his active and talkative son about now.

Surprised when he arrived home at noon to find his house empty, Thomas could not imagine where his mother had taken Tres. Although she didn't know anyone in town, he figured she had gone out and made friends in the couple of days he'd been gone. She was outgoing and would see nothing wrong with introducing herself to his neighbors.

He and Tres usually kept to themselves, but he knew if he had more time he would enjoy getting to know his neighbors. In fact, he was looking forward to meeting that cute little shorty across the street whose son seemed to be about the same age as Tres. He saw her frequently working in her yard, always digging around putting out flowers. She looked real good in her shorts.

Of course, she didn't seem to approve of him. Once when Tres had wandered over there, she'd called to let him know where Tres was. When he didn't panic, he sensed a censure in her comments. What was wrong with a little boy crossing a street in a cul-de-sac to go visit neighbors? He'd also noticed she had tons of friends. Cars were always coming and going at her house. Maybe she'd invite him over one day.

Since his mother and Tres were out, he decided to

head to his office in the Raven Athletic Center on campus. Once there he was not able to get much done. In between answering the phone, which rang incessantly, he called home throughout the afternoon. He had planned to work on his travel vouchers, but his phone demanded all of his attention. When it rang again at three-fifteen, he thought it was more basketball business and was surprised when he heard a very pleasant female voice.

"Mr. Simmons?"

"Yes?"

"I'm your neighbor. Justin's mother," the voice said tentatively.

"Oh, yes, Mrs. . . . ?" he couldn't remember her name to save his life. This was the cute little shorty across the street he'd thought of earlier. Her name completely escaped him.

"Lovejoy—Ms. Lovejoy. I called because Tres has been staying with me. I—uh, your mother brought him over because she needed to return home. Everyone is okay," she hurried to assure him. This was more difficult than she'd anticipated. Expecting Mr. Simmons to be away from his office, she'd only called to see if she could reach someone there who might have a better number for him. She paused and swallowed, preparing to go on.

"Did you say that my family is okay?" he asked, trying to understand why his mother had left Tres with a stranger.

"Yes, your mother—"

Impatiently Thomas interrupted her. "I'll be right there. I should be at your place in fifteen minutes."

Before Regina could answer, Thomas had ended their connection. Minutes later he was on her front doorstep. Tres ran to the door yelling, "Daddy! Daddy!

Daddy!" Justin looked on in misery. He knew that the end was coming to his visit with his friend.

After Thomas had given Tres a bear hug and placed him back on his feet, Tres said, "Daddy, I want you to meet my friend Justin. Justin, this is my dad."

Justin stepped forward in a very mature manner that Regina had never seen before and gave Thomas a handshake. "Do you know my mommy?" Justin asked. "Mommy, this is Tres's dad," Justin said seriously, continuing the introductions.

Regina accepted the hand that Thomas offered her. "I believe we've met before," she said, drawn deeply into Thomas's gorgeous brown eyes that were fringed with velvety eyelashes. His eyes captured her and she could not break the spell that held her. When she finally looked away, her gaze settled on his one-dimpled smile. He wore an amused expression, as if they were sharing a private joke.

"I am so pleased to meet your mommy," Thomas said, holding Regina with his intense gaze, before he finally broke the silence between them. "Thank you for taking care of Tres for me," he said, turning to include Justin.

"Anytime," Justin said, surprising Regina again. When had her little boy become so grown up? she wondered.

"Boys, why don't you go out back and swing until we call you? I need to talk to Mr. Simmons for a few minutes," Regina said after greetings had been exchanged all around.

"What happened that my mother went home so suddenly?" Thomas asked when the boys had left the room.

"She said that your father had been hospitalized. It was an emergency. They thought he'd had a heart attack. But this morning when she called, she said he was

much better and they'll release him in a day or so,"
Regina said, trying to reassure Thomas that everything
was all right.

"My father always has some excuse for my mother to
come home as soon as she gets here. They've been
married thirty-five years and you'd think that he could
stand for her to be out of his sight for a minute."

"Why didn't he come with her?" Regina asked.

"He doesn't want to leave home. He likes his routine, and part of that is to have Mom there with him. I
thought they'd worked things out this time. Since she
hasn't seen Tres since Christmas, I thought she'd want
to stay the week."

He paced around the brightly colored family room.
Regina had the distinct impression that he'd forgotten
her presence for a moment. She was certain of that
fact when he said, almost to himself, "Oh, well, I guess
I'd better call to see if Dad was actually ill or if he was
just crying wolf again."

"I would think that would be a good thing to do,"
Regina said, interrupting his thoughts.

"I care about my father," Thomas began to explain,
defensively, after seeing Regina narrow her slanted
eyes. "It's just that I'm up against a deadline here.
There are very specific rules on when schools can
make contact with prospective players and I can't miss
a day of the contact period."

Regina noted that he looked exhausted as he ran his
hand over his smooth, closely cut hair. "So you really
do need to get back out on the road?" she asked.

"Yes, there's a kid in Dallas that I really wanted to
sign to our team. In fact, we were going to fly directly
out there. But their exhibition game is not until tomorrow night, so I decided to come home first, which
I'm very glad that I did. But this kid is terrific. He's
six feet ten inches tall, averages eighteen points and

twelve assists per game. I'm surprised that he's not signed yet. But his parents are waiting to talk with me. I really need to go."

"I'll take care of Tres for you," Regina found herself offering. "Another child is no problem. Just promise to call him at bedtime. He lost a little sleep waiting for your call last night."

"I'm sorry," Thomas said. "It was so late when I got back to the hotel that I didn't want to wake him. Besides, I would just have gotten the answering machine at my house because I didn't know he was over here."

"That's true," Regina conceded. "And another thing. Your cell phone is absolutely useless. I called and got the recording about fifty times since yesterday morning."

"I'm sorry about that too," he said sheepishly. I forgot the adapter for my charger and ran out of juice. I promise to do better," Thomas said.

"Don't apologize to me. Tres got homesick last night and we wanted to tell you about your father. Frankly, I'm surprised that you're not more concerned about him," Regina said.

"I love my dad, but I doubt that he's ill. Every time Mom has ever come to visit, he has an accident or an illness, which causes her to shorten her visit. The last time she came to visit us, he called within a day to complain that he had thrown his back out working in the backyard and had to have complete bed rest. He wasn't able to warm up the meals that she had prepared for him. She had to rush home to take care of him," Thomas explained, wondering why he felt the need to explain things to Regina. Once again he felt as if she were reprimanding him.

Quick as a wink, Regina's demeanor changed and she flashed him a big, tummy-tingling smile. "It sounds like they understand each other. She doesn't mind too much, does she?"

"No, not at all. She says that if she doesn't take care of him, there are plenty of women willing to do it for her. Can you imagine that after nearly thirty-five years of marriage?" Thomas laughed.

"No, I can't, but it sounds sweet to me. I'm cooking dinner and I need to check on it. I'm not really good in the kitchen and I'm not sure how long these things are supposed to take. Would you like to come into the kitchen with me? Or do you need to get back to your office?"

"If you don't mind, I'd like to run home and call my mother to be sure that Dad really is okay. This could have been the big one, you know? Then I'd like to come back and have dinner with you guys."

"You want to have dinner with us?" she repeated, sounding surprised. "Well, of course you're welcome, but I have to warn you, I don't cook often. One of my friends gave me a recipe that I've gotten pretty good at. It should be safe for you to eat with us tonight. Why don't you leave Tres over here? I can look out the window while I'm cooking and see what they're doing in the backyard."

What had gotten into him? He'd just invited himself to dinner and felt good about it, too. Within thirty minutes Thomas was back with a bottle of white zinfandel. He knew that was a favorite wine for most women. He hoped that Regina was like most women.

After talking to his mother and receiving her assurances that things were under control at home, Thomas had rushed through a shower and changed clothes. He'd felt grimy standing in Regina's immaculate house, smelling her wonderfully sensuous perfume and looking at the nice crisp outfit that she wore. Surely she'd not chased around with two preschool-aged boys all day and still looked so fresh in her starched white shirt and creased jeans. Her only concession to being at home was that she was shoeless.

He stood at her door ringing the doorbell as nervous as a boy on his first date. He knew that she'd only allowed him to come to dinner because he'd invited himself. All he wanted was a little company with a nice neighbor. That was all. His son seemed to be enjoying her son's company. That's all. But, what if there was something more? No, she wasn't his type. She was too petite, barely five feet five, if that. He usually went for the long-legged, athletic types. His wife had been a long-legged athlete.

While his wife had been tall and slender, Regina was petite and more rounded, soft looking with an ample bosom and curvy hips. Now why was he comparing Regina to his wife? She was gone and as everyone told him, he had to move on with his life, especially for the sake of their son. He almost never thought of her when he thought of other women. She belonged in a reserved part of his mind and heart. His memories of her were sacred. No one would ever take her place.

He was trying to gather his wits, when Justin answered the door. "Hi, Mom told me to take you to the family room and Tres and I will entertain you. She took us upstairs to clean us up for dinner, but she's not down yet. She looked in the mirror and said that she needed to clean up, too," Justin explained.

"Oh, I see," Thomas said, trying not to smile at the boy's candidness. He followed Justin to the living room.

"Hi, Daddy," Tres said, barely taking a glance away from the video game he was playing on the large-screen TV.

"Do you want a controller?" Justin asked.

"No, I'll sit over here and watch you guys," Thomas, said, taking a seat on the love seat that faced the TV.

"I'll take that bottle for you," Justin said, noting the wine that Thomas held in his hands.

Thomas looked from the bottle to the little boy. "Show me where the kitchen is and I'll put it in the refrigerator." The large room was bright and pretty with white cabinetry and fancy peach and green curtains framing the bay window. But pots were spilling out of the sink, the cutting board still held bits of apple core, and all the countertops had flour and curry on them. Obviously housekeeping was not Mrs. Lovejoy's forte. He set the wine on the refrigerator rack next to a six-pack of Miller Lite and returned to the boys.

The house smelled good—like spices. The colors of the rooms he passed were warm and inviting. He looked at the pictures on the bookshelf. There were many pictures of Justin, Justin and Regina, and Justin with an older couple, grandparents perhaps? But none of Justin and any man who could be his dad. He wondered where Justin's father was. *I'm just over for a neighborly dinner,* he reminded himself. *She did not ask you for a date.* In fact, she had not even invited him to dinner.

Upstairs Regina hurriedly stepped out of the shower and wrapped herself in a towel. Looking in her vanity mirror, she realized that she'd still have to wait to pluck her eyebrows. The mirror was too steamed up to see. She dashed to her closet to find something suitable to wear. It had to be something casual and comfortable so that Thomas would not think that she had changed clothes just for him. She discarded one outfit after another, tossing them on her bed. Settling on purple linen slacks and a pale lavender linen blouse, she hurriedly dressed and slipped her feet into sandals with three-inch heels. If she didn't wear heels, she would have to hem the slacks.

Passing the vanity mirror, she remembered that she still needed to shape her eyebrows. After all, her eyebrows had started this whole process. She'd simply come upstairs to take some of the surface dirt off the boys before dinner, but when she had finished washing the boys off, she'd decided to freshen her makeup. Adding makeup made her feel so soiled that she'd washed all the makeup off. Once her face was clean, she had noticed that her eyebrows needed shaping. However, it was too painful to pull the eyebrows without steaming them first; thus the shower. Now she'd better hurry downstairs before her neighbor began to wonder if she'd called off dinner.

Thomas smelled her delicious scent before he saw her. She must have floated down the steps because he had not heard her descend the stairs, nor had he heard her come into the family room.

"Everything is ready," she said entering the room. "Come on, boys, let's eat," she called to the boys, who were still engrossed in the video game. To Thomas she said, "I hope you're hungry. I made an apple and chicken curry and I always make too much."

"Oh, that's what I'm smelling. That's a delicious aroma. I know it's going to be as good as it smells," he said, following her from the room.

"I don't know about how good it's going to be," she said apologetically. "I'm not one of those natural, down-home cooks that can take a pinch of this and a handful of that to make things taste right. I have to use cookbooks and recipes."

As soon as they were seated for dinner, Tres let Regina know what he thought of her efforts. "What is this stuff? I can't eat this."

"It's good, Tres, give it a try," Justin said immediately.

"We don't eat stuff that's all mixed together, do we, Dad?"

"Not usually," Thomas answered easily. "But I see things on this plate that we really like. Don't you like apples, Tres?"

"Yes, sir," Tres answered.

"Don't you like raisins?"

"Yes."

"So let's eat."

"No. I don't like that smell."

"I can find something else for him," Regina said, half rising from her chair.

"No, we won't put you out. Either Tres eats this or he waits to eat his next meal tomorrow morning," Thomas said firmly.

Regina was surprised at the firmness in Thomas's voice. Tres had given her the impression that he was undisciplined and ran the show at his house. Maybe she had been wrong.

Tres sat staring at his plate while everyone began eating. During dinner Thomas talked about the many basketball games and dunks he'd seen over the past couple of days. The boys were fascinated with his stories. Regina smiled at her son, who was trying his best to be mature for Tres and his father. Again, she wondered what had become of her baby boy. One thing was sure, Justin seemed to be eating up the male companionship to the point she no longer existed for him.

Slowly, during the course of the meal, Tres had taken one bite and then another, until the awful curry disappeared from his plate. No one made any comment.

Chapter 2

Thomas cleared the table while Regina loaded the dishwasher. When he'd brought the last dish in from the dining room, he leaned on the counter and watched her work. She scraped dinner remains into the disposal as if it were the most distasteful task she'd ever done. Again, he had the distinct impression that she did not enjoy kitchen duty.

Bent over the counter, he was eye level with her beautiful, heart-shaped face. He noticed her short, dark, and permed hair was cut into a style that beautifully framed high cheekbones and almond eyes. Her face became completely animated when she flashed one of her big, bright smiles.

There was nothing pretentious about her, including her laughter. A deep, belly laugh had escaped her several times during dinner. He wondered what he could do to elicit that delightful sound again. It had bathed him in joy, inviting him to join in on the big joke. It had been a while since he'd shared a deep, stress-relieving, soul-freeing laugh with anyone.

As he was looking at the dark-skinned, petite figure before him the thought occurred to him that he'd like to get to know her. "I talked about my work straight through dinner. Now tell me what you do for a living," he said.

"My work is not nearly as interesting as yours. I enjoyed hearing you talk about your recruitment efforts. There's a lot more to it than I ever thought. You want the best, the brightest, and the most athletic. That must be quite a challenge," she said, scrubbing the pot that the rice had been cooked in, with a look of utter disgust.

"It certainly is," he agreed, "but we've talked enough about me. Let's talk about you. What does my lovely and capable neighbor do all day?"

She flushed at the compliment, but brushed aside her pleasure. He probably did not even realize he'd called her lovely.

"I don't exactly work all day," she hedged.

"Oh, then you work at night? Are you a lady of the night?" he guessed jokingly.

"Yes, one could say that," she said, deliberately misunderstanding him. When she saw the puzzled look on his face, she began to sputter before she released one of her big, soul-deep laughs. "Oh, Thomas, don't look so startled. I'm legit. I'm a songwriter and I do much of my writing at night."

"You are? You mean you can support yourself writing songs? Don't you have a day job?"

"Not anymore. I'm under contract with Honeysuckle Records and I'm completing an album for one of their artists, Alison McKenzie."

"Alison who?"

"Surely you've heard of Alison McKenzie. She's right up there with Dolly Parton, Reba McIntyre, and Martina McBride," Regina informed Thomas.

"I guess I may have heard one of her songs and didn't pay attention. Have you written anything that I might recognize?" Thomas asked, feeling totally out of his element.

"Maybe. I hope I don't sound like I'm bragging, but

more than a few of my songs have gone to the top of the charts. Have you heard 'All Alone in a Crowd'?" Regina asked.

"No."

"What about 'It's Not Your Turn'?"

"No."

"'Highway 75 Heartache'?"

"No, I haven't heard of any of those," Thomas admitted, puzzled.

"They've all been on the Top 40 Chart," Regina assured him.

"I listen to the radio all the time. Of course, when I'm with my players, they flip to the rap stations, but I usually listen to R-and-B."

Regina laughed one of her deep from-the-gut laughs again. "Oh, I don't write R-and-B. I write for country artists. I wrote those songs that I asked you about for Mary Lou Hatchett, Stuart Ranger, and Track 29."

"I can't believe this," Thomas said. "I thought that country music was closed to African-Americans. I never dreamed that I'd actually meet someone in country music when I moved to Nashville. Of course, this is Music City U.S.A."

"Most people think that Nashville is called Music City because of the Grand Ole Opry, but the moniker actually came about when the Fisk Jubilee Singers toured the world giving concerts to raise money for their university."

"I stand corrected, Mrs. Lovejoy. You're a fountain of knowledge," Thomas said. "Are there many African-Americans in your business?"

"Not nearly enough. Just like any other industry, it's been difficult for us to break into the business. Do you know who Charlie Pride is?" Regina asked.

"Of course I do. I'm not that culturally isolated," Thomas responded.

"Most Americans do, but he wasn't the first African-American in country music and he certainly won't be the last. I bet you didn't know that one of the original members of the Opry was African-American?"

"No, I didn't know that. Who was he?"

"Deford Bailey. He was a harmonica player and he became one of the original stars of the Grand Ole Opry radio program," she explained.

"You really know your stuff, don't you?" he said, respectfully.

"Stick with me and you'll learn some things," Regina said and winked at him.

Her beautiful, almond-eyed wink nearly floored him. It was a simple gesture full of promise and sensuality. Visibly lifting his dropped jaw, Thomas was speechless. He had to gather his thoughts to remember what they'd been talking about before her flirtatious wink.

"Why do you write country music? Didn't another style appeal to you more?" he finally managed to ask.

"I grew up listening to country music. My grandmother always had the country station on in the kitchen. I like the song lyrics because they tell a story and that's what I wanted to do," she said, casually shrugging a shoulder.

"I never imagined that black folks were that involved in country music," he commented, hoping to keep her talking just so he could enjoy the melodious sound of her voice.

"Well, we are. I think that country music will always be a part of us, whether we're welcomed in the front door or the back door."

"Did you come in through the front door or the back door?" Thomas asked curiously, forgetting all about his goal not to ask her any personal questions so that she wouldn't ask him any.

"Do you want the long version or the short version?" Regina asked.

"I think I'd like the long version. Give me the details," he ventured, hoping that his curiosity would not backfire on him.

Regina slid the lever to lock the dishwasher and pushed a button, before drying her hands. "Let's get something to drink and we can sit over here," she suggested, gesturing toward the breakfast nook. When they were seated, she told Thomas how she had become a songwriter.

"I majored in advertising in college and got a great job in New York immediately after I graduated. It was so exciting and I was going to climb the corporate ladder to make my mark in the advertising world. I thought that my job was a dream come true. But after two years of that rat race, I wanted to come back to the South."

"Where are you from originally?" Thomas asked, realizing that he was sinking deeper the more questions he asked her. He figured time for his answering her questions would come soon enough.

"I'm originally from Bessemer, Alabama, but this is not my first time living in Tennessee. I graduated from the University of Tennessee in Knoxville."

"So from the University of Tennessee you went to New York to make your mark in advertising and became disillusioned?" Thomas prompted, hoping that she would go on without his having to ask more questions.

"Not exactly. I worked for an advertising agency in Nashville briefly before I accepted the job in New York. I did a good job, got promotions, and made more money than I ever dreamed, but I couldn't get used to the big city. I went back to Bessemer and did some freelance work there. While in Bessemer, I came up with the idea that I could be a songwriter. I'd gone to enough songwriter showcases while I lived here and had a good feel for the industry. When I worked in advertising in Nashville, the agency that I worked for represented many of the record companies here. I sent a demo tape to a record company. They liked the song, flew me to Nashville, and the rest is history."

"What is the history?" Thomas asked.

"They asked me if I had any more songs like the demo. I performed almost every song from my portfolio. They liked the songs, but not my voice. When they asked if I would mind having another artist sing my songs, I was relieved. I had never intended to be a singer. I get sick at the thought of performing, but I knew that I had to do my own demo to protect my songs. After I promoted my demo, I wanted to be behind the scenes. I've never had to hang around clubs or record companies waiting to be discovered or any of that. I have been truly blessed."

"It sounds like you have. Do you write your music, lyrics, and everything?"

"Yes, but I don't always have to do all the compositions for all of our songs. My record label put me with two other writers. After I get a song started, sometimes one of my partners will finish it and I do the same for theirs. Sometimes I'll take a song from start to finish with very little input from anyone. It just depends."

"Are your partners easy to work with?" Thomas asked, still fascinated with learning more about this unknown industry.

"Oh, yes. They're fun. When I first looked at Jimmy Bob, I thought, okay what kind of trouble is this good old boy going to give me? He looks like the epitome of the country boy with his scuffed-up boots, big belt buckle, and cowboy hat. But he's a real kind, considerate gentleman. My other partner, Kent, has a master's degree in literature from Yale and he looks the way you would expect a liberal intellectual to look. Anyway, we began with a deep respect for each other because we all had successful track records. We have fun together because there's nothing in the world we'd rather do than what we're doing now."

Regina talked about her business and Thomas could tell that she had pride in her craft and obviously enjoyed her work. He listened, totally captivated by the light in her eyes as she talked about her work, the way she moved her hands to punctuate a word, and her joyful spirit.

He asked questions from time to time, hoping that she wouldn't realize the time and send him home. He could have listened to her talk about anything and would have been totally engrossed. She was making a subject in which he had little interest sound positively intriguing.

"Where were you before moving to Nashville?" Regina asked, abruptly changing the subject as she set her empty glass back on the table.

"I worked for a school in North Carolina," he answered tentatively. He'd known his turn for answering questions would come and dreaded what she might ask.

"Is it a school I may have heard of?" Regina asked, noting his evasiveness.

"Probably. I was at St. Luke."

"You left St. Luke to come here? Isn't that school in a better class or league or whatever than Renaissance?"

"Conference." He supplied the word Regina was looking for. "Of course it is."

"Why would you come here?"

"I was looking for new challenges. I wanted to get out of my comfort zone as a coach, to face different challenges." With that he looked at his watch and said,

"I guess Tres and I had better get home. I believe we've overstayed our welcome."

Before Regina could respond, Thomas was up, out of his chair and leaving the room. She was confused by the sudden change of demeanor. If she'd said something wrong, she wasn't sure what it was. By the time she'd risen from the table, he was in the family room. And before she made it to the family room, he'd pulled Tres from the video game and was at the front door.

"Thanks for everything, Mrs. Lovejoy. I really appreciate your taking care of Tres for me." With that he was gone. Regina shook her head at the closed door before following Justin back into the family room. "I need to do some work in the music room, do you want to come with me?" she asked her son.

"No, Mama, I want to watch *Dragon Ball Z* on TV. I'll check on you later," Justin answered absently.

Regina sat at the keyboard, but music just wouldn't come. She was completely confused by Thomas's abrupt departure. His evasive answers to her questions had not gone over her head either. On the other hand, she admitted that she'd not practiced full disclosure in telling him about her past either. She'd left out the part about why she'd gone to New York. Neither had she been totally honest about her move back to Bessemer.

Dinner with Thomas had been a total pleasure until she'd asked him about his move to Nashville. It had been a long time since she'd spent so much time alone with a man, other than those with whom she worked. But she was totally not attracted to either of her cowriters. But this Thomas was another story altogether. Waving at him from a distance across the street had not prepared her for his powerfully masculine good looks. Well over six feet tall, he was slender with an ath-

letic build and a golden brown skin tone that reminded her of a freshly baked sugar cookie. His
close-cropped, jet-black hair was neatly trimmed with
a sharply defined, precise razor line. He was so handsome that just looking at him set her blood to boiling
in her veins.

But it was more than his outward appearance that
made him attractive to her. It was his demeanor, his
confidence and infectious charm. While his dimpled
smile and playfulness had made him seem boyish, she
was aware of his mature self-confidence. It was a confidence that led her to believe that he was accustomed
to being in control.

Maybe she would not think about Thomas so much
if she had any other man in her life. When she'd seen
him on her doorstep earlier, her heart had nearly
stopped. If she didn't stay away from this man, he
could make her forget her pledge to keep men out of
her life until she finished raising her son.

A devoted and totally engaged mother, she did not
want to confuse her son by having men revolving in
and out of his life. After several unsuccessful attempts
at dating and building romantic relationships, she did
not like the way her son responded when they ended.
At that point she'd decided that it would be best if she
focused on rearing a healthy, mentally balanced child.
Her social life could wait.

From time to time, she attended awards dinners and
other events related to the music industry. She usually found someone more than willing to escort her.
However, they were usually one-time-only deals and
her escort was always surprised to learn there would be
no follow-up to their date. That was just the way it had
to be. She didn't want to bring in some man who'd in-
terfere with how she wanted to raise Justin.

She leaned one elbow on the keyboard and absently

stroked the keys. Now Thomas had her all confused. She was rethinking her pledge after just one afternoon in his company. When he'd come back to her house for dinner wearing his nicely fitted jeans and silk shirt left open at the collar she'd been overwhelmed by the energy emanating from him.

As much as she tried to ignore it, she was deeply aware that he was a man. His sensuality had engulfed her and wouldn't let her think of him as just another parent of one of Justin's friends. His loose-fitting shirt did not hide his broad shoulders, or the well-defined muscles in his chest. Though his jeans had a relaxed fit, she could plainly see the musculature of his thighs. "Yes, siree, it's time for you to get out more, girl," Regina said, fanning her face with one hand.

Realizing her Muses would not grace her with a visit tonight, Regina gave up trying to create anything new. She lifted her violin from the case and began to play a familiar song with a slow, sweet melody. Her thoughts were so scattered that the tune helped her to focus and soothed her troubled mind. As she played, Justin ran from the family room into the music room. He sat on the floor in front of the chair where Regina was seated and quietly listened until she finished her song.

"I'm finished watching TV, Mama. I came to keep you company. Will you play my song now?" Justin asked when she ended the song. She played the theme from one of Justin's favorite television shows. The boy could barely contain himself. He jumped up, clapped his hands, and began to dance around the room as his mother played.

Following three more requests from Justin, Regina said, "Now it's your bedtime. Let's go up and find the sandman."

"Tres said that there is no sandman. His daddy told

him that it's just something grown-ups made up to make children go to sleep."

"Is that what he told you? Maybe his father doesn't know about the sandman. Remember how your eyes hurt and you can hardly hold them open when you're real tired? That's the sand in your eyes. And what is it that comes out of your eyes when you wash your face in the morning?"

"I don't know," Justin answered, beginning to doubt his friend's wisdom.

"It's the sand that's gotten all mixed up with the moisture in your eyes," Regina explained as they climbed the steps.

"Oh," Justin said thoughtfully and remained silent for a moment. "Do you know why Tres is called *Tres*?" he asked, ready to move on to another topic as they entered his room.

"No, I don't know," she answered, pulling Justin's shirt over his head.

"His name is Tres because he's the third Thomas Milton Simmons. Tres means three, did you know that, Mommy?" Justin asked proudly.

"I think I knew that," Regina answered.

"Is Tres going to come over tomorrow?" Justin asked.

"I don't know. We'll have to wait and see," Regina answered, unsure of what Thomas might do after his sudden bolt out the door.

The next morning Regina jumped out of bed, running late as usual. She'd hit the snooze alarm three times before finally turning off the radio alarm completely and snuggling back under the covers. The early April air was still chilly and the house seemed to have gotten cooler overnight. It was the absence of all outdoor noise that had awakened her. No longer did the sound of her neighbors leaving for school and work invade her dreams, no more garage doors opening and closing, no more trash cans rattling, not even the occasional sound of a delivery truck cruising the cul-de-sac.

She rushed to Justin's room, telling him to dress himself while she got dressed. In less than ten minutes they were in the kitchen eating breakfast before racing off to Justin's school. When she rushed Justin into his classroom, the class was already in a reading circle.

Tres jumped from his seat and rushed to her. "Daddy said that I'm going to come stay with Justin tomorrow. I can't wait."

"Oh, okay," Regina said, slightly surprised that Thomas would leave his son with her since he'd left her house so abruptly the night before. Maybe she was just projecting her thoughts onto his actions. She was the one who'd been all discombobulated at having a man in the house.

"Good-bye, boys," Regina whispered, trying to ignore the teacher's dirty looks at her for coming into the classroom late and disrupting the children's activities.

Regina hurried to the studio on Music Row where Alison McKenzie was recording one of the songs that Regina had written with Jimmy Bob and Kent. When Regina walked in, the petite blonde rushed over and gave her a hug. "Regina, I'm glad you're here. These boys are getting on my nerves. We have a slight difference of opinion on how this song should sound," Alison said before Regina could get settled on a stool.

Jimmy Bob came over. "What's up with you, girl? Have one of those late nights hitting the juke joints again?" Everyone laughed because the standing joke was that Regina never went anywhere, but frequently overslept. If they needed to stay in the studio all night, they could count on Regina to be there, but not early in the morning. When the musicians and writers went out after a big show or a stressful time in the studio, Regina could be counted on to hurry home to her son.

Plenty of men hit on Regina, including Jimmy Bob, but she quickly put them in their place. Regardless of their ethnic group, wealth, or looks—or lack thereof—Regina was not going out. She explained that she had a son to raise and going out was for the rare award show or some other such event.

Alison, Jimmy Bob, and Kent had a disagreement over some of the words to the song that would not flow quite right. "Instead of saying, 'I like it like that,'" Alison suggested, "can't I just repeat la-de-da there?"

"Let me hear it," Regina said. She listened with her eyes closed as Alison's strong voice belted out the song. When she got to the change, Regina shook her head, but Alison continued singing.

"Wait, wait," Regina said, struggling to be heard above Alison's strong, raspy voice. "You don't need to change the words to the song. What you need to do is breathe." Regina rose from the stool and walked over to Alison. "Go deeper, pull it from here," she said, pressing a hand over Alison's diaphragm. "Say all five words without taking a breath."

Alison nodded her head and tried again. They knew that Regina had an indisputable ear when it came to these things. While she was not always tactful, she was usually right. She'd taken singers to the top with her lyrics and music more than once.

The rest of the day was filled with other problems and sped by without Regina glancing at her watch until three o'clock. She was shocked at the time and flew from her office without pausing. Now she was going to be late picking up Justin. She broke all kinds of speed limits getting to the school, but luckily she did not get a ticket. When she got there, some kids were still sitting outside waiting for their rides, but Justin was nowhere to be found.

She parked and hurried into the school's office. The clerk said that she had not seen Justin. Regina then went to look for his teacher. She found her in the teacher's workroom. "I was a little late picking up Justin and I can't find him," Regina said in a near panic.

"I let him go home with Tres," the teacher answered. "The boys told me that Tres had been staying with you and since you brought them in and picked them up yesterday, I thought that it was some kind of trade-off."

"You could have called me first. You have my cell phone number, my studio number, my office number, and my home number. Why didn't you call me?"

"I thought that it would be okay since Tres had been staying at your house," the teacher explained again. "Tres's father is a very responsible man. He works with boys all the time at the university. My son has been in his summer basketball camp. He's a good person," the teacher explained to Regina's retreating back.

"Okay, you're right," Regina said, rushing out of the workroom.

Regina pulled into Thomas's driveway and was out of the car almost before she stopped the engine. When he answered the door, she said, "I wish you'd called to let me know that you were bringing Justin home with you. I panicked and ran through the school looking for him like a madwoman. When I didn't find him, I found his teacher and I chewed her out."

"Calm down, Regina," Thomas said, putting his hands on her shoulders. "Why are you so stressed out?"

"I thought something had happened to him," she answered with tears in her eyes. The stress had built up to a point where she knew that she might cry now that the crisis was over, but she didn't want to cry in front of Thomas. "Look, I need to run home," she said.

Before she could turn away, he tightened his grip on her shoulders. "Regina, come on in here. Tell me what's got you so upset. Justin is okay. He's in the back playing with Tres's train set. Do you want to see him?" Thomas asked, his voice all tenderness.

He led her to a small family room that was furnished with a giant sofa facing the fireplace and two large overstuffed chairs at either end of the sofa. It was a crowded but tidy room. This obviously was not a room that he and Tres used frequently.

Never taking his hand from Regina's elbow, he seated her at one end of the huge sofa and sat in one of the large chairs next to her. When he removed his hand from her elbow, Regina felt cold all over. Though he'd touched her lightly, she'd been aware of his strength and had been infused with his warmth. She imagined that she could still feel the warmth of his thumb and forefinger on her elbow.

"I'm a little confused," Thomas said. "Please forgive me if I don't ask this right, but can you tell me why you're crying?" From experience he knew that he might not get a comprehensible answer. He knew that at times he certainly could not explain his feelings or emotions either. Like now, why was he so hot from merely touching this woman's elbow? After all, she was nothing special. Not at all his type—too short, too hippy. At the thought of her hips, he found himself wondering how her lush, curvaceous hips would feel in the palm of his hands.

She looked up at him with unshed tears illuminating her large, dark eyes and he felt instant guilt. How could he think about feeling her up at such a time? He wanted her to trust him with what was bothering her and here he was lusting after her.

Digging around in her purse, she finally came up with a raggedy little piece of tissue. Thomas quickly reached into his back pocket and offered her his big white linen handkerchief. She blew her nose soundly into the handkerchief and then flashed him one of her big mischievous smiles. "I guess I'd better throw this in with my laundry. I'll bring it back when it's clean."

"No, you don't. I lose more handkerchiefs that way. A little snot doesn't scare me. For the past three years I've raised Tres all alone. Believe me, I've been up to my elbows in snot," Thomas said, laughing, and Regina joined him.

She was so beautiful when she laughed and it was the sincerest sound in the universe. Her laughter ran deep and pure. When she spoke, his body was washed in waves of warmth. "So, you have a lot of crying women on your doorsteps, Mr. Simmons?"

"What?" he asked, perplexed.

"You said you lose more handkerchiefs this way. I assume you mean by giving them to crying women," Regina explained.

"No, that's not what I meant. Well, not exactly. It's just that when you loan out your handkerchief, no one gives them back. Don't try to avoid my question. Tell me why you were crying," Thomas said, anxious to change the subject.

Knowing that he would keep asking her, she decided to try to explain. "Since Justin was born, I've been alone with him. I've never had any help except during vacations when he's with my mother. He's been my total responsibility. I've taken that responsibility very seriously, but today I got all caught up in a session and I completely lost track of time. I try to let nothing come before my child and when I thought I'd lost him I was so scared. I knew that it was my punishment for being an unfit parent. I know it sounds stupid, but that's how I felt."

She was mortified that she'd spoken her fears aloud, but she had to be honest since he'd asked an honest question. She still felt uncomfortable that she'd not been completely honest with him the night before.

When he nodded his head to what she was saying, Regina was totally amazed. He said, "I know what you mean. Tres has been my sole responsibility for so long that I almost forgot how to ask for help. When I was at St. Luke, I had a full-time housekeeper, but I don't have that luxury now. I was hoping that my mother would help out, but I see that nothing has changed there."

"It can be so hard sometimes," she said, reaching out and covering his hand that rested on his knee with her own. The warmth of her hand immediately spread throughout his body and enveloped him. She was stirring things in him that he thought were long gone. If they kept it up this way, it would be no time at all before they were discussing their past again.

"I guess I'd better go check on the boys. Do you want to see the setup we have back here?" he asked, clearing his throat and rising from the chair to move away from Regina as quickly as possible.

A little thrown off by his sudden change of subject, she blinked twice before standing and following him to the back of the house. The room that she used for a music room in her floor plan was a giant playroom in this house. That would explain why his family room was so small. All of the houses in the subdivision had about the same square footage, but the space could be customized. In his floor plan, he'd opted for putting most of the square footage for the first floor in the entertainment room. On one side of the room where the boys were playing, an elaborate electric train station, with all kinds of scenery and buildings, was laid out on a homemade table. The train set began on the table; however, it didn't stop there. The railroad tracks traversed the room, running across ledges in the ceiling, down to baseboards surrounding the floor, and ending back up on the platform. Boys young and old would be entertained for hours with that setup.

The room also contained a full-sized pool table and a Foozball table sat in a corner. A projection television was on the wall opposite the entrance to the room with several rows of theater-style seating facing it. The room was a male paradise—she could practically see the testosterone dripping from the walls.

"Hi, Mom," Justin said with one of his fingers on a switch for the train. He barely spared a glance her way.

"Look at this, Daddy," Tres said, putting the train in reverse as it crossed a bridge.

"It's going to crash," Regina yelled without thinking. But Justin threw his switch and the train changed tracks and went through a tunnel. The boys laughed to see that they'd gotten Regina with their trick.

"You guys are some tough engineers. Good job," Thomas said and they all high-fived each other.

"Let's go home, Justin," Regina said when the celebration was over. "You haven't had an afternoon nap."

"We don't take naps anymore," Justin answered.

Regina rolled her eyes heavenward. "Yes, *we* do," she answered.

"Mrs. Lovejoy, if it's okay, I'll keep Justin with us while you go do whatever you need to do."

"Are you still calling me Mrs. Lovejoy? I thought you'd gotten over that yesterday. My name is Regina. Besides, it's Ms. Lovejoy. Lovejoy is my maiden name. If you want to call me Mrs. you'll have to use my ex-husband's name," she explained in the spirit of full disclosure.

He did not respond to that. Another bit of her past had been laid out before him. What would he have to reveal in exchange for this bit of information?

"Okay, Regina, could you leave Justin over here? That way they can entertain each other while I finish up some work that I need to take back to campus before I hit the road tomorrow. By the way, will you still baby-sit for me on Thursday and Friday?"

"Certainly I will. There's one thing I need you to do, though, please be sure that Justin takes his naps when he's with you. I believe that Tres should take naps, too, but since he's your child I'll keep my opinion to myself," Regina said in her fast-paced manner.

"Actually, you didn't keep your opinion to yourself at all," Thomas said with the dimple showing deep in his right cheek.

"No, I didn't, did I?" she said pointedly, fixing him with her stern gaze.

"No. I prefer that they not take a nap. It's too hard getting Tres to go to bed at night as it is. Tres's bedtime is eight o'clock," Thomas said, certain that Regina had expected his complete obedience without any discussion.

"We usually go to bed a little bit later," Regina answered. "That's why Justin needs a nap."

"If you went to bed earlier, you wouldn't always run late in the morning," Thomas said without rancor.

"Who told you that we always run late?" Regina asked defensively.

"Justin," Thomas answered and shrugged a shoulder as if he really didn't care to discuss it anymore.

Regina paused and considered Thomas's point. Finally she said, "I'll be back in an hour. I'm trying to find a song to finish a CD that we're already recording in the studio."

"Good and when you come back, I'll have dinner

ready for you. I promised the boys that I'd grill hot dogs for them. Would you like a hamburger and grilled corn on the cob and a salad?" Thomas asked, hoping he could entice her with his menu.

"That sounds great. Anything that I don't cook is good to me," Regina said.

In exactly one hour, Regina returned to the Simmons house, bringing a red velvet cake with cream cheese frosting with her. Their earlier disagreement forgotten, the adults had as delightful an evening as the children. The dinner conversation was light-hearted and easy. After dinner they went into what Regina couldn't help thinking of as the "men's room" and played games.

"Well, how do you like them apples?" Regina asked when she'd beat him in another game of pool.

"How did you learn to play like that?" Thomas asked, impressed with her ability.

"Pool was my first major in college," she explained, laughing. "That is until my mother got my grades at the end of the year."

Thomas laughed with her. "My ego is bruised. We'll have to play something else," he said.

"Well, Tommy, name your poison," Regina teased.

"I hate being called Tommy," Thomas answered.

"But your mother called you Tommy," noted Regina.

"I know, but I can't help what my mother does. I would rather you call me by my name."

"Then I'll never call you Tommy again, Tommy—I mean, Thomas." She couldn't help teasing him one last time.

"I'm going to get even with you for that," he challenged her. "Let's play pinball."

After several games where the score was too close for either to gloat, Regina called it a night. Even after being together all afternoon, the boys still did not want to separate when it was bedtime. The only thing that made their separation palatable was the promise that Tres would sleep over the next night.

When Thomas brought Tres over the next morning, he gave Regina a key to his house. "I think I have everything in this bag, but here's a key in case I forgot something. Tres can tell you where his things are."

"I'm sure that if he needs something, he can use what Justin has," Regina said, reluctant to accept the key.

"You never know. I'd feel better knowing that all of our bases are covered," Thomas insisted.

He got on his knees and hugged his son again. Seeing the longing look in Justin's eyes, he pulled the boy into his embrace, too. He must have missed the same look in Regina's eyes. "I love you, son. You be sure to obey Ms. Regina and don't give her any trouble. Do you hear me?"

"Yes, sir," the small, mature voice answered.

With Thomas's departure, the house seemed lonely. After school, she and the boys had a lonely dinner and Thomas's absence was pronounced.

Regina managed to get the boys up on time and to school before the first bell rang on both Thursday and Friday. She found that having two boys had its advantages. They entertained one another and she had more time to write during the evenings.

When Thomas returned Friday night, Regina was startled to find that she was just as excited by his arrival as the boys were. She felt a slight tinge of envy when he lifted one child in each of his arms and gave them big hugs.

"Guess what, guys, I have tickets for us to go to the *Blue's Clues Birthday Party Show*. Who wants to go?"

Both boys yelled, "I do," simultaneously.

Regina smiled at their enthusiasm, but said nothing.

"I have a ticket for you, too, Regina. Can you go? I know it's short notice, but I ordered them on-line and forgot to mention it to you when I called last night. It's spur-of-the-moment, I know."

"Please, Mommy, go with us," Justin pleaded.

"Yeah, Miss Regina, we won't have fun without you," Tres added, surprising her.

"Come on, it'll be fun," Thomas said, making the decision for her.

Saturday afternoon Regina found herself nervously dressing for a performance of *Blue's Clues*. One would have thought it was a first date. *Come on,* she said to herself, *we're just two adults taking our sons on an afternoon outing. That's all.* What does one wear to a live-action performance featuring a big blue dog, anyway? Finally settling on a pale blue cotton pantsuit with a matching T-shirt, Regina hurried out of her bedroom before she changed her mind.

She and Justin laughed when they saw Thomas back his Navigator from his driveway straight into theirs. Regina was about to follow Justin to the car when Thomas jumped out and met her before she could close her front door.

"Here, let me do that for you," Thomas said, taking the key from her. After locking the door, he returned the key to her still outstretched hand.

"Thank you," she said, surprised by his courtesy.

"You look real nice," he said, placing her hand in the fold of his elbow. He led her to the car, opened the door for her, and helped her in. Waiting until she was settled in the seat, he closed the door and hurried to sit behind the steering wheel.

"Lady and gentlemen, we are off to have fun," Thomas said, starting the vehicle again. The boys giggled in sheer glee at the prospect of the adventure that they were about to embark upon.

When the show was over and the final clue had been used to find Blue's birthday wish, the foursome left the theater still laughing and singing songs from the live performance.

They were halfway to the car when Justin said, "Mama, I'm hungry. Let's go for pizza."

"It's a little early for dinner," Regina noted, looking at her watch.

"I'm hungry, too," Thomas said. "We didn't get to eat any lunch because we had to start getting dressed to leave right after breakfast. Let's go for pizza."

The boys began to chant, "Piz-za, piz-za, piz-za!"

"There's a good pizza place near the university and it shouldn't be that crowded this time of day," Thomas suggested. "Their pizza is unusually good."

In less than fifteen minutes they were on Jefferson Street just beyond the four-campus area where Tennessee State, Fisk, and Renaissance Universities met Meharry Medical College, constituting the capital of black intellect for the mid-South area. After they placed their pizza order, the boys were allowed to play video games while they waited for their orders. Thomas fed quarters into the games and came back to chat with Regina.

"These boys are a bundle of energy, aren't they?" he said.

"I wish I had that much energy," Regina answered. "I have a to-do list a mile long and am tired before I complete half of it. Unfortunately I have to stop and sleep."

"The boys don't realize it, but they have to stop and sleep too. They fight it as long as they can and then after a while they just fall over to the side. Tres fights going to bed every night, but he's practically asleep before his head hits the pillow."

"I know. The same goes on with us. That's why I think five-year-olds should be taking naps still." Regina returned to their old argument.

"I thought you agreed with my reasoning when you left the other night. I should have known that you gave in too easily," Thomas said, laughing at her attempt to try to win the battle again.

"I left because I was already drained from my fright at not finding Justin at school when I went to get him. You never even listened to my rationale for naps," she answered coolly.

"Which is?" Thomas asked, lifting one of his thick, glossy eyebrows.

"I'm a writer. Sometimes I'm up late at night in writing sessions. I frequently take Justin to the studio with me when I work at night. Things go better for us if he's had a nap."

"I don't buy your reasoning at all," Thomas said bluntly. He could tell that she enjoyed the debate. "He's in school now and will be for the next twelve years. The boy needs his rest. As I understand it, you set your own work schedule. You have the flexibility to work when it's convenient for you."

"It's not that simple and you know it. I am an independent contractor for a major record label. That means that I have to earn every penny that I get. I'm not on somebody's payroll where I get paid for doing nothing," Regina said, looking directly into Thomas's eyes.

"I don't get paid for doing nothing," Thomas said.

"I didn't say you specifically, but if the shoe fits . . ." Regina said, before continuing to make her point. "During the day I have to take care of business matters.

Writing music is a business—or did you know that already?" she asked sarcastically.

"I figured as much," Thomas conceded.

"If I don't take care of myself, I'll end up penniless and broke like so many other artists who trusted others to take care of their business," she said, driving her point.

"I know, but—" Thomas began.

"Don't interrupt, I'm not finished," Regina said. "Sometimes I even have to go to recording sessions in the day. They are not all at night. Then at the end of a very long day, I am still a songwriter and I will not have residuals to track and royalties to invoice, if I don't write songs."

"I know you have a busy schedule to juggle, we all do. But now you have to consider what's best for Justin. You need to change your work habits," Thomas said, resolutely.

Regina opened and closed her mouth without making a sound. It was so seldom that she lost an argument that she didn't know what to do. "Are you accusing me of not putting my son first? Why were you so comfortable leaving your son with me if you think I'm such an awful mother?"

"I'm not accusing you of being an awful mother. Sometimes we single parents need a second opinion. My opinion is, you need to change your work habits. Otherwise you are a wonderful mother," Thomas said, pulling out all the charm he could muster to keep her from being angry with him.

Regina said thoughtfully, "I've always considered myself extremely fortunate that I can take Justin to work with me. He's gone in with me since he was an infant. He enjoys the musicians and I think he has respect for the whole process."

Thomas wondered again where Justin's father was,

but knew that if he asked such a question, he would leave himself open for a similar question. So he simply responded, "The same here. I don't think I could do my job if I couldn't take Tres with me." He looked at Regina and she seemed to have dismissed him. He wondered at her thoughtful demeanor.

Regina sat quietly looking at Thomas. If any other person had talked to her the way he had, she would have become defensive and angry. Somehow, coming from him, it all made sense. She looked at him thoughtfully. His stern expression was hiding his boyish quality today. His ideas on child rearing were obviously well thought out and he was serious about them.

In spite of his serious demeanor, she couldn't help noticing how absolutely mouthwatering delicious he looked. He was wearing a brown-and-cream-colored loosely knitted cotton sweater that was open at the neck and khaki slacks. The colors looked good against his caramel-brown skin. Sitting across from him, she found being forced to look at his gorgeous face downright disconcerting. She wondered if she would be more comfortable sitting next to him. No, that wouldn't work either. She'd probably melt from the contact.

She let the argument on naps end without further rebuttal. As the silence lengthened she began to stir her soda with a straw and hum softly. Thomas was certain that her silence was not an indication that she was angry with him. At least he didn't think she was angry. She was humming a happy tune.

She looked so delectable today that he had to keep his hands flat on the table to keep from reaching over and touching her. "What are you humming?" Thomas asked.

"I don't have a name for it yet," she said as if she was having difficulty returning her thoughts to the present. "Sometimes I compose in my head," she said shyly.

"Every time I'm around you, I learn a little bit more about how creative genius works," Thomas said, admiringly.

She looked at her hands and smiled again, a smile that sent warm sparks shooting through his nervous system before settling in his groin. If he was going to keep hanging out with her and the boys, she'd have to stop smiling like that.

"I wouldn't say that I'm a genius. I'm no Stevie Wonder for sure. Every song that I've ever written has been rather difficult to pull together. I've never been able to let a song go without several rewrites," she said self-deprecatingly.

"I'd like to hear some of your music sometime," Thomas said.

"You're so kind," Regina answered. "But I didn't think that you'd be interested in country music."

"I'd like to hear some of yours," Thomas said, looking boldly into her sensuous, slanted eyes.

"Sure," she said nervously. "I can loan you some of my CDs."

"Won't you treat me to a live performance? Justin told me that you play the violin, guitar, and piano. I'd like you to play something for me when we get home," Thomas suggested.

"I never play for anyone. I go to my instruments when I'm writing and need to hear the music and lyrics together. I'm really not a performer," she said, becoming agitated at the thought of playing for Thomas. She nervously smoothed the tapered hairline at the nape of her neck; then she fidgeted with her watch.

"Don't get upset, Regina," Thomas said, placing his hand over hers to still its nervous motion. As soon as he did, he regretted his action. A pleasant warmth surged through his body and Regina looked up at him, holding his eyes steadily with hers. This time he was certain that she'd felt it, too. He couldn't move his hand away from hers, nor could he look away.

He sat spellbound until a small voice said, "Mr. Thomas, we need more quarters."

Thomas jerked his hand away as if he'd been burned and hurried to the boys. While he was feeding the game machines, the waitress came with their order. Tres and Justin finished their game before hurrying over to devour the pizza.

To make matters simple, Regina and Thomas had ordered one pizza with everything. Thomas picked up a slice of pizza and began to pick off all the mushrooms.

"Don't you like mushrooms, little Tommy?" Regina teased.

Thomas rolled his eyes at her and took a bite from the slice of pizza in his hand.

Chapter 3

Throughout the spring recruitment season Regina baby-sat Tres, and when Thomas was in town he returned the favor by taking care of both Justin and Tres as much as possible. He would pick them up from school and take them with him back to his office on the university campus. There they played in the gym and were entertained by students who were glad for the diversion. Many of the students were homesick for younger siblings and welcomed their time with Tres and Justin.

Realizing that Regina's culinary skills were extremely limited, Thomas routinely prepared dinner for the two families and had it ready by the time Regina came over to retrieve Justin. They were diligent about maintaining a friendly relationship. Whenever they were alone, they kept the conversation generic and never touched one another, for they realized that to do so would be inviting spontaneous combustion. They were aware that the fire between them was so hot that it could easily blaze into an all-consuming flame.

One night Regina sat on the steps leading from Thomas's deck as he watered the flowers that she'd planted in his backyard earlier in the day. "Tin Pan South begins next week," Regina reminded Thomas. "Will you still be able to take care of Justin for me?"

Thomas stopped the flow of water with the hand-held nozzle. "What's Tin Pan South?"

"I told you all about it. Don't you remember?" Regina answered.

"I know you told me about it, but I guess you were talking faster than I could think again. Sometimes when you get going I don't know whether to listen to you or try to read your hands," Thomas joked.

"Okay, tease me if you must. I'll keep my hands in my lap and you watch my lips, okay?" she said as if talking to a very slow pupil.

"I love to look at your lips," Thomas said, hoping that his husky voice did not betray his emotions.

"Stop it—you're not being serious and tomorrow night you'll ask me what Tin Pan South is again," Regina said primly.

"Sorry—I forgot how serious you are when it comes to music," Thomas said, not quite sincere in his apology.

"Tin Pan South is a songwriters' celebration sponsored by the Nashville Songwriters Association International. Over the next few days we'll have a couple of big events at the Ryman Auditorium and the Music House. But we also have something going on at almost all the nightspots around town. I need to be out there to see what the trends are. So, can you take care of Justin?" Regina asked, trying to talk slowly but beginning to pick up her normal rapid speech pattern before she reached the end of her request.

"That sounds like fun," Thomas said, surprising Regina. He was showing more and more interest in the country music world after listening to a few of her CDs.

"Do you want to come with me?" she asked, tentatively.

"No, you need me to take care of Justin," he answered quickly.

"You were the first person I thought of since Justin would rather be with Tres, and of course you, than anywhere else in the world. Why don't you come with me? We can get one of the teens in the neighborhood to baby-sit. I think you'll enjoy it," she suggested.

"Hanging out with a bunch of country music folks and bar-hopping sounds like my kind of fun," he said with an ironic expression on his face.

"Don't knock it until you try it," Regina answered. "At least join us one night. I know you'll like it. Admit it—you are a little curious."

"I am. And I was serious when I said that it sounds like fun," Thomas admitted.

"That settles it then. I'll ask Keisha or Leah to come over and take care of the kids. The best night for you to come with me would be Friday. My label is hosting a big show at the Exit/In that night."

"It's a date then," Thomas said, looking intently into Regina's eyes.

She began to feel warm and flushed under his intense scrutiny. She smoothed the hair at her tapered neckline and then looked away from him. "I think it'll be fun. But it won't be a date. Remember, we agreed, we're just friends. Just two friends hanging out, right?"

"Right," he repeated.

Before they could say more, Tres came running from the far end of the yard where they'd been digging holes and hauling dirt with their construction trucks. Justin followed him closely. "Daddy, spray me with water. Put some water on me," Tres said playfully.

"Yeah, me too," Justin chimed in.

As Thomas turned the hose on the boys, Regina stood and yelled, "Thomas, don't do that! It's still too chilly out."

"No, it's not," he countered, not looking at her. "It's been warm all day."

"They'll catch pneumonia out here," she said, a little calmer.

"It feels good," Thomas said. "See?" He turned and sprayed water on Regina's open-toed sandals.

"Thomas, you'll ruin my shoes," she said before taking one off and throwing it at him. He caught the shoe and was about to throw it back when she took off running.

He chased her with the hose, spraying water on her legs and back. The boys wanted to get in on the fun and ran through the water that Thomas had aimed at Regina's back.

"You're going to pay for this, Thomas Simmons," she yelled.

She grabbed a bucket of dirt from the boys' construction site and threw it on Thomas right before he blasted her with water again.

"You want to play in dirt, huh? Is that it?" Thomas grabbed her and tackled her to the ground. Pinning her beneath him, he took some of the dirt that she'd tossed on him and smeared it all over her arms and face.

"Stop, stop! I give up," she yelled, laughing.

"Get her dirty, Mr. Thomas. Get her dirty," Justin urged. Thomas reached into the boys' mud pile and smeared more dirt onto Regina's face.

"Don't mess up my hair. I just got my hair done," Regina pleaded.

"What will you do for me if I don't mess up your hair?" Thomas asked, pulling away from her so that he could look into her face.

"I'll buy you a drink when we go out Friday night," she bargained.

"That's not good enough. Your hairdo should be

worth more than that," Thomas said, beginning to enjoy the feel of her body under his way too much.

"You name it—I'll do it," Regina said desperately.

"I'll let you up, but remember, you owe me big time," Thomas relented, realizing that he would be too embarrassed to get up if he lay on her much longer. Her squirming and bucking to throw him off of her body was doing nothing to quell his growing arousal.

Thomas stood and offered his hand to help her up. He should have been warned by her mischievous smile, but his mind had taken a sensuous turn. He was completely taken off guard. As she rose from the ground, she caught the handle of the beach bucket and tossed its liquid contents on him.

"You don't give up, do you?" Thomas yelled, chasing her into the house. The boys laughed gleefully and followed the adults into the house.

"I'm sorry. Something came over me," Regina pleaded when Thomas caught her around the waist as she ran through his kitchen.

"Give me one good reason why I shouldn't take the hose from the sink over there and wash your hair in dishwashing detergent," he demanded, pulling Regina's back against his chest as she squirmed to get away. "You know you can't get away," he said in her ear as she struggled to break his hold on her. He lifted her off her feet and carried her to the sink.

"Please don't do that. I can't get another hairdresser appointment until next week. I can't go out if you wet my hair," Regina pleaded.

"You beg now, but I can't trust you. How do I know you don't have another trick up your sleeves?"

"Because she doesn't have any sleeves," Tres offered.

"Okay, boys, you tell me, should I trust her? Should I let her go?" Thomas asked their audience.

"Let her go. We'll watch her," Justin said.

"Okay, since my boys have my back, I'll let you go this time," Thomas said.

"Look at this mess," Regina said, when she turned to face Thomas.

"You look worse than I do. We'd better take hot showers before we get chilled," Thomas reasoned.

"Justin's sneakers are all wet," Regina complained. "He can't even walk they're so squishy."

"I'll give him a taxi ride home. Hop on, buddy," Thomas said, stooping low so that Justin could board his back. "While I take Justin home, you go to the laundry room and undress," Thomas directed Tres.

After Thomas had deposited Justin on the floor of the Lovejoys' foyer, he turned to hurry back home.

"Wait," Regina said. "Here's your door key. I've been meaning to give it back to you."

"Keep it. You'll probably need it this week since Justin will be staying with us more than he'll be at home. That way you can leave his clothes or pick up his things at your convenience," he said, closing her hand over the key she held out to him.

"Thanks," Regina said, removing her hand from his. She watched his retreating back as he loped across the street. She'd had about all the contact she could handle with her *friend* for one night. She had not yet recovered from the intense pleasure she'd experienced from his body pressing hers to the ground. Her attraction to this kind, handsome, playful man was intensifying rapidly. And she had no hope of avoiding him. It seemed that their lives were inextricably interwoven. She needed some space to regroup. Maybe she could handle him better another day.

After she closed the door on Thomas, she went to the family room where she found Justin sitting wrapped in a towel, watching TV.

"Where did you put your clothes?" she asked the boy.

"In the washer," he answered.

"Why is the TV on?"

"I just want to watch for a little while," Justin explained.

"Justin, it's a school night. You need to take your shower and go to bed. Turn off the TV," Regina ordered. "Now," she added when he did not move.

The following week was hectic for Regina. Each night she was at a different venue listening to traditional and new country. She heard new artists and old. Some of the music sounded more like pop or rock than country. The variety was there and she listened to as much as possible. She heard some familiar voices, but most of the artists were newcomers.

Friday night she was more than a little nervous. She was about to introduce Thomas to her world. What would he think of her after he met her colleagues and saw her working the shows?

Thomas rang her doorbell promptly at six-thirty. "Are you all set?" he asked.

"Yes, I'm ready. Tres and Justin are upstairs coloring. Come on in the family room and meet Keisha, she's your next door neighbor's daughter."

Meeting Keisha was the first of many introductions for Thomas that night. At the Exit/In, a local nightspot known for impromptu performances by stars, he and Regina joined Kent and Jimmy Bob. The two men were so different, both visually and personalitywise, that Thomas had no trouble distinguishing between them.

Kent was slight and under six feet tall. His dark hair was long and unkempt. Jimmy Bob, on the other hand, was just as tall as Thomas, but much heavier. While Thomas was built like Michael Jordan, Jimmy Bob had the physique of a Tennessee Titans linebacker. When they shook hands, it was a battle of domination to see who would wince first. When Thomas withstood the pain stoically, Jimmy Bob slapped him on the back before letting go of his right hand and said, "It's good to have you join us. We've heard some good things about you." With those words, they all sat down.

"What did I miss?" Regina asked, adjusting her seat so that she could see the stage.

"We have an intermission right now, but you've already missed Shelby Webb. She came over looking for you after she performed," Kent told her.

"It doesn't look like the waitress is going to make it over this way. She's apparently overworked today," Jimmy Bob said, rising from his seat. "I'll go to the bar. What would you like, Thomas?"

"Anything on tap is fine with me," he answered.

"And I guess you want your usual—a Miller Lite on tap?" Jimmy Bob said to Regina, smiling a little bit too intimately to suit Thomas.

While Jimmy Bob was at the bar, Kent talked with Thomas, who was surprised to discover that Kent knew a great deal about Renaissance University's team. "I'm a real sports junkie. I'll watch any sport that comes on TV, including bowling," Kent admitted.

"This year is going to be a real good year for Renaissance. Tell Kent about the player you recruited from New York," Regina prompted Thomas.

"Our game is going to be almost as exciting as anything you see in the NBA. We're building a powerhouse team. I'm working on getting my team to play the full ninety-four feet of the basketball court. They all want to be inside players, but I've got to get them to move their feet. They have to keep moving, using the whole court to their advantage. I want them to own the place," Thomas said.

"Hot damn. I can't wait to see you all play. How long have you been there now?" Kent asked.

"This will be my second season. The university's president wants winning athletic teams at all costs. He's given me a full-time recruiter who's on the road all the time. I've also just gotten a nice budget increase to add more staff," Thomas said, warming up to the conversation.

"After you've built your team up, they'll be something to see. I hope the Renaissance game doesn't change too much though. I enjoy the kind of ball those boys play. They play for the joy of the game, good honest ball. It's so refreshing. They don't showboat waiting for that big NBA contract."

"Very few of our players will go to the NBA, but all of them will have degrees when their playing days are over," Thomas boasted.

Their discussion was interrupted by Jimmy Bob's return. "Here you are, doll," he said, placing a drink before Regina.

Wondering if Jimmy Bob came on to Regina like that all the time, Thomas looked at Kent to see if he had any reaction to his partner's flirting. Maybe this was just innocent, Thomas decided.

"Do you know if Shelby's left yet?" Regina asked.

"I don't believe she has. She's probably around here somewhere," Jimmy Bob answered, looking around the crowded bar.

"It's been so long since I've seen her. She's been on tour for almost a year now. I can't wait to catch up with all that's going on," Regina said, thinking of the phone call she'd received from her friend upon her arrival in Nashville. Shelby was one of the first people to welcome her to Music Row with open arms.

"I think she was sitting over there toward the windows. I saw her husband at the bar a while ago," Kent said.

"I've been thinking about writing a song for her. I don't know if she'd be interested since she's had so many hits," Regina explained.

"She ought to be. We gave her the first hit she ever had," Jimmy Bob said.

"What do you have in mind?" Kent asked.

"I don't have it all together yet. The words just came to me when I was watching her at the Country Music Awards show. She seems to have it all, a wonderful husband, two healthy children, and supportive parents. Do you know that they live at her estate so that they can be close to their grandkids? I guess I was thinking of how thankful I would be if I were in her shoes."

"You could be, sweetie. Just give me the word." Jimmy Bob winked at Regina.

"Don't pay him any mind," Regina said, wanting to put Thomas at ease, sensing his tension. He goes on like this all the time. He flirts with anything in a skirt."

"Not anything. Don't sell yourself short," Jimmy Bob replied.

"Let me hear what you have," Kent said, ignoring the tangential conversation.

"Okay, this is still in the very early stages," she warned. She hummed a little bit to find her key, then sang the words: "'Thank you for my family, friends, and sunlit days/ The life you've given me is so enchanted/ The answers to all my prayers you've granted / When I think of all you've given me, I'm filled with praise. . . .' That's all I have," Regina said, stopping abruptly.

Jimmy Bob took out a napkin and began writing. "Let's say those last lines again, then 'Enchanted, enchanted, my life is so enchanted/ Praise, praise, praise for my deepest desires you've granted,'" he sang.

The three worked on the song together, rubbing out words and moving them around. They had a stack of napkins around them before the next show started. Thomas was amazed as he watched the three heads together. He didn't feel left out; rather he felt as though he was being treated to a rare event. He forgot his momentary jealousy and admired the way each songwriter fed off the ideas of the others. This was the same kind of teamwork that he encouraged from his players.

When the houselights went down and the show was about to begin Kent folded the napkins together and asked Regina if she minded putting them in her purse.

The performer onstage was a relative newcomer. He had a clean, clear voice with a slight twang and was wearing the requisite cowboy hat and boots. He sat on a stool and held a guitar over his thighs.

Thomas actually found himself caught up in the performance. The singer did have a certain stage presence. To his chagrin, Thomas noted that Jimmy Bob had his arm draped around the back of Regina's chair and from time to time he would lean closer to whisper to her.

When the singer had left the stage, Kent said, "I'll make the bar run this time. Will it be the same all around?"

When everyone had responded in the affirmative, Jimmy Bob turned to Thomas. "What did you think of that last singer?"

"I'm the amateur here, but he sounded pretty good to me," Thomas replied.

"Your opinion is just as good as mine. We don't write songs for the critics; we write them for the music-buying public," Jimmy Bob said. "I was just telling Regina that he has a good voice. If he was on our label, we could write something that would make better use of his good rich tenor voice. We could work with him."

Kent returned with the drinks to hear the last of the conversation. "Let's find out if he has a contract. I was thinking that he could sing that song we were going to pitch to Allison. He could probably do more with it."

Before they could pursue the idea, another performer was onstage, followed by five more. At intermission Regina excused herself to go to the ladies' room. As she was freshening her lipstick she saw a familiar face behind hers in the mirror. "Shelby— Shelby Webb. I was just about to go table-hopping to find you. I hoped that I hadn't missed you." She turned and hugged her old friend.

"I was going to call you at home tonight, see if maybe we could get together before I hit the road again on Tuesday," Shelby said, stepping away from their embrace. "Girl, you look better than ever. The older I get, the younger you look. We used to be the same age," the celebrity continued.

"Don't give me that. I love your haircut. How's the road treating you?" Regina asked, eager to catch up.

"Try touring with two buses and two kids and a husband and get back to me on that." Shelby laughed.

"It can't be that bad," Regina said.

Shelby raised one eyebrow and let her expression speak for her. "Actually it's not all bad. My sons have to stay with my parents when I tour since they're in school now, but Artie's still my road manager. The only problem I have is that we have no social life out there. It's just Artie, the band, and me. I really miss you and our good long talks," she said. "Otherwise, it's all good."

"Great," Regina said. "Please don't disillusion me because I believed all the press I've read about your fairy-tale life."

"It's exactly what we said we wanted when we sat down in that coffee shop talking about where we wanted to be in the next five years—and to think it only took us three years. I have a platinum album and touring the world and you have songs that are being covered by every major artist out there," Shelby said joyfully.

"We have come a long way. In fact, we were just writing a song for you," Regina said.

"For me—not you geniuses. Let me hear it," Shelby said excitedly.

Regina sang it and Shelby hugged her. "That's beautiful. It brings tears to my eyes because it's so true. When I finish my tour I'll be working on a new album. I want that song."

"By the time you return I should have recovered from Tin Pan South," Regina said, laughing as they left the rest room together.

"This thing is bigger than ever," Shelby said, fanning herself with a slender, delicate hand as they left the ladies' room. "I know you worked hard on it this year. It's fantastic."

"Yes, it's wonderful. Come on over and say hi to the boys," Regina said.

"Is there a special someone over there you want me to meet?" Shelby asked as they neared the table.

"He's my neighbor," Regina said neutrally, not wanting to encourage Shelby because she would surely embarrass her in front of Thomas. In their early friendship, Shelby had tried to match Regina with every man they met. Shelby claimed that it was because she wanted to spread the joy that her marriage gave her.

"He's your neighbor, huh? Are there any vacancies in your neighborhood? He's a real cutie pie," she said, grinning.

Regina knew Thomas was in trouble. The charismatic Shelby had Thomas eating out of her hand in five seconds flat. *That's why she's the star and I write the songs*, Regina thought.

When they hugged in parting, Shelby whispered in Regina's ear, "This one is a keeper. I want to be matron of honor." Regina's mouth flew open in surprise and she remained speechless as Shelby said charming good-byes to the men.

In the wee hours of the morning, Thomas and Regina dragged themselves from the third nightspot that they'd visited that evening. They'd left the Exit/In in time to catch the "open mic" show at the Blue Bird Café. From there the group had moved on to Twelfth and Porter to hear Kirk Whalum and other world-famous musicians.

As they walked toward the Twelfth and Porter parking lot, Jimmy Bob asked, "Do y'all want to go somewhere and get something to eat?"

"No, I'm calling it a night," Regina answered instantly. "My feet hurt and I'm sleepy. This has been a rough week."

She wrapped her arm through Thomas's and leaned on him as she picked her way across the graveled parking lot in strappy, four-inch-heeled sandals. They had driven Regina's car because she knew where she was going and did not have the patience to give Thomas directions.

"Do you want me to drive now?" he asked, noting the fatigue in her voice.

"Please," was all she said and handed him the keys. Before he had backed from the parking spot, Regina leaned her head on the leather, padded headrest and closed her eyes. It seemed to her that only seconds later Thomas was trying to awaken her.

"Regina, we're home. Wake up, baby," he said gently in her ear. He smoothly pulled the car into the attached garage and turned off the motor.

Curled in the passenger seat, she turned to her side and covered her head with her hands. "Just leave me here. I'll be all right," she mumbled, not opening her eyes, trying to hold on to her restful sleep.

"Baby, you've got to go inside. Come on," he said. She didn't stir. He walked around to the passenger side of the car and opened the door. He touched her gently on the shoulder, urging her to wake up.

"My feet hurt and I'm so-o-o tired," she said, moving away from his hands.

Thomas lifted her into his arms and carried her up the three steps that took them from the garage into the house. She put one arm around his waist and the other over his shoulder as she snuggled her head against his chest. She was surprisingly lightweight for an avid dessert eater and beer drinker.

Walking through the dark, quiet house that was now as familiar to him as his own, he decided to take her up to her room. He hoped that Keisha was sleeping in the guest room and not Regina's. Finding Regina's bed empty, he carefully laid her there and removed her sandals before covering her with the afghan from the chaise.

He paused and looked at the beautiful woman that lay before him. Without realizing it, she had captured a part of his heart and he didn't know what to do. His deepest desire at that moment was to lie next to her and to hold her in his arms through the night.

"Is my mommy all right?" a small voice asked, interrupting Thomas's wayward thoughts.

"Yes, she's very tired. Is Tres still asleep?" Thomas asked, pulling his attention to the small child standing behind him in the doorway.

"Uh-huh. Do you want to spend the night over here so that you won't be home all alone?" Justin asked, looking up at Thomas with deep brown, almond-shaped eyes so like his mother's.

Involuntarily, Thomas's gaze returned to the woman sleeping peacefully on the bed. When he'd carried her upstairs, she'd felt so warm and soft in his arms. The thrill of her body against his had left an imprint on his mind.

With Thomas's hesitation, Justin spoke again. "You can sleep in my bed with me," the child offered.

Thomas cleared his throat and whispered, "I'll go home. We need to be real quiet so that we don't awaken anyone else. Let's tiptoe."

After he had tucked Justin safely into his bed, Thomas returned to the garage and took the automatic garage door opener from the sun visor of the Volvo. He exited the garage and pressed the remote control button to secure the house.

Chapter 4

In May when school closed for the summer, the boys were enrolled in summer activities at the Cumberland Science Museum and the pace became a little more relaxed. The two families continued to attend all kinds of events together, frequent each other's homes, and share meals together.

The foursome was shopping the supermarket one day, when Thomas was greeted by one of the professors from the university. "Hi, Coach, how are things going for you this summer?" the older man greeted Thomas.

"They're going pretty well," Thomas answered. "Are you teaching in summer school this year?"

"Yes, first session only though. I need some time to get away," the professor answered.

"That's great. I'll see you around." Thomas turned to continue selecting tomatoes, but was stopped by the professor's voice.

"By the way," Dr. Henry said in a loud voice that would carry to the rear of a three-hundred-seat lecture hall, "I am the president-elect for the faculty senate."

"Yes, I've heard. Congratulations," Thomas responded, offering his hand for a handshake. "I work closely with the faculty to address issues of common concern. Maybe you'll put me on the agenda for one of your meetings in the fall before basketball season starts."

"It would be better for you to utilize your faculty representative on the athletics committee. You know how it is. Our faculty doesn't have much respect for athletes; things are more credible coming from another faculty member. We believe that university policies and procedures should be faculty driven. Besides, we don't want to lose sight of the fact that Renaissance is an academic institution," Dr. Henry said pompously.

"No, we don't," Thomas said evenly. "My top priority in recruiting has been to find players who can meet the university's rigorous academic standards as well as they manage the round ball. Except for a few players recruited by my predecessors, I believe you'll be proud of the academic quality among our athletes."

"We'll see. I just want to put you on notice that we'll be watching you," Dr. Henry warned. Thomas was about to turn away again when Dr. Henry's voice stopped him a second time. "By the way, the Faculty Social Club is meeting in Kalante Hall tomorrow morning. Why don't you join us?"

"I'm very sorry, but I can't. Sunday morning is one of the few times that I have with my son and I don't like to leave him," Thomas said, sincerely apologetic. The Faculty Social Club was obviously an influential group. This was about the fifth time he'd been issued an invitation to attend one of their meetings.

While Thomas was making his apologies, Regina returned to the cart with several boxes of rice and pasta. Thomas wanted to avoid introducing her to the man whom he was finding to be quite antagonistic. But seeing Dr. Henry's intent gaze on her, Thomas knew that it would be rude to ignore the professor. "Wait a minute. I have someone I want you to meet," Thomas said, taking Regina's hand to slow her departure. "Dr.

Henry, I would like for you to meet my friend, Regina Lovejoy. Regina, Dr. Henry."

"I'm pleased to meet you," Regina said, gracing the man with her dazzling smile. "Excuse me, please, I left our sons choosing cereal. I'd better get back over there," Regina said and dashed away.

"She's a pretty little thing," the professor said, obviously unable to take his eyes from the gentle roll of her hips as she walked away. "A young fellow like you can come to town and draw the prettiest women we have. Do you two have a thing going on?"

"Yes, she's very pretty. Our sons play together," Thomas said stiffly, choosing to ignore the professor's salacious implication.

"And are you playing with her?" the professor asked, anxious for information to feed the campus rumor mill.

"No, we're just friends as I said. Our sons like to spend time together," Thomas explained with a growing sense of discomfort.

"Oh, I see," Dr. Henry said, trying to remember her name so that he could have all the details right at the meeting of the Faculty Social Club. If the coach knew how often he was the topic of discussion at their meeting, he'd certainly find a way to attend. All the women had been excited over his arrival and had speculated on his marital status, bank account, and sexual orientation.

The fact that he'd remained aloof during his first year only served to feed their hope and gossip. He was a good-looking, single man with one of the highest paid positions at the university—make that one of the highest paid positions in the city. He certainly earned more than any tenured professor, even one who had been in the classroom for more than twenty-five years.

Thomas thought no more about Dr. Henry for a

long time. He was much too busy. As the weeks went
by, Thomas and Regina managed to honor their tacit
agreement never to be alone together. Their sons
served as a buffer to the growing attraction that neither would admit to feeling.

One day in early June the three males came into the
music room where Regina was writing. Earlier in the
day, they had offered to wash her car and she'd reluctantly agreed. Now she wondered at her wisdom. They
were nearly as wet as if they'd gone swimming.

She smiled at the motley crew, and looking at the
sparkles in their eyes, she thought it was obvious that
they were up to some kind of mischief again. She carefully laid her pencil down on her desk and waited to
hear what scheme they had up their sleeves now. It was
always something. If the boys weren't planning something, Thomas would put ideas in their heads. He was
almost as bad as they were.

Although he had not gotten wet with the water hose,
Thomas's profuse perspiration had his T-shirt clinging
to his body. He was the most perfect specimen of mas-
culinity that Regina had ever encountered. The
thought had popped into her mind before she could
censor it. Embarrassed, she looked away to gather her
composure and had difficulty focusing on what was
making the three boys so excited.

"Regina, the boys and I have been talking about
going camping. I know that some ladies don't like
camping, but we sure would like to have you join us,"
Thomas said, hardly able to contain his glee.

"Please, Mommy! Please, Mommy!" Justin shouted,
dancing around Regina.

"I don't know. My idea of camping out is checking
into the local Holiday Inn," she said.

"Nah, we want to camp for real. We plan on roughing it. We'll go to the Great Smoky Mountain National

Park and sleep out under the stars. But we'll make it easy on you. We'll pitch your tent and you won't have to carry your own water or backpack. Will she, boys?" Thomas asked, including the boys with a wave of one arm.

"We'll take care of you," the boys said in unison, as if they'd rehearsed their attack on her.

She was grateful that Thomas was such a strong, positive male influence in her son's life, but she was also well aware that she couldn't leave it all up to her neighbor. She'd have to make some concessions to raising a male child. Her son liked to do the stereotypical male activities and she figured she'd have to get with the program. But three or four days of intense closeness to Thomas in near isolation would be trying. About to say no, she looked at the plea in her son's eyes and found herself saying, "Okay, count me in. But I'll have to go shopping. I have nothing to wear camping. Who wants to go with me?"

"Mom!" Justin exclaimed, hitting his forehead with the palm of his head. "Why do you always have to go shopping?"

"You can go shopping if you like," Thomas said, "but we're not taking any clothes with us. Clothes are too heavy to carry."

"You mean you're not changing clothes! I can't stay in the same clothes for three or four days," Regina exclaimed.

"Well, the rule is, don't pack more than you can carry on your back," Thomas said.

"I can pack strategically, but I can't be out there without a daily change of clothes," Regina said emphatically.

"Sure you can," Thomas assured her. "Give it a try."

"If I'm going, I'm changing clothes," Regina said.

"And I need to go shopping," she repeated firmly, folding her arms across her bosom.

Conceding that he would not be able to convince her not to change clothes during the trip, Thomas began to offer her advice. "Don't buy shorts because we'll be in the woods and the insects will eat up your legs in shorts. Get some jeans from Wal-Mart or somewhere like that. Don't go out and buy any expensive designer jeans, because management of this operation can't guarantee what might happen to them, okay? And although I—we—love your fragrances, please don't wear any perfumes, scented lotions, or soaps," Thomas continued, listing the dos and don'ts of camping. Regina listened carefully, making mental notes.

"Anything else?" she asked when he finally paused for a breath.

"You'll need comfortable hiking boots. None of your heels out there," Thomas teased her, although he loved to see her walk in heels. They made her hips sway a little more.

"I know that—don't be a doofus," Regina said, throwing a pencil at him. "Now seriously, tell me what else."

"Bring a bathing suit," he added, relishing the thought of finally seeing more of Regina's luscious body. They'd been practically inseparable for nearly three months and they were still in the *just friends* stage. *Very good* friends, he corrected, but nothing more. He was enjoying his friendship with Regina, but he was confounded by his desire for her that continued to grow with each encounter. However, he didn't know if a romantic relationship between them could work. After all, he'd already been head-over-heels in love once and that was enough for him. He still suffered from that loss. He didn't know if he could survive loving and losing again. He just couldn't take that risk.

As she prepared for the shopping trip, Regina quickly became as excited as the boys. As she talked to her friends on Music Row, it seemed that most of the men were really into this camping thing. Almost all of them had been Boy Scouts and at the very least they had that experience as a reference point. She had no experience at all. Her only experience with camping was limited to staying in a chalet in the mountains.

Over the next few days she finished her shopping and was left with one final concern. After they went swimming, what would she do with her hair? That was one issue that her friends on Music Row wouldn't understand. She decided to talk it over with Rosemary, her beautician, at her next appointment.

Rosemary thought for a few minutes after Regina posed the question. "We could let the perm grow out and you could wear a natural," she suggested.

"I could, but I don't have time. They're talking about going next weekend."

"Do you want to get extensions and have your hair braided?" Rosemary asked, running her fingers through Regina's coarse and thick hair.

"I don't know. I've never really thought about extensions."

"We can make it look real natural. We'll weave them into your hair and no one will know where your hair ends and the weave begins. Almost all the stars are wearing some kind of weave now."

"They may be, but that doesn't seem right for me," Regina said. "You know how I am." None of Rosemary's suggestions were appealing to Regina, but she kept pushing her hair care professional for more ideas.

After several more that involved additional hair, Regina said, "I'm not sure if I would be comfortable with a lot of hair. I've worn my hair short for so long now and it's easy to take care of."

"A weave is almost no extra care," Rosemary assured her.

"Look at how short my hair is," Regina said, indicating her short, tapered haircut.

"I can still weave more hair into it. You should let your hair grow out. I don't know why you have me cut it every time you come in here," Rosemary said.

"Because I like my hair short," Regina answered, telling the beautician what she already knew. Contrary to the myth of the scissor-happy hairstylist, Rosemary was always encouraging Regina to let her hair grow longer.

Rosemary continued to think about hairstyles she'd seen at the last hair show in Atlanta. She snapped her fingers. "I've got it. Obviously you don't want the weave. Let me relax your hair as straight as I can get it. That way you can let it dry in the sun and fluff it out in spikes all over your head."

"Now that I can live with," Regina said, relieved and visibly relaxing in her seat as the stylist cut her hair before applying the cream relaxer.

Regina attempted to read the newest issue of *Essence*, but today happened to be one of the days that Rosemary felt like having a conversation. Sometimes during her two-hour appointments with Rosemary, the beautician would barely utter two words beyond a greeting. Regina knew that her friend was moody, but chalked it up to her artistic temperament. When she had met Rosemary at church after her return to Nashville, a friendship between the two blossomed almost instantly. They were both members of the Sisters of Ruth women's prayer group at church. Regina respected the woman's experience and commitment to her craft.

"When I asked you about your relationship with Tres's father, you told me that *just friends* story," Rosemary said as she applied the cool cream to Regina's hair. "Now I hear that you two go grocery shopping together and everything."

"Where did you hear that?" Regina asked, somewhat taken aback that her business was in the street.

"It's common knowledge. You know that you can't hide when someone with a high profile like the head coach of our major university is involved. I'm just hurt that you didn't tell me that you were more than just friends," Rosemary said softly so that they wouldn't be overheard in the busy shop.

"But we are just friends," Regina said just as softly.

"Is he the *friend* that you and Justin are going camping with?" Rosemary asked, making a part with a rat-tail comb and applying more of the creamy chemicals to the exposed growth.

"Yes, you know how close the boys are. There's no way that Justin was going to let Tres go away without him. And although I don't want to go camping, I can't leave it up to Thomas to expose my son to these masculine activities that Justin loves," Regina answered.

"No wonder you're worried about how your hair is going to look. I would be worried about how I look if I were going somewhere with him. Girl, he's a TYM if I've ever seen one."

Realizing that Rosemary was setting her up, Regina asked the question anyway. "What is a TYM?" she asked, feeling like the straight man in a comedy act.

"You know, a tender young morsel. Don't you listen to the radio in the morning? I know, you're probably listening to your songs on the country stations."

"I listen to all kinds of music. That's where I get my ideas from."

"Back to your man—I know, but if he's not your man now, he soon will be. Don't try to change the subject on me," Rosemary said, waving away Regina's attempt to interrupt her again. "How can you keep your hands off him? Don't you want to feel those big muscles? O-h-h, he's so fine. Those long legs with that little bow in them—and those shoulders—and he's got a totally buff body." Rosemary was practically drooling when she met Regina's eyes in the mirror.

"Don't look at me like that," she said to Regina's reflection as she positioned her before the mirror.

"Well, I was just wondering if I should mention this to Harold," Regina said, barely able to suppress her smile.

"I might be married, but I'm not blind. I know you've thought the same thing yourself. I'm not the only one who's noticed him either. You know, when he first came here, there were so many female spectators coming to watch their practice that they had to start locking the gym doors. Do you think that many women were suddenly interested in basketball? No, word had gotten out that he was single, superfine, and a real gentleman to boot—the total package."

"I hadn't heard about that. I guess I missed that bit of gossip," Regina said dryly, subtly reminding Rosemary that she discouraged gossip.

Rosemary leaned toward Regina and whispered into her ear as she worked the cream through to her roots, "Well, you know we don't like gossip in this shop, but I hear that it's more than just the women over there at the school that are interested in him. If you want him at all, and I don't see why you wouldn't, you'd better use this camping trip to make your move on him."

"What makes you think that I haven't made my move already?" Regina asked.

"For one thing, because I know you, but if you have made your move you'd better send out notices. Rumor has it that a certain woman in the English department has made no bones that she's waging an all-out campaign to get his affection. Girl, take my advice now. Use this camping trip to make your move."

"Rosemary, you know I can't do that. Our sons will be with us," Regina said impatiently.

"You act like you're so bold and independent all the time. Now you're being timid when your boldness would come in handy. I know your problem, though. You're scared. That's what your problem is," Rosemary said as if it had just dawned on her.

"I am not scared. I'm just not about to begin chasing after some man because everyone else wants him," Regina said.

"Suit yourself, but think about this. Your boys will fall asleep way before you adults do. The sunshine, fresh air, and swimming will have them so tired that they'll pass out in no time," Rosemary advised.

Regina gave up on trying to read and laid the closed magazine in her lap. Rosemary was encouraged by her friend's attention. "I hope you didn't go out and buy any of those drip-dry-looking camping clothes," Rosemary continued, beginning to enjoy her advisory role.

"I think I did," Regina admitted.

"At least get you a knock-'em-dead two-piece bathing suit," Rosemary suggested.

"I'm too big for any two-piece," Regina said.

"No, you're not. I wish I had your hourglass figure— those big boobs and hips with that tiny waist."

"My butt and thighs are too big," Regina tried explaining.

"Yeah, yeah, you never act like they're a problem. You walk around carrying your booty like it's some kind of prize," Rosemary said.

"What else can I do with it? It won't go away," Regina said, laughing at her friend's assessment. "Isn't it funny that we're never satisfied with our figures?"

"I would like to be just a little more shapely. You

know what they say." Rosemary laughed. "Nobody wants a bone but a dog and he buries it." She roared heartily at her own joke and Regina joined her. "Now seriously," Rosemary said, wiping tears of laughter from her eyes, "you go get a nice bathing suit and flaunt those voluptuous curves of yours. You know that's the kind of figure that brothers go crazy over."

"I don't know about that," Regina began.

"I do. Honey, when Erica was born and my breasts grew a couple of inches my husband was so excited you would have thought he was the one being breast-fed. Now listen to me." Rosemary paused and looked at Regina's hair before saying more. "Come on to the shampoo bowl. Let's get this chemical out of your hair."

When they reached the shampoo bowl, Rosemary continued, "Now where was I? Oh, yeah, as I was saying, as sweet as this man has been to you, you should at least let him know that you're interested." As if to verify the accuracy of Rosemary's assessment the timer buzzed, indicating it was time for the relaxer to be rinsed from Regina's hair. "Is it burning yet?" Rosemary asked before applying the sprayer.

"No, it's not burning at all," Regina answered.

As the beautician rinsed her customer's hair and applied a neutralizer, she continued until Regina was ready to go under a hooded dryer.

As she sat under the dryer, Regina thought about Rosemary's advice. Maybe she should be bolder in her approach to Thomas. He was certainly attractive and more than once he'd let her know that he found her appealing. Yet, there was always a reserve between them. Whenever they began to talk comfortably, he would go only so far before he would erect a barrier between them.

He never talked about his job at St. Luke University

beyond generalities and he'd never once mentioned Tres's mother. In all the time they'd spent together, she did not know the woman's first name or where she lived. Then again, he could say the same about her. She'd never mentioned Justin's father except that one time. And that day, he'd not even bothered to ask what her married name was. She would be more forthcoming, she reasoned, but he seemed to discourage such revelations. Usually if their conversations went in that area, he would run for cover. Now that's what they should be revealing in the woods. Not her body, but the secrets that lay between them.

In less than twenty minutes, Rosemary was taking her from under the dryer. "Your hair is still damp, but I'm going to finish with a blow dryer," Rosemary said, adding mousse and then spiking the hair away from the young woman's head. "I know that you can't wear a gel in the woods, but this mousse has no scent. It should be safe to use. After your hair is nearly dry, but still damp, apply this and style it," she instructed. "You'll look good enough to eat and he just might," she continued and winked at Regina.

"You're too much," Regina said, shaking her newly styled, lightweight head. She felt as if she could float on air.

Wednesday night, Justin was too excited to sleep. Regina allowed him to lie in her bed and keep her company while she finished packing. While she rolled her shorts and shirts into neat piles in her backpack in the order she would wear them, Justin fell asleep. She wanted everything to be neatly organized so that she could dress as quickly as possible. She did not want the boys to complain about her need for a daily shower and change of clothes.

Early the next morning the ringing doorbell awakened her. She opened her eyes and found that the room was as dark as midnight. She was about to cover her head and go back to sleep when the doorbell rang again. Then she remembered the camping trip. She stuck her feet into the house shoes and threw on a robe before hurrying down the stairs to the front door.

"Did you oversleep?" Thomas asked when she threw the door open.

"Yes, I sure did. I forgot to change my alarm clock for an earlier wake-up time," she said. "Give me a minute. We have everything packed. It won't take us long to dress."

Tres was about to follow her upstairs until his dad held him back. "We'll wait down here," she heard him say as she fled the room.

In less than ten minutes, she and Justin were dressed and headed out on their adventure. The boys fell asleep before the car was out of the driveway. "We'll eat breakfast after we get a little bit farther down the road. Is that okay? I'd like to get through Knoxville before their rush hour begins," Thomas said.

"Yes, sure. Do you need me to read the map or anything?" Regina offered.

"No, I've been up here a couple of times before. I've got it pretty well figured out. It'll take us about four hours. By the time the boys are good and awake, we should be there."

"That sounds good to me," Regina said and then promptly fell asleep. Thomas looked over at the sleeping figure next to him and was filled with a sense of contentment. For the first time in years, he was at peace. The boys asleep behind him and the woman next to him had given him more joy than he'd ever expected to feel again.

Regina had proven to be a godsend. Not just because of her easy acceptance of Tres, treating him as if he were her own son, giving him the cuddling and attention that he'd never gotten from his own mother. But, she was so good for the father, too. When they talked, she understood the words he said, as well as those he did not say.

Sometimes when he vented his frustration with some administrative nightmare at work, she'd look at him with her large expressive eyes and simply say, "I feel you," and he knew that she really did. She could be cutting and sarcastic at times, placing the blame for some of his problems at work squarely on his shoulders where they belonged. But the thing was, she was always right on target.

He admitted that he didn't know what was next in their relationship, but for now he knew that she was his best friend—even if she didn't like to play basketball. He wouldn't mind getting her into a little game of one-on-one. His mind had moved into a more lustful direction when he felt Regina awaken. She opened her eyes first, then shifted in the seat and stretched.

The sun was high in the sky. "Where are we?" she asked.

"We're about fifteen minutes outside of Knoxville," Thomas answered, not taking his eyes from the road.

"Do you need me to take over the wheel for a while?" Regina offered.

"No, I don't want to stop the car until the boys wake up," Thomas responded. "Unless you need a pit stop," he said, taking a quick glance at Regina.

"I'm fine. I agree with you, let's ride while we can. When the boys wake up, we'll have to stop for sure."

"I love riding through east Tennessee," Thomas said. "The terrain is so varied with the rolling hills and then the miles of plateaus. The scenery is magnificent, it reminds me that there is a higher power."

"Only the majesty of God could create these wonders," Regina agreed. "It's beautiful until you hit Knoxville."

As if on cue, the road curved and they were riding through Knoxville. "You see the Cumberland Avenue exit up there?" Regina asked. "That's the exit that took me to the dorm where I lived for four years."

"I can just see you now, a cute little freshman in her college sweatshirt, baggy jeans, and nappy hair," Thomas teased.

"Now why did you have to go there? Why do you imagine that my hair would have been nappy?" she asked.

"Because you were a minority freshman on a majority campus. You hadn't found your way into the city yet and didn't know how to hook up with a black beautician."

"Well, you're wrong about one thing—my jeans were not baggy and I was wearing a natural back then. I was happy to be nappy. I wasn't looking for a beauty shop. What makes you think you know so much about women, anyway? You're always saying things like that," Regina said, more interested in his answer than perturbed with him.

"Because I spend all my time around young men. And when young men aren't talking about the game, they're talking about women. They're always asking the coaches why this and why that. I leave it up to my assistant coaches to answer their questions and I learn a lot that way. They're all younger than I am and they have all the answers," he said, only half joking.

"And here I was thinking you were extrasensitive to the needs of women," Regina said, poking him in the arm.

"UT sure does have a big campus," Thomas observed. "Have you come up here since you graduated?"

"Not much. I've been up for an alumni tea and for a

homecoming event," she said, remembering when she'd come up the fall after her May graduation to spend some time with the man who became her husband. During her visit he'd told her that he was moving to New York. She'd told him that she was going too. He already had the job in New York and left immediately. She had gone back to Nashville, given a two-week notice on the job that she'd started only months earlier, packed up her bags, and moved on.

She shook her head in disbelief at the memory. That time seemed like a distant dream. She'd been so immature at that time. She'd argued with her mother over her drastic actions. Her mother had been upset for many reasons, including the fact that she'd not been allowed to see her only daughter married.

Her mother could not accept the fact that Regina was more interested in being married than having a wedding. All her mother would talk about was how Regina was disappointing the people who'd watched her grow up and wanted to be included in this special event.

Regina could finally admit that she'd been extremely selfish. She could have included her mother in some way. There was certainly a big difference between being twenty-two years old and thirty, she thought ruefully. She suddenly realized that Thomas was looking at her as if he was expecting an answer.

"I was asking if you ever went skiing in Gatlinburg while you lived up here." Thomas seemed to be repeating himself. He stole a glance at her, wondering where her mind had been that she had not even heard him. She'd completely missed his question the first time.

"I'm sorry, I think I'd drifted back to my good old school days," Regina said, with a tinge of sarcasm in her voice. "But to answer your question, yes, I did go skiing a few times. I never enjoyed it though. Have you ever been skiing?"

"Yes," he answered in his don't-ask-me-any-more-questions way.

Determined that she wouldn't let his short answers shut her out this weekend, Regina ventured to ask more questions. "Where?"

"I've skied in Colorado and Pennsylvania." After a pause he added, "We lived in Japan for a couple of years and I skied while we were over there."

"What were you doing in Japan?" Regina dared to ask, wondering if he realized that he'd revealed more about his past than ever before.

He sighed deeply and plunged ahead. "When I graduated from college, I was so far down on the NBA draft that I went to play for the Toyota team in Tokyo. We played about twenty-eight games a year and the pay was good, especially for me. Most of the teams in the Japanese League have one or two Americans playing for them and we're paid at a premium rate. All in all, it wasn't a bad gig."

It felt good to talk openly with Regina. He was tired of guarding his tongue and playing games of being evasive when she asked simple questions that required a straightforward answer. No more, he decided, whatever she asked this week he'd tell her. He knew that Regina never seemed to run out of questions and she might go on for hours, but it was time for full disclosure.

"What did you like most about living in Japan?" she asked.

"My son was born over there," was his immediate response.

"So he was really born and not hatched as you've led me to believe," she shot at him.

"There you go with one of your zingers again. If you

keep being so sarcastic, I'm not going to talk with you. You know how sensitive I am and you hurt my feelings when you do that," he said dramatically, imitating Regina's mannerisms and speech pattern.

"I do not."

"Yes, you do"

"Okay, I'll be sensitive to your thin skin. Although I don't know why you pretend I'm hurting you."

"Regina, sometimes you say things without thinking and they are pretty tactless."

"Okay, I'll grow tactful. Where is your son's mother now?" Regina asked, without missing a beat. Maybe she was a little tactless, but she planned to ask questions while he seemed to be in a mood to answer them. He couldn't run away from her now. All the doors to the Navigator were locked.

"She's dead," he answered flatly.

At first she thought he was joking, but seeing the stricken look on his face, she knew that he was being truthful. "I'm so sorry," Regina said, instantly filled with regret that she'd been so inquisitive.

"So am I," Thomas answered emotionlessly.

"What happened?" Regina ventured.

"She had lupus. Do you know what that is?" he asked.

"I know that it's a chronic disease with no cure, but most victims of the disease live long full lives," she answered.

"Not my wife," Thomas said, still without emotion. "She had systemic lupus, which attacks various systems in the body. When she became pregnant, the disease was exacerbated, attacking her kidneys. After Tres was born she went into total renal failure and had to have kidney dialysis treatments. We decided to come back to the United States so that she could receive benefit of the research being done here. It's not that they didn't have advanced medicine in Japan, but since lupus affects African-Americans four times more than it does Caucasians, we thought she'd have a better chance of living with the disease here."

Regina felt an overwhelming sympathy for Thomas. As he was talking, she could feel the pain that she'd awakened in him. No wonder he never talked about his past, it had to be much too painful to discuss. However, she was relieved that he finally trusted her enough to reveal as much as he had.

"Are those all of your questions?" Thomas asked when Regina remained silent.

"No, I have one more. What was your wife's name?"

After a pause so long that Regina didn't think he was going to answer her, he said, "Her name was Paulette." He gripped the steering wheel so hard that she could see the tension around his knuckles, but he drove along as if they were having a normal conversation.

It had become too difficult to avoid talking to Regina about Paulette. He and Regina spent so much time together that it was wearing on him to keep blocking her from his past. He hoped that he'd told her enough to satisfy her curiosity so she would leave the subject alone.

Regina sensed Thomas's emotional turmoil and remained silent. She knew that it had taken a lot out of him to reveal so much and she wanted to give him a chance to relax again.

"Listen to this," Regina said, increasing the volume on the radio. "That's Alison McKenzie singing one of my songs." She began singing along with the radio. Thomas smiled at the sheer nonsense of the lyrics. It was a song about a woman dyeing all the family wash blue because she was so blue. The woman who belted out the song sang in a rough raspy voice and Regina did a good job of imitating the voice and acting out the song.

When the song ended Thomas laughed again and commented, "That sounds like the blues."

"It's very similar to the blues. I think it's a little more like honky-tonk though. You know, a lot of the country music used to have that honky-tonk sound. You don't hear it much anymore. Everything's so homogenized to appeal to everyone that it ends up appealing to no one. It's all too mainstream," Regina said.

"Then there's Hank Williams Jr. and Wynnona Judd. They can get down with their honky-tonk sounds," Thomas said.

"You do know something about country. All this time and you've been pretending that you've never ever listened to country music before," Regina praised Thomas.

"That's something hard for a black man to admit." Thomas laughed. "But anybody who's ever watched the beginning of *Monday Night Football* has heard Hank Williams Jr. sing out 'Are you ready for football?'"

"You must be familiar with Whitney Houston's hit from the *Bodyguard* soundtrack?" Regina asked.

"I sort of remember it," Thomas replied.

"Did you know that Dolly Parton wrote it? It fact, she recorded it first. But it was never as successful as Whitney's version."

They chatted comfortably through Knoxville and continued until they left Interstate 40 and got on Highway 441. Somewhere in between Knoxville and the entrance to the Great Smoky Mountains National Park, the boys awakened. "I need to go to the bathroom," said one.

"I'm hungry," said the other.

Thomas pulled over at the next restaurant. They had a relaxing meal of pancakes, omelets, and juice.

After they'd eaten, they let the boys run around the picnic area that surrounded the restaurant before re-boarding the SUV and heading up the mountain for the final leg of their journey.

Chapter 5

Once in Gatlingburg, they drove through narrow streets lined with shops and tourist attractions on either side. The scenic atmosphere was reminiscent of a small English village with the antique lampposts and attractive little shops. When they pulled into the parking lot of a supermarket just like the one at home, it was like being snatched from a beautiful movie scene back to reality. Its thoroughly modern facade was in sharp contrast to the artsy little village scene that they'd just left.

"We'd better stop and get our supplies here. I can't think of any store closer," Thomas said.

They entered the store and were greeted by a friendly clerk. "You folks headed up the mountain?" he asked.

"Yes, we'll be camping out up at Deep Creek over in Bryson City."

"You still have a little ways to go yet," the clerk noted. "Where are you folks coming from?"

"Nashville."

"Well, I hope you and the missus have a good time. I know your twins will."

"Thanks," Thomas said, seeing no need to correct the clerk. "What have you heard about the bears this year?"

"The usual. A few sightings," the friendly clerk answered. "Do you need any of those big plastic containers to put your food in?"

"No, I brought those with me. But I will buy some rope," Thomas decided.

"I'll get it for you." The clerk rushed to the back of the store.

As Regina began taking things from the cart and placing them on the conveyor belt at the cash register, she whispered, "Why didn't you tell him that I'm not your missus and that the boys aren't twins?"

"Because it's none of his business. We'll probably never see him again anyway," Thomas whispered back. *And because I like the thought of us being a family unit,* he added silently.

After they'd put ice in the cooler and loaded the groceries in the back of the SUV, they continued their journey. They followed the Blue Mountain Parkway to Newfound Gap Road. As the road climbed, the dignified, centuries-old maple trees gave way to majestic evergreens. "Look at all the Christmas trees!" Justin exclaimed gleefully.

"They're beautiful, aren't they?" Regina replied.

"Let's take one home with us," Tres suggested.

"If we could cut one down, where would we put it?" Thomas asked.

The boys grew silent, contemplating an answer. All around them the scenery continued to change as the road went through sharp turns and steep elevations. It rose 3,600 feet from Gatlinburg to its end in Newfound Gap. The boys laughed when their ears began to pop. Regina gave a stick of gum to each of them.

She was uncomfortable with the elevation and hairpin turns, but she tried to talk with the boys as they discussed the deer and other wildlife they spotted in the woods. "Why did you need rope?" she suddenly re-membered to ask Thomas.

"You'll see," was his noncommittal reply.

Finally they crossed the Tennessee state line into North Carolina and saw the sign directing them to Bryson. "We don't have much farther before we reach Deep Creek," Thomas said when they were on an even steeper and more narrow road than the one they'd just left.

Thomas drove the Navigator into a paved parking area and announced that they'd reached their desti-nation. The boys jumped from the vehicle and wanted to begin their explorations, but Thomas stopped them. "First we have to secure our area," he told the group.

"What does that mean?" Justin asked.

"We've got to decide where we want to put our tents, and then we have to move all the rocks and sticks from the area. You don't want to sleep on rocks and sticks, do you?" Thomas asked.

"I sure don't," Tres answered. The four headed for the campground and after locating and clearing an area, they returned to unload the SUV. They set up tents and placed their sleeping bags in them before they unloaded the groceries. After placing the food into two huge plastic storage containers, Thomas tied rope around them and devising a pulley, he hoisted first one and then the other high into a tree.

"Why did you do that, Daddy?" Tres asked.

"It's for the bears, isn't it, Mr. Thomas?" Justin an-swered.

"It sure is. We want to keep the food away from us and away from the bears. When we eat, we'll take out what we need. Eat all of it and put the rest away, high in the trees," Thomas explained.

Regina shuddered at the thought of bears roaming

around just waiting for them to make the mistake of leaving food out. She didn't have much time to dwell on her fears because the energetic little boys were ready to go. They'd done all of their chores and wanted to take their first hike.

"We don't have time to go far today," Thomas said. "It's getting late and we don't want to be too far from our campsite when it gets dark."

The walk felt good after being cooped up in the car since before daylight that morning. Regina was concerned that the hike would be too much for the two five-year-olds, but discovered that she was having trouble keeping up with the pace they set.

When dinner was over that night and the boys were in their sleeping bags in the tent that they were to share with Thomas, Regina sat at the campfire thinking about the day. She was tired, but her mind wouldn't stop.

She sat in a low, cloth camp chair before the fire when Thomas came to sit next to her. "What do you think of your first day of roughing it?" he asked.

"Most of the day we were in the car, but it's been beautiful out here in the wilderness. The mountains are so awesome that it's unbelievable. When I look at all this beauty, I feel like I've been put in my place. I feel so insignificant before the majesty of God. Then I remember that He put us in charge of all of this. He made us just a little bit lower than the angels. Our relationship to nature and God is so awesome," she said meditatively.

"That's the same way I feel. As a matter of fact, I've felt overwhelmed by the scenery for most of this trip. Wasn't that sunset something to see?"

"It was beautiful," she responded.

"Camping out like this helps me to keep things in perspective. Sometimes I get so caught up in my job that I forget that there's a whole world outside the gym. Then something, like this sunset, reminds me that I'm just a small part of the universe. When I look at winning or losing a basketball game from that perspective, I realize that it's just a game. A game that I enjoy immensely, but it is just a game," Thomas said, thoughtfully, somehow certain that Regina would understand.

"I think life is a game, but it's a fun game. Those boys at Renaissance need you to teach them to succeed in this game we call life," Regina said earnestly. "I think you emphasize to them that basketball is just one aspect of what makes them important."

"I suppose so. I guess it's just a matter of keeping everything in its proper place," Thomas said.

"How much of that hiking trail should we tackle? I don't think we should go overboard and try to do all twenty miles at once," Regina commented after they'd listened to the night noises of the surrounding forest for several minutes. "I'm glad you started me off on the short trail."

"Are you feeling okay?" he asked, ready to tease her if she could accept it. "I know how much you hate exercise."

"I'm okay. It was all rather inspiring. In fact, I was composing a song in my head when you came over. Want to hear it?"

He wondered at the laughter in her voice and readily agreed to hear the song. He was relieved that she had finally gotten over her shyness of singing for him. "Sure, I'm game," he answered.

She sang in a voice with an exaggerated country twang, "Pain in my back, numb to my toes/ Water from the creek up in my nose/ Twigs in my hair, rocks in my shoes/ Bears looking at me, like I'm a fool/ Oh, camping, camping's a delight/ Camping, camping's a delight/ Now I know, I'll never get it right."

Thomas laughed heartily. "Do you think you can get it published?"

"I don't know. It's more for personal relief than public consumption. I just need to express my pain," she answered.

"It's not as bad as all that. We only hiked six miles today." He laughed.

"That must have been the same six miles you told me about when you had me hike from that downtown parking garage in five-inch heels," she said, referring to a long walk where he'd motivated her to keep walking, telling her it was only a short walk to the arena.

"At least you have on proper foot attire this time. Take your boot off and let me see your foot," he ordered.

She took off her hiking boots and socks, holding one foot toward him. He kneeled before her and examined her foot carefully. His tender touch removed all the pain and sent a flood of pleasure through her body.

"Well, at least you don't have any blisters." He began to gently rub her tired, aching foot.

"Don't do that," she murmured, leaning back in the low chair.

"Why? Doesn't it feel good?" Thomas asked.

"Because it feels too good," she answered through half-closed eyes. "And because I know my feet must stink after I stepped into that creek today and now my socks have dried on my feet."

He didn't remove his hand from her foot, but continued the gentle massage. "Your feet don't stink all that bad," he said. "I've changed diapers that smelled sort of like this," he teased.

She raised a hand to hit him, but was too tired to complete the effort.

"What do you have planned tomorrow?" she asked, feeling very relaxed.

"We'll drive a little, then hike up to Clingmans Dome. It's the highest point in the Smokies and you can see seven states up there. I think the boys will get a kick out of it," Thomas said.

"Then I think I'd better get to bed," Regina said, not wanting to end their time together, but realizing that she'd soon be too tired to drag herself to her sleeping bag.

Before breakfast the next morning, Thomas told the boys to dig a hole not far from their campsite. He checked their progress from time to time as he worked on other parts of the meal. When it was finally big enough, he took out a big, lidded cast-iron Dutch oven and tested to see if it would fit in the hole.

"Why are you going to put that pot in the hole, Daddy?" Tres asked.

"Who wants apple cobbler for dessert tonight?" Thomas asked.

"I do," the boys answered.

"Then we have to put this pot into that hole, but first you have to help me make the cobbler."

After they'd eaten breakfast, Regina cleared away the remaining food while Thomas and the boys began to make the cobbler. They lined the Dutch oven with a premade piecrust, then tossed in canned chopped apples, cinnamon, and sugar.

While they were making the cobbler, Regina lined the hole with charcoal and let them flame before they settled to a red glow. By the time the ingredients for the cobbler were in the Dutch oven, the fire was ready. Thomas set the pot in the hole and covered the whole thing with dirt. "This should be ready by the time we get back today," he told the boys.

They had a full day of hiking and sight-seeing. For lunch they ate sandwiches from their backpacks and drank water from bottles they carried with them on the trail. Regina was tired again, but refused to let a couple of five-year-olds outdo her. Maybe she should join the gym when she got home. The few calisthenics that she did before her shower each morning were not working to keep her heart fit.

That evening after the boys were asleep, she and Thomas sat before the fire and discussed their day again. "Are you ready for your massage?" he asked.

"Yes, everything aches today," she said without thinking.

"Well, I can massage your everything if you like," Thomas said, raising one eyebrow.

"I didn't mean—just start with my feet, okay?" she said, trying not to show embarrassment at her slip.

He massaged her feet and she sighed heavily. It was such a relief. "You have a knot in your muscle right here," he said, gently massaging her right calf.

His touch melted all that was aching inside her. "You have a nice touch," she practically purred in her totally relaxed state.

"I'm a trained masseuse," he answered.

"Seriously?" she said, rising in her seat to look at him.

"Yes, it was an extra-credit class. Since then, I've worked a lot with our trainers and learned a little more than what I learned in class." He lifted her leg and said, "Try this. See, when I touch this, it should relax your spine," he said, giving a deep push to a muscle in the back of her thigh.

"It worked," she said, amazed. "I feel new. My pain is gone."

"Now go to your tent," Thomas ordered. "Tomorrow we're going to ride horses around the trails and see what else is around here. We might go to Indian Creek Falls if you're up to it."

After breakfast the next morning, they drove to one of the ranger stations and rented horses. Thomas assured the ranger that they would not need a guide; they would follow their map.

The falls were completely secluded when they got there. They anchored their horses, stripped down to the bathing suits that they wore under their clothes, and splashed and played in the water most of the morning. Regina was nervous that one of the boys would slip on a slick, moss-covered rock, but Thomas was helping her keep a close eye on them.

While she had not worn a two-piece bathing suit as Rosemary had suggested, she looked good to Thomas in her simple one-piece. Thomas noted that her soft curves amply filled the conservative cut of the suit. Although it was not low-cut, he could see the promise of the soft rise of her breasts. He looked at her appreciatively, thinking that there was nothing he would change about the woman frolicking before him. She joyfully played in the water with the children, while her body seduced him with each movement.

When they'd first gotten in the water, it had been a relief after the long, hot horseback ride. But after a while it became too cold and they sought a sunny spot to eat their lunch.

Totally wiped out from the water play and lunch, Regina stretched out on her towel after eating. Thomas promptly placed his next to hers, after warning the boys to stay within sight of the adults.

Regina lay serenely on her back with dark glasses on and her arms behind her head. She stole quick glances at his long, muscular body without moving her head.

She watched as he turned toward her, resting on one elbow. His gaze did not stray from her body and he did not attempt a conversation. He must have thought that she was asleep.

Without moving, she asked, "Why are you staring at me like that?"

"I thought you'd fallen asleep. Aren't your eyes closed?" he asked, feeling like he'd been caught doing something wrong.

"No, I'm not asleep. I was looking at you looking at me," she said provocatively. "Do you like what you see?"

"Yes, as a matter of fact I do. You're good to look at. Those colors in your suit contrast against your skin beautifully. What are those colors?" he asked, trying to recover from his embarrassment.

"Do you really want me to start naming all the colors in my suit?" she teased.

"No, I don't give a damn about the colors in your suit. I want to know what you'd do if I held you in my arms and kissed you until we had to stop for air," he said truthfully.

She could not let him know that the thought of being in his arms again stayed with her all the time. She'd frequently thought of how comfortable and secure she'd felt in them on their Tin Pan night when he lifted her from her car and put her to bed. She flushed when she thought of his deep, husky voice calling her *baby*. It would be so easy to give in to the temptation he offered. She realized, however, that if she gave in, there would be no turning back. So instead of giving in, she threatened, "Don't even think about it. Friends don't kiss friends."

Thomas immediately rose from his towel and walked away, saying that he needed to check on the boys. She hadn't meant to hurt his feelings, but she was afraid that she had. She couldn't mess up their friendship with her desire for something more. It was best to leave things as they were.

That night after the boys were in their tent, Thomas came to sit next to Regina at the fire. He did not offer to massage her feet or legs as he had the previous nights. After an uncomfortable silence, Thomas said, "Excuse me if I offended you today. I thought that maybe you were beginning to feel some of the things that I feel for you. I apologize."

"Think nothing of it," she said breezily, with a wave of her hand.

They sat several more minutes, listening to the sounds of the night that surrounded them. Finally Regina rose and said good night.

The next day, they decided to try fishing. Regina hated the thought of putting bait on a hook and catching unsuspecting fish. "Whatever you catch, we'll have for dinner," Thomas promised the boys.

They drove the Navigator into Bryson to get a fishing license, and then they went back up to Dry Creek, near their campsite to a little pond they'd seen on one of their hikes.

"What kind of fish are we going to catch?" Tres asked.

"Can we catch a whale?" Justin asked. The boys were so excited over the thought of catching dinner that they couldn't stop talking.

"If you don't get quiet, you'll scare the fish away," Thomas whispered.

The boys became quiet and Regina stretched out in her lounge chair to read a magazine she'd brought along with her. When no one had caught anything after an hour, they decided to take a swim.

"That doesn't look like safe water for swimming.

This is not one of the designated swimming areas,"
Regina warned.

"We'll be okay," Thomas said.

"Don't go out too far," Regina cautioned, fighting
the impulse to absolutely forbid their swimming altogether.

"We'll be okay," Thomas repeated.

"How do you know that?" Regina asked.

"Because we are great swimmers," Thomas said and
started walking toward the pond. The boys picked up
their gear and followed him.

Regina followed behind the boys. Instead of seeing
a clean, crystal-clear pond, she saw danger. "You know,
there could be slippery rocks in there. You could fall
and bust your head open," she said doubtfully.

"We could, but we won't," Thomas answered positively. "Okay, who's ready to go?"

"I am," both boys said.

"Look, here's a vine," Thomas said, excited. "Since
we don't have a diving board, we can swing out into
the middle of the pond."

"You may not swing on that vine," Regina said firmly.
"Do you think you're Tarzan?"

"Relax, it's going to be fine," Thomas said. "I've
done this many times before. We used to have vines all
around the ponds back home."

"Now you're going too far. It's bad enough that you
wanted to swim in this hole, but now you want to swing
from a vine? This is insane. You may endanger your
son, but I'm not going to let you put my baby at risk
like that," Regina said firmly, looking up at Thomas
without blinking.

"I am not putting any baby at risk. You know that
your five-year-old boy doesn't like being called a baby.
And you know that I'd never tell the boys to do any-

thing that would put them at risk. The water in this pond is not that deep."

"You have no idea how deep it is," Regina challenged

"I have some idea," Thomas said. "Look, the water is so clear that we can see the bottom."

"You may not be concerned about your son's safety, but I am concerned about mine," Regina said, now full of righteous anger.

Thomas stopped in midstride, surprised at the anger in her voice. "So it's like that," he said, turning to look at her angry face. To the boy that he loved as much as his own son, he said gently, "Justin, you need to stay with your mother."

Justin and Regina watched as Thomas helped Tres grip the vine and push him as far out as possible, nearly to the middle of the pond. Tres splashed around in the water and his father quickly swung out to join him. They swam to the other side and warmed themselves in the sun, before jumping into the water again.

Regina found herself longing to escape the heat and humidity clinging to her by jumping into the cool and inviting water. It did look like Tres and Thomas were having fun, she realized.

"Mama, I'm not a baby. I can swim better than Tres and you know it," Justin said as he looked at his friends waving to him from the other side.

"Don't use that tone of voice with me, young man. We came to fish. You can fish where you are. This pond is not one of the designated swimming areas," Regina said impatiently.

Justin glared at his mother, but knew better than to say anything more. He sank to the ground with tears in his eyes, staring at his friends and wishing that his mother could be reasoned with.

Thomas and Tres jumped into the water again. This time they only stayed in for fifteen minutes before they gave up. Swimming was not fun without Justin and Regina, but Thomas hated to face Regina. He knew that she was angry with him. Well, he should be angry with her for not trusting his judgment, again.

When the two groups reunited, Thomas could see that Regina's anger still simmered. Any word from him and it could easily reach the boiling point. Thomas decided that his silence would be the better part of valor. She did not utter a single word all the way back to the campsite.

From time to time, he felt her shooting poisonous darts at him with her eyes. She was usually very talkative, especially when angry. This was the woman who usually debated with him without thinking twice. Now she was not saying anything at all. He did not recognize this new level of anger.

Sensing the mood of the adults, the boys ran ahead, stopping from time to time to examine an insect on their path.

When they reached their campsite, Regina rushed into her tent without a word to anyone. Once inside, she could think of nothing to do. She'd rolled her sleeping bag before they'd left and her things were packed away since they planned to leave early the next morning.

She sat on the small camp stool in the center of her tent, resting her chin on her hands. Perhaps Thomas was right, maybe she was overprotective of Justin. She thought of Justin's sad little face and his tears while he watched his friends play in the water and swing from the vine. She wanted to make him happy, but she was the parent. She couldn't do anything that would put him at risk just to make him happy. Sometimes a parent had to be firm and say no. But this time Thomas had made her look like the bad guy to her son. Things were so much easier when she was parenting solo. She wished that Thomas would act like a responsible adult sometimes.

This wasn't the first time that they'd argued about her smothering Justin, as Thomas called it. There was no way she would ever let anyone put her son in harm's way. Since this was such a problem for Thomas, perhaps they'd better stop planning activities together.

Before she could finish her thoughts, she heard the signal for dinner. The boys had insisted that while they were at camp, the call to dinner would be the sound of a metal stick ringing a large metal triangle. They looked forward to ringing the triangle each night.

When she joined the group, they joined hands around the picnic table that served as their dinner table, and said grace. Regina felt her anger dissolve a little. The boys were watching her, but they directed their conversation toward Thomas.

The meal was delicious. It was a savory beef stew that had been cooked the same way as the cobbler had been the previous day, over charcoals in a hole in the ground in the Dutch oven.

"Was the food good, Mama?" Justin asked when the meal was over.

"Yes, Justin. The food was very good," Regina answered.

"Ms. Regina, are you still mad at me and my daddy?" Tres asked.

Regina looked at the boy's big brown eyes in the small round caramel-colored face and her anger was washed away by the wave of love that swept over her. "No, sweetheart, I'm not angry with you," she answered. "Come here and give me a big hug."

The boy rushed to Regina and threw his short arms around her neck. Then he planted a kiss on her cheek. "What about my daddy?" Tres asked, while he was still in Regina's embrace. She pulled away from the boy and looked at his sincere face, but did not answer. "Are you still mad at my daddy?" Tres asked again when Regina did not answer.

Regina's and Thomas's eyes met over the boy's head. She silently pleaded with Thomas for help. He held her gaze and waited for her answer. He offered no help.

"Well, are you?" Justin chimed in.

"No, I'm not angry at anyone," Regina answered.

"Well, give him a hug, too," the ever bossy Tres instructed.

"Go ahead, Mama, give him a hug and kiss like you gave Tres," Justin echoed.

Thomas held his arms open wide and Regina stepped into them. He wrapped her in a warm, firm embrace that felt to her like a welcome home. She stood close to him, enjoying the warmth of his body and listening to the rhythms of his heart.

"You've got to kiss and make up," Tres said, giggling.

"Yeah, kiss him," Justin agreed.

Regina rose on tiptoes and moved to plant a kiss on Thomas's cheek at the same time that Thomas lowered his head. Her lips missed their target and their lips met. The instant his lips touched hers, a thrilling warmth swept through her body.

When she attempted to move her mouth away from his, she realized that he held her firmly to him with gentle fingers on the back of her head. Slowly and gently, he coaxed her mouth open with his tongue. At first, she was shocked by his boldness, and then she gave in to the burning pleasure, hoping that she would not self-ignite.

Forgetting everything, Regina gave herself completely to the feel of his lips on hers, his tongue teasing

hers. She was in a timeless place until she heard the applause.

She pulled away from Thomas and he looked as lost
as she. The boys laughed and ran to them. The four
were caught up in a group hug when Tres said, "I knew
you couldn't stay mad at us. You like me and my daddy,
don't you, Miss Regina?"

"Yes, I do," Regina said somewhat breathlessly. She
still felt the warmth of Thomas's lips on hers and her
legs felt as if they might give way at any moment.
Thomas still had one arm firmly around her shoulders
as he turned to include the boys in their circle.

"Is it time for our campfire?" Justin asked.

"Yes, it is. Go and get the wood while we put our
food away," Thomas answered.

The boys ran to do their chore and Regina turned
to gather up the remains of dinner. Thomas leaned
against the table and pulled her between his legs.
"Would you like to finish what we started?" he asked.

"Don't you think we should seal this food up before
a bear comes visiting?" she asked.

Thomas took the bowl from her hand and set it next
to him on the picnic table. "Come here," he said and
gathered her closer. This time he didn't have to coax
her, her mouth eagerly accepted his. She felt faint with
the heat that rose between them. His big hand rubbed
her back through her T-shirt and she leaned into him,
holding on for dear life as her legs became weaker.

She was just as soft and delicious as he'd thought she
would be. He was lost in the softness of her lips, her
body against his, and the warmth that surrounded
them. He knew he was losing himself fast and should
put the brakes on, but she was so sweet, how could he
stop?

Thomas opened his eyes and saw Tres and Justin
standing with wood in their arms and mischievous

smiles on their faces. "It looks like we have company," Thomas whispered.

She pulled herself away and busily began storing the food while Thomas directed the boys on making a fire. That night as they sat around the campfire, Thomas told the boys one ghost story after another. Regina stared into the fire, but was not really hearing the stories. She was wondering about the wisdom of getting involved with Thomas. As it stood, he was a very good, dependable friend. What would happen if they began a romance and things didn't work out? She'd lose her friend and things would be awkward between them. It would be a hardship on Justin if she and Thomas had a bad relationship and Justin couldn't be around Tres anymore. No, this would never work.

After the boys were in their tents and all movement had stopped, Thomas returned to her side.

"Thomas, we have to talk."

"I know," he answered.

"We can't have a romantic relationship. If it doesn't work out, things would be uncomfortable between us and that wouldn't be fair to our sons. We'll break up and then we can't resume our friendship, so what do we do? Let's not even start something that won't work. Let's be glad for what we have. I mean, look, we're good company for each other, the boys enjoy being together. Let's not mess up a good thing. I like the way things are now," she said hurriedly.

"Now take a deep breath," Thomas said, smiling.

"Don't make fun of me. This is serious."

"I'm very serious, too," Thomas answered. "What makes you so sure things won't work out between us?"

"Because—because—I don't know why. It may be irrational, but it's my fear. I know that we can't get back to the way things were if a romantic relationship doesn't work out. What if I care more for you or you care more for me? Then one of us will want to end it and we'll end up avoiding each other. Then it'll get all icky," she said emphatically.

"I'd like to give a relationship with you a try. We're compatible in so many ways. I like talking with you and joking with you. When you're not being real bossy and contrary, you're a pretty nice person," Thomas said, trying to keep the mood light.

"But the fact is, I am a bossy and contrary person by nature. You know that," she reminded him.

"I can deal with it," Thomas said. "I like you, Regina. When we get back to Nashville, I'd like to get a baby-sitter and go out to dinner—just you and me. Somewhere with white tablecloths, china, and crystal. No paper plates, clowns, or tokens. Would you like to go out with me?" he asked.

"You make a very tempting offer, Mr. Simmons, but I think not," Regina answered. "It would be a step in the wrong direction," she managed to say around the lump in her throat.

Thomas stared at her incredulously for several long moments. "You can't be serious, Regina. I know that we've been attracted to each other for a long time and we each have our reasons for not wanting a romantic relationship, but we can't deny our feelings. Right here and now we're more than neighbors. Why are you going to turn down the chance we have to build on a wonderful relationship?"

"Because you let Tres cross the street without worrying about him. Because you don't want the boys to take naps. Because you've never once asked me about Justin's father or any other personal question beyond my work and education. Because you think it's okay to jump into a pond clinging to a vine without knowing where the bottom is," she said, quickly without taking a breath.

"What are you talking about?" he asked, wondering if she were speaking a foreign language.

"I don't really know," Regina answered. "I don't know you. All I know is that you scare me and I don't like to be scared. I don't usually scare very easily."

"How do I scare you?" he asked, getting more confused by the moment.

"I just—I—I can't say exactly," she stammered.

"Okay, let's start with something easy. Tell me what you said about Tres crossing the street," Thomas said, still confused.

"I can't. I'm going to my tent now. I know you want to make an early start in the morning. We're out here isolated in the wilderness. Once we're back in the city, we'll start seeing things in their proper perspective again," she said, easily rising from her stool and retreating to her tent.

On the drive home, Justin stuck his head from the backseat in between the front seats occupied by his mom and Thomas. "Didn't we see you guys kiss and make up last night?" he asked.

"Sit back and fasten your seat belt," Regina answered.

"But we did, didn't we, Tres?" Justin persisted.

"Uh-huh," Tres answered.

"So what's wrong now?" Justin asked, sounding as if he were at the end of his patience.

"Stay out of grown folks' business," Regina answered. "Is your seat belt fastened?"

"Yes, ma'am." Seeing that his mother was in a permanently irritable mood, Justin didn't utter another word.

The boys settled into their seats and played their handheld video games. Thomas wanted to start a conversation with Regina, but didn't know what to say. He still wasn't sure that he'd ever understand her.

She was not in the mood to talk. So far, talking things out had gotten them nowhere. They stopped only once on the way home, and even then there was a cloud over the group that had been so happy when they began their vacation.

At four o'clock in the afternoon the glum foursome was back on Sonata Drive. Thomas efficiently unloaded the Lovejoys' camping gear, before pulling across the street to unload his own.

After they were settled in the house, he remembered that he'd forgotten to ask Regina if Justin would still be going to his basketball camp the next morning. When he called to ask her, her cool response was, "Of course."

Managing a basketball camp for boys eight to eighteen was difficult, but it was a wonderful public relations opportunity for his department and for the university. On the first day of camp, Dr. John Morgan, the president, had come over to welcome the boys to the Renaissance campus. Dr. Morgan was very paternal toward Thomas and very supportive of his many activities.

As the week progressed things ran smoothly at the camp. Thomas sat at his desk on Wednesday afternoon going over plans for the closing ceremony. He was proud of the way his coaching staff and members of the college team had pitched in to make the camp go smoothly for their youngsters.

The good thing about all the activity that week was that he had little time to dwell on Regina's rejection. It was probably for the best. It was too soon for him to start dating. His wife had been gone for a little more than four years. He didn't know what got into him around Regina anyway. He knew that he wasn't ready for the kind of commitment that a relationship with her would require.

He stared at the plans that his camp manager had insisted that he approve today, but he was having difficulty taking his thoughts away from Regina. He looked up when a woman who looked vaguely familiar entered his office. "Are you busy?" she asked.

"No, I'm just finishing up here," he answered cordially.

"Do you remember me? I met you at Dr. Morgan's Christmas party. You mentioned that we might get together sometime," she said.

He was embarrassed because he didn't remember her. He had been so new at the school then that everyone was unfamiliar to him. Obviously she did not frequent the athletic department. She saw the look on his face and continued. "My name is Rosa Johnson. I'm chair of the English department."

"Oh, yes, I see," he said, still not remembering meeting her before. "We talked on the phone a couple of times. Are you getting an early start on our tutors for the fall?"

"No. It's a little too early for that. Actually, I came by to ask you if you'd go to the Blue and Gold Gala with me. You don't already have someone to go with, do you?" she asked nervously.

"Dr. Johnson, I, a-h-h-h," he began.

"Please call me Rosa. I already have the tickets. I would really like for you to go with me," she said persuasively, sitting on his desk and crossing one long slim leg over the other.

He'd planned to ask Regina to go with him. In fact, until yesterday, he'd assumed that Regina would go with him. Now he didn't know what to do. "Rosa, I have a son and I don't have a baby-sitter, yet. Since the ball is a couple of months away, perhaps I could get back with you?" he asked, feeling guilty for using his son to get out of making a commitment.

"I can help you get a sitter," the woman said eagerly. "That shouldn't be a problem." She leaned closer to him, almost sprawled across his desk. He stood and walked around his desk, moving closer to the door.

"I'm real selective about who cares for my son. I hope you understand," he said, opening the door that she'd closed when she came in.

The woman looked at him for a moment before standing. He had not noticed when she entered his office how attractive she was. She was tall and slender, wearing a beautiful pale yellow, short-sleeved summer suit. Her nails were well manicured and she seemed to be a well-maintained woman. She had none of Regina's soft curves, nor did she have Regina's lively spirit. But she looked good enough to make Regina jealous.

Well, hell, Regina wouldn't even give him the time of day. Since his wife had died he had felt nothing for any other woman. Now the one woman who made him feel like a man again was constantly running away from him. Before he thought, he said, "The Blue and Gold Gala is not until fall. I'd like to take you out before that. Are you busy this weekend?"

"No, I'm not." She flashed him a big bright smile that was almost as bright as Regina's. "What do you think about going out to dinner and maybe to a play at the Tennessee Performing Arts Center?"

"I think it sounds great. What time shall I pick you up?"

"I believe the play begins at eight o'clock. Why don't you come by at five? Maybe we could have a drink before we leave. Then we'll have plenty of time for dinner before the show," Rosa suggested.

As Dr. Johnson was leaving his office, one of his players brought the boys to him. "Who was that?" Tres asked.

"That was Dr. Johnson," Thomas answered blandly.

"What did she want?" Justin asked.

"She asked me for a date," Thomas answered. *Now go and tell your mama that,* he thought, becoming immediately embarrassed at his immaturity. That's when he realized that Regina Lovejoy was driving him crazy.

He immediately had another crazy thought. What if he asked Regina to baby-sit while he went out with another woman? Would she care? She had made it painfully clear that she wanted no personal relationship with him.

Although the boys were together every day, from the start of basketball camp each morning until dinner each night, Thomas had not seen Regina since the camping trip. She would let Tres into her house or send Justin out, but he'd not seen her.

When he took Justin home that evening, he stood next to the children while they waited for Regina to answer the doorbell. She opened the door and greeted Justin and Tres warmly as she drew them into the house. Thomas followed on their heels so that she wouldn't shut him out.

The first thing Justin said was, "Mama, Mr. Thomas has a date. That means he's going out with a lady. Can Tres stay with us while his daddy goes out? Tres doesn't like to stay with anyone else, do you, Tres?"

"Please, may I stay with you, Ms. Gina?" Tres asked.

Without thinking Regina looked at Thomas and he was surprised to see her slanted eyes shooting daggers at him. Thomas felt like a kid caught peeing in his pants. Embarrassment was all over his face. He shrugged. "I didn't know that they'd discussed it."

"Apparently they have," Regina said in a voice that would freeze fire.

"Can Tres stay for dinner?" They looked at both adults.

"Yes, you may stay for dinner with us unless your father has other plans," Regina said, looking pointedly at Thomas.

The boys skirted around Regina and rushed to the kitchen. Thomas continued standing in the foyer, not knowing what to say next. He had thought that it would be fun to tell Regina he had a date with someone else, but it had not turned out that way.

"Well, when is your date?"

"Friday night."

"Why don't you bring Tres's bag over when you bring them from camp Friday afternoon? He'll spend the night," she said. Before he could answer, she had walked away. She caught him staring at her swaying hips when she turned and asked, "You will be able to bring them home from camp before your date Friday night, won't you, or should I plan on picking them up?"

"I'll bring them home," he answered, wondering why his mouth was so dry he could hardly speak.

Chapter 6

Friday came much too quickly. Thomas felt as if he were about to take the graduate school entrance exam as he prepared for his date. He was nervous and looked forward to the evening with a sense of dread. How long had it been since he'd had a date? Could he count going to Tin Pan South with Regina? No. Surely he couldn't count going to *Blue's Clues* or any of the events that they'd taken their sons to. Then he would have to say that his last date was with his wife.

Again, Dr. Rosa Johnson was dressed in a stylish outfit and was well coiffed. She greeted him warmly and invited him in.

He looked at his watch and said, "I'm sorry I was running late—sitter problems. I think we'd better get to the restaurant, we have early reservations."

"Okay, maybe you can come in for a nightcap later," she said, before she hurried from the foyer to get her purse.

Throughout dinner, Thomas stole glances at his watch. At six o'clock, he wondered what the boys had had for dinner. Surely, Regina had not cooked on a Friday night. She'd probably ordered out for pizza. At six-fifteen he wondered if they were watching a movie. At six-thirty he wondered what games they were playing. He wished desperately that he were at home with them.

"Isn't your fish good?" Rosa asked, looking at his barely touched plate.

"Oh, yes, it's pretty good. I just have a lot on my mind this evening," he answered.

"Tell me about it. Perhaps it's something that I can help you with," Rosa offered kindly.

"No, I don't think so. I appreciate your offer though."

"Who did you find to take care of your son? You told me that you're very selective about who takes care of him," Rosa said, trying to find an avenue for conversation.

"My neighbor. She has a son the same age as Tres, and the boys spend a lot of time together."

"Oh, is it the same neighbor that Dr. Henry saw you with at the grocery store?" Rosa asked.

"Yes, we—our boys—spend a lot of time together," he hastened to explain.

Rosa took her napkin from her lap and folded it carefully before speaking again. "You know, Coach Simmons, you are a really nice person. I was looking forward to getting to know you better and I still am. Just not in the way I'd hoped. I look forward to seeing our basketball team go to the nationals and I'll do anything that I can do to be sure that our team is successful. But I'm not willing to sit here as a substitute player for the woman that you really want to be with. I thought we'd have a fun, stimulating conversation. You struck me as someone who is intelligent and could talk about more than sports, but right now you're boring me to death. Don't look at that watch again," she said with an edge to her voice when he couldn't resist the temptation to look at his watch one more time.

Thomas felt terrible. "Look, we're out now. I'm so

rusty at dating that I probably didn't do it right. I find you attractive and I hoped to show you a good time. Could we start over?" he asked, sincerely.

"You should know that I'm used to being the center of attention and you've paid me none," she said with the edge gone from her voice. He smiled tentatively and she returned the smile with one of her own.

"Could you give me a little more of your time?" he asked, flashing her a boyish smile with the dimple flickering in his right cheek.

"You don't want to go home this early, do you?" Rosa asked, smiling.

"No."

"Did you plan to use me to make your neighbor jealous?" Rosa guessed.

"No—yes—I didn't think of it as using you. But I did want Regina to know that I had other options. I don't want to make you feel bad, but I had to go out with someone who was pretty enough to make her jealous."

"You haven't made me feel bad. Not since I know that you realize that I am attractive. Well, since you've already paid for the tickets, I'll go to the play with you. Eat up. Big as you are, I can't imagine that you've ever missed a meal," she said, laughing.

Thomas felt a lot more relaxed and discovered that he did have an appetite. The food was delicious.

"Why do you have to make your neighbor jealous? Why aren't you out with her tonight?" Rosa asked.

"She said that she's afraid of me. I don't understand," he said, as he bit into one of the big, succulent shrimp that dressed his freshwater trout.

"You two must have it bad for each other," Rosa said, shaking her head.

"What?"

"I'm sure that she's not afraid of you. You're as gentle as a spring rain. No, she's afraid of her feelings for you. What else did she say?" Rosa leaned forward on her elbow and watched Thomas intently. Since they'd started talking about Regina, he'd become a lot more animated.

"She said that if things didn't work out between us, our sons would be devastated and that our friendship is too good to mess up with romance," he said, trying to remember everything that Regina had said.

"Um-m-m. Let me see if I can decipher this code," Rosa said, enjoying her new role. If she couldn't have a romance with Thomas, she could at least help him get with the woman he wanted. "I've been in and out of relationships since I was sixteen. I think I have this thing figured out. Did she say anything else?"

"She said that I never ask her personal questions and something about letting my son cross the street without worrying," he said, his voice full of confusion.

"I don't understand that one," Rosa said. "But I know that you and your lady need to talk. You have a strong attraction to one another, but you're letting words get in your way. Now, as an English professor, I've got to tell you that words are important. They can bring people together and they can tear them apart. They're a basic means of communication for humans, even though sometimes what we do speaks louder than what we say. What time does that play start?" she asked, glancing at her watch.

"Eight o'clock," Thomas said, absently. He was engrossed more in what Rosa had told him.

"Do you still want to go to the play?" Rosa asked.

"Of course I do."

The next morning Thomas went to pick up Tres from Regina's. He stood on the porch thinking about what he would say to her, when the door was thrown open. "Hi,

Daddy. Ms. Regina's back in the music room. I don't think she heard you," Tres said, before running back to the family room.

Thomas followed the sound of Regina's voice to her music room. She was singing a hauntingly beautiful song that he'd never heard before. He listened at the door as she sang:

> *"This is no longer a silly game of chance.*
> *Baby, you stole my heart with your very first glance.*
> *Come on with your sweet romance.*
> *Come on, baby, end this flirtatious dance.*
>
> *Please, baby, don't make me wait.*
> *This romance that began with our first date*
> *Is now a dance of sweet romance.*
> *Come on, baby, with your sweet romance.*
>
> *Let it begin, baby, this sweet romance.*
> *Take a chance, baby, with this sweet romance.*
> *It's all a chance, this sweet romance.*
> *Let it begin, baby, this sweet romance."*

When the words ended, she continued playing the melody on the piano and looked so wistful that his heart hurt. This was the most beautiful song that he'd ever heard. She looked up, noticing him in the doorway for the first time.

"Hi, how long have you been here?" she asked.

"Just a few minutes. I wondered if you'd like for me to take the boys off your hands."

"That would be nice. I got a call from Shelby last night. She reminded me that she needs my songs before she goes to the studio in September. She wants us to write the whole album and she's got an idea for a theme," Regina said, talking in her normal rapid fire speech pattern.

"What is her theme?" Thomas asked.

"Did you hear the song I was playing just now?"

"Yes, I did."

"Well, that will be the first cut. She wants to tell about her romance with her husband from courtship to marriage and maybe even a peek into the future with something like two old people sitting in a rocking chair, sharing their memories," Regina related enthusiastically.

And to think that the words to that song might have been meant for him, Thomas thought wryly. "What was the name of that song?"

"'Sweet Romance.' Did you like it?"

"It was absolutely beautiful," he said with feeling.

"Good. You are my inspiration for it."

"I am?"

"Don't stand there gloating. Yes, you are and I won't answer any more questions about that. How was your date last night? I hope it was awful," Regina said, not quite smiling with a shimmering glow in her eyes. She'd tried to sound cavalier, but couldn't quite pull it off.

"It wasn't so bad. We were having an awful time until she asked me about you and then I told her that the only reason I took her out was that you and I are fighting a mutual attraction for each other," Thomas said, huskily.

"You didn't?" Regina exclaimed, carefully setting her guitar on the floor next to her before standing in front of him with her hands on her hips.

"I did. She asked me where my mind was and I had to admit that my mind was on you," he said so sincerely that Regina had no immediate response. He continued in a neutral tone. "She had some good advice for the lovelorn."

"What was her advice?" Regina asked.

"She said that we need to talk." He put his arms around Regina and pulled her to him. "I've missed you this week, Regina. Why did you cut me out when you knew how much I care for you?" he asked, looking down into her beautiful almond-shaped eyes.

"I told you why, Thomas," she answered, trying not to sink into the inviting depths of his eyes.

"Then help me understand what you were talking about. I swear I try to understand you, but sometimes you chirp faster than a blue jay and I don't understand. No one would believe that you are a southern girl," he said, lightly lifting her chin so that she would have to return her gaze to his eyes. "Tell me again so that I can understand what's wrong with our being together."

"We've been together day and night for the past few months, yet we know nothing about each other. We never talk about our past or our future. I don't know what your hopes and dreams are. We laugh and joke, but it doesn't go any deeper," she said, waving her hands, accenting her words as if to help him understand.

"You know that I'm from a small town in Michigan. That my mother and father are still alive and in love. And my father is a hypochondriac. You know that I want to take my team to the championship—"

"Be serious," Regina interrupted. "We talk about work all the time and I know about your mother from your mother. She calls me from time to time. But when things get deep between you and me, you run. You know how to get out of my house so fast, you should conduct fire drills," Regina said seriously.

"Okay," Thomas said. "Tell me all about you." His intense gaze made her uncomfortable and she looked away.

"What do you want to know?" she asked, turning

away from his scrutiny and wondering if she'd opened a can of worms that she couldn't get the lid back on. He touched her narrow chin with his fingertips to turn her face back toward his. Her eyes became transfixed on his lips. Without warning, she remembered how soft and warm they were when he'd kissed her at the campground.

As if reading her mind, he leaned down and pressed his lips to hers, letting her get used to the pressure before he slipped his tongue into her mouth. She felt light and heaven-bound. He felt her tremor and took it for nervousness.

"What are you afraid of? Your attraction to me?" he asked hoarsely, his hand lightly touching her cheek.

"Yes," she answered, taking his hand into hers. "I'm afraid of losing control and when I'm with you, I'm not in control."

Thomas laughed, nervously. "You think you're out of control? Damn, I can't even control my own thoughts anymore. You control my mind, my dreams, my goals, everything. I don't know why I do half the things that I do anymore."

She shook her head. "You're exaggerating."

"No, I'm not, Gina," he said, touching her cheek again.

"Before we get too deep into this conversation we need to check on the boys. Let's take them outside where we can keep an eye on them—"

"And where they can't hear us talk," Thomas finished for her.

Thomas led the boys to the backyard while Regina stopped in the kitchen to get a pitcher of orange juice and four plastic tumblers. By the time she got outside, the boys were trying to see how high they could swing. They waved at their parents and continued swinging. If they were surprised to see Regina and Thomas together after the week of strained silence between them, the children did not let on.

Sitting the tray of liquid refreshments on the table in front of the glider, she said, "Now where were we?"

"We were right here," Thomas answered. He slid across the glider and put his arms around Regina. He gave her a long, soul-stirring kiss this time. When she thought he'd never let up, he did and she felt like she'd been abandoned.

"You were about to start telling me all about you. Tell me all your secrets."

"I don't have any secrets." She laughed.

"Okay. I'm curious about Justin's father. You never talk about him, nor does Justin. I've told you about Paulette; now will you tell me about Justin's father?"

Looking at her hands, Regina thought for a moment. She'd asked for this, and now she'd have to go where she'd never gone with any other man. "Where do you want me to begin? What do you want to know?"

"Is he still around?" he prompted.

"No, fortunately I have no drama to tell you about," she answered and paused, waiting for another prompt from Thomas.

"What was his name?" he asked.

"Peter Oku," she answered and paused again.

After a somewhat lengthy silence, as if trying to determine how much he wanted to hear, Thomas asked, "What happened? Why aren't you two still together?"

"We were separated before we knew that I was pregnant. I don't think I would have done anything differently if we had known, though. It would have been more difficult for him to leave, that's all," she said a little bit less reluctantly. Then she fell silent again.

"Regina, this is a lot like pulling teeth. Do I have to keep asking questions? Just tell me about him. What was he like? Where did you meet?" Thomas said, sensing her reluctance and hoping to convey to her that he was sincere in wanting to hear about her previous relationship.

She took a deep sip of her juice, wet her lips, and began talking. As usual, she talked rapidly. This time it was like someone swallowing a bitter medicine, hurrying just to get it over with. "He was a bright and intelligent student from Nigeria. When I entered college, he was a senior. I felt special that he chose me, a lowly freshman, to receive the benefit of all his knowledge and greatness. When he graduated and stayed on campus as a graduate student and then as a Ph.D. candidate, I was elated to have him near. His major was engineering." As if she had said all she was going to say, she stopped again. She seemed to wait to see how much he wanted to hear. She was cautious. Sometimes people thought that they wanted to hear things that they could not handle.

Sensing her reserve, Thomas finally asked another question. "Was he still on campus when you moved to New York? I thought that Justin was born in New York."

"I graduated and moved to Nashville where I was working for the advertising firm that represented the country music labels that I told you about. While I was living in Nashville, I returned to Knoxville every weekend to be with him.

"Later that year Peter finished his Ph.D.program and got a job offer in New York. We decided to marry immediately so that I could accompany him. At first it was fun and exciting, but then he began to work longer and longer hours. There was no reason for me to hurry home, so I began to work longer and longer hours. Pretty soon we only saw each other in passing. I thought that if he saw less of me, he'd want to see me more, but that never happened."

She stopped again and looked so embarrassed that Thomas's heart went out to her.

"Regina, maybe this is too personal. You don't have to tell me anything more," he offered, holding her hand.

"No, it's okay. I'm a little embarrassed, but I guess we've all been a fool over someone at some point. I want you to know as much as you want to hear. Do you want me to go on?"

He nodded his head.

She continued, "Anyway, I kept trying to get us back to where we used to be before New York, but that wasn't happening either. My fascination with Peter ended as my fascination with New York was ending. After I'd been there two years, I was ready to head South again, but I hated to admit defeat, so I kept hanging on to both long past the time to let go. I couldn't figure out what to do next."

"So what did you do?" Thomas asked.

"The decision wasn't mine to make. One day Peter was at home when I came in from work, which was very unusual. I immediately knew something was wrong. He didn't waste any time telling me his father needed him to come home to take over the family business. He'd been a dutiful son and gotten the education the family needed. Now it was time for him to end his carefree life to fulfill his familial obligations."

"Did you know that he was expected to leave the U.S.?" Thomas asked gently.

"I knew his family expected him to return to Nigeria eventually. He'd explained that to me before we married. When he told me, I had planned to go with him. I'd thought I would follow him anywhere. After all, I'd already followed him to New York. But as he was telling me what I needed to do to prepare for the trip, I realized that I didn't love him enough to give up everything I was familiar with to make the journey with him.

"About two days later, he came home and asked me

if I'd given notice on my job. When I told him I hadn't, he wasn't surprised at all. Two weeks later he left without me. In those two weeks we conceived Justin."

"Did you think about going to Nigeria when you found out about the baby?" Thomas asked, encouraging her to continue.

"I thought about it—I thought about it a lot. By the time I knew I was pregnant, we were already seperated and I wasn't sure what I should do. But in the end I stayed in New York and Justin was born. My mother came to take care of me and tried to encourage me to come home, but I was determined to handle things on my own. I put my six-week-old baby in day care and returned to work."

"That must have been hard to take care of a baby that far from home all by yourself. When Tres was born, we had live-in help until we came back to the States."

"It was extremely hard. By the time Justin turned a year old, I gave up and went home to Bessemer. I've already told you the rest of the story. All of that was true. I just left out some of the parts that made me look real stupid," Regina finished, suddenly looking as if telling the story or the memories had drained the energy from her. Her usually animated face was void of expression.

Thomas touched her chin and turned her face toward him. She looked up at him nervously, before licking her lips and saying, "I hope I haven't scared you away with the messy details of my life. I feel so stupid when I think back to that time in my life."

He noticed the question in her nearly breathless voice and hurried to reassure her. "The details of your life are not messy at all and nothing you did was stupid. You should hear what some of the kids on campus are going through. I believe that all babies born are gifts from God, regardless of the circumstances under which they are born. Justin is a wonderful gift. Did you ever tell Justin's father about him?"

"The funny thing is I was relieved that Peter had returned to Nigeria. That way I had my baby all to myself and I didn't have to debate with anyone but my mother about how my son would be raised. Not until I met you, that is," she teased Thomas. He took her small hand in his and kissed her fingers before she could poke him.

Regina continued, "But, yes, I did tell him that I was pregnant. Of course, he demanded I come to Nigeria right away. He wanted his firstborn son with him. I knew that he had a right to his son and when I married Peter I knew that our cultures were different, but I didn't think it through. I didn't think about what that would mean in my life. Going to Nigeria would have required me to leave everything I knew so that he could have his son with him. If I decided that I couldn't make it there, would I have to leave my son with his father? Besides, by the time I knew I was pregnant, the feelings that I had for Peter were gone."

"Does Justin know his father?"

"He has come to see Justin a couple of times. It was amazing to me that the man that I had acted such a fool over—picked up stakes and moved to New York without a job—meant absolutely nothing to me anymore." Regina shrugged her shoulders as if she were still surprised.

Thomas commented, "Sometimes as we mature our needs change." He still held her hand and his warmth was comforting.

"Okay, enough about me. I don't like being too analytical. If we study our navels too long, we come up with all kinds of reasons explaining why we act the way we do. Now it's your turn."

"What do you mean?" Thomas asked.

"Tell me about your past loves. More specifically, tell me about Paulette. How did you meet her?" Regina asked.

Thomas took a deep breath and began talking. "I met her in an orientation class during our freshman year. We were both physical education majors and took classes together. We began dating in our sophomore year and married immediately after graduation."

"It's still hard for you to talk about her, isn't it?" Regina asked.

"I can't pretend she never existed. I have wonderful memories that are supposed to sustain me, but mostly I'm still very angry," he answered, trying to hold back the rush of emotions that he still felt when he talked about his wife's death.

"Why are you so angry?" Regina asked.

"That's a long story. Longer than we have this morning. But I can tell you that I'm mainly angry because she died so young and she left me with a baby who never knew what it was like to be pampered by his mother. By the time Tres was born, she was barely able to hold him. She had so much to live for that it is totally unacceptable to me that she was taken away from us." Thomas hoped that his answer would be sufficient. Even in their spirit of shared confidences, he was reluctant to say much more about Paulette's death. The guilt was too overwhelming.

Regina did not offer any platitudes about the Lord's will. She sensed that Thomas had heard them all before and decided not to press him for more answers. Their glasses of juice were empty and the sun was high in the sky. The boys were still running around the backyard enjoying their summer freedom.

"Okay, we've covered our past loves. What's next on the list?" Thomas asked.

"List of what?" Regina asked, puzzled.

"You said that we need to get to know each other," he reminded her.

"That's true. I did say that. Why haven't you asked me about Peter before? You were obviously curious."

"I didn't know that it was okay for me to ask. I'd been curious, but I wanted to respect your privacy, that's all," Thomas tried to explain.

"So that I would respect yours?" Regina asked, astutely.

Shocked by her intuitiveness, Thomas answered honestly, "That's part of it. But I sensed that you needed your space, too."

"It's not a story that I relish telling. I'm giving it to you warts and all, but it's embarrassing for me. It's just hard for me to realize that my big love affair in which I invested so much was all one-sided. It was just a figment of my imagination. After he was gone, I realized that Peter never took our marriage seriously. I don't believe he married me for love, at least not the way I loved him. If he had, he would have put more time into our relationship, he wouldn't have been away so much. Realizing that our relationship had been so one-sided made me feel very vulnerable," Regina explained.

"So you've avoided men since Peter left?" Thomas ventured.

"Not entirely and we don't want to go into any more details, do we? But I will say that I've tried to keep to myself. It's too difficult to handle men and a child. I made a pledge when Justin was born that I would not have men rotating in and out of my life while I was raising my child. I wanted to focus on giving him the best childhood possible."

"I can understand that. You've given a lot of thought to how you want to rear your son and you seem to think that you have all the answers for being a model parent, but you don't give me credit for giving any thought to how I'm raising my son," Thomas said seriously.

"What are you talking about? I think you're an excellent father," Regina replied incredulously.

"What was that about Tres crossing the street?"

Regina had the decency to be embarrassed over her irrational behavior. "I apologize. I was angry with you. But when Tres first visited Justin and me, I thought that you should have reacted differently when I called to tell you that he'd crossed the street alone."

"Oh, I see. I'll try to be more hysterical the next time," he said dryly. Then in a high, mimicking voice with both hands on his cheeks, he exclaimed, "Oh, my God, the boy has crossed the street. Not the street. This street that's at the end of a cul-de-sac. All those fast drivers with children of their own live on this street."

Regina did poke him on his hard biceps that time. "I hope you're not mimicking me. Try to be serious. This parenting thing is serious business and sometimes you take too many risks with your son."

"I can't believe you're serious when you say that. Don't you know I'm a recreation specialist? I make my living taking care of other people's sons. As careful as you are, you still seem relaxed when Justin is with me," Thomas pointed out.

"Your ego is inflated, but you're right. There's something about you that, well, I don't know. From the beginning Justin took well to you and Tres and you just sort of inspired our confidence."

"So you agree that my child-rearing methods are as valid as yours? I know that we have our differences on how our children should be raised, but I don't think that there is any one answer. Sometimes it helps me to hear another person's point of view," he said tentatively, hoping not to start another argument about child rearing with her.

"I know. Well, I guess I'm sort of figuring that out as I debate with you. I grew up in a single-parent household. It was just my mother and I and sometimes my grandmother. My mother rejected any suggestion that my grandmother made. Mother had to be right all the time and I see her in some of my responses to you. Sometimes I scare myself."

Regina surprised Thomas with her confession. "Now was that so hard for you to say? I'm glad that I came over here to talk with you and to iron out our differences. No matter what happens between us, I want you to know how much I value our friendship. At first, I was going to sit over there at my house and wait for you to come begging me to be your friend again. But I'm crazy about you and I miss you," he said earnestly.

"I missed you, too," she admitted.

"Is that why you wrote that song for me?"

"Don't get your ego all inflated. All I will admit is that you inspired me to write it," she answered.

"Then are you ready to begin our romance?"

"I'm ready to get to know you in a boy-girl kind of way," Regina said, giggling shyly.

"Then will you go to the Blue and Gold Gala with me?" Thomas asked.

"What is that?"

"It's a formal fund-raiser that the athletic department has each year. It's mandatory that all faculty and staff attend. I sure would like for you to go with me, because if you don't I'll have to go with Dr. Johnson and she might hurt me this time if I spend the evening discussing you," he said, imitating Regina's rapid speech pattern.

"What?" she asked, not sure if she should take him seriously.

"Dr. Johnson asked me to go with her, but I'd rather go with you."

"I don't believe Dr. Johnson wants to go anywhere else with you after you spent the evening discussing another woman with her."

"You're probably right," he admitted.

"So, Thomas, will I be your mercy date? Are you using me to protect yourself from the predatory women on campus?" Regina couldn't resist teasing him.

"I wouldn't exactly call it a mercy date. More like a favor for a friend," Thomas answered around his growing embarrassment.

"I'll go, but you're going to owe me big time," she finally answered. Watching Thomas squirm, waiting for her answer, was not as much fun as she'd hoped.

"Speaking of owing big time, don't you remember the night I was tempted to wash your hair in the kitchen sink? The only thing that saved you was your begging and pleading. You said you'd do anything if I didn't wet your hair," he said, regaining his old confidence.

"I remember. I promised," Regina said, smiling up at Thomas and wondering what he was leading up to.

"Then it's time for you to pay up. I'd like to let my colleagues know that you and I have a—you know—relationship. I don't want another fiasco like last night. I think we should be seen together without the boys. What do you think?" he asked.

"You're pushing it now," she began. "A relationship—a romance?"

"But you owe me so much," Thomas said, wrapping his arms around Regina and pulling her back against his chest.

"Are you asking me to go steady with you, Tommy?" she asked with a mischievous gleam in her eyes.

"Yeah, Gina, will you be my girl?" Thomas asked in a goofy, teenagerish voice.

"I don't know, I have to talk it over with my mom," Regina answered.

"Let me talk with your mother," Thomas said.

"Believe me, you wouldn't want to. My mother is a real trip. She would have to have a complete family tree and bio before she'd even interview you," Regina said, no longer joking.

"Okay, when will I meet your mother? I think I can withstand the mother check," Thomas said, gently, noting Regina's agitation.

"She'll be coming to get Justin for the summer in about two weeks. You'll get to meet Madam Julia then," Regina said, relaxing inside his arms.

"Tres will be leaving at about that time. His grandparents are coming to get him next weekend. We can paint the town with the kids gone," he said gleefully.

"Oh, is your father well enough to travel now?" she asked curiously.

"Yes, I told you that my father was never ill. But it's not my parents who are coming. Tres's other set of grandparents is doing the traveling. He stays with them for two weeks each summer, and then they take him to my parents. They'll keep him until school starts," Thomas explained.

"Justin is going to die when he gets back if Tres is not here. I'd better line up some big-time activities to keep him occupied," Regina noted.

"Well, I'll be here. I'll help you out as much as I can," he offered.

"Yeah, right. You get rid of your kid to spend time with mine."

"Honestly. I'll enjoy being around Justin. I miss Tres

terribly when he's gone. The only reason I let him go is that I think knowing the older generation enriches his life. Sometimes I've gone to stay with my folks while Tres is there because I get so lonely. Maybe you and Justin can go with me this year?" Thomas asked with a new animation in his voice.

"I don't know," Regina began.

"That's still some time off. We'll see," he said quickly to keep her from turning him down without any consideration. "By the way, you mentioned that you need to go to the studio this afternoon. Did you want to leave Justin with me?"

"Now that you're here, that'll work out fine. I was going to take him with me, but he needs to go to bed early. Tomorrow we're having a program to celebrate the children's move to new classes in Sunday school and he wants to be there. I'll come get him as soon as I finish at the studio so that I won't have to wake you guys up early in the morning."

"That's mighty decent of you. But, we might decide to go with you. This will be a good time to start Tres in Sunday school since new classes are forming."

Chapter 7

Immediately after lunch, Regina headed to the studio to meet Kent and Jimmy Bob. They worked productively for several hours, causing Regina to lose track of time and stay at the studio later than she intended. When she called Thomas at nine o'clock, he told her that Justin and Tres were already in bed. She decided to put in a couple more hours, hoping that they would be as productive as the first hours had been.

Two hours after her phone call, she pulled into Thomas's driveway. The house was dark and still. Although she was certain that everyone was in bed, she decided that she'd let herself in with her key. She planned to take Justin home without disturbing the household. It would be so much easier to take him now instead of waiting until the next morning.

She tiptoed up the steps leading to the bedrooms and was surprised to meet Thomas standing at the top of the stairs. "I wondered who was breaking and entering this time of night," he said softly.

"It's just me. I saw how dark the house was and didn't want to awaken you by ringing the doorbell. I thought that I could get Justin and we could go on home," she responded. Her breath caught in her throat when she looked directly at him. Though the only light was coming from his bedroom behind him, she could plainly see his rippling pectoral muscles, six-pack abs, and rock-hard biceps. He was wearing knee-length basketball shorts and no shirt. Her mouth became dry and she tried looking beyond him. She didn't want him to know that she was awed by his brawn. After all, she'd seen him without a shirt plenty of times. Of course, those times had usually been in the daylight. Somehow, this was much more intimate.

"You look so tired. Why don't you go on home and get some rest? I promise to get Justin up on time, and knowing you, I'll probably have to wake you up, too," Thomas whispered.

"I don't know. It'll be easier if I take him now. I promised his Sunday school teacher that we would be there. He wants to be there to walk to the front of the sanctuary to receive his promotion certificate and shake hands with our pastor. It's a big thing for the kids. I really don't want him to miss Promotion Sun-day," Regina whispered.

"Let's talk in here before we awaken the kids," Thomas said, leading Regina down the hall to the mas-ter bedroom suite. "I should have known I couldn't get a simple yes from you," he teased. Can't you admit that you're too tired to take Justin home right now?"

"I am tired,"she admitted.

"How did it go this evening?" he asked.

"Grueling. We finished '*Sweet Romance,*' and several more songs to go with it," she said, stretching and yawning. They want to suggest to Shelby that she name the album *Sweet Romance.* That's the theme that's run-ning through all our songs we've written so far."

Her face was painted with exhaustion and tired lines were drawn around her beautiful eyes. They were no longer the big, beautiful almond eyes he loved, but half-closed slits. "Come here," he said, pulling her to his bed. He sat with his back against the headboard and with her between his outstretched legs. He gently massaged her neck and shoulders, working all the knots and kinks in her tired neck.

"Oh, that feels good," she moaned when he moved from the nape of her neck up to a point right above her hairline.

"Loosen your blouse a little. Massage works better if it's skin-to-skin. You'll hardly feel anything through that cloth," Thomas explained.

Regina obeyed without thinking twice. Her white cotton blouse wrapped around her torso and tied at the waist. She loosened it and leaned into Thomas's strong hands. He kneaded the muscles in her shoulders and the center of her back. Through closed eyes she asked, "What did you and the boys do tonight?"

"I tried to teach them to play Scrabble. It's a difficult game to play when most of the words that they can spell have three or four letters. We had to customize the rules, making them up as we went along."

"That sounds like fun," she said drowsily.

He continued talking and in a few minutes she was asleep. He let her rest against his chest with the intention of leaving her in his bed and going to the guest room when her sleep was deep enough that his movement would not disturb her. However, since her arrival had awakened him from a deep sleep, he too was unable to stay awake. Before he knew it, he was sliding down in the bed, trying to get comfortable on his king-sized pillows.

Through the night, Thomas slept with Regina sprawled across him. When he turned to his side, she was tossed next to him. He awakened the next morning to find one of Regina's arms across his waist and her leg across his thigh. Seeing her next to him brought a smile of contentment to his face. It felt so right to have her there. She was in a deep sleep and was completely relaxed.

Though he tried to be as still as possible, she must have sensed that he was awake because her eyes flew open shortly after he awakened. For a moment or two, she did not seem to know where she was. She lay motionless, staring blindly for several moments. From past experiences, he knew that she was slow to wake up and she hated facing mornings.

Becoming alert slowly, she was not instantly aware that she was in bed with Thomas. When his proximity hit her, she gingerly removed her leg that was thrown over his thighs. Then she tried to smooth her skirt that was bunched up around her hips. Last she tried to pull together the blouse that had become totally unwrapped during the night, revealing a lacy, snow-white bra.

"It's too late for a show of modesty now. We've already slept together," he said playfully.

"Why didn't you wake me up so that I could go home?" she asked in dismay.

"I wanted to hold you in my arms all night," he said in a teasing voice that he hoped would mask the truth of his statement.

She grabbed a pillow from the other side of the bed and tried to smother his face with it. He threw up his arms to block her blow and tossed her to the mattress. All of their wrestling only put her clothes in greater disarray. In her eagerness to best him, she seemed to have forgotten about her appearance. Looking down at her animated face and flashing eyes, Thomas wanted desperately to feel her beneath him without any clothes on at all. Pushing the thought aside, he decided to continue their game.

"Why do you always think you can get the better of

me, Gina?" Thomas asked when he had her flat on her back, pinned to the bed with her arms above her head.

"Because I can and I will one day. I just haven't caught you right yet," she answered, smiling up at him.

Captured by her irresistible smile, he was no longer able to resist her as a woman. He leaned down, intending to plant a safe, chaste kiss on her lips. She wrapped her arms around his neck and the safe little kiss became intensely erotic.

Suddenly aware of where they were, Thomas ended the kiss. He lay next to her and wrapped his arms around her. "You are beautiful in the morning," he said, huskily.

"Thank you, but I don't believe you," she answered. "I know how horrible I must look. My hair hasn't seen a comb since early yesterday."

Thomas wanted to kiss her again so badly that his body ached, but he knew that it would not be sensible for him to start something that neither of them would be able to end until they were both satisfied. Suddenly he moved from her and sat on the side of the bed. "If you don't get up now, you're going to be late for Sunday school. In fact, you may miss Sunday school entirely."

Regina quickly rose from the other side of the bed and adjusted her clothes, hastily tying the blouse around her waist again and smoothing out her skirt. By the time she came out of the bathroom, Thomas and Justin were waiting for her at the other end of the hall.

As she crossed the street, she fleetingly wondered if any of their neighbors noticed her. What would they think about her leaving Thomas's house at seven o'clock in the morning? *Well, I can't worry about the neighbors. I have other problems. What am I going to do about us? This man is too gorgeous for me to be around without los-*

ing my mind. I forget my goals, my principles, everything when he's around.

Justin apparently had had enough sleep; he was talkative and raring to go. He wanted pancakes for breakfast and promised his mother that he could make them for her. She got the package of frozen pancakes from the freezer and set it on the counter for him. He promptly placed four in the toaster and put butter in the microwave to melt.

Luckily, her son had enough to tell her about that did not require any focus from her. Her mind was still on Thomas. It suddenly dawned on her that she was more than physically attracted to the man. He had occupied her every thought since the first day they met. Even when she'd tried to stay away from him, he was on her mind all the time. She thought that her feelings were reciprocated, but she wasn't too sure. Her only relationship as an adult had been with Justin's father and she didn't feel that that relationship had gone too well. What was she supposed to do?

Justin, Tres, and Thomas were ready and waiting for her in the family room by the time she'd taken a leisurely bath and dressed. She told herself that she'd taken no greater care in preparing for Sunday service than she usually did, but if she were honest she'd have to admit that she'd dressed for Thomas. She knew that she looked particularly good in a peach-colored linen sheath with almost off-the-shoulder cap sleeves. The skirt of the dress was very slim and stopped several inches above her knees. She wore a natural-colored straw hat decorated with perfectly matched peach flowers.

"You look like the perfect picture of summertime this morning," Thomas said when she walked into the room.

"Yes, Ms. Regina, you look pretty," Tres said.

"You sure do," Justin agreed.

"Thank you, gentlemen. Was I worth waiting for?" she asked, turning like a model so that they could see her outfit. Thomas whistled and the boys tried to follow suit. "Well, we don't want to be late. We might miss Pastor Bender calling your name for your certificate," Regina said.

Thomas looked at his watch. "We've only been waiting for you for about thirty minutes, but we should be able to make it in time. And you were worth the wait," he added as he escorted her to his car.

Of course, Tres had already been to church with the Lovejoys several times. Most of the church members knew him and greeted him warmly. It was his father who drew the attention today. Most of the members of the black community had read about him in the weekly newspapers and were big supporters of Raven basketball, but few had actually met him.

"I heard that you were seeing Coach Simmons. I've been trying to meet him since he moved here. How did you sneak that one in?" one of the sisters of the church asked.

"Come on and introduce us," another whispered to Regina

"I'll introduce you after church," Regina whispered.

"I want to meet him, too," the woman on the other side of her whispered.

"Honey, he's holding a seat for you up there with the boys up front," the pastor's wife said. "The kids are so excited. You should be with them. Go on and take your seat. We'll get the goods on him later."

After the ceremony, orange juice and pastries were served in the church's fellowship hall. Several women, and a few men, lined up to be introduced to Thomas. Pastor Bender and his wife came over to congratulate

Justin on his promotion and invited Tres to join in the activities for children.

"I don't believe we've met," Pastor Bender said, looking at Thomas.

"Pastor Bender, Mrs. Bender," Regina said, "this is my friend Thomas Simmons. He's the coach at Renaissance University."

"Yes, I know. I've heard the buzz this morning," the pastor said. "We attended several of the games last year. We're real pleased with the new rules you've introduced and the on-court courtesies. Being nice won't keep you all from having a championship season either."

"No, it certainly won't. I've promised President Morgan a championship season and I believe we have the makings of a great team. I'm pleased to meet both of you. I hope to see you at some of our games," Thomas said, shaking hands with Mr. and Mrs. Bender.

"You can count on us at your games if I can count on seeing you here at church. I guess if I were doing my job right, I would have invited you here long ago. Have you joined with a church in Nashville yet?" the minister asked.

"No, I haven't, but if it's left to my son we'll be back. He seems to like it here," Thomas said, indicating Tres, who was sitting with a group of children his age.

"Come anytime. We look forward to having you. I'm glad Regina brought you today," Mrs. Bender said.

When the Benders had moved on, Regina said, "If we don't make our exit soon, we'll end up staying for eleven o'clock service and I'm not up for that today. Let's go to lunch."

During the rest of the week Regina and Thomas were extremely busy with their respective jobs. Thomas had to go to several meetings, both in town and out of town, to solidify the schedule for the coming basketball season. He felt that in his second season, he needed to raise the ante by adding some razzle-dazzle to the schedule.

"I want to play a couple of exhibition games beginning in late October and I'm looking at getting our games televised," he told Regina with excitement one evening after a late dinner.

"Who are you talking with about televising your game?" Regina asked.

"Right now, just the conference folks. I have to have their approval before I go to one of the networks."

"Do you think it's going to happen this year?"

"I'm almost certain that it will. I have some of the most exciting players you'll find anywhere playing for us. My recruiters have done a tremendous job. I just need to let the right people know what we have going on. If we don't get it this year, at least I'll plant a seed for next year."

"I'm sure you'll get it this year," Regina said encouragingly, gently stroking his arm.

"Thanks for your vote of confidence," Thomas said, feeling ten feet tall. "By the way, don't forget my in-laws—Tres's grandparents—will be here Saturday morning. Will you come over when they get here? They have heard so much about you and Justin that they're anxious to meet both of you."

"I'll be over," Regina said, noting that he still called his son's grandparents his in-laws. She reasoned that attachments like that didn't end just because a loved one was gone. "What are their names?" she asked.

"Paul and Sara Evans. I've always called them by their first names because I met them when I thought I was grown and they let me get by with it," Thomas explained with a self-deprecating chuckle.

After discussing the Evanses' arrival, Regina told Thomas about the deadline for the songs for Shelby

Webb's album. They needed to have everything written and ready for recording by the time Shelby was off of her tour and ready to return to the studio. She explained to Thomas that the songwriting for that project was still exhilarating. It was almost like writing an opera because all the songs were interconnected to tell the story of Shelby's life.

The week dragged on with Thomas and Regina continuing to share responsibility for two active boys. When the Evanses arrived bright and early on Saturday morning, Regina and Justin were watching out their window and saw Thomas pull into his garage.

Earlier Thomas had called Regina to awaken her when he and Tres had left for the airport to retrieve their guests. Now, fully awake and neatly dressed, Regina and Justin hurried across the street to meet the new arrivals.

Before she could ring the doorbell, Thomas threw the door open. Putting an arm around her, he led Regina into the living room. "Paul and Sara Evans, I'd like for you to meet Regina Lovejoy," he said with a big smile on his face.

"We're so pleased to finally meet you. For the past few months your name has been in every conversation that we've had with Tres and Thomas," Paul said. Regina offered him her hand, but he pulled her to him like a long-lost daughter, smothering her in a bear hug.

When he let her go, Sara Evans pulled Regina to her heavy bosom, reminding Regina of another disadvantage of being shorter than most people. She turned her head so that she wouldn't suffocate. "We're so glad that you are here to take care of our boys. You mean everything to my grandson. He tells me that you sing to him and you're teaching him to play the piano. He thinks you can do anything," Mrs. Evans said with her hands on Regina's shoulders.

"Don't forget Justin. Grandma, Grandpa, here's Justin," Tres said, pushing his playmate to the center of the circle that the adults had formed.

"Hello, Justin," Sara said, leaning over to greet the boy. "I'm delighted to finally see your face. I've heard your voice over the phone so many times. You have a nice face," she told the child, pinching his plump cheek.

"Where are those trucks you guys told me about?" Mr. Evans asked.

"They're in the backyard at our construction site," Tres replied. "Want to go see?"

"Go on to the back," Thomas said. "I'll have breakfast ready in a few minutes."

"So you cook now?" Mrs. Evans asked with something akin to amazement in her voice.

"I have to. Tres and I got tired of eating out," Thomas explained.

"Well, this I've got to see. I'll help you," Sara offered.

"I know that you didn't travel this far to hang out in my kitchen. Go spend time with the children. I have everything under control."

At her doubtful look, he said, "I do. Now scoot." When Regina remained in the kitchen with him, he put her to work setting the table and mixing the frozen juice. In no time at all, everyone was sitting down to a breakfast of grits casserole, scrambled eggs, sausage, bacon, biscuits, sliced oranges, and orange juice.

"This is quite impressive," Sara said as she spread a napkin across her lap. "Everything is colorful and looks delicious."

"All I can say is I'm hungry now that you've put all of this before us. It had better be edible," Paul said.

After the food was blessed, silence reigned at the breakfast table for several minutes. The silence was punctuated only by a request for a platter to be passed or the offering of more juice. As everyone finished buttering their biscuits and filling their plates, conversation began again. "I hope you and Tres have found a church to attend. We'd like to go with you in the morning," Sara said.

"We went to church the other morning. You know, that morning that Miss Regina was in your bed, Daddy?" Tres said.

Regina paused in stunned embarrassment. She carefully set her glass of juice back on the table, hoping that her trembling hand would not slosh juice on the white tablecloth. Thinking back, she had not been aware that either of the children had seen her in Thomas's bed. She did not want the child's grandparents to think that she and their son-in-law were having an intimate relationship, but for now she was incapable of speech.

"It was last Sunday," Thomas said smoothly, seeming not to notice the stricken look on her face.

Regina wondered what she could say that would not sound defensive. When she had found her voice again, she stammered, "I don't—I was in Thomas's bed because I came home late and fell asleep."

"No explanation is in order here," Mr. Evans said. "We don't meddle in grown folks' business."

Before Regina could say more, the conversation quickly moved to other topics with Tres telling his grandparents about basketball camp and the big kids he and Justin had beat in a game of HORSE.

"I'll clear the table since you did all the cooking," Regina offered when the meal was over.

"Let me help you," Mrs. Evans said, picking up plates as she moved quickly around the table.

When the two women were alone in the kitchen, Mrs. Evans said, "You became awfully quiet after Tres made his announcement. I know that he embarrassed you, but I agree with my husband, what two adults do is none of our business."

Regina paused in rinsing a plate and looked at Mrs. Evans. She saw nothing but kindness on the woman's face. "I guess I shouldn't be embarrassed by what either of the kids say anymore, but they still manage to shock me at times."

"I know—out of the mouths of babes. Honey, I know you're a real sweet girl. I've been anxious to meet you since Nadine called and told me all about you when she met you back in April. We were so worried about Thomas after our Paulette died that we weren't sure if he would be able to go on. I took Tres and cared for him for a while; then I gave him back to his father because I realized that Thomas needed something to live for—a reason to get up every day. Over the past few years, he's become an exceptional father, but he's merely gone through the motions of living. We loved Paulette with all our hearts and we know that she can't be replaced. But we also know how much she loved her husband and child. Now we only want what's best for them. We think you've been real good for our boys."

"Thank you. They've been good friends to Justin and me, too. We have a lot of fun together. We have a lot in common, having sons and all," Regina said, rambling because she had not expected such a frank conversation with Mrs. Evans. Remembering something the older woman had said casually, Regina added, "Nadine—Mrs. Simmons—told you about me? But we only met for about thirty minutes right before she left town. What could she know about me?" she asked, surprised.

"First of all, she said that you were pretty enough to take her son's mind off his grief and that you were a serious mother who spends a lot of time with her son. She thought that you must be pretty outgoing because there are always a lot of people coming and going from your house," Sara said, trying to focus on the details that Nadine had given her that had made them agree that Regina was the one for Thomas.

"A lot of people at my house," Regina echoed in surprise. "I never have people at my house. Oh, she must have been here when I hosted the Tin Pan Alley planning meeting. That's just a group of people in the music business. We were planning a songwriters' celebration. Of course, it could have been when I had the songwriting sessions at home. Sometimes I don't want to take Justin out. Maybe she noticed my ladies' night group," she explained, at first confused by the reference to the activity at her house. As far as she knew she lived a pretty quiet life.

Sara continued as if Regina had not spoken. "Oh, yes, she liked it that you were directly across the street. That way Thomas can't get depressed and try to avoid you. And with the boys being the same age, it was a godsend," she said, smiling at the memory of the conversation she'd had with her friend.

"Was her husband really ill?" Regina asked, wondering if she'd been set up.

"Probably not. But Nadine didn't make up his phone call or her concern for him. Of course, she could have brought the boy home with her, but she felt that you and Thomas needed to meet." Seeing the disconcerted look on Regina's face, Mrs. Evans quickly added, "Please don't be upset with two old matchmakers. It's worked. You and Thomas are in love with each other and the boys are happy."

"I'm not sure if Thomas and I are in love with one another. He hasn't said a word about love," Regina answered.

"But it's obvious that you're in love and you were in his bed—"

Regina interrupted before Sara could finish, "I was in his bed because I had fallen asleep when I came to pick up Justin and I was too tired to keep moving. We don't have an intimate relationship."

"Well, whatever the reason was, you were there and it's obvious to me that you two are in love. I'm a keen observer of human nature and I know what I see," Sara said stubbornly. "It's the touches, the caring, the communication without words, the cooperation and agreement. You have it all. I'll be happy to report to Nadine that her plan worked."

"But it hasn't. We haven't even had a date without our children present yet."

"Sometimes things don't happen the way we expect, but they work out okay in the end," Mrs. Evans said, rinsing a dishcloth and wiping the stove. She hummed as she worked and Regina continued loading the dishwasher in silence. Usually she respected the opinion of older people, but these two old women had gone too far. In the first place, they had no business playing matchmaker with her and Thomas. And to think that Mrs. Evans had already decided that they were in love. They didn't know anything about Regina.

Hmmph—she'd thought that she was in love with Peter and how long did that last? Not long enough to carry a baby full term. No, she'd been a fool in love once and that was one time too many. So what if Thomas was the best-looking man she'd ever seen in her life, the most thoughtful man she'd ever met, a wonderful role model for Justin who happened to spark her passion? That didn't mean she had to fall in love with him.

No way, just because she came close to asking him to make love to her when she was in his bed did not mean she was in love with him. Was that why she was so embarrassed over Tres's announcement? If she'd actually spent the night and had good sex with Thomas, maybe she wouldn't be so embarrassed now. But the truth was, Thomas had pushed her away before she got enough nerve to do what she really wanted to do in that bed. She certainly didn't want another one-sided love affair.

She'd have to be more in control in the future. She wouldn't let things get so out of hand again. Wasn't she the one who didn't want her son around people having casual sex? She certainly didn't want her son around a lot of temporary *uncles*. She helped Thomas entertain his guests the rest of the weekend, but tried to avoid further personal discussions with Sara.

They all attended her church on Sunday morning. Sara and Paul were introduced to the congregation as first-time visitors. When given a chance to speak, Sara stood in her wide-brimmed and high-stacked royal-blue straw hat that was covered in a concoction of royal-blue netting and sequins to say that she and her husband were visiting their son-in-law and grandson and they were pleased to have been invited to this church by Ms. Regina Lovejoy and her son, Justin.

As Sara Evans talked on and on about her wonderful visit, Regina began to worry that she had no control over her tongue. There seemed to be no connection to her brain and mouth. Regina hoped that she would not give out too many personal details after she'd already called Regina "the wonderful girl" that her son-in-law was seeing. Surely she wouldn't dare mention that Regina had arrived in church last Sunday after spending a lustful night in her son-in-law's bed. At a couple of points, Regina thought that was what the woman was leading up to.

At last Sara finished responding to their welcome

and service ended. The congregation gathered around the visitors after service to personally welcome them to Nashville and to their church. Several members commented on Justin and Tres's impending summer separation. They were concerned about the boys' survival during that time.

After Sunday dinner at a nearby restaurant, the older married couple and the younger couple sat on the deck in back of Thomas's house. They idly watched the boys play in the mud at their construction site. Neither Regina nor Thomas was surprised when Mr. and Mrs. Evans offered to take Justin home with them. "One more boy won't be any additional problem for us. In fact, he'll save us from having to be so active with Tres."

"I wish he could go with you, but my mother is looking forward to spending time with Justin. In fact, she's planning to take him to the Space and Rocket Center in Huntsville. He's too young for Space Camp, but they're going to participate in a program for younger children. My mother is almost as excited as Justin. They've been on a waiting list for months and she chose next week because that's when the center had space available for them," Regina explained.

"We'll plan earlier for next summer," Mrs. Evans said. Leaning toward the glider where Regina was sitting next to Thomas, she added in a whisper, "By then you and Thomas will need some time alone together." Thomas and Mr. Evans exchanged a look, but neither spoke.

"Tell me again what time you're going to leave in the morning?" Regina asked.

"We need to be at the airport by four-thirty. We want to get our car out of the airport parking lot before business travelers start coming in," Paul explained to Regina.

"We'll try to come over and see you off," Regina said, yawning at the thought of getting up so early.

"Why don't you say good-bye tonight, Regina? And you could leave Justin with me. I'll drop him off before I go to the campus in the morning." Thomas smiled indulgently at her. She'd been a real trooper getting up earlier than her usual summer schedule over the past couple of days.

"I just might take you up on that," Regina answered, unaware of the look that passed between the Evanses.

Regina went home without Justin that night and received a wake-up call at ten o'clock the next morning. "Were you waiting for me to bring Justin to you?" Thomas asked.

"To be honest, I'm still asleep," she answered.

"Good. We decided to go out for breakfast on our way home from the airport. Since it was still so early, I didn't want to awaken you but I decided to come to the office to work on our schedules and budgets while it's still quiet. Justin is taking a nap on the sofa here in my office."

"Thank you, Thomas," Regina answered quietly.

"I'll keep him here all day, if it's okay with you. I'll have some students coming in later who'll keep him company."

"Okay. Just be sure that if he goes to the pool they watch him carefully."

"Yes, ma'am," Thomas quipped.

Regina lay in bed thinking of how nice it was to have the luxury of lying there with no responsibilities. It felt good to have someone in her life that she could trust to take care of her son. But she was not in love with him, she insisted to herself stubbornly. She turned over on her back and stared up at the ceiling. Okay, she admitted to herself, she was very attracted to Thomas. That was for sure. However, she could not even consider the possibility of being in love with him. She should not have let Mrs. Evans plant that thought in her head. How was she going to face Thomas if all she thought about was being in love with him?

What a waste of time, she thought as she sat up in bed. Her time would be put to better use writing songs *about* love than thinking about love like some silly teenage girl. She still had an album to complete and needed to get to work on it. She sat on the side of the bed for a few minutes and held her head. Yeah, this would be a good time to work on lyrics for the Shelby Webb album.

She ended up staying in her music room well into the evening. She didn't hear from Thomas or Justin, but she didn't worry because she knew that sometimes Thomas got caught up in activities on campus—everything from counseling students or staff to impromptu meetings with the athletic director or others in administration. There would be no way she could catch up with him. She also knew that there was no need for her to worry because he always made certain that Justin was well cared for. Or he would call her if he needed her to come pick up her son.

It was close to eight o'clock before Thomas brought Justin home. The boy was full of news about the people he'd met and the meetings that he'd attended.

"What's in that bag?" Regina asked, looking hungrily at the large brown, grease-stained bag that Thomas held in one hand.

"You have to guess," he teased her.

"From the way it smells, I'd say you've been to Mary's Pit Barbecue," Regina guessed, sniffing the air with exaggerated motions near where Thomas stood with the bag.

"What did we get you, Mama?" Justin asked, enjoying the game.

"You got me—let me think. Can I still read your mind like I could when you were little?" she asked, putting a finger to her temple. "I can see it now. You were in Mary's and you ordered a shoulder sandwich and a cup of potato salad for me and you guys have already eaten."

"How did you know? Can you really read my mind?" Justin asked.

"All mothers can read their children's minds. It's a special gift we have. And I see barbecue sauce on your shirt," she said, touching a spot on Justin's shirt, then tickling him and hugging him. She didn't get as many hugs from him anymore since he started hanging with the tough guys.

"Do you want me to put this bag in the kitchen?" Thomas asked, after she was standing again.

"Yes. Do you want to join me while I eat?"

"It's been a while since Justin and I ate our meal. We stayed at the restaurant shooting the breeze with some of the guys; then we placed an order for you and had to stay longer. I got a couple of extra sandwiches so that we could eat with you. I don't know about Justin, but I'm hungry again," Thomas said as he followed Regina to the kitchen.

Regina watched Thomas wolf down a chopped pork sandwich in two bites. She stared at him and shook her head.

"What—what did I do?" he asked innocently, making his eyes big and round.

"I admire the way you can put away the food. What did you do with that sandwich? Are you some kind of magician?" she teased him.

"No, I need nourishment. I'm still growing, that's all."

"I wish I were," Regina said, thinking of how every extra ounce showed on her petite frame. Didn't she read somewhere that some birds ate their total body weight in food every day? She wondered if that could possibly be true for Thomas as well.

"You're still staring at me," Thomas said, wondering what was on her mind.

"You're so tall and muscular and I feel so short and—oh, never mind," she said. "I'm going to enjoy this sandwich because it's good."

"Baby, I love your body. It's a cute little compact body. If you have any extra fat on you, it's right where it's supposed to be because you look good to me. In fact, I like a sister with a little junk in her trunk," he said, briefly holding her hand.

"Good, because I really like this sandwich," she said, removing her hand from his and breaking off a piece of the meat and bread. Closing her eyes she moaned softly, "Umm, this is good. I'm not going to let the threat of a few pounds keep me away from something this good."

While they were eating, Thomas asked, "When does your mother get here?"

"She'll be here Friday afternoon. She's driving because they'll stop in Huntsville for Space Camp on their way back to Bessemer," Regina answered, taking the pickles off of her sandwich.

"I should have told them to leave your pickles off. I forgot," Thomas said, noting the pile of pickles she had on her plate.

"No, I like the taste of the pickles. I just don't like to bite into them with my bread and meat so I set them aside," she explained. "Why were you asking about my mother's arrival?"

"I was trying to get our schedules in perspective. I have traveling that I need to do. A couple of conferences and things like that. I thought it would be fun if you could get away and go with me," Thomas said with a hopeful look on his lean, handsome face.

Regina had broken off a piece of her sandwich and was about to put it in her mouth when she heard the question in his voice. She looked at him and wondered what was on his mind. He took business trips all the time and had never asked her to go with him before. Of course, they'd never had this luxury of being childless before.

"Well, don't just sit there staring at me. I'm not going to eat you up. You can have a separate room if you like. The conferences are planned for business and pleasure and I thought it would be a good treat for us to do some adult things—I mean some things we couldn't do if we had the children with us," he hurried to explain when he saw the look of reprimand on her face.

She slowly chewed on her bite of sandwich, vying for time. Finally she swallowed and asked, "Where are we going?"

Thomas smiled, but did not question Regina's use of the pronoun *we*. Instead he answered her question without comment. "My first trip is in two weeks. I leave on a Monday for a coaches' retreat at the Sunriver Resort in central Oregon. Nike sponsors it and I assure you, everything is first class. I know you don't care much for golf or tennis, but there'll be plenty of other things for you to do. The scenery alone is worth the trip. If you want to go, I'll have my secretary make reservations for you and she'll see that you're added to the guest list."

"So you think I'm going to enjoy watching a bunch of fat-bellied old men sit around chomping on cigars and discussing a sport that they can no longer play?" Regina asked.

"That's the Regina that I know and love. You're getting some of your old sarcasm back. But to answer your question, you will not be required to sit around with the pot-bellied old men. They have a wonderful arts community and I thought you would enjoy visiting some of the museums and crafts shops. Or you can have a spa day. It's your choice. You just have to promise to save a little time for me. Is that too much to ask?"

"No, it's not." She smiled, relishing the thought of spending some uninterrupted time with him. "I take it that this is a trip for coaches and their wives?" she said with a question in her voice.

"Wives—girlfriends—anyone we want to spend a week with and who can tolerate us for a week," Thomas said.

"So, am I your girlfriend?" Regina asked playfully.

"Gee, Regina, I thought I already asked you to go steady with me. Didn't you already say yes? Would you like my class ring to make it official?" he said in his goofy teenage voice.

"No, Doofus, I don't need your class ring. You probably don't even know where yours is anymore, do you?"

"To be honest with you, I don't. But I remember the girl that I gave it to."

"And now she's probably happily married with three kids. You mentioned that you have a couple of trips. What is the other?"

"It's to Boca Raton, Florida. It's more of a seminar and I'll be in classes all day, but I'll have the evenings free to spend with you. At least in Boca, the hotel will be close to two big malls," Thomas explained.

"That sounds great, but I think I'll go for the trip to Oregon. That's in two weeks and I should have made some headway on that Shelby Webb project by then," Regina reasoned.

"I know we'll have fun," Thomas said.

"I'm going to need to fit in some shopping between now and next week," Regina said, thinking aloud.

"Why do you need to go shopping again?" Justin asked, coming to get juice from the refrigerator as Regina was making her comment.

"I'm going on a trip while you're away and I need new clothes. You like me to look pretty, don't you?"

Justin rolled his eyes heavenward and left the room.

Chapter 8

By the time her mother arrived Friday afternoon, Regina was a nervous wreck. She loved her mother, but she could be so critical sometimes. Nothing missed her eagle eyes and she was not the most tactful person to be around. Regina dreaded having her mother meet Thomas. Feeling protective toward him, she had tried to warn Thomas about her mother, but he'd simply laughed her off and told her that he was looking forward to meeting the famous Ms. Julia Lovejoy.

Regina had spent all day Thursday washing, ironing, and packing Justin's clothes. Though she never ironed his T-shirts and shorts, she knew that if she didn't she'd get a lot of grief from her mother.

Her mother's pessimism regarding her endeavors often stunned Regina. Julia had warned Regina that she'd never make it in the music business, asking her to name the number of African-Americans who'd made it in county music. When Regina won her contract with a major record label almost immediately, her mother had not rejoiced with her. Instead, she'd told Regina that she'd waste her money and she'd come crawling back home looking for help. Julia had never understood how Regina could walk away from her corporate office in New York to go write country music with a bunch of hillbillies.

Rather than celebrate Regina's being able to own a big two-story all-brick house in one of the better neighborhoods in Nashville, her mother had accused her of wasting money and being a show-off. To prove that she'd not spent nearly as much on the house as she was qualified to spend, Regina had shown her mother her investment portfolio. Instead of congratulating her daughter on her shrewdness, her mother had said, "Don't brag to me, girl, it's not becoming."

Regina's grandmother had explained to Regina that Julia Lovejoy believed in tough love. She was afraid that showing Regina how much she loved her would make her weak and Julia felt that a woman had to be strong to survive. "Well, I should survive a long time because my mother sure has been tough on me," Regina had answered. With that, her grandmother had folded her in her arms and given Regina the love that Julia withheld.

Now her grandson was another story indeed. Whoever coined the expression "black women raise their daughters and love their sons" sure had it right in Julia Lovejoy's case. She catered to her grandson's every whim. One of the reasons that she'd hoped for Regina's failure in Nashville was that Regina had dared take her grandson from her. She looked forward to her annual indulge-him-fests with her grandson. During his time with Gran Julia, he was catered to totally and completely. When he was smaller, it would take weeks for Regina to restore discipline and order to her son's life after a summer with Gran Julia. That was one of the reasons that he only stayed two weeks now instead of the whole summer.

Thomas had wanted to be at her house when her mother arrived, but Regina asked him to wait until she called him. She wasn't sure how her mother would react to Thomas. She wasn't sure if he was up to her mother's kind of abrasiveness. When she'd told Julia about him, she'd described him as the father of Justin's best friend.

A dark blue Taurus wagon pulled into Regina's driveway at about four o'clock. "That's not Gran Julia's car," Justin said.

"It must be the car she rented to drive up here," Regina said, throwing open the door and holding Justin back until the car was still. When the driver-side door opened, Justin rushed to his grandmother.

"How is my love? How is my precious grandson? You have grown so much this summer. You're not a baby anymore, are you? I can't pick you up anymore," she said, kneeling on the pavement, having to steady herself to prevent being knocked over backward by the rambunctious boy.

After she'd covered the boy's face with kisses she stood and smoothed her white knee-length walking shorts. "Hi, Regina, it's been a long time. I thought you would have come home as soon as school ended for a short visit. I see you're still keeping your hair chopped off," she noted, smoothing her French roll from which a single hair dared not stray.

"I'll get your bags, Mother. Justin, take your grandmother inside," Regina said in a flat voice.

How many pieces of luggage does one need for a weekend trip? Oh, yes this is luggage for all of next week while they're in Huntsville. Then should I take it all in? She went back inside looking for her mother. She found her in the back watching Justin show her how high he could swing. "Mother, which piece of luggage do you want me to bring in?" Regina asked.

"All of it! You could have had it in by now, while you were looking for me. Some of it is for Huntsville, but I don't want to leave my bags in the car over the weekend. Do you mind pulling my car into your garage when you're finished?" she added, not looking away from Justin.

When Regina returned to the front, Thomas was striding down the driveway toward the garage at the back of the house. "I know that you told me to wait for your call, but sometimes you don't know how to ask for help so I came over anyway."

"It certainly looks like I need help now," she admitted.

After the luggage was in the first-floor guest room, Regina took Thomas to meet her mother. "My goodness, Regina, do you have to have a man do everything for you? There weren't that many pieces of luggage. If it was too much, I could have helped you," she said, sounding annoyed.

"I thought your mother was coming, Regina. I didn't know you had a sister," Thomas said, pouring on the charm.

"Don't try that with me, young man. I've heard that line before. I am old enough to be Regina's mother, although I was very young when she was born," she said, smiling at Thomas. "I'm Julia Lovejoy and you must be Thomas."

"I am. I'm Thomas Simmons," he said, accepting her offered hand. He wasn't sure if he should kiss it or shake it. She seemed to expect a bow and a kiss. He simply took her hand in his and held it as he told her how beautiful she was. She actually blushed. Regina could detect a flush spreading beneath her mother's dark skin. Thomas had actually made her mother's temperature rise and he'd managed to take her attention away from Justin for a moment.

"I would recognize you as Regina's mother anywhere," Thomas was saying. "You both are striking beauties and you have those same beautiful, almond-shaped eyes. That must be the family's symbol of beauty," he said as he helped her to the glider.

"Yes, they are. Everyone notices our eyes. My mother also has the very same eyes," Julia gushed.

"They're absolutely gorgeous. And if the eyes weren't a dead giveaway, your delicate figure is," he commented, not sure of how many more compliments he would have to pay her, but relieved that she seemed to be eating them up.

"Thank you." She smiled up at Thomas.

Good, he thought, *she considers being tiny a compliment.* Her daughter certainly didn't. When he'd called her a "shorty" she'd let him have a piece of her mind. He was relieved that he'd guessed correctly when he'd made note of Julia's petite stature.

He returned his focus to what she was saying. "I walk at least five miles every evening after dinner. I've been after Regina to exercise more. You know, once you're over thirty, your metabolism changes. You have to exercise to keep any kind of figure. Have you started exercising yet, Regina?"

"Yes, ma'am," was Regina's only answer. She almost dropped her jaw with all the flattery Thomas was pouring on her mother. She marveled at how easily her mother accepted the compliments.

"What do you do?" she asked in an accusatory tone. "I could never get her interested in tennis or any outdoor sport," her mother said in an aside to Thomas.

"I usually do a few stretch exercises every day before I dress," Regina answered.

"That's not enough, is it?" Julia said, touching Thomas's muscular arm. "Now you surely work out every day."

"I do, but I work with athletes. We spend our summers in conditioning and training in the weight room.

I try to motivate them by showing them what an old man can do," Thomas explained.

"Maybe you could get Regina in there with you," Julia suggested.

"Regina can go anywhere with me that she chooses," Thomas said pleasantly.

Julia raised an eyebrow and looked at Regina, who tried not to smile. At any rate, she'd had enough of the two of them. "Are you about ready for dinner, Mother? We have early reservations so that Justin wouldn't be too tired and grouchy."

"I need to go and change. Are you going to wear that?" Julia asked, looking pointedly at the three-piece suit of linen capri pants, sleeveless top, and jacket that Regina was wearing.

"Yes, I changed shortly before you got here," Regina answered.

"So we're not going anywhere nice?" Julia asked.

"I think it's a very nice restaurant—one of the best in Nashville in fact. You'll love the food," Thomas said. "And they even accommodate children, so it's one of our favorite places."

"Okay, I'll be right back," Julia said, hurrying into the house.

"Whew! I'm not going to make it through the weekend," Regina said when the door had closed behind her mother. She stood staring at the closed door as if waiting for her mother to return.

"Yes, you will. I'll be here for you," Thomas said, taking her hand and pulling her into his lap. "Relax for a moment. You know, you're a lot like your mother. That's probably the reason that you and she sometimes have difficulty communicating. You two have lively discussions, don't you think?"

"I am not like my mother," Regina said, fitting herself against Thomas's chest.

"I was serious when I said that you're both beautiful. You really are," he said, wrapping his arms around Regina. "And as for those zingers that you're so good at, I see you got your training at the feet of the master," he added, pulling her closer. "Let's try something different this weekend. Instead of arguing with her, we'll be so supersweet to her that she'll have nothing to complain about. For the next twenty-four hours, let's try to keep everything sweet and light. Are you willing to give it a try?"

"If I don't argue with her, she won't enjoy her visit," Regina replied, only half in jest.

"Have you ever tried anything other than arguing with her?"

"No," Regina said slowly.

"So, let's set a new tone in your relationship with her. We'll keep it sweet and light, okay?" he said, kissing Regina lightly on her neck.

"Okay, but I think she'll have you crazy before she leaves. You're already acting kind of strange. What's with all of those compliments?"

"Like I don't pay you compliments?" Thomas questioned.

"You were just pouring them on. Don't you think you overdid it?"

"No, I don't. She liked each one. Watch me work and learn from a pro."

When Julia returned, Regina attempted to rise from Thomas's lap, but he tightened his hold on her. "Not yet. Sweetness and light."

"Oh, am I interrupting something?" Julia asked.

"Nothing that we can't save for later," Regina answered. "Mother, entertain Thomas for me while I go and wipe off Justin's face and hands."

"You're not going to bathe him?"

"No, Mother. He and I bathed and dressed for din-

ner when you called to let us know that you were just
an hour away. We're ready to go. I just need to remove
some surface dirt from him," Regina answered her
mother in an exasperated tone.

"Remember, sweetness and light," Thomas whispered in her ear before he let her rise from his lap.

"I thought Regina said that you and she are just
friends," Julia said as soon as the door was closed.

"We are at a turning point in our relationship. We
have been just friends, but we're very attracted to each
other. I'd like for our relationship to be something
more. You're her mother, so tell me, how do I win your
daughter's heart?" Thomas said, hoping that by involving Ms. Lovejoy she would not try to thwart the
relationship. He could tell that she still had a great
deal of influence over Regina's thoughts and actions.

Julia looked at him carefully. Putting both hands on
her hips, she took a step back as if to get a full view of
him. He towered over her, but she made him feel like
a small child. "I think you'd be good for my daughter,"
Julia finally said. "She works much too hard. Maybe
you can teach her how to laugh and relax. She takes
herself much too seriously."

"Regina does?" Thomas asked, surprised at her
mother's assessment. She obviously did not know that
side of Regina. As far as he knew, Regina was pretty
playful.

Julia continued talking as if Thomas had not interrupted. "You know what I think, since your son is gone
and I'm about to take Justin away, perhaps you
should—now don't get me wrong, this is just an idea—
but I think you should sweep her off her feet and take
her away somewhere."

"That's a great idea. What do you mean by don't get
you wrong?" Thomas asked.

"I'm not suggesting that you two become more involved than you're ready for, but I think some time away from your cares and burdens may be just what the doctor ordered," Regina's mother advised Thomas.

"I like that idea. I'll talk to her about it right away," he said, hoping that Regina would not let anything slip about the trip already planned before he'd had a chance to talk with her. He wanted Julia to think that the trip was all her idea. He needed desperately for Julia to support his relationship with her daughter. He was almost certain that Regina had not confided anything about the trip to her mother yet. But she would have to soon because she would want her mother to know how to reach her in case of an emergency. He'd have to get Regina alone as quickly as possible.

There was no time before or during dinner, but later that evening, after they'd returned from the restaurant, Thomas and Regina sat out on her deck all alone. He told her of her mother's suggestions.

"I can't believe she would even suggest that I go away with you. She is so prim and proper. She wanted me to have a big wedding in Bessemer when I married Peter so that everyone would know we were married. She didn't want anyone to think that I was in New York living with him out of wedlock. Now she's suggesting that I go away with a man? Who is this woman and what have you done with my mother?" Regina asked in mock terror.

"I don't know. I just met her today, but go along with the program. I believe that I'm on the right track. I think she needs to feel needed and involved. After all, you did elope with Peter and she wasn't included in your wedding. Maybe you should get her to go shopping with you tomorrow. Let her buy you something if she offers. Don't you want her blessing on our relationship?" Thomas asked.

"Yes, I do. What makes you think that this is the way

to get her approval? She never approves of anything that I do and I don't expect my relationship with you to be any different."

"Well, I do. I think everything is better when the people that we care about get along."

"Do you really think you can win her over?"

"Of course I do. I'm the coach, remember? Ninety percent of my job involves diplomacy and negotiations. I can solve everybody's problems but my own."

"Which is?"

"I have so many, it'll take all day to begin telling you," he quipped.

"Try me," she challenged.

"I'll tell you about it—them—one day," he answered and closed up.

Early the next morning, Regina told her mother that she and Thomas had talked last night and he wanted to take her away. Julia glowed, feeling good that Thomas had taken her advice so quickly. She and Regina made plans to go shopping right away. As if on cue, Thomas called, offering to keep Justin while the mother and daughter went shopping.

They really did look almost like sisters. Both women slightly more than five feet five inches tall with small waists and wide hips, their beautiful heart-shaped faces with keen chins were accented by high cheekbones. Both were cursed with wildly growing eyebrows that had to be maintained with tweezers on a daily basis. While Regina wore her thick, coal-black hair in a modern, tapered cut, Julia wore her shoulder-length hair in a bouncy flip, which gave her a youthful appearance.

"Mother, you don't look like you've aged since I was a teenager," Regina remarked as they were trying on clothes. *Sweetness and light,* Regina thought to herself.

"You know what they say, 'Good black don't crack,'"

her mother quipped. Then more seriously she said, "Actually, with the melanin in dark skin we're less likely to wrinkle. Take care of yourself, Regina. I know people like to say that looks aren't important, but looks will always be what attracts a man to a woman— at least initially. Thank God different men are attracted to different things."

"What do you mean?" Regina asked, surprised at her mother's frankness. Maybe Thomas was right about involving her.

Julia sat on the tiny shelf that served as a seat in the otherwise spacious dressing room. She began putting some of the outfits that they'd tried on back on the hangers. "To be honest," she said softly, "I'm pleased and surprised that Thomas is attracted to my little dark-skinned girl. You know most of those NBA players have wives who are white or as close to white as possible."

"Stop stereotyping, Mother," Regina reprimanded her. "Anyway, Thomas never played for the NBA."

"But he was a professional athlete. Same difference. Stereotypes are based on some truth," her mother quickly rejoined.

"Mother!"

"Okay, okay. I forget how politically correct you are. But I would think that Thomas would have one of those tall, leggy models on his arm."

"Well, for now all he has is little ole' me," Regina said and was surprised to see her mother join her in laughter.

The rest of the shopping trip was fun, with Julia enjoying the opportunity to dress her daughter again. Julia seemed surprised when Regina readily accepted her advice on various purchases. With all the battles they'd fought in recent years, they'd forgotten how similar their tastes were. And as the day wore on, they discovered many other things that they had in common that they'd long forgotten.

By the time they were on their third mall for the day, Julia said, "Okay, I'm not your sister. I'm an old woman. I'm ready to go home. I give up."

"I'm ready to go home, too. There's one more stop I need to make. My favorite little boutique is on our way home. It's not in a mall so I'll be in and out quickly."

By the time they got home, the warm summer night had turned totally dark. She took her bags up to her room and called to let Thomas know that she was at home. "Would you bring Justin to me?" she asked. "I'm worn out."

Not only did Thomas bring Justin, but he also brought over a skillet of stir-fry. "You are a man I could easily love," Julia told Thomas, flirtatiously batting her lashes at him.

"If my heart wasn't already taken, you are the kind of woman I could love," Thomas answered.

"Who took your heart, Mr. Thomas? Where is it?" Justin asked.

"Your mother has it," Thomas answered.

Regina was warmed by Thomas's remark but told herself not to take him seriously. He was just making conversation. She realized, however, that her mother and son took Thomas very seriously. They both sat with big grins spread across their faces.

Julia watched as Thomas and Regina loaded up the Taurus immediately after church service on Sunday. "We should be in Huntsville before it gets dark," Julia said, looking at her watch.

"Call me when you get there. Give me the number to the hotel when you call," Regina said, stooping to hug her son one more time.

"You have my cell phone number. Just call me on that," her mother snapped.

"Sometimes when you're traveling, your cell phone doesn't connect well or you forget to charge it," Regina said patiently.

"You're right. I forgot," her mother relented easily.

Maybe this sweetness and light thing was working. She'd have to remember to thank Thomas for his lesson in interpersonal skills.

As soon as Julia had backed the Taurus out of the driveway, Thomas began courting Regina relentlessly. It was not a plan on his part; he was just doing what came naturally. Courting her was just as natural to him as shivering on a cold day. He enjoyed being around her and could not get enough of being with her. Of course, if anyone had accused him of persistently pursuing her, he would have denied it. He was oblivious as to why he felt a deep attraction to her. He was simply going on instinct.

On Tuesday when she declined his invitation to go to lunch with him because she needed to go shopping for their upcoming trip, he canceled his afternoon appointments and went shopping with her.

"I thought you hated shopping," Regina noted as they walked toward the mall.

"Well, you need someone to carry your packages and I need a couple of shirts," he said, opening the door to Parisian's for her. He waited patiently while she tried on shoes in the department store before they headed out into the mall. Luckily, since it was a weekday and early afternoon, the mall was fairly quiet.

As they passed the window display at the Baby Gap store, Regina stopped to ooh and ahh over the pretty little sundresses. "They are just so precious," she said. "Can't you see a little fat-legged girl trying to stand alone in one of those?"

"Do you ever think of having more children?" Thomas asked.

"Of course I do. Don't you? But I know that I can't. I have to focus my attention on raising Justin and I don't have time to build a relationship with a man, so my chances of becoming pregnant again are slim to none."

"You mean you won't have any more children. But what I'm trying to tell you is that I can't."

"What do—" she began.

"Sit down over here for a second, baby," Thomas said softly, leading her to a bench in the center of the mall.

"What is it? What's wrong?" she tried to continue as they walked to the bench.

"You were talking about having more children and I need to tell you—I want to tell you—that I had a vasectomy while my wife was ill. We couldn't risk the possibility of her becoming pregnant again." Thomas spoke so quietly that Regina was not quite certain that she'd heard him correctly.

She turned toward him and searched his face. She couldn't read his expression, so she had to ask, "Why did you feel compelled to share that information with me?"

"Full disclosure, remember? I offer you this information in the spirit of full disclosure. We don't know where our relationship is going, but I don't want to hold any facts from you that may come back to haunt me later."

"Okay, I appreciate your honesty. But for now the child that I have is quite enough for me and you're fortunate to have Tres. Now let's go in Joan Steven's and see if I can find a nice dinner dress for that 'First Night Reception' at the conference," Regina said, slipping her hand in his.

For the next two weeks they were together whenever Thomas was in town. In the final days before their departure, Regina had a beauty shop appointment to get her hair done, then another to get a pedicure and manicure. Rosemary and the other operators teased her about traveling with her *neighbor*, as Regina had referred to him in the beginning of their relationship. This time Regina didn't try to deny the attraction that they held for each other.

She was more than a little jittery when they boarded the plane for Oregon. As she glanced at the tall, handsome man sitting next to her, she wondered how she would fit in with his associates. She knew that this trip would take their relationship to another level or all of the close contact without their children as buffers could end their relationship.

Three days after their arrival at the resort, Regina sat in the hotel lounge waiting for Thomas to join her. To her surprise and pleasure, things had gone extremely well. He had offered to decline his many invitations to play golf and tennis to spend time with her, but she'd encouraged him to spend time with his friends, most of whom he had not seen since leaving St. Luke University.

She'd selected seminars to attend during the day, and over the course of several she'd met many of the women who were attending as spouses. After the morning seminars, she and Thomas usually spent some time together before joining the group for dinner. They'd lounged at the hotel pool, gone sight-seeing, and he'd even accompanied her when she'd gone shopping in the arts and crafts district. She smiled, thinking about how much fun it had been shopping with him. He was really getting the hang of it.

On the first day, while they were checking into the hotel, a tall, heavy man who seemed to be in his mid-to-late thirties had gotten out of his registration line as soon as he'd seen Thomas enter the hotel lobby. Slapping Thomas on the back and pumping his arm up and down, he'd practically yelled, "Hey, man, you've resurfaced. Where have you been? Everybody's been asking about you."

"I wasn't in hiding. Didn't you read any of the press about my new job at Renaissance?" Thomas asked in a quieter voice than the one he'd been greeted with.

"No, I'm afraid I missed out on that. I guess I was too caught up in going to our championship game," the man answered.

"Oh, yeah, that was a nasty loss you had in the last few seconds of the game," Thomas said with a smile on his face. Pulling Regina closer to him, he said, "Moon, I want you to meet my friend Regina."

The man gripped Regina's hand in his hard, bear-claw hand and pumped it up and down enthusiastically. While he was still pumping her arm, Thomas asked, "Where is Chantay?"

"She's waiting for me at the bar. You know, we've been married over ten years now. She takes me for granted, there's no way she'd stand in a line with me. How are things for you down there in Tennessee?" Moon asked in a quieter voice.

"Real good—real good. I've got some good opportunities and a lot of potential down there," Thomas answered.

"I'm glad you came out all right. It was really messed up what they did to you at St. Luke, but I knew a brother couldn't keep a plush job like that for too long."

"Yeah, well, that's the way it works out sometimes. But, you know," Thomas said thoughtfully, "it's all for the best. Things have worked out for me okay," he said, wrapping an arm around Regina's shoulder.

Moon looked from one to the other and a big grin

spread across his face. "Oh, I get it. She's your lady. Well, all right. Things did work out for you then. After Paulette died—well, we'll talk later," he said, stumbling and becoming embarrassed at the mention of Paulette.

Before they were checked into the hotel, Thomas had introduced her to about twenty other men and their spouses or significant others. To her surprise, many of those attending the conference were university presidents, athletic directors, and others in administration.

The next morning after Thomas had gone to his session, she had dressed slowly for a coffee she planned to attend for "spouses and others." The topic of discussion for the coffee was how audiences at basketball games had changed over the years.

When Regina walked into the room, several women were already seated and talking softly. One woman stood and welcomed Regina to the group. "My name is Audrey Morgan," she said, extending a long delicate hand to Regina.

"I'm pleased to meet you," Regina responded, recognizing her as the first lady of Renaissance.

"You're here with Thomas Simmons, aren't you?"

"Yes, I am."

"My husband is so pleased with himself for having recruited Thomas to our campus. He's rather proud that he snatched Thomas up before other universities even knew that he was available. I've heard nothing but good things about the coach over the past year. He's done some smart recruiting and we're looking forward to this coming season. Do you follow the game at all?"

"Just a little. I work around a bunch of men, and of course the conversation always goes back to sports. I usually watch the championship games in March. That to me is when basketball gets exciting," Regina replied.

"Oh, yes. The championship games are an exciting

time and my husband, John, believes that Renaissance will get an invitation to participate this year. But my favorite time in the season is right at the beginning. That's when anything is possible. All teams are even," Audrey Morgan said enthusiastically. "I hear that you're in the music industry," she said as they moved to a sofa and love seat.

Regina began to enjoy talking with the medium-brown-skinned woman with auburn hair and freckles, who continued asking questions about Regina's profession. The other women came over to listen to Regina talk about the music industry in Nashville, and as the room filled, everyone gathered around Regina and Audrey.

Finally it was time to begin the official program. "Before we begin," Audrey said, "I'd like for us to go around the room and introduce ourselves. As you can see we have a couple of newcomers this year."

After the introductions, everyone was anxious to jump right into addressing issues that were of common concern to the group. Regina soon realized these women had concerns that no one else in the world, other than those in the room, would understand. Audrey facilitated the lively discussion with a sense of humor, but maintained order.

One tall, fashion-model-looking woman asked, "What do you do when you're sitting next to someone who's hurling insults at your husband? How do you take it?" Regina remembered that her name was Chantay and wondered if she was the same Chantay that Thomas had asked his friend Moon about the previous day. Her question was quickly answered.

"Surely no one is hurling insults at Moon," Audrey said in a teasing manner with a big smile on her face.

"Believe it or not, not everyone in Marlin loves my

husband," the tall, beautiful woman with a long flowing hairstyle answered.

"Well, Chantay, at Renaissance, we believe that protecting the coach's wife is up to the administrative staff and those in positions of influence in our community. With our previous coach, we protected his wife as much as possible. We'll do the same with Regina if she comes to our games," Audrey said, smiling directly at Regina. "Our seats are at center court, but we decide in advance who is going to sit to her left, right, and directly behind her. We'll protect her physically and as much as possible from the verbal barbs."

"What's with these people nowadays? They want to argue with the coaches, they want to argue with the refs, and they even argue with the boys on the team that they're supporting," a tall blonde with green eyes and a southern accent said.

Another blond-haired woman with a serious face reasoned, "We live in a democracy and everyone feels that they have a right to say whatever they want to whomever they want wherever they want. It you correct them, they'll yell that it's their right."

"I still want to know how you can stand having all those people yelling at your husbands," Chantay said, bringing the group back to her original question.

"We can't stand it. None of us can stand it, but we can't avoid the games either. I know that Mike would curl up and die if he could no longer coach, and we both know that the second-guessing and emotions go with the game," the serious-looking blonde said.

"I don't worry so much about the insults tossed at Rich," another woman said. "I worry at the panties tossed at him and the offers that he gets on the road." Those remarks started another flurry of discussion.

When the meeting officially ended, everyone

seemed reluctant to leave. Chantay sought Regina and they made a spa date for the next day.

The seminars, sight-seeing trips, and receptions were interesting, but Regina still wondered at Thomas's intent in bringing her to this particular conference. Especially after Audrey's comments about protecting her at the games. She decided that for now, at least, she would accept his explanation at face value. Perhaps all he wanted to do was get away. These were certainly luxurious surroundings. She could not complain about the first-class accommodations.

While she sat in the bar waiting for Thomas, Audrey Morgan entered the lounge. She smiled when she saw Regina and walked purposely toward her. "Mind if I join you?" she asked.

"Not at all. I'm waiting for Thomas. He was just coming to the suite when I was leaving, but I didn't want to stay up there any longer. I was getting claustrophobic."

"As big as these suites are?" Audrey asked, incredulously.

"They are extremely large and luxurious, but sometimes I just have to get up and get out. I can't stand being confined," Regina explained.

"I know. We're getting a foursome together for golf tomorrow morning. Would you like to join us?" Audrey asked.

"No, I promised Chantay that I'd have a spa day with her. Besides, I've never tried golfing."

"I don't enjoy the sport as much as my husband does. I think he could play eighteen holes two or three times a day if he had the time. I get tired of the sun and heat, but here the weather is perfect. Maybe next time you could sign up for lessons," Audrey suggested.

"Maybe I will," Regina answered, wondering if there would be a next time.

"There's John now," Audrey said, indicating a

distinguished-looking man with graying hair and ebony skin coming through the lounge entrance. Regina recognized him instantly from his pictures in the newspaper and on TV. Audrey waved at her husband and he smiled as he strode toward them.

"John, I'd like for you to meet Thomas's Regina," Audrey said when her husband had joined them at the table.

Regina accepted his hand and was warmed by a very firm handshake. "It's a pleasure to meet you. I've heard so much about you. Welcome to the Renaissance family," John said in a voice as firm as his handshake.

"Thank you," was all Regina could think to say. How had she joined the university family? she wondered. What had Thomas told his colleagues about her? Maybe Thomas had been serious about spreading the word that they were an item to keep his admirers at bay.

"Is it okay if I call you Regina?" John was asking her.

"Yes, certainly. I'm a part of the family now," she said with a bright smile on her face to take some of the bitter sting from her sarcastic remark.

They chatted for another couple of minutes, before Dr. Morgan got to the real reason for his joy at meeting her. "Regina, Thomas has been under tremendous pressure to bring his basketball program to a world-class level. Of course, that takes money. While he's spent time recruiting the right players and coaches to the university, he's spent just as much time or perhaps more raising money. It's been a challenge, as it is at all historically black colleges and universities, but he's done extremely well." He paused as if waiting for her response. Regina let the pause linger and the university president continued speaking.

"This is an exciting time for the basketball program

at Renaissance. We anticipate something wonderful happening for us this season. Business leaders from almost every industry in Nashville have invested in the program. The one industry not represented is country music." He paused again.

Finally Regina spoke to fill the void that surrounded his last comment. "We tend to give most of our support to music programs in the public schools. But if you would like, I'll talk with the people at my label."

"Yes, yes, that's a wonderful idea. I sincerely appreciate your offer." He flashed what he'd probably been told at some point was a million-dollar smile. "But, since you're so involved in our program, we wondered if you would also like to make a personal contribution."

"Certainly, but you must know that although I'm a songwriter, I'm not as wealthy as you might think. What amount do you have in mind?"

"If you contributed ten thousand we could put your name on our gymnasium wall," Dr. Morgan suggested.

"I'd like that," Regina said impulsively. "Yes, I think I could do that. Do me a favor. Don't tell Thomas yet, I'd like to surprise him."

"No, we don't have to tell him just yet. I think the Blue and Gold Gala would be the perfect time to tell him. All of our big donors will be there and Thomas will be happy to know that you've helped the athletics department make its goal," the president said, beaming.

"I thought maybe we could just walk over and show him my name on the gymnasium wall one day," Regina suggested.

"No, no, this way will be better," Dr. Morgan said. "Just you wait. He'll be delighted to know that he's exceeded his fund-raising goal."

"Thomas is coming now," Audrey whispered.

Chapter 9

After greetings were exchanged, the foursome agreed to go to dinner together. Throughout the meal, Dr. Morgan could talk of nothing but basketball. "Do you know what a conference championship could do for our fund-raising?" he asked Thomas at one point.

"I'm sure that the positive feelings that will result from a championship will carry over into increased giving in other areas," Thomas ventured, knowing that fund-raising was one of Dr. Morgan's favorite topics.

"It certainly will, especially among our alumni. I want a championship this year and I want it bad. I know you're the man who can bring that trophy home for us," Dr. Morgan said.

Back at their hotel suite after dinner, Thomas briefly touched Regina's arm. "Can you stay out here and talk with me for a minute? We haven't spent much time together over the past few days," he told her. "And that defeats my whole purpose for bringing you here."

"So what was your purpose for bringing me here?"

"To relax, enjoy ourselves, and well—" He hesitated a moment before continuing. "Do you like our accommodations?" he asked in a sudden change of subject.

"I love them, they're quite plush," Regina said, looking around at the living area of their suite, but she couldn't help wondering why he'd changed the subject.

"Would you like something to drink?" Thomas asked, heading for the bar at the wall opposite a bay of windows that in the day displayed a scenic view of the golf course, but now in the dark night reflected the room.

"I'll take a Heineken. I'll go upscale with an import since I'm in these luxurious surroundings," Regina joked.

"What have you thought of our conference so far?" Thomas asked, bringing the drinks to the sofa with him and taking a seat next to Regina.

"It's been a real eye opener. I had no idea that so much went into coaching."

"You've met the coaches' wives. Do you think that you could lead the kind of life that they lead?" he asked.

"So now we get to the rest of the story," she said, crossing her legs and sinking into the soft sofa. "You want me to see firsthand the kind of lives the coaches' wives lead. Is that why you invited me here?" she asked, reality dawning on her.

"Yes. I want you to be this coach's wife," he said, jabbing a finger at his chest. He seemed to be as surprised as she was, but he continued valiantly. "I want you to marry me, but I want you to walk into our marriage with your eyes open. I love my work and I can't think of anything that I'd rather do. But if this is not the kind of life you can lead, I'll have to find something else to do," he finished earnestly.

When Regina didn't answer, he searched her face, wondering what was going through her head. "Surely I haven't caught you totally off guard?" he asked.

"But you have," Regina said, setting her drink on the

elaborate glass-topped coffee table. "I wondered what was behind this trip, but I had no idea that marriage was on your mind."

"It just sort of hit me a few days ago. I can't eat, drink, or breathe without thinking of you. It dawned on me so suddenly that we should marry that I don't have a ring for you yet. I guess I should have a ring to propose?" he asked.

"No, the ring doesn't matter," she said, still feeling dazed. "Why do you want to marry me?"

"I want you to marry me because I can't imagine Tres and me living without you and Justin. It just makes sense for us to marry. We're together all the time anyway and we enjoy each other's company," Thomas said, taking Regina's small, cold hand in his. "Your hands are cold. Are you as nervous as I am?"

"Yes," she said in a soft, distant voice. "This is a big decision. Not just for me and you, but for our children, too."

"Regina, you and I both know that we're extremely attracted to each other. We have a chemistry that scares me to death. I can't keep my hands off of you and you enjoy my touch, don't you?"

She smiled and looked away. His intense gaze let her know that he could read her thoughts and right now she was shivering at the thought of his touch on her skin. So he knew that he could drive her wild with the mere touch of his fingertip on her arm. Did he also know how much she loved him? He hadn't mentioned love. What if she asked him? No, he had to say the word of his on free will. She didn't want a "me too" response from him. Where did love fit into his perfect little family wedding plans?

Holding his breath, he watched an array of emotions dance across her face. First a dreamy, romantic smile had slowly risen on her face like the birth of a new day. Replacing the dreamy smile, a frown seemed to have been drawn on her face. It seemed as if she'd mentally shrugged her shoulder when the frown was followed by a look of intense concentration.

Not able to take her silence a moment longer, he said, "Regina, say something. What's going through that gorgeous head?"

"I don't know, Thomas. I don't know what to say. Obviously, you've lived with this idea longer than I. Give me some time to absorb the thought. If I give you any kind of answer up here, in this setting, it may not play well back home. Everything is idyllic on vacation. Do you understand what I mean?"

"At first I couldn't move you off that friendship thing. Once I did that, I realized that what we have is unique," he said, walking away from her and beginning to pace the room.

When he turned around to reverse his walk around the room, Regina blocked his path. Standing directly in front of him, she held out her arms. "Don't be upset with me, Thomas. Please give me a minute to think this thing through."

He stepped into her arms and she closed them around his waist. Wrapping his arms around her shoulders, he pulled her closer to him. "I hope you know, Ms. Regina Lovejoy, what waiting for your answer is doing to my ego," he said after holding her tightly to him for a while. He rested his chin on the top of her head and she listened to the rapid beat of his heart.

Stepping away from him, she looked up at him. "My granny told me that if you marry in haste, you repent in leisure. I don't want to repent for marrying you. I want to be sure that we're marrying for the right reasons and not just because it's convenient or because it will make our sons happy."

"It will make our sons happy," he said, shoving his

hands into his pockets and beginning to pace around the room again. Regina folded her arms across her chest and watched him for several moments.

Finally, she said, "It's been a long hard day and I have another one coming up tomorrow. I think I'll call it a night."

He watched her until she closed the door to her sleeping room at the opposite end of the suite from his. He turned off the lights in the living room and went to his bedroom. He knew he should have waited until they returned home before proposing to her. Maybe he should have waited until he had a ring to put on her finger. Maybe he should have gotten down on one knee. Surely he'd done something wrong and he didn't know what it was.

Regina put on the clear plastic shower cap supplied by the hotel and stepped into the spray of warm water. She needed time to think. She was so in love with Thomas that when she was around him, she wasn't sure if she was thinking clearly. Having him in the bedroom at the other end of their suite also caused fuzzy thinking on her part. She thought that maybe the shower would isolate her and allow her to think clearly.

What could possibly be wrong about marrying a man that she already spent every free second of every day with? A man that her son adored? A man who made her feel adored? A man who was totally unselfish and caring?

Coming to a quick decision, she stepped out of the shower and dried off quickly before slipping on the mint-green terry robe supplied by the hotel. Racing through the living room, she tapped lightly on the door to Thomas's bedroom.

"Come in," he called out, looking at the door expectantly.

He was sitting up in bed with a magazine in his

An Important Message From The ARABESQUE Publisher

Dear Arabesque Reader,

Arabesque is celebrating 10 years of award-winning African-American romance. This year look for our specially marked 10th Anniversary titles.

Plus, we are offering *Special Collection Editions* and a *Summer Reading Series*—all part of our 10th Anniversary celebration.

Why not be a part of the celebration and let us send you four more specially selected books FREE! These exceptional romances will be sent right to your front door!

Please enjoy them with our compliments, and thank you for continuing to enjoy Arabesque.... the soul of romance bringing you ten years of love, passion and extraordinary romance.

Linda Gill
PUBLISHER, ARABESQUE ROMANCE NOVELS

P.S. Don't forget to check out our 10th Anniversary Sweepstakes—no purchase necessary—at www.BET.com

A SPECIAL "THANK YOU"
FROM ARABESQUE JUST FOR YOU!

Send this card back and you'll receive 4 FREE Arabesque Novels—a
$25.96 value—absolutely FREE!

The introductory 4 Arabesque Romance books are yours FREE (plus
$1.99 shipping & handling). If you wish to continue to receive 4
books every month, do nothing. Each month, we will send you 4
New Arabesque Romance Novels for your free examination. If you
wish to keep them, pay just $16* (plus, $1.99 shipping & handling).
If you decide not to continue, you owe nothing!

- Send no money now.
- Never an obligation.
- Books delivered to your door!

We hope that after receiving your FREE books you'll want to remain
an Arabesque subscriber, but the choice is yours! So why not take
advantage of this Arabesque offer, with no risk of any kind. You'll be
glad you did!

In fact, we're so sure you will love your Arabesque novels, that we
will send you an Arabesque Tote Bag FREE with your first paid ship-
ment.

**Call Us TOLL-FREE At
1-888-345-BOOK**

* Prices subject to change

THE "THANK YOU" GIFT INCLUDES:

- 4 books absolutely FREE (plus $1.99 for shipping and handling).
- A FREE newsletter, *Arabesque Romance News*, filled with author interviews, book previews, special offers, and more!
- No risks or obligations. You're free to cancel whenever you wish with no questions asked.

INTRODUCTORY OFFER CERTIFICATE

Yes! Please send me 4 FREE Arabesque novels (plus $1.99 for shipping & handling). I am under no obligation to purchase any books, as explained on the back of this card. Send my free tote bag after my first regular paid shipment.

NAME

ADDRESS _____ APT.

CITY _____ STATE ____ ZIP

TELEPHONE ( )

E-MAIL

SIGNATURE

Offer limited to one per household and not valid to current subscribers. All orders subject to approval. Terms, offer, & price subject to change. Tote bags available while supplies last.

Thank You!

Accepting the four introductory books for FREE (plus $1.99 to offset the cost of shipping & handling) places you under no obligation to buy anything. You may keep the books and return the shipping statement marked "cancelled". If you do not cancel, about a month later we will send 4 additional Arabesque novels, and you will be billed the preferred subscriber's price of just $4.00 per title. That's $16.00* for all 4 books for a savings of almost 40% off the cover price (Plus $1.99 for shipping and handling). You may cancel at any time, but if you choose to continue, every month we'll send you 4 more books, which you may either purchase at the preferred discount price. . . or return to us and cancel your subscription.

THE ARABESQUE ROMANCE CLUB: HERE'S HOW IT WORKS

THE ARABESQUE ROMANCE BOOK CLUB
P.O. BOX 5214
CLIFTON NJ 07015-5214

PLACE
STAMP
HERE

hand. During the four days that they'd shared the suite, she'd never set foot across the threshold to his bedroom. To say that he was surprised to see her would be putting it much too mildly.

She rushed over to him and sat on the side of the bed. "What are you reading?" she asked.

"Did you come in here to ask me about my reading material, Regina?" he asked, looking at her intently and wishing that he could pull her into his arms. She smelled like fresh peaches on a sunny day.

She looked at him shyly, which was another big shock to his system. Regina was never shy. "I've finished thinking," she said softly.

"And?" he prompted, sitting straighter and leaning toward her.

"Is the offer still good?"

"I didn't put a time limit on the offer," he said quietly, realizing that his voice was about to stick in his throat he was so nervous.

"I want to marry you, Thomas," she said, smiling.

He pulled her across his lap and began kissing her wildly. He held her to him and felt that his heart might burst with the joy he was feeling. "I'll do everything in my power to make you happy. You'll never regret marrying me," he said, with his face against her neck.

"I know, baby, I know," she said, wrapping her arms around his neck.

He stopped kissing her and just held her against him, slipping his hand into her robe and caressing the soft, damp skin of her back. "You are the most wonderful person I know. We're going to have a good, long-lasting marriage. I promise you that."

"There's just one thing, Thomas, that I would like you to do for me."

"What is that?" he asked, moving away slightly to look into her face.

"Help me to remain chaste until we're married," she said, tightening the belt on the terry cloth robe.

"I don't know if I can promise that. It's been all I can do to keep my hands off of you as it is. What good will waiting do?"

"I know we have a deep physical attraction for each other and I know that the sex between us will be good, but I'd really like to wait until we're married," she said quickly.

"Why?" he asked dumbly.

"I think it's the right thing to do. I'd like for us to be married the first time we make love. I think that it will be such a powerful emotion to be made love to by my husband. I can't explain it to you, but I hope that you can do this for me without understanding," she said, pulling away from him to look at his face because he was so still.

"Are you having doubts about us, Regina?"

"No, I'm not. I'm honest when I say that everything is going to be good between us, but I think waiting is better. I will feel like such a hypocrite if I'm sleeping with you and trying to hide from our children. Or if we don't hide from our children, how can we tell them that they shouldn't do what we've done?" she said, talking faster still.

"Okay. I'll buy that. Do you want to set a wedding date then?"

She smiled brightly and said, "The sooner the better. How about Easter weekend?"

"Next year?"

"Yes. Easter has already passed this year," she said, wondering at his question.

"That's not soon enough. You heard Dr. Morgan. The pressure is on this year to bring home a trophy. I don't want to go through that trying period without being able to take you with me. I'll be working long hours and the only time I'll have to see you is in bed. If we're married you and the kids can travel with me. We won't have to worry about separate hotel rooms or anything like that. Let's get married before our first game."

"Halloween weekend?" she asked, raising one recently arched brow.

"No—are you being sarcastic again? I was thinking of something sooner."

"Like when?"

"Labor Day weekend," he said firmly.

"I can't plan a wedding that quickly," she said, panicked.

"You want a wedding?"

"Of course I do. Nothing grandiose, but I do want to celebrate. I want to be surrounded by my family and a few friends," she said, beginning to pout at the thought that he would deny her a wedding.

"Okay, baby, whatever you want," he said, pulling her close to him again. "But can't you plan something wonderful and perfect that can take place within the next four weeks?"

"I guess—yes, I can," she said decisively.

"That way, when my parents bring Justin back, they'll already be here for the wedding and your mother can have the whole weekend to visit. Since she doesn't have to go back into the classroom until after Labor Day, maybe she'll take care of the boys while we honeymoon. And your friends will have a four-day weekend off from work. Do you have any friends who work a nine-to-five?"

"Yes, I do, silly. All of my friends are not musicians. In fact, few of them are. My friends from college are teachers, artists, bankers, you name it. Their careers are just as varied as your friends' careers."

"My friends do not have varied careers at all. They're either P.E. teachers or coaches," he said, laughing.

As the bright yellow sun slowly rose above the Cascade Mountains, Thomas and Regina continued to talk. It was as if they were suddenly free to talk about all the things that they'd never discussed before. Their conversation was focused on their future together, both eager to leave the bitter past behind them. A sixth sense told Regina that Thomas was holding something back, but she figured that it couldn't be anything important enough to change her mind about marrying him.

Thomas's stomach growled loudly. "Are you hungry?" she asked.

"I'm starved. Let's order room service. I need to shave and get ready for my seminar. This is one that I really need to attend today; it's on facilities administration. Otherwise, I'd like to stay in with you."

"I won't be here. I'm supposed to have a spa day with Chantay. We're getting pore-cleansing mud packs, facials, and massages."

"You know, I can give you a massage you won't forget," Thomas said, sexily rubbing his big hand across Regina's back.

"I know you can, but if you did I don't know if I could stop with a massage. I'd better go downstairs to the pros. They give massages without any emotional attachment."

Regina fell asleep after breakfast and was startled when the phone rang. "Regina, I'm waiting for you in the lobby. We were supposed to meet at ten o'clock," Chantay said.

"I'm sorry. I'll be right down," Regina said, hanging up quickly.

When Regina walked into the lobby, a big grin spread across Chantay's face. "For someone who was sound asleep ten minutes ago, you sure do have a bright glow on your face. Girl, you don't need a facial. Give me some of what's making you glow."

Regina could barely contain her excitement. "Thomas asked me to marry him last night," she squealed.

"Congratulations," Chantay said, hugging her.

They talked excitedly as they walked across the courtyard to the spa. "Where is your diamond?" Chantay asked.

"I think my proposal was impromptu. I don't have a ring yet," Regina explained.

"Well, don't settle for just any old thing. This gives you a chance to go shopping with him. He gave Paulette a three-karat diamond. You should at least hold out for four," Chantay advised.

"I don't know if I want a diamond," Regina said. "I'd cherish anything that Thomas wants to give me."

"Girl, you've got to be practical. You already have a son and Thomas is pulling down good money. You need to think about your future."

"My future is secure. I want Thomas, not the things that he can give me," Regina said pointedly.

"Okay. Just don't say I didn't try to tell you. When you've been married as long as I have you start looking at things differently."

"I hope I never get to the point where Thomas is just spending change to me," Regina said.

Chantay opened her mouth and closed it. When they were escorted to the mudrooms another word still had not passed between them.

After the mud was removed and they'd had deep massages, they were finally alone waiting for their facials. "I hope you don't think that I'm some kind of gold digger," Chantay said. "Men don't care as deeply as we do. I can see that you're in love with Thomas and it's obvious that he's in love with you. But I bet you fifty to one that he has a hard time saying that he loves you. Those words don't flow out of a man very easily. When I talk to my husband on the phone while he's at the office, do you know what he says when I tell him that I love him? *Me too!* He says *me too.* You just have to guess that they love you by what they do and what they buy you," Chantay said with a sense of hard-earned wisdom.

"I only met you and Moon this week, but you seem to care for each other. I know that you two have more than material possessions between you," Regina said, feeling sorry for the disillusioned woman next to her.

"Marriage is no fairy tale and sometimes it's rough. They don't always have a happily-forever-afterward ending," Chantay said. "You won't always talk so positively."

"Don't you think that you can do things to ensure that you have the ending that you want?" Regina asked.

"Sometimes it gets out of control. If anyone had a perfect marriage, it was Thomas and Paulette. I don't mean to be rude bringing up his former marriage again, but they were. He cherished her beyond reason and when she died, a bit of him died, too. He was never the same again. I've seen him more alive this week than I have in five years. Even before she passed, when she was ill he was like an old man grieving. You're good for him, but don't think you're in control," Chantay warned.

The silence between them grew. Regina was sorry that she had agreed to spend the day with this gloom-and-doom woman. She'd never seen anyone suck the life out of joy so thoroughly before.

She still had a sense of hopelessness when she returned to her suite. "What's with you?" Thomas asked.

"After a spa day, you're supposed to be reenergized. You look like someone's just stolen your best milk cow."

Regina laughed. "You can't get our country sayings right to save your life, can you?"

"I try. Now what's up with the grim reaper facade?"

"I spent the day with Chantay. Why didn't you warn me about her?"

"What about her?" he said, taking Regina's hand in his and pulling her down to the sofa next to him.

"She's so materialistic. Her only advice to me as a newly engaged woman was to see how much I could get from you before our marriage ends. I hope you weren't planning to have Moon in the wedding."

"I haven't thought about who to have in the wedding. I thought you'd let me know who I could include," Thomas joked.

"I'm not that controlling. Come on, now. Give me a break," Regina said, hitting at Thomas.

"I like Moon. We were real close once, but I don't know. I let a lot of people down because they were excited for me when I got the job at St. Luke and then I walked away from it without a fight or any attempt to defend myself. You know there's a lot of pressure when you're in one of those 'first black' jobs and I was the first black person to have a coaching position at St. Luke and some folks felt that I let them down."

"Is that what he was talking about in the lobby on our first day here?"

"Yes. I left St. Luke under a cloud. The NCAA investigated our program and everything seemed to say that I had committed major rule violations in giving money to players. I was never sanctioned, but our program did receive penalties."

"Is the NCAA like the FBI or something?"

"The NCAA is the National Collegiate Athletic Association and it's a voluntary organization. Colleges and universities choose to become members, but it's a self-governing body to be sure that all institutions follow the same rules to equalize the playing field so to speak."

"And what rule were you accused of breaking?"

"Getting boosters to give spending money to our players when we went on road trips."

"Did you do that?"

"No, but I didn't have the energy to defend myself so I just left. They couldn't prove that I'd done anything wrong and I couldn't prove that I was innocent. I was too tired to fight."

"I guess you were still grieving over Paulette's death?"

"Yes. I sort of dropped off the basketball radar screen for a while. People tried to reach out to me, but I was unresponsive. I pretty much isolated myself from all my friends."

"And you thought you could hide out at this obscure little school way down South where none of your friends would deign to enter."

"No, Regina, it's not like that. I was tired. All the fight was out of me. When Dr. Morgan offered me the opportunity to be a head coach, I realized that this was the perfect position for me. I wanted to be a head coach and I knew that I couldn't be that at one of the traditional basketball powerhouses. I hadn't paid my dues yet. I'm not even thirty-five and my father doesn't head a program anywhere. I thought I'd go to Nashville to make a name for myself. And I knew that if I was in control, I could be sure that my school didn't play around with NCAA violations."

"Do you think the St. Luke head coach played around with the NCAA rules?" Regina asked, trying to understand the whole NCAA thing.

"My head coach was constantly skirting the rules and

looking for loopholes to play through. We just got too close on that one, and as usual, an unsuspecting assistant coach was set up as his scapegoat. I got the job that time. He wrote glowing letters of recommendation for me because he knew that I hadn't done anything wrong. But with me gone, the NCAA officials were satisfied that things were now in order at St. Luke. Now I've been the focus of their attention since I've been at Renaissance. They're just waiting for me to mess up."

"So, we'll just have to be careful, won't we?" Regina said, stroking his arm.

"Regina."

"Yes, baby?" she answered absently.

"You've got to stop touching me like that. You make me hot all over when you stroke my arm like that. It makes me want to turn around and—" He grabbed her and kissed her passionately. She returned his passion eagerly, wrapping her arms around his neck and fitting her body to his.

Just as suddenly, he let her go. "That's how I feel when you stroke my arm. Is there anywhere else you would like to stroke me?"

"After that display, I'm afraid to touch you."

News about their engagement spread quickly to all the conferees, and over the next two days Regina and Thomas were feted with several impromptu celebrations. Whenever they entered a gathering of conference attendees, someone would propose a toast to the engaged couple and before anyone knew how it happened they would be in the midst of a full-blown party. Often others at the resort would join in the festivities.

On the last night of the conference, Chantay and

Moon hosted a surprise reception in Regina and Thomas's honor. When Chantay expressed her sincere best wishes for their marriage, later that evening Regina had to admit to Thomas that she might have misjudged Chantay. Perhaps Chantay was only cynical because she was disillusioned.

They enjoyed the celebrations, but were relieved when they finally returned to Nashville. Feeling the pressure of having to plan a wedding in such a short time period, Regina began making lists. Number one on her list was to find a wedding coordinator.

The morning following their arrival back in Nashville, Regina was dialing the number for the beauty shop before she remembered that Rosemary would not be in the shop on a Monday.

She called Rosemary's home number and left a voice mail message. Still anxious to locate a wedding coordinator, she decided to call her cellular phone. She couldn't remember the phone number and began hunting for her business card.

"Rosemary? Hi, this is Regina," she said excitedly.

"Hello, stranger. Are you back already? Don't tell me you need to get your hair done today. You must have had a lot of fun at that resort with your *friend*," Rosemary teased, putting emphasis on the word "friend."

"I do need to get my hair done as soon as possible, but I'm calling you to get the phone number for your mother's friend who coordinates weddings."

"Who needs a wedding coordinator?" Rosemary asked, now on full alert.

"I do. My friend is now my fiancé," Regina said, barely able to keep her voice level. She wanted to shout the news she was so excited. She knew that Rosemary would share her joy without reservation.

"Oh-h-h, girl, you did it. You got your man," Rosemary said.

"You mean the man got me. He's the lucky one," Regina said with laughter in her voice.

"Yeah, you best keep trying to convince him of that," her friend said. "When is the wedding?"

"Labor Day weekend. We're looking at that Saturday. I want to sit down with a coordinator before I get too far into making plans. All we know so far is the date," Regina explained.

"I'm so happy for you. Hold on, I need to pull over to a parking lot so that I can get that number for you."

In a few minutes, Regina had arranged for her and Thomas to meet with the wedding coordinator the next evening.

"Do I have to go?" Thomas whined like a small kid when she told him about the appointment.

"Of course you have to go. It's your wedding, too," she said, failing to hide the hurt that she felt at his reluctance to get excited about the wedding.

"Baby, don't look at me like that. You know men don't get into this wedding thing as much as women," he said, reaching out to lift her chin.

"I just want you to be as excited as I am about our wedding," she said sadly.

"I am excited about marrying you, Regina. If it takes a wedding to get us married, then I'm all for a wedding."

In a flash her solemn face changed and she graced him with one of her mischievous smiles. "If you don't help me with the wedding plans, it may be a year or so before we can get married."

"I knew I was in trouble when I saw that smile. You drive a hard bargain, woman. Tell me what I need to do."

"Be there tomorrow at four-thirty. I have to meet you there because I have a meeting at three and won't have time to come back home," she instructed him.

* * *

The wedding coordinator's office was a concoction of pink and white froufrou, with lace and netting everywhere. Regina was wondering if she'd made a mistake and was considering leaving when a slender woman in a tailored suit walked briskly into the reception area to greet them. "Hello, my name is Goldie. And you must be Regina and Thomas," she said, offering her hand first to Regina and then to Thomas. Regina felt an instant affinity to the tall, dark-skinned woman. She was a little taken aback by the woman's golden blond hair that was cut stylishly. Her clothes, hairstyle, bearing, and voice conveyed a stylish sophistication, which was in contrast to the displays in the outer office.

"I hope you can help us," Regina began immediately, not wanting to waste anyone's time. "My fiancé and I are both over thirty and we don't want a fairy-tale wedding or something out of a storybook. We want to have a fairly simple, but elegant affair to celebrate our marriage. I hate pink and I don't care for those southern belle dresses."

Goldie smiled at Regina and refrained from telling the bride-to-be that she and her fiancé looked as if they were still babies to her. She did say, "I've been in this business for over thirty years. I've done any kind of wedding that you can think of. Those pictures out front are to attract a certain clientele. I target specifically those who can afford me, and the more fantasy I add, the more it costs. However, I believe I understand what you are looking for and we can do that, too. Please come into my office where we can sit down and talk."

They followed the sophisticated-looking older woman into a spacious, formally furnished office. A large mahogany desk anchored one wall and a large round mahogany Queen-Anne-style table loaded with several sample books was in the center of the room. The chairs surrounding the table were upholstered in a pink and green floral pattern that almost exactly matched the wallpaper. Regina eyed the four bookshelves surrounding the office and noted that they were loaded with books on any subject related to a wedding, from invitations to in-laws.

When they were in their seats, the receptionist served them champagne in tall, fluted crystal glasses. Quietly and efficiently, Goldie opened a white leather portfolio and began completing a questionnaire. After getting the wedding date, she asked, "Where do you want the wedding?"

"At my church," Regina answered.

"Don't you think that the church sanctuary is too large for the number of guests that we will have?" Thomas asked.

"How many guests do you plan to invite?" Regina asked.

"About twenty," Thomas answered without thinking.

"After all of your years of playing ball, working at universities, and attending school for eighteen years, all you can come up with to attend your wedding is twenty people? Are you telling me that you want to keep your wedding a secret or something?" Regina asked caustically.

"No, not at all. A wedding is very personal and I prefer to think of it as a private affair. I would invite only a select number of people to such a private event, but I haven't really made a list yet," Thomas hedged, realizing that he'd made another mistake. Regina was serious about this wedding and he realized instantly that he'd better pay attention and put some thought into the plans.

"I think you're being selfish, Thomas. I'm sure that there are many people who have played a major role in your life who'll be hurt by not being invited to your wedding. Just think of the people here in Nashville alone—you play a major role on campus—and you're telling me that people won't be hurt by not being invited?"

"How many people are you inviting?" he finally realized he should ask.

"One hundred fifty, easily," she said. "I started making my list last night."

"But we didn't get home until nearly midnight last night," Thomas said. "I'm amazed that you weren't exhausted when we finally got home last night."

"I was too excited to sleep," Regina said. "You've given me four weeks to plan this wedding and I want it done right." She pushed away from the table and folded her arms across her ample bosom. Fixing her gaze on Thomas, she waited for his response.

Goldie broke the silence that had begun to fill the room. "We can take some of the pressure off of you and help you have your ideal wedding. Mr. Simmons, I see that you work at Renaissance University," she said, scanning the application that they'd completed while they waited to see her. "They have a lovely chapel right there in the center of the campus. It will seem cozy with about two hundred fifty to three hundred guests. Do you think that can work?" she asked, looking from Regina to Thomas.

"If you had your heart set on having your wedding at Mt. Joy Baptist Church, I'll go along with you," Thomas said, taking one of Regina's hands and holding it in both of his.

She looked at him thoughtfully and realized that he was not deliberately trying to keep her from having a wonderful wedding celebration. "It will work. Let's look into the chapel."

"May I make another suggestion?" Goldie asked.

"Certainly," Regina and Thomas replied simultaneously.

"Move your date from that Saturday to the Friday night. It will give you more flexibility as you seek accommodations and services. Labor Day is the last weekend of the summer and there are already quite a few weddings that weekend. For instance, I know that there is no banquet hall, country club, or ballroom space left in town that will hold three hundred people for a reception."

"We can change the day," Regina readily agreed.

"Do we have to have the wedding at a private club or hotel room? Let's have it in our backyard," Thomas suggested, regretting opening his mouth as soon as the words were out. He did not want Regina to think that he was not willing for her to have some kind of fantasy setting for her dream wedding.

He had nothing to fear from Regina though. She replied immediately, "What a great idea. Our homes sit on at least an acre of land. We should be able to do something at home."

"I think it's a wonderful idea," Goldie said. "But before we order tents or anything, I'd like to come over and look at the property. You know your kitchen will have to be accessible to the caterer."

The next day, Goldie came over to inspect Regina's lawn and kitchen facilities. "This is perfect," she declared instantly. "The lot is nice and level and you certainly have the space for two tents."

"Why two tents?" Thomas asked.

"One will be for the banquet. We'll set up thirty to forty round tables that will seat eight guests each. Under the other we'll lay the dance floor and stage for the band. By the way, I called the university and the chapel is available that Friday night, but was already booked for the Saturday. Also, the tent can be installed on Thursday and be ready for Friday. Everything's a go, so far."

After that, the wedding plans moved along rapidly. Thomas had his guest list ready for Goldie by the end of the week and the invitations were mailed immediately. Even with a wedding coordinator taking care of the details, Regina still had a great deal to do. Goldie called or met with her daily, with new ideas and things to add or remove from her numerous lists, causing Regina to be extremely glad that she'd thought to hire a professional coordinator.

When Dr. John Morgan discovered that the wedding would be on his campus, he called Regina and asked what he could do to facilitate arrangements. She said that she could think of nothing. He called back a day later and said, "I just left a meeting where Thomas was in attendance also. He tells me that your father is not active in your life. I would be greatly honored if you would allow me to give you away. After all, the wedding will be on my campus and we are all family," he said with a smile in his voice.

"I really don't like the idea of being given away since no one owns me. I've been on my own for a long time now," Regina answered in her usual straightforward manner.

"I can understand that. I hope you don't think I'm trying to horn in on your wedding, but it is a very special day for you. I wouldn't exactly give you away. I would escort you down the aisle. You do plan to walk down the aisle, don't you?" the president asked persuasively.

"Actually," Regina said, trying to find the tact that she so seldom used, "I had planned to enter the sanctuary from one of the side doors the same way the groom does."

"No, no, no. Don't half-step with the walk down the aisle. Don't you want to show off your wedding finery? You need that walk so that everyone can see you. Aren't you wearing something special?"

"I don't know what I am going to wear. I haven't found anything suitable yet. But, I didn't know that I needed to walk down the aisle to show off my outfit."

"The bridal march is essential. It's like the old-fashioned Victorian promenades. Do you know that the word 'prom' comes from promenade? Of course couples don't promenade at their high school proms anymore, do they? But I digress. Regina, I like Thomas and I'm glad that he's putting down roots in Nashville by marrying you. I don't have a daughter, so this may be my one chance to escort a bride to her waiting groom."

Finally relenting and not wanting to argue anymore, Regina said, "Let me talk this over with Thomas. Do you mind if I call you back?"

That evening Regina told Thomas about the phone call from Dr. Morgan. "Thomas, he's your boss and I don't want to make things difficult for you, but I can't see why he wants to get involved in our personal life."

"Actually he's my boss's boss, but that's beside the point. I think he sees himself as a mentor for me. In order for me to be considered for the job here, he had to go to bat for me with the NCAA. You know about the NCAA sanctions against me?"

Regina nodded her head and Thomas continued. "He went to the show-cause hearing and took on a lot of responsibility by hiring me. I feel indebted to him, Gina. And I think that it would mean a lot to him to be able to tell everyone that he had a major role in our wedding," Thomas explained.

"He took on the added responsibility because you're the best coach in the world and he knew that he was lucky to catch you when you were down on your luck. How else would he have gotten someone of your caliber, already an assistant at a Big Ten school, to come to a Division Two school? Chantay told me that they were expecting you to take over the position at the University of Connecticut or Duke before the scandal at St. Luke's. And I think you've already been extremely kind to Dr. Morgan," Regina argued.

"You may be right about all of that, Regina. But I still feel a great deal of loyalty and gratitude to Dr. Morgan. I was down and out when I got his call. Please let him do whatever he wants in our wedding," Thomas asked.

"You are the sweetest, most understanding man on earth. That's why God sent you to me. He knew that I needed a little sweetness in my life," she said, leaning forward to plant a kiss on his lips. "If you want Dr. Morgan involved, then Dr. Morgan will be involved."

On top of planning the wedding, Regina continued to work on songs for the new Shelby Webb album, which was due to be recorded in mid-September. Luckily, when Regina had called her mother with the news of her engagement, Julia insisted that Justin stay with her until she came to Nashville for the wedding.

Regina decided on her bridesmaids and was delighted when each agreed to stand with her. Rosemary and Shelby were right there in Nashville. Her third attendant, Morgan, her college roommate, lived in Washington, D.C. Shelby's tour was ending in the Southeast and she was now able to come home during the week from time to time to check on her boys.

After getting commitments from each of the women, the next problem was getting dresses selected for them. Morgan was short and curvaceous like

Regina, while Rosemary was tall and extremely slender. Shelby was as slender as Rosemary and shorter than Regina. And on top of that, their personalities ranged from shy to flamboyant. Now how in the world do you dress such different figures and personalities?

Goldie convinced Regina that the dresses did not have to be the same style if they were the same color. Two weeks before the wedding Goldie joined Rosemary, Shelby, and Regina as they shopped for dresses. As they buzzed around the shop, Goldie's critical eye found several suitable selections for each bridesmaid. Following Goldie's instructions, each woman took several dresses home to try before making a choice. They also sent three to Morgan. Within a week each had selected the perfect style and color. By now Regina was convinced that Goldie was a true miracle worker.

The unselected dresses were returned and Regina still had not found a suitable one. She wanted something so stunning that the way she looked on their wedding day would be imprinted in Thomas's memory forever, even after he was old and his memory began to fade.

One day while she was in the beauty shop, her cell phone rang. Goldie excitedly told her that she'd found the perfect wedding dress at Davenport's. "How soon can you get here?"

"Hold on for a second. I'm under the hair dryer. Let me ask Rosemary."

"Tell her to give us thirty minutes. It will take me fifteen minutes to put some curls in your hair, but we'll be there. Tell her not to leave us."

"Us?" Regina asked when she'd ended her conversation with Goldie.

"Sure thing. I'm going, too," Rosemary assured her.

* * *

As she was about to try on the dress that Goldie held out to her, Regina paused. "Wait, should I get this dress in white or ivory?"

"Which do you prefer?" Goldie asked in return.

"I'm not sure, but before I make a decision I don't want to be out there all wrong and tacky. I don't want to give Thomas's colleagues something to talk about. Audrey Morgan says I should be aware that Thomas has a prominent position in the community. She's been giving me pointers on being a good university spouse and I don't want to embarrass Thomas. Since I have been married before, will people talk if I get married in white?"

"Not your friends and you don't care about the people who aren't your friends," Rosemary said loyally.

"I wish I had the luxury of not caring, but I do," Regina said, uncharacteristically.

"You have it bad, girlfriend," Rosemary said. "This man has changed your personality."

Goldie got back to business. "Actually, from all I've read, white is no longer a symbol of virginity or purity. It is a symbol of happiness and joy," she advised seriously.

"Well, I'm certainly happy and joyful." Regina smiled, holding the beautiful dress in front of her and looking in the mirror.

"Anyway, you're a lot purer than many of those girls getting married in white," Rosemary continued in her loyal vein.

"Which do you suggest then?" Regina asked, turning from Goldie to Rosemary.

"They only have white in your size in stock. If you want the ivory you can't get married next week," Goldie warned. "Besides, since you're having a candlelight ceremony, I think the white will be beautiful in that dim lighting. White will be more dreamy, almost surreal in the shimmering candlelight."

"And I think your dark skin contrasts beautifully with the white. Besides that, white looks better with the bridesmaids' dresses," Rosemary decided.

Regina slipped on the dress and modeled it for the two women. They agreed that it was a perfect fit.

"It is sophisticated, yet demure. Perfect for a *mature* woman's church wedding," Goldie assured her client.

The slim, beaded lace dress was sleeveless with a high, pearl-encrusted collar that fit snugly around Regina's slim neck. The chiffon train was detachable.

"You are absolutely darling," Rosemary said, wiping a tear from her eye.

"This style is perfect for you. It makes you appear taller than you would in a full dress," Goldie noted, stepping back and surveying the bride-to-be. "It's almost a perfect fit. You should probably have it taken in an inch or so on each side at the waist," she added, pinching an inch of fabric between her fingers.

"You look so regal," Rosemary said, giving Regina a hug.

"Of course, you know that if you choose that dress, you won't be able to kneel at the altar," Goldie warned, noting the snug fit around the knees before the dress flowed to form a puddle at her feet.

While they were at Davenport's, they also found the perfect pearl-and-babies'-breath headpiece. Rosemary was so inspired by the headpiece that she immediately whipped out a comb and styled her friend's freshly coifed hair around the glamorous confection. The result was sheer perfection.

By that time Goldie had returned with long gloves and white satin bead-and-pearl-encrusted shoes. With those purchases, Regina was fully outfitted a full week before the wedding.

Chapter 10

Thomas considered himself fortunate that three out of the four weeks of their engagement he had conferences and meetings out of town. At the meeting of the Cumberland River Conference, the region in which Renaissance University competed in athletics, the schedule for the upcoming basketball season was finalized. Thomas, Dr. Morgan, and the athletics director were jubilant. The conference committee had accepted Thomas's ambitious schedule.

The university had been given permission to play several much larger schools, which would garner them a great deal of credibility as an upstart team. Thomas had convinced the president and athletic director that this ambitious bid was a win-win situation. The games would be televised, resulting in more revenue and exposure that went with such an endeavor. If the team won, that would be great, but if they lost that would be all right too. No one would expect a Division II school to beat a Division I school. Yet, many fans would cheer for the underdog.

Coming straight from the airport to Regina's house after the conference, Thomas could barely wait to tell her his good news. "We got the schedule that I proposed," he said as soon as Regina opened the front door. He lifted her in his arms and kissed her exuberantly.

When her mouth was free again, she said, "Congratulations, baby. But did you have any doubt? That was a sound schedule, I knew it would be adopted." She threw her arms around his neck and kissed him again.

He spun her around the foyer and into the family room before setting her back on her feet. "Get dressed in your finest, Gina. We're going to Mario's or Valentino's to celebrate."

Regina looked distressed. "I can't go, baby, not tonight. I've got to get with Jimmy Bob and Kent to pitch some songs that I've been working on. I've missed so many sessions over the past few weeks that I told them I'd come with something tonight," she said, watching Thomas's face carefully.

He was clearly disappointed, but he said, "That's okay. I know you have a lot going on. We can't just hang out on impulse like we used to." He thrust his hands in the pocket of his jeans and headed for the door like a bereft little boy. "I'll go home and let you do what you need to do."

"Wait, Thomas, don't leave like this. I've missed you so much. I want to spend some time with you," she said, touching his arm lightly to slow his retreat.

"You were obviously about to leave," he said, looking at her purse on the table in the foyer.

"What time do you have to be on campus tomorrow?" she asked.

"No particular time," he answered, shrugging a shoulder.

"Could I come to your place for a midnight snack when we finish tonight? I'll pick up Chinese," she teased to sweeten the offer.

"Sure," he said. The smile had returned to his face.

During the songwriting session that evening, Regina was focused and productive, determined to be with Thomas before the night was over.

"You've got a groove going tonight, girl. You're really with us," Jimmy Bob teased.

"That's because I'm on a meter and I've got to get out of here. I don't want to spend the night with you guys," she said, resting her violin on her legs.

"What's up?" Kent asked.

"Thomas has been out of town all week and I had to rush out just as he was coming in. I didn't expect him until the morning, but I felt bad leaving him since we haven't spent much time together lately. Before he left for his trip I barely had time to say good-bye because I was wrapped up with the wedding coordinator and working on this music that you guys love so much. Have I contributed enough yet?"

"I'd rather have you spend the night with us, but I've never been one to stand in the path of true love," Jimmy Bob said.

"You've contributed more than enough. Since you supplied the lyrics, we'll do the rest," Kent promised. "I think with these new songs, we have enough for Shelby's new album. Let's call it a night."

Regina drove swiftly through the Music Row Roundabout and headed for home, making one stop at an all-night Chinese restaurant on West End Boulevard. She hoped that Thomas would not be asleep. She had seen so little of him over the past few weeks and she had a lot that she wanted to talk to him about. She wanted to tell him about all of his friends from high school, college, professional sports teams, and St. Luke University as well as Renaissance University, who had responded to their wedding invitation.

As had become her custom, she let herself into his garage using the automatic door opener that he'd furnished her with. The plan was for both families to move to Thomas's house until they had time to build a new house at the end of the basketball season next spring. They would put her house on the market immediately and his on the market after they began to build the new house.

Coming into the kitchen from the garage, Regina heard only the distant sound of the television in the "men's room." She set the food on the counter and followed the sound. Thomas was stretched out in his recliner, remote in one hand with a thumb on the "channel up" button as if he had fallen asleep in the midst of changing channels. He looked so good in his lounge pants and T-shirt that she couldn't resist leaning over to place a featherlight kiss on his lips. As if a reflex, his left arm rose and caught her around the waist. She let out a startled yelp, as he pulled her into his lap.

"Don't you know by now that you can't sneak up on me?" he asked.

"I thought you were asleep. I didn't want to disturb you."

"You wanted to be able to tell me that you came back, but I was asleep. You were going to leave without waking me, weren't you?"

"Wrong. I didn't want to miss you. I want to be with you. And I was wondering what I would do with all that Chinese food out there in the kitchen," she said, nuzzling his neck and taking in the intoxicating scent of his cologne.

"Woman, you entice me. You need to stop teasing me this way," he said, gently stroking her back and hips with one hand and holding her close with the other.

"Are you hungry?" she asked.

"It's not the food that's enticing me. I'm talking about your body," he said, huskily. His hand lingered at the side of her soft breast and he began massaging it, before he reached around to find the already hard nipple. "How many days is it?"

"Eight," she said, practically breathless from the thrills his hands were creating on her body. "Are you ready to eat now?"

"No, I want to enjoy being with my fiancée. You don't have to run from me; I know when to stop," he said, preventing her from getting up. "I missed you so much this trip. Next year, I want you to plan to travel with me as much as possible. Audrey was there with John."

"I will," she promised. "Speaking of Audrey, did she tell you that she is having a tea for us Sunday?" Regina asked, sitting up straight and away from Thomas so that she could look at him.

"Yeah, I think she did," he said. "I told her that she should be having a keg party for a beer guzzler like you."

"You'd better not ruin my reputation with my new best friend," Regina said, socking Thomas's hard biceps.

"I'm sorry I mentioned Audrey and John. I don't want to talk about the wedding tonight," Thomas said, rubbing his arm where she'd punched him. When she tried to move away he tightened his arms around her waist to hold her still.

He felt her body tense when he said that he didn't want to talk about the wedding and tried to soothe her by rubbing his hands over her tense muscles. "It feels like you're losing weight," he said, cupping her buttock in his big hand. "You used to be a perfect handful, now you're barely a pinch," he said.

"Good. Then my diet is working. Goldie picked out this slim, little wedding dress, but I can't have a bulge anywhere."

"Sweetheart, don't you know how much I like your bulges?" he asked, kissing her passionately.

She quickly forgot about wedding dresses, bulges, and teas. She gave in as his touches, kisses, and whispered words sent heat streaming through her veins as if it were a part of her blood. The thrills and pleasure his touch ignited filled her with a fire that made it almost impossible for her to remember to take her next breath.

"Gina, baby."

"Yes, Thomas?"

"It's time to stop."

"What?"

"You've got to get up, sweetheart."

"Am I too heavy? I thought you said that I'm light as a feather."

"That's not the problem. Your sitting on me feels entirely too good. I feel like you're giving me a lap dance."

"What are you talking about? What do you know about a lap dance anyway?" she asked, pulling away from his neck to listen to him carefully.

"I won't answer that. But I told you that I know when to stop. This is when."

"When?"

"You've got to get up, sweetheart, if you don't want me to throw you to the floor and ravish you. Your lap dance is entirely too arousing."

She understood him then and hopped from his lap immediately. "I'm sorry. I don't want to make things hard for you. I mean, I don't want it to be hard for you to keep your promise," she said, becoming embarrassed at her blunder.

"You've made only one thing hard on me," he said with a big dimple appearing in his cheek.

Ignoring his implication, she said, "Come on, let's

go have our midnight snack." She reached out a hand
to help him from the chair.

"Go ahead and start warming the food. I need a moment to gather my composure."

Against her will, her eyes fell to the lump in his lap
where she'd been sitting and she felt a warm flush
cover her face. Feeling rather pleased with his obvious
desire for her, she felt bad that she was subjecting him
to such misery. She promised that after their wedding,
she would never deny him anything again.

Eight days later Regina stood at the door to the
chapel next to Dr. Morgan with one sweat-drenched
hand resting lightly in the fold of his tuxedo-covered
arm. After her eyes adjusted to the soft glow of the candlelight in the sanctuary she could see Thomas
standing at the altar with Justin and Tres on either
side.

Standing slightly behind Thomas were his attendants and the bridal party stood opposite them. Pastor
Bender, with a large white Holy Bible in his hands,
stood front and center, at the altar, completing the
tableau.

The candles flickered in the seven-branch cande-
labra lining the stone walls as the air conditioners
increased power to cool the humid, early September
air. As Regina mentally adjusted to the crowd of people in the pews, the harpist began strumming
Mendelssohn's "Wedding March." She was suddenly
gripped with an attack of stage fright.

As Dr. Morgan was about to step forward, Regina remained glued to the spot where she stood. He couldn't
get her to budge. Feeling her, Dr. Morgan touched her
hand that was resting in the crook of his arm and
whispered, "Take a deep breath. This is your day. You
may lean on me, child. Now just relax and walk." His

words steadied her and as the harpist played their cue
the second time, they began the march.

A sense of calm swept over her, enabling her to
enjoy her stroll down the aisle and make eye contact
with many of their guests and nod at others. She
smiled brightly for Thomas and the three hundred
guests who cared enough to use the last holiday weekend of the summer to witness their marriage.

At the rehearsal dinner the night before, they'd entertained their wedding party and all out-of-town
guests. They had not counted on the record label brass
and the university's administration wanting to be included in the festivities, which brought the party total
close to two hundred.

Thomas had been emotionally overwhelmed and totally surprised by the enthusiastic response to his
wedding invitation. Regina had never gotten the
chance to tell him about all the people who'd responded positively to the invitation because he never
wanted to talk about the wedding. Goldie's office had
carefully typed up the message from the many people
who had called with regrets, but sent Thomas their
best wishes.

After his wife's death, Thomas had become emotionally isolated from their many friends and they had
given up on trying to reach out to him. He had not
seen many of his guests since his wife's funeral. He realized that he'd made a mistake by deliberately cutting
himself off from those who could have comforted him
through his grief.

The rehearsal dinner had turned into an all-night
party with someone requesting that the disc jockey go
way back and play old tunes from their high school
and college days. He had even played a few requests
from their parents. Everyone danced together, old
friends blending quite well with new ones. Of course,

it all ended with everyone moving into the Electric Slide. Two hundred bodies moving to one rhythm was like a giant wave rising out of the ocean.

Pastor Bender's melodious voice brought Regina back to the ceremony. She smiled at her groom, who appeared to be anxious for the ceremony to proceed. Dressed in his black tux and stark-white shirt, he looked absolutely delicious. In just a few moments they would be joined together for life. He would be hers to love and cherish from this day forward.

"Who presents this woman to this man?" Pastor Bender began the ceremony.

"I have that pleasure," Dr. Morgan responded in his clear sonorous voice before taking a seat in the first row next to his wife, who sat beside Julia. While he was moving to his seat, Alison McKenzie sang a joyful song of praise that Jimmy Bob and Kent had composed for the wedding.

When that song ended, the Mt. Joy choir began singing very softly, almost in a whisper, "Sweet, Sweet Spirit," as Regina and Thomas held the boys' hands and met their parents at a large silver urn placed on a pedestal to the left of the altar.

Using four silver chalices, each parent called the names of departed ancestors and poured libations in memory of those who had gone before them. Regina emptied the contents of her cup into the same urn and watched it mingle with the wine from Thomas's cup, which signified the blending of their two bloodlines. Finally, each of the boys was lifted so that they, in turn, could pour the wine from their cups, signifying the mingling of the future with the past. In the end wine representing both families, as well as their past, present, and future, mingled in the urn, which would be carefully stored until it could be poured on the ground at Regina and Thomas's new home in the spring.

When Thomas and Regina were again at the altar, the minister spoke. "Real love is not something that you fall into. It is something that you commit yourself to and sacrifice for," Pastor Bender intoned. "I have watched these young people in their courtship and I know that they have entered this most holy covenant thoughtfully and reverently."

He continued, "Let marriage always be thought of as precious. Let it be treasured like silver or gold or the rare jewels that you'll exchange today. Let it be revered and respected like the noblest, most precious person you know. Let marriage be held in honor among all," Pastor Bender went on in his deep, eloquent voice.

The couple would now exchange vows, the minister said. Thomas spoke first. "Regina Joyce Lovejoy, my friend, comforter, counselor, and joy, I promise to protect, honor, and care for you as long as there is breath in my body," he said in a distinct voice that had become hoarse with emotion. He took both of her hands in his and looked directly into her beautiful, almond-shaped eyes.

"Thomas Milton Simmons," Regina began in a trembling voice that became stronger as she spoke, "my love, my heart, my peace, my joy, I promise to you my unconditional love and devotion for the rest of my life."

To Regina's surprise, Tres moved forward then and joined hands with her and Thomas. He lifted his little face toward her and said, "Ms. Regina, I promise to honor you as my mother that my days may be long upon the land which the Lord thy God giveth me."

Before Regina could contain the tears threatening to overflow her eyes, Justin came forward, completing their circle, and said the same words to Thomas.

After that, she became so emotional that she barely paid attention to the prayers and songs that followed until it was time to exchange wedding rings.

Things had happened so quickly following Thomas's proposal at Sunriver that she had not given another thought to a ring. She'd commissioned a handcrafted gold ring for Thomas from a local artisan immediately after their return to Nashville, but she had no idea if he'd gotten her a ring.

Uncontrollable tears flowed from her eyes when he placed a ring on her finger that was made by the same artisan. It was a bold gold ring set with an emerald stone, her birthstone. She was overcome with emotion by his thoughtfulness and the knowledge that he knew her well enough to know what she'd like to wear every day for the rest of her life.

The smile through tears that she gave him reassured him and brought sunshine to his heart. He'd gone back to the artisan the day after they'd selected his band and commissioned this piece of art for his Gina. He was glad to know that she understood what had gone into selecting the ring for her.

While the couple held hands and continued smiling at one another, the minister finished the ceremony. Opening his large Bible, he said, "Hebrews chapter thirteen, verse four, tells us that 'Marriage is honorable among all, and the marriage bed is undefiled.'" He looked around to let the message sink in before he continued, "I tell you that a marriage is spiritual, physical, and psychological. We pray that God bless you with all these benefits of marriage." With those words, all heads bowed in prayer.

During the recessional, Regina was so overcome with emotion that she could not stop the tears from flowing. She was thankful for the man that God had sent her way, she was thankful for her sons and she was thankful for the guests who had come to share this most joyous, solemn, and holy occasion with them.

The solemnity of the wedding ceremony gave way to a righteous good time at the reception. By the time the wedding party arrived, the festive reception was in full swing. Thomas had insisted, "I don't want our guests to sit around with their bellies growling while they wait for us to finish taking pictures." Goldie had agreed and arranged for the caterers to begin serving guests as soon as they arrived.

When the wedding party was finally released from taking the arduous formal photos at the chapel, they too rushed to the reception and were served immediately. Regina and Thomas were so caught up in the antics on the dance floor that they barely ate a bite.

When they arrived the old school generation challenged the hip-hop crowd in a *Soul Train* line competition. Thomas was surprised to see his usually reserved father clowning down the *Soul Train* line. Tres and Justin were in the midst of things, taking their turns going down the line.

After allowing the free-for-all dancing until the bride and groom arrived with their attendants, Goldie was anxious to get the ceremonial aspects of the reception under way. Although Regina and Thomas did not want to stop the fun, the guests cheered them on when Goldie announced that they were about to dance together for the first time as husband and wife.

For their first dance, they chose a rumba. Goldie had suggested a popular slow dance tune, but Regina had countered, "I will not dance that close to Thomas. It will look ridiculous because instead of being cheek to cheek, I'll be under his armpit."

"You won't be at my armpit. Think of it as reaching my heart, shorty," Thomas had teased her."

Goldie had a compromise as usual. "Children, children, why not rumba?" Three days before the wedding, they had perfected the rumba in Goldie's office and now they impressed their guests with their elegance.

After the dance, they went through the traditional ceremony of cutting the cake. Both refused the photographer's instructions to smear cake on their beloved's face. Nor would they feed each other. The photographer had to settle for a picture of Thomas's hand on Regina's as they cut the first slice of cake.

The crowd roared with laughter when it was time for Thomas to toss Regina's garter to the bachelors. Instead of allowing him to pull her dress up and search for the garter on her leg, Regina turned her back to the crowd, and when she turned around the garter was in her hand. To cheers and laughter, she tossed it to a surprised and disappointed Thomas, who in turn tossed it to the waiting hoard of eligible bachelors.

With the final ceremony of tossing the garter, the party resumed. Regina was swept into the arms of her new father-in-law, who complimented her on the weekend activities and her well-mannered son.

"Now that you've seen where we live, won't you come more often?" Regina asked her father-in-law.

"Now that Thomas is married, I'll definitely come more often. I guess I sort of stayed away because my son was down and out for so long that I felt helpless not knowing what to do for him. I sort of thought that if he didn't have his mother and me to lean on, he'd have to—you know—move on with his life. He leaned on us so much in the beginning that we had to help him. He was right pitiful, all alone with a baby not even a year old yet. But I told my wife, I said, you're making it too easy on him. He's got to get on with living. He's got to live for that child. Well, anyway, I'm real glad that he found you. I haven't seen him smile like this in years."

Regina refrained from telling the elder Mr. Simmons that perhaps his son had needed him more, not less, as he dealt with his grief. But since this weekend was her first time meeting the man, she bit her tongue and held her silence.

Before she caught her breath from dancing with Mr. Simmons, Dr. Morgan claimed her as his partner. He put her through some fancy swirls before he pulled her into a two-step where she was able to carry on a conversation with him.

"Dr. Morgan, thank you so much for escorting me down the aisle tonight. I'm awfully glad that I had you to lean on when I got struck with a bad case of stage fright. We really appreciate your support and everything that you and Audrey did to make our wedding special," she said.

"Anytime," he replied, uncharacteristically laconic.

"No, this is my only time." She laughed. "But you were right, it was better walking down the aisle and I did need you tonight."

His face beamed with pride. "Sometimes our women don't know when they need help. You think you can do it all, but it's all right to lean on a man sometimes. That's my only bit of advice that I'll give you as a newlywed."

"Thank you. I'll remember that," she said, smiling, with a growing admiration for the energetic administrator.

After a few more dances, she found herself with Thomas again. "Are you about ready to get out of here?" he asked.

"I was ready an hour ago. When Mom put the boys to bed, I wanted to go with them," Regina answered.

"Let's go tell our mothers good-bye. They're sitting over there."

Thomas led her to a table where their mothers were sitting with Rosemary and Goldie. As they neared the group they could hear a lighthearted argument under way.

"I'm the one who told her that if she didn't make a play for him, she'd lose him. You don't know, a young handsome, eligible bachelor like that in town and the sisters were after that man from day one," Rosemary told the group.

"Well, if I had never made that march across the street, neither one of them would ever have met," Nadine argued.

"You only arranged for them to meet. They still were trying to figure out what to do next when I came to town. I'm the one who told him he should—oh, look, here they are now," Julia said, stopping in midsentence when she spotted them.

"You all wouldn't be talking about us, would you?" Thomas asked.

"Don't be silly, boy, who else would we be discussing at your wedding?" his mother replied, swatting at him.

"If you two are finally deciding to leave, I would suggest that it's about time," the usually professional Goldie said, letting just a bit of her professionalism slip.

"We are leaving," Regina said, suppressing a yawn. She leaned over and kissed her mother on the cheek. "Thanks for everything, Mom."

"Come here and give me some sugar," Nadine said, holding out her arms for Regina.

"Thank you, too, for all your help," she told Nadine.

"What about me?" Rosemary asked, holding out her arms.

"Don't worry about kissing me," Goldie said. "Wait

until you see my bill. Giving a person four weeks to plan a wedding of this magnitude. You should be ashamed of yourselves."

"You're not finished yet," Regina reminded Goldie. "What time will you be here for opening gifts tomorrow?"

"What time did you decide?" Goldie asked, turning the question to Julia, who had turned out to be an expert at planning events.

"We won't be able to get your attendants out of bed before eleven o'clock, but since they're either staying here or right across the street, we could say twelvish? That way we can have brunch first. What time can you get here, Rosemary?"

"I'll be here in time for brunch, unless this wedding has made Harold feel real romantic. Then I may have to sleep in a little later. If you don't see me by the time you start serving, don't hold brunch for me," Rosemary answered.

"Would you like to have brunch with us, Goldie?" Julia asked.

"No, thanks. I'll be here at twelve," Goldie replied.

With the time settled, the newlyweds headed for their honeymoon suite at the finest hotel in Nashville. When they entered the capacious room, Regina kicked off her high-heeled shoes that had begun to make her feet ache. Goldie had tried to talk her out of wearing heels so high, but Regina had insisted that she didn't feel dressed unless her heels were at least four inches high. She had claimed that flats hurt her feet worse than heels. Well, now she was in pain.

In bare feet, she rushed to the bathroom to begin preparing for the intimate part of their celebration. She wanted to take a quick shower before she dressed in the negligee that Shelby had given her. Finding that she couldn't get out of the tight-fitting dress alone, she pulled off her panty hose and rushed back out to the bedroom to get Thomas's help with the zipper. Backing up to the chair where Thomas was sitting, she asked, "Will you unzip my dress, please?"

"Of course I will. I'll be more than happy to help you out of this dress, but before I do, let me look at you again." He stood and walked around her, taking in her stunning appearance. She shivered under his intense scrutiny. "You are extremely beautiful tonight. I believe that you are the most beautiful woman on earth," he said, lifting her hand and gently kissing her fingertips.

After releasing her hand, he stood behind her and slowly unzipped her dress, kissing her back inch by inch as it was exposed by the release of the zipper. When the zipper was low enough, he kissed the part of her buttocks left exposed by her thong underwear. Then he moved in front of her to pull the dress from her shoulders. "Do you want to pull the dress over your head or step out of it?"

"I want—I want—" She couldn't quite remember what she wanted. His gentle kisses and probing eyes had left her addled.

When she couldn't answer, he let the dress fall to her feet. She stepped out over the puddle and stood helpless before him. He sucked in his breath, finding it nearly impossible to breathe, as she stood before him in a strapless bra and lacy thong panties.

"All evening I wondered what you could possibly have on under that tight dress. This is better than I imagined," he said, huskily.

"I wore the thongs so my panty line wouldn't show," she said apologetically.

"You don't have to explain to me. I think this is what you should wear under all your clothes," he said softly, unable to take his eyes off of her. She looked at him and looked away, unable to stand the intensity of his eyes.

He stood back and walked around her again. "You're even more beautiful without the dress," he said, looking at her as if he were appraising a piece of art. "I'm not disappointed yet."

"You're embarrassing me, Thomas," Regina whispered.

"You're too beautiful to be embarrassed. Looking at you is like looking at a work of art. Please don't cover up," he said and gently took her hands in his so that she wouldn't put them across her bosom again.

"I love looking at you and I get excited knowing that we have the rest of our lives to get to know each other better. It makes me want to take my time and appreciate you even more," he said, taking her into his arms. Leading her to the chair where he'd been sitting, he said, "I'm sorry if I embarrassed you. Please sit down."

When she was seated, he knelt before her and buried his face in her bosom. "Your breasts are so soft and pretty, I've wanted to do this since we first met. I was jealous every time I saw one of the boys resting his head on your bosom." He turned and buried his face in her cleavage, before unsnapping her bra and tossing it aside.

"Perfect. They're more beautiful than I'd imagined."

"You've been imagining my breasts?" she asked in wonder. She was relieved to know that her feelings for him were reciprocated. She'd been lusting after his body, but often wondered if he would find her attractive.

"You'd better know I have." His touch sent shivers through her body. She rubbed her hands over his back and urged him to continue.

She felt light-headed and intensely aroused. Her voice was barely a whisper. "Thomas."

"Yes, baby?"

"I was going to take a hot bubble bath and put on my honeymoon negligee for you," she managed to say. But what he was doing to her breasts was so delightful she could barely remember what her plan had been.

"Could you do that for me later?" he asked. "We'll be married a long time. This is our first time, but it certainly isn't our last."

"But I'm even hotter and sweatier from the humidity and dancing," she complained.

"In a few minutes, you'll be hotter and much more sweaty," he said in between nibbles on her breasts. "You can put on your negligee in the morning while we have breakfast."

"In the morning then," she answered before relaxing her head on the back of the chair and giving in completely to the pleasure he was sending through her body.

"Regina."

"Hmm?"

"Want to go to bed?"

"I'm too stimulated; I'm not tired anymore."

"Neither am I. Let's go to bed."

On Saturday Regina and Thomas went home to open wedding gifts and to again thank their families and out-of-town guests for celebrating their wedding with them. They laughed, talked, and caught up on the goings-on in everyone's life.

On Sunday, although many of their guests were still in town, they decided to enjoy their last day of free sitters and spend the day alone. It was the only honeymoon that they would get for a while so they stayed in all day to enjoy being together.

Regina's mother, who'd been staying with the boys, had to return home on Monday to prepare to go back to her job as an elementary school teacher. When Julia was finally out of the house, Regina closed the front door and leaned on it. "Whew, we're finally alone again."

"Don't you like having Gran Julia visit?" Tres asked when he overheard Regina.

"I do, baby, but we've had so much company lately that it's nice to have just the four of us again. We haven't been alone together for nearly two months."

"Is that a long time?" Justin asked.

"Sometimes it feels like it. I sure did miss my boys," she said, wrapping an arm around each boy's shoulder.

"But you just saw me Saturday," Tres reminded her.

"I know but you were gone a long time this summer," Regina answered.

"Do you guys want to help me move some furniture around? I need a music room, so I think I'll move furniture around in the living room to make space for my instruments," she explained to the boys.

Chapter 11

Settling into their new home with Thomas and Tres was relatively simple for Regina and Justin. They had shared the same routine for such a long time that it was just a matter of blending their household furnishings.

Now that was a problem. Stuffing all the furniture from two households into one house was almost impossible. Thomas moved all of his clothes to the closet in the guest room so that Regina could have both closets in the master bedroom. He was floored when he saw how many pairs of shoes and hats filled Regina's closets, even after she made sacrificial donations to the Goodwill.

Regina put most of her household items in storage until she could see what they'd need in their new house when it was built next spring. Still trying to make a space at home suitable for her work, she removed the overstuffed furniture from Thomas's living room and replaced it with a love seat and club chair from the music room in her house. With a few more adjustments, she had the perfect workspace. It was far enough away from the "men's room" that she was not bothered by the noise of the boys while they played.

With less than two months before their first game, Thomas had started two-a-day practices with his team.

They practiced before classes at seven o'clock in the morning and again at four o'clock in the afternoon. In between the practices, he was rewriting the team's playbook with his three assistant coaches and working on the media guide with the sports information director; his time was almost totally consumed by work.

When school first started in September, Thomas had taken the boys there in the morning. But, once his morning practices began, Regina stepped in and started taking them and picking them up. Since the boys were now in the first grade, Regina realized that some adjustments had to be made in her personal work habits. She discontinued her all-night writing sessions and tried to get more done while the kids were at school, which left less time for her to manage the business end of her craft. From time to time, Jimmy Bob and Kent made the trek out to her house to work, but her facilities were no longer as accommodating as they had been previously.

The fun part was that most days, Thomas did come home after the morning practice to shower and spend some time with her. She looked forward to that time alone with Thomas and rushed home after she dropped the boys off at school.

One morning she walked into their bedroom, just as he was coming out of the shower. She paused and looked at his hard chest glistening with water. She felt warm all over and couldn't remove her eyes. She sat on the bed and watched him move around the bathroom as he towel-dried himself and applied his toiletries.

He smiled when he caught her watching him. "Hey, little girl, do you like what you see?" he called from the bathroom.

"Don't be so vain. I was just waiting for you to come out," she said, flushing with embarrassment. Thankfully, she was so dark that her flush would be unnoticeable. But her husband knew her too well.

"Gina, don't go getting all embarrassed on me again. You talk a good game, but sometimes you act like a shy little girl. Come here," he said, pulling her off the bed and into his arms. "You owe me a lap dance, or don't you remember?"

"I don't know anything about a lap dance," she said, smiling.

"Put on that CD you were listening to last night and I'll help you learn," he said with promise in his voice.

She walked to the CD player and pressed the "play" button. When she turned around, Thomas was sitting in the big chair and his towel was on the floor beside him.

"Let me watch you take off your clothes," he said in a soft, tender whisper.

She slowly unbuttoned her shirt, one button at a time. Before she was halfway finished, he'd gotten impatient and stood to help her. "I thought you liked me to take it slow," she said in his ear as he was nibbling her neck and unfastening her bra.

"I thought I did, too. But sometimes you drive me crazy. You know I can't get enough of you and you always want to make me wait. Come on, baby, give me what I've got coming to me."

He helped her out of her jeans and panties and pulled her to his lap facing him. "You are so perfect, Gina. You're absolutely beautiful."

When he went back to work, he was totally satisfied and Regina felt real pleased with herself. She stayed in bed and took a nap before she started working again. She decided that she'd better relax while she could, because the next week would be pretty intense. She, Kent, and Jimmy Bob needed to polish and have ready for recording the songs that they'd completed for *Sweet Romance*.

When she got to the studio, Jimmy Bob said, "Hey, girl, married life is totally agreeing with you. You're prettier than ever. I'm just sorry that it wasn't me who put that glow there."

"Thanks, Jimmy Bob, I think. What've you got?"

"My new contract. I was about to turn it in, but I see I need to get it notarized. Did you bring yours?"

"I haven't really had a chance to look at it. Isn't everything about the same as it was last year?"

"Not quite. We have a big four-cents-per-song increase. Didn't you notice that? And a premium bonus if an album with even one of our songs goes double platinum."

"You're joking, aren't you, Jimmy Bob?"

"No, girl, I'm dead serious. You need to read that contract with a magnifying glass," he answered, without the usual smiling smirk on his face.

Regina finished the session with her cowriters but she had a strange feeling that something wasn't right. She and Jimmy Bob did not discuss the contract anymore after Kent arrived. Both instinctively knew that Kent would not discuss something that personal.

When Thomas came in that evening, Regina was sitting at the desk in her newly appointed music room. "What's wrong, baby? Why the glum look?" he asked.

"It's just work. Don't you want dinner? I picked up your favorites from Gourmet to Go."

"Regina, don't stall. You know that I know good and well when something is wrong with you. So save us some time and spit it out."

"It's my contract. You know I told you that I got it last week?"

"And I told you to take it to an attorney."

"Yeah, you told me not to sign my life away without

legal counsel and I told you that it was okay because I trust my record company. After all, Honeysuckle Records has been good to me. Look at how all the big brass showed up for our wedding—they treat me like family," she spat out angrily.

"What's this about, Gina, baby? You sound like you're about to cry," he said, sitting on the arm of the love seat and leaning toward her.

"You can't trust anybody. They're treating me like I'm ignorant and I was about to let them get away with it. Jimmy Bob's new contract calls for him to get eight cents per song instead of four cents per song. They left me at the old, beginner rate and I've been under contract with Honeysuckle longer than either Jimmy Bob or Kent."

"Don't be upset with yourself, Regina. We've had a lot going on around here. Have you signed the contract?"

"No, luckily I never got around to it. I was so busy with the fund-raiser at the boys' school last week and working with Audrey on the Blue and Gold Gala that I kept putting it back into my desk until I had time to read it. Jimmy Bob didn't have an attorney either. He took his to a notary, but he still got more than I ever could."

"You haven't lost anything. Look on that contract as a first offer. You can always counter. Get an attorney and negotiate what you want. Don't stop with what Jimmy Bob got. Since you have to pay an attorney, factor that in," Thomas advised.

Regina jumped up with a big smile on her face and hugged him. "And I thought that you were just a pretty face. Thank you, baby. Can you suggest someone for me to call?"

"Of course I can, we're full service here. There's a guy—a big-shot attorney in town—who used to play ball at Renaissance. When I get to the office in the morning, I'll call you back with a number. Since we can't solve any more problems about your contract, can we eat? What's for dinner, wife?"

"Liver, onions, mashed potatoes, peas, green beans, corn on the cob, and rolls," she sang as they walked into the kitchen.

"Sweetheart, you really know how to keep me happy," he said, watching her hips sway as she walked in front of him.

"You should see what we're having for dessert." She smiled at him wickedly.

He caught her around the waist and pulled her back against his chest. "Where are the boys?"

"They're up in their room reading, waiting for you to say good night," she answered, relaxing against his firm muscles.

"Good. I could have a quickie before dinner."

"Yes, you could. But you've had enough already. Weren't you satisfied this morning?"

"Yes, but that was this morning. I've been thinking about you all day. You smell so good," he said, nibbling her neck.

"You love that liver and onion smell, don't you?"

"When you had me on that sex fast before the wedding, you promised me that you'd never deny me again," he moaned in her ear.

"But this good stuff is for the needy, not the greedy." She laughed as he turned her toward him for a kiss. "I love you so much, Mr. Simmons."

"I adore you, Mrs. Simmons."

Still no *I love you* back, she thought. He had not even said *I love you* in their marriage vows. Not even in his proposal had he once said that he loved her. Perhaps she'd assumed too much by assuming that he loved her.

Well, that's okay, she reminded herself once again. She loved him so much that she had enough love in her heart for the two of him. He didn't have to say, "I love you." All he needed to do was keep treating her the way he did. She was totally and completely head over heels in love with her husband. There was nothing in the world that she wouldn't do for him. She'd live with him whether he loved her or not.

As they ate dinner, he filled her in on the latest happenings of the Renaissance Ravens. "Our players are in real good shape. You can tell the ones who spent the summer lifting weights and getting into condition. They're light-years ahead of the others."

"How's that kid from New York doing? Is he still homesick?"

"Howard—his name is Conway Howard. I think he might be a little homesick, but he's a good kid. He's serious about getting into shape and he hasn't missed one class or practice. I was right about him. He has what it takes. I wouldn't be surprised if we make it to the NCAA tournaments this year. I don't expect to win, but I sure would like an invitation. Just to play in the Sweet Sixteen would be enough for me."

After dinner, Regina cleared away the remains while Thomas went upstairs to say good night to the boys. Rather than having Justin move into the guest room, the boys had decided that it would be more fun to share a room until the new house was built. To them it was like a permanent sleep-over.

"Hey, what are you guys up to?" Thomas asked as he entered the boys' bedroom.

"We heard you come in, Daddy but we thought we'd give you and Ms. Gi—I mean Mommy—some time alone," Tres offered.

"We know you want to go kissy-kissy-poo, like you did at the wedding," Justin said, giggling.

"Are you going to get us a baby?" Tres asked.

"No, Tres, it's going to be just you and Justin. You guys are enough for us."

"Don't you want a baby?" Justin asked.

"A baby would be nice, but we're happy with the family we have. Aren't you?"

"I guess so," the boys answered.

"It's time to turn out the lights. It's almost nine o'clock," Thomas said, pulling the cover over first Tres and then Justin. "I love you both."

"Wait, Mommy is coming up to hear us pray," Tres said, as Thomas was about to turn off the light next to his bed.

"I'm here," Regina said from the doorway. She tried hard to concentrate on the boys' prayers but she couldn't help thinking about overhearing Thomas easily tell the boys that he loved them. At least her son had the love that she'd wanted him to get from a father when she married Thomas. Why should she complain?

Fall was beautiful in Nashville. The weather remained mild until late October with children wearing sweaters to school in the morning, but leaving them at school in lockers because the days grew so warm. The maple and oak trees all along Sonata Drive had turned yellow, gold, and orange.

The night of the Blue and Gold Gala, Regina dressed in a shimmering gold formal that highlighted her dark chocolate skin. Thomas was the perfect escort in his black tuxedo, white shirt with black studs, and black bow tie. His beautiful dark eyes reflected the gold from Regina's dress when he gazed at her admiringly as she sauntered down the steps at their home.

"I truly will be the envy of every man in the ballroom tonight," he said, when she touched the last step.

"You look good enough to be with me." She smiled

at him. "On you a tux is more than a mundane backdrop for a woman's formal. You clean up well."

"Can you believe that I'm the same man that wore that scruffy sweat suit this morning?" he said, swelling with boyish pride at her compliment.

"Don't get too proud, now. Remember, I'm the cute one and you're my foil, okay?"

"Oh, yeah, that's why you get to wear gold and look like a goddess while I'm in this plain black tux that everyone's already seen. This is the same tux that I wore to our wedding, but you had to have a new formal," he said, teasing her again for always having to shop for something new to wear. "As if anyone had seen the formals that you have already. I should have gone shopping for something new," he noted.

"You'll do. Let's go tell Keisha that we're about to leave."

The ballroom at the Opryland Hotel was filled with royal-blue and metallic gold balloons, producing an explosion of color. Tiny white lights surrounded the stage and lined the ceiling. There was excitement in the air because the football team was already eight-and-zero and expectations were equally as high for the basketball team

Regina and Thomas sat at a table with John and Audrey Morgan; Veronica, the athletics director, and her husband; the football coach and his wife; Sonia, the sports information director, and her husband. After a dinner of steak and lobster, the program began. John Morgan went to the microphone to introduce significant donors to the athletic program.

Regina didn't pay much attention to what John was saying because she was rewriting a new song in her mind. She was tempted to hum it aloud, but she didn't want people to think that she was odd.

"And the newest member of the President's Circle is

a very talented young woman who is a Nashville country music songwriter, a woman that I had the pleasure of giving away in marriage just last month, the newest member of the Raven family, and the wife of our very own head basketball coach, Mrs. Thomas Simmons—Regina Simmons. Please come forward, dear."

Audrey nudged her from the side and Regina stood in a daze. She'd forgotten to tell Dr. Morgan how much she hated crowds and standing in front of people. It wasn't that she was shy, she just didn't feel that all of this attention was necessary when she had done nothing but write a check.

As she walked to the platform and accepted her plaque, she hoped that she smiled pleasantly enough for the photographer. When she returned to her seat, she noticed Thomas standing and applauding along with the rest of the audience. Yet, somehow she knew that he wasn't pleased at all.

During the rest of the evening, Thomas was fairly quiet. He danced with her once and didn't seem to notice when she danced away with Dr. Morgan and others. Regina, as usual, was the life of the party. When everyone jumped to the floor to do the Electric Slide, he stayed in his seat while she lined up with the others from their table.

When the affair was over, they drove home in silence. Neither was in the mood to begin the conversation that would lead to their first fight. In their bedroom, he unzipped her dress without any of the affection that he usually showed her. After it was unzipped, she stepped away from him quickly. She wanted to let him know that his touch would not be missed.

She placed her dress in the garment bag and hung it in the closet. In no mood to have an angry man ogling her, she dressed in the bathroom for the first time in their marriage. When she was in her gown, she stood before where he sat propped up against the upholstered headboard of their bed. "Okay, buddy, what's up?"

"Why did you donate so much money to our basketball program?" he asked, without hesitation.

"Because you've convinced me that this program is worthwhile and since you work the hell out of the boys, the least we can do is provide a couple of scholarships."

"Why didn't you tell me about your contribution?" he growled.

"I forgot. It was no big secret—well, actually it was. I made the pledge while we were at Sunriver—that's when Dr. Morgan first solicited me. At first I wanted to keep it a secret because, well, I didn't know where our relationship was going and I didn't want you to think that I was assuming anything about us. I figured one day you'd just see my name on one of those plaques in your gym and then you'd know. That was back when we were still just friends, but you proposed the next day and I simply forgot in all the excitement of getting married," Regina answered in her rapid-fire speech pattern.

Instead of finding amusement in her rapid speech and waving arms as he usually did, Thomas stared at her with his arms folded across his chest. "People are going to think that my wife had to buy my job."

"That's not true. My contribution is just a fraction of your salary. What's really bothering you?" she asked, putting a hand on her hip.

"Your contribution is significant compared to the other donations we receive. That's why you were onstage receiving a plaque tonight while I watched in surprise. Right now I feel the way Steadman must feel."

"You're not as handsome as Steadman and I'm not

as rich as Oprah, so don't worry about what the secretaries on campus are saying about you," Regina said sarcastically.

He tried again. "You could be in violation with the NCAA. We're supposed to have the coaching staff and players over for a barbecue in two weeks. What if you're considered a booster now?"

"Dr. Morgan wouldn't have let me violate any NCAA rule, would he?"

"Dr. Morgan wouldn't give a damn about NCAA violations. He leaves that for his staff to figure out. He just goes after the money."

"Should I take the check back?"

"I'm sure that your check has been cashed, you'll never get it back," he said with less anger in his voice.

"Okay, Thomas. I'm still trying to be nice here and you're still cruising for a fight? Are you going to tell me what this is really about?"

He stared at her with his arms folded and she stood looking at him with a neutral look on her face. She couldn't begin to fathom what was on his mind. And she would be the first to admit that she just couldn't figure men out. All those women who claimed to know and gave her all of their advice had more interest in figuring them out than she did. She preferred the straightforward method. Just ask.

"Okay, does this have something to do with money?" she asked.

"Regina, go to bed. I don't want to play with you tonight," he answered grumpily.

"Well, that'll be a first," she answered airily. "How in the hell am I supposed to know what's wrong with you when you don't tell me?"

"There's nothing wrong."

"Okay and Peter Pan wasn't gay," she shot at him.

Laughter burst from him; this crazy woman could always make him laugh, even when he didn't want to. "You know he was gay. Why else would he run around in panty hose?" Then he remembered that he was angry and became stone-faced again.

"Are you going to tell me why you're angry?" she asked again.

"No," he said and folded his arms the way she'd seen Tres do a hundred times.

"I'm not going to sleep with a grim bear. I'll go to the guest room," she said and sauntered toward the closed bedroom door. He watched the soft roll of her hips as she walked away from him.

"No, don't you dare," he said, rushing toward the door.

"So, are you going to talk to me?"

"I don't know what's wrong, so how can I tell you? Your donation caught me by surprise. I didn't know that you had that much money to give away," he tried to explain.

"We finally get to what this is really about. We never got around to talking about money, did we? I assumed that you were doing well because you live in this neighborhood and I assumed that you knew that I had enough money to take care of Justin and me. We're not suffering economically," she explained patiently.

"But I don't have huge sums of money to give away on a whim."

"I believe that the more I give away, the more I get. Some years I make a lot of money. Sometimes I don't. I try to put as much as possible away like an ant. I put some money in reserve several years ago in anticipation of lean times, but times have been good. I have been blessed. This new CD that Shelby is working on is going to earn us some big bucks because I wrote or cowrote everything on it. Of course, I have to split my four cents, or eight cents, with Kent and Jimmy Bob."

"But you can't spend based on what you might earn," he remarked.

"I know that. I don't spend all I earn. Take my house for instance. The Realtor was disappointed because I qualified for a much more expensive house, but I didn't want to go that high. I needed to put away money for Justin's education and to begin a retirement fund for when I no longer want to work. I also have some other mutual funds. Now what about you?"

"I put aside some money when I played in Japan. They were good to me over there. So I guess I'm not broke either, it's just that, well, like I said, you surprised me."

"Did I hurt your male pride? Will the people of Nashville really spread the rumor that the great Thomas Simmons had to let his wife buy his job?"

"I had the job before I met you."

"That's right. You said it, buddy. So what's your beef?"

"I guess I'm still a little nervous about the NCAA. We'd better check to be sure we're not in violation of any rules," Thomas said, not willing to let go of his anger and still trying to sort out his feelings.

"While you wrestle with that, may I come to bed now? My feet hurt," Regina said from the doorway where she'd been standing since she threatened to leave the room.

Within the next few days, Regina reluctantly met with the attorney that Thomas recommended and liked him instantly. He had an easy, southern manner that belied his sharp mind. She was impressed by the many diplomas and awards on his wall, but totally unimpressed with his game ball. She chuckled when she saw it encased in glass and exhibited in the center of the reception area.

"Hello, I'm Andre Drummond. Congratulations on

your recent nuptials," he said, extending his large hand.

"Thank you. I see you have your priorities in order," she said with a smile, which masked her sarcasm.

He looked at her with a question on his face. "What do you mean?"

"Your diplomas and professional certifications are hidden in here, but that game ball is proudly displayed in your reception area," Regina said, smiling. "That ball must inspire your clients with respect for your professional abilities as a basketball player, but my question is about your legal skills."

"Oh, yes, my game ball. It's a great conversation starter. But I guess you're not impressed, living with the great Thomas Simmons. You must have them all over your house."

"No, I haven't seen any of Thomas's. He's rather modest and keeps them packed away somewhere."

"I'd never pack mine away. It reminds me that I can overcome any obstacle because I have before. I received it when we won the NCAA championship. It was the first time Renaissance had ever been invited to the NCAA championship playoffs. We were not expected to go at all and no one ever dreamed that we would go all the way. When we were invited to the playoffs, all the prognosticators predicted that the big schools like Indiana or Maryland would knock us out. When we were still hanging in at the final four, everyone was surprised, including our coach. Then we did the impossible, we won a national championship. It was a good time," he said, smiling with the memory.

"You don't charge by the hour, do you?" Regina asked.

"No, of course not. Why do you ask?"

"Because that was a pretty lengthy story. I don't mind you wasting my time, but I don't want you to waste my money, too," Regina explained without rancor.

At first the man was taken off guard by her bluntness, but then he leaned back in his executive chair and roared with laughter. "You're insulting me, aren't you? Did Thomas send you here under duress?"

"No, it's my choice to get help. I'm upset that I have to pay someone to speak for me, but that's how it is sometimes in a man's world. I just want to be sure that you're up to snuff in all this legal stuff. You've got to know more than I do or I don't need you."

"A man doesn't have to wonder where he stands with you, does he?"

"Let's hope not," she answered with a sincere smile this time.

"You must give Thomas a good run for his money."

"I try," Regina answered, indifferent to the possible compliment in his statement.

After that exchange, rapport was established and respect grew between client and attorney. Regina presented her contract to Andre and he took copious notes as he asked her questions about the role she played with the record label and what she really wanted in the deal.

While he was studying the contract, Regina looked around his office again. He had a picture of himself with CeCe Winans, Bobby Jones, and Otis Blackwell. "Otis Blackwell!" Regina said aloud. "Did you represent Otis Blackwell?" she asked when she realized she'd actually spoken the revered songwriter's name.

"Yes, he took a chance on me when I had just gotten out of law school and was trying to build a practice focused on entertainment law," Andre said, surprised by the awe in Regina's voice. "Did you know him personally?"

"Yes, he was a wonderful, talented man. When I first

moved to Nashville, he granted me an appointment to sit down and talk to him about the ins and outs of Music City. By that time, he had already penned more than one thousand songs that were recorded by Elvis Presley, Billy Joel, Ray Charles, Kris Kristofferson, and just about everybody. He's the one who advised me to continue singing my demos. He said that was the way to control how they would be recorded," Regina said with more enthusiasm than Andre had heard from her to that point.

"I take it you were a fan of Mr. Blackwell's?"

"He was very encouraging to me. He wasn't into country, but his music crossed all genres. Did you know that he wrote 'All Shook Up' and 'Don't Be Cruel' and 'Breathless' and 'Handy Man' and 'Great Balls of Fire'?"

Andre smiled real big. "Of course, I'm the man that made sure he kept getting his royalty checks when those songs were played. I also know that he's in the Nashville Songwriters Foundation Hall of Fame. This is my business, I have to know these things."

"Now you've really impressed me. If Mr. Blackwell trusted you, so will I."

A week later Andre called Regina to let her know that a record company executive wanted to meet with them in person to discuss her counteroffer on the contract. She had been surprised that the CEO of Honeysuckle, Tony Stone, was actually interested in meeting with her. She had thought that the meeting would be relegated to one of his staff attorneys.

Regina woke up nervous that morning and things were not going well around the house. Thomas had left for his early morning practice, and the boys wanted to dawdle and talk over breakfast. She needed to get them to school so that she could come back home and spend some time getting dressed for this important meeting.

"Brandon Rucker says that me and Justin can't be brothers," Tres said between spoonfuls of Cheerios.

Regina wanted to ignore the child because she knew that this could be the beginning of a long discussion, and it was, because she asked anyway, "Why is that, Tres?"

"He said I'm light skin-ded and Justin is dark skinded."

"Did you tell him that Justin looks like your mother and you look like your father?"

"Is Daddy light skin-ded, too?"

"I guess some people would think so. His skin is the same color as caramel candy, don't you think?" Regina answered, relating skin color to something sweet and good so that both children would have positive associations.

"Yes, it sure is," Justin said, giggling. "And what do we look like, Mama?"

"I don't know. What would you say?"

"You and Justin look like Hershey bars," Tres said.

"We're different on the outside, but we're just as sweet on the inside, just like caramel and chocolate. Wouldn't it be boring if you could have only one kind of candy?" Regina asked.

"Yes, because sometimes I want Snickers and sometimes I want Now-and-Laters."

"It would be boring if all people looked the same. Aren't you glad that you don't look exactly like Justin? Then no one could tell you apart," Regina explained, feeling hopeful that both boys realized that their skin colors were different shades of brown, but each was just as good as the other. Before she had time to congratulate herself on what she thought was a successful explanation, the boys had moved on to another subject.

"But I want to have the same name that you and Dad and Tres have," Justin said.

This caught Regina off guard. She was about to tell the boys to hurry with their food, but she knew she couldn't ignore the child. "I didn't know you wanted your name to be Simmons."

"I do. I used to be a Lovejoy when your name was Lovejoy, but your name is not Mrs. Lovejoy anymore. Now at school they say 'Mrs. Simmons' is here to pick up her sons. Then they say, 'Tres Simmons and Justin Lovejoy, please come to the office.'"

"I'll see what we can do about that," Regina promised her son. "We really have to get a move on, fellows. Could I have one chocolate kiss and one caramel kiss before we get in the car since no one at school can see you kiss me anymore?"

Tres turned his pockets inside out. "I don't have any kisses. Do you, Justin?" Both boys thought that the joke was so funny that they rolled with laughter.

"Stop teasing me," Regina said, reaching for the boy and giving him a hug before kissing him. "You'll never be too big for one of my kisses."

Chapter 12

She hurried back home after leaving the boys at school and was out the door again in less than an hour. Dressed in her red power suit with black accessories, Regina sat in the executive offices at Honeysuckle Records with Andre waiting for Tony Stone to meet with them. She tapped the toe of her black kid heels impatiently as she waited.

"Don't get impatient," Andre said softly. "This is part of the game. He's letting you know who's in charge. Just keep your cool."

"Everyone around here knows how much I hate to be kept waiting," Regina shot back.

"Obviously. That's why he has you waiting now. This is a power play and if you let them get under your skin, they'll have the upper hand before we start," Andre advised.

After several more minutes, a slim, trim secretary came through the double doors that led to the inner sanctum of the executive suite. "Mr. Stone will see you now," she said in a very un-Nashville, almost British voice.

"Regina, my dear. How are you? I haven't had a chance to tell you how much fun Grace and I had at your wedding. That reception was a blast. We'll have to do that again," Tony said, coming from behind his desk to embrace Regina as if she were his favorite love child.

Regina stepped from his embrace and looked at the well-tanned, fit, and fiftyish executive with his manicured hands and newly dyed, curly brown hair. He had success written all over him. "That's not likely," Regina answered dryly.

"We're not here in an adversarial role," Tony said, acting hurt and surprised.

"Why are you acting all hurt that I don't want to do it again?" Regina asked.

"Frankly, I'm surprised because I thought we'd grown so close over the years. I thought now that you're married you would have us over from time to time and we could invite you all over or take you out."

"Hold it—slow down. I meant that I'm not likely to have another wedding for your pleasure. I don't want to get married again because I have the husband I want," she explained to the embarrassed Tony. "I did not mean that I didn't want to entertain you again. I don't know that yet. It depends on how things go today."

"I guess you jumped the gun that time," Andre said, cocking a finger at Tony and taking a mock shot at him.

"Let's have a seat and regroup," Tony said, some of his composure lost. When Meg, the slim-hipped secretary, entered the office, he asked his guests, "What will you have to drink?"

They made small talk about the industry in general until Meg returned with bottled water for Regina and coffee for the men. Meg sat down, took out a stenographer's pad, and waited with pen in hand.

"Our attorneys shall be up shortly. I just wanted to talk with you off the record before they get here," Tony said, looking at Regina.

"Well, my attorney *is* here."

"That's all right. Frankly, I was a little surprised by your counteroffer. It seems that you place a lot of value on the work you do for us."

"Yes," was all Regina said. Andre had instructed her not to offer too many comments. He had warned her that an innocent remark could come back to haunt her later. "I'll do the talking since you tend to get carried away," he'd instructed as they rode the elevator up to the executive suite.

"You know we offered you a contract when you were untried and unproven. We took a risk on you," Tony reminded her.

"That was one gamble that has paid you well," she answered.

"Ms. Simmons's songs have been consistently on the Top 40 charts since she signed with you," Andre said.

"That's true and she's been well compensated for her success," Tony answered. Turning to Regina, he continued, "I read in *The Tennessean* that you received an honor the other night for your philanthropy. What was that you contributed to?"

"The Renaissance athletic program," Regina answered, succinctly.

"That was a beautiful, very expensive-looking designer dress that you had on. We can't be paying you that poorly. You are a philanthropist now and you were dressed like one," Tony said snidely.

"I use my money how I see fit. I notice that you have on an Armani suit right now in the middle of an ordinary workday. And you have a building named for you at Vanderbilt University. How much money did you have to contribute to get a whole building named for you? It must take a lot of songs at mere pennies per song to get your name on a building," Regina retorted.

"Ah-h-h, here is my backup right on time. Guys,

we've just been chatting about Regina's contributions to Honeysuckle Records."

Quickly dispensing with all pleasantries, the attorneys opened their portfolios. The older legal man spoke first. "Your contributions have been significant, but the things you've asked for in your contract are not quite in line with what we've offered our other writers this year."

"Is that right?" Regina said, leaning forward and unconsciously putting her hand on her hip. Andre put his hand on her arm to silence her.

"Gentlemen, may I direct your attention to the contract?" Andre suggested.

Each pulled out his copy of the contract and they went through it line by line. On some things they were flexible; on others they would not budge. Regina was becoming more impatient by the moment and left no one in the room wondering how she was feeling. At one point, while the men were discussing her future, she began to pace the room.

Andre had urged her to trust him since he was the expert on these matters. She decided that she would and fought to remain silent. When the session had been going on for several hours, she said, "Do these things usually take so long?"

"Sometimes," Andre answered.

"I'm an artist. I could be writing while we're doing this. Instead of earning money, you have me paying out good money. I've been listening and frankly, Tony, I don't think you have been bargaining in good faith. Don't you think that I'm familiar with what you willingly gave Kent?" she bluffed, taking a guess that Kent's contract would have been more lucrative than Jimmy Bob's based on his more businesslike personality alone.

"Well, that's, ah-h-h—"

She interrupted, standing before his desk with one hand on her hip again and blocking his view from the attorneys. "Don't bother to answer. When we are in the studio, I'm the one who calms your artists. I'm the one who sings the demos to give the artists a template for the style that they usually try to emulate. I'm the one who taught Alison to breathe and Carter to be less nasal. There's no recognition in here for my production time whatsoever."

"But you're not a producer," Tony retorted.

"I haven't been paid to be a producer," Regina corrected. "So why do you always have your producer call me to the studio when you're having trouble? I'm just the girl with the ear. You expected my gratitude to carry you forever, didn't you? The little black girl should be grateful to get her foot in the door. Well, now I have a name," Regina said.

"Don't do this, Regina," Tony said, standing.

"You can't intimidate me," she said with laughter in her voice. "I'm not sure if I want you to wield your power over me anymore. I respected you, Tony, and I'm hurt that you have no respect for me."

"You should let your attorney do the talking for you. You're getting all emotional," Tony warned.

"That's what women do. It's that emotion that makes our songs sell. But for now, I've had enough. We'll go over what we have now and we'll get back to you," Regina said calmly. She turned on her black kid pumps and strutted out of the office, her head held high.

Andre quickly stuffed his papers into his briefcase and ran to catch up with her. "We'll get back to you," he repeated.

On the ride back to his office, he said, "Regina, you may have backed yourself into a corner. Are you okay with that?"

"I don't know. I didn't have a plan. I went in there completely resolved to stay quiet and let you handle everything, but he upset me by arguing over a penny here and point five cents there. I don't want to be bothered with those details. I know a good deal when I hear one and we were nowhere near a good deal."

"Tell you what. Let me pull together what I have and get back to you tomorrow morning. Is that okay?" he asked, looking at her closely, trying to gauge her temperature.

"Sure. I'm not that difficult to work with, am I?"

"One does know where he stands with you," Andre said with admiration in his voice.

When Thomas got home that evening, Regina was in the kitchen dumping a premade tossed salad from a bag into a big serving bowl. "How did it go at Honeysuckle Records?" he asked.

"Not so well. I'm not good at the negotiating process. I got tired of their playing around with numbers, going from four cents on a dollar to four and a half cents on a dollar, so I walked out," she explained.

Thomas roared with laughter. "You just walked out in the middle of negotiations. It must have been priceless to see the look on Stone-Cold Tony's face."

"I was surprised that Tony Stone wanted to negotiate with me in the first place. I'm so insignificant in the organization and he's the big exec. I assumed that we'd meet with the attorneys. But, I didn't see the look on his face because when I headed for the door I never looked back. I saw the look on Ms. Fake British Accent's face and she looked like she smelled puke. I waited for Andre at the elevator and we went straight to the garage."

"Andre said that he doesn't know whether to thank me or shoot me for sending you to him," Thomas said, still laughing.

"He knows I give him energy to get off his butt and do something. I keep him thinking. In fact, I don't know how he caught up with me so fast, because I was really strutting when I left that office."

"Gina, you're too much."

"When did you see Andre anyway? You two haven't been discussing me, have you?"

"Not much. He came over to watch practice one day. You know we're having open practice."

"So you can unlock the gym doors again? Do you feel safer since you're married?" she asked.

"The doors weren't locked because of the female on-lookers. That was just a rumor. We locked the doors because we had five freshmen last year who were nervous and had to be put through a lot of un-pretty drills. We're opening the doors for our scrimmages because that's what the public wants to see," he explained.

Regina put the bowl of salad in the refrigerator and took out the plates and cutlery that they used when they ate on the deck. "Okay, if that's your story, I'll buy it. Let's take this outside and you can start the grill," she suggested.

"Oh, I forgot I was supposed to be grilling today. You caught me completely off guard with your story. I'll run to the shed and get the charcoal."

"Then I guess it's best that I keep this other thing that I want to talk to you about until after dinner," Regina said.

"What is it? I guess I can do two things at once."

"Go get the charcoal and I'll get the other vegetables ready."

They got involved in preparing dinner, then eating and chatting with the boys, and Regina did not get a chance to tell Thomas the other thing she needed to discuss with him until the boys were in bed.

"Let me do that for you," Thomas suggested as he

watched Regina, fresh from a shower, smooth lotion over her arms and hands. "Slide into bed so that you're comfortable," he instructed; then taking the lotion bottle from her, he poured some into his hand and began rubbing it into her feet and legs.

"What is the other thing that was on your mind?" he asked when she was practically purring from his ministrations.

"The other thing—oh, it's Justin. He's concerned because he's the only one in the family who's not a Simmons. I promised him that I'd talk to you about that."

"Can't you legally change his name without his father's permission?"

"I don't know," Regina answered.

"Why don't you ask Andre to take care of that for you?" Thomas suggested.

"You don't mind changing Justin's name to Simmons?"

"Of course not, his mother has already done damage to the name, what have I to lose?" Thomas said playfully.

"What have I done to damage your name?"

"Walk out on meetings with record company executives. Tell people what you think about various issues whether they want your opinion or not. Little things like that," he said, rubbing the lotion up higher and higher on her leg.

"You're the one who's corrupting me. You have me doing things that would embarrass my mother," Regina said, giving in to the sensuous pleasures his hands were producing as they stroked the sensitive skin on the inside of her thighs.

"You'd better not tell your mother about what I'm getting ready to do," he said, untying the belt of her robe and tossing it aside.

He lay next to her and looked in the eyes that he adored. "You are so precious to me. I thank God every day for making you my wife," he told her and took her into his arms.

"I love you so much," she whispered to him.

He kissed her nose, her neck, shoulders, breasts, stomach, thighs, legs, and feet. "You're absolutely delicious," he said, when he took her into his arms again. "You're the sweetest thing I've ever known."

She wrapped her arms around him and surrendered to the ecstasy that she'd grown to expect when they were alone together.

The next morning, Thomas was slow to leave for his morning practice. "Why aren't you rushing off today?" Regina asked.

"It seems like you and the boys have been having some heavy conversations in the mornings, but they're so tired and worn out by the time I see them in the evenings that we don't have any fun," he explained.

"Help yourself, but what about your practice?"

"They're running drills this morning. I have three assistant coaches, a trainer, and an equipment manager. I should be able to spend a morning with my family."

"Well, all right then, Mr. Big Stuff. You have the staff and you are the boss," Regina joked, snapping her fingers and wagging her head. "If you really want to know what the kids are thinking, you should drive them to school," she suggested. "We have great conversations in the car because I can't get away and they have my complete attention."

"Uh-huh. I'm the boss. So who's bossing me now?" he said, coming up behind her at the kitchen counter as she poured cereal in bowls for the children's breakfast. Pulling her back against his chest, he lightly kissed her on the neck and slipped his hand inside her robe to stroke her soft breast.

She relaxed and let her head rest against his chest for a moment. "When you get back I'll have a surprise for you," she said suggestively.

"Now I know you're trying to wear me out," he said in a mock complaint.

"I just want to hear you say *when*," she teased.

"What are you talking about?" he asked, puzzled.

"I'm referring to the night that you told me that you were in complete control and you knew when to say you'd had enough. You said that you knew when to say *when*," she reminded him.

"Oh, that. Wasn't I a glutton for punishment? I figured out how many cold showers one man could endure while I was waiting to marry you. Never again. I've endured enough celibacy to last a lifetime," he said and kissed her neck again, before she interrupted.

"That feels good, but do you mind going up and telling the boys to get some speed on?" she asked.

"You're afraid you're going to get weak for me, aren't you?"

She laughed and threw a dish towel at his retreating back. When he returned, she said, "Andre is coming by to discuss the contract with me. I'm glad you'll be here so that I can get your opinion and you won't have to hear anything secondhand."

"Do you really want me involved in your professional life like that?" he asked, pleased that she wanted his opinion.

"You're all up in my personal life. I might as well let you in my professional life, too," she said, playfully. "But right now, your first priority is getting the boys to school on time."

* * *

Having been forewarned about the lack of coffee in the Simmons household, Andre arrived with a large cup of latte from Starbucks. By the time Thomas returned, contracts, notes, and clippings were spread all over the kitchen table.

"These are some of the other artists I represent. They are doing quite well as independents," Andre was telling Regina. "As prolific as you are as a writer, you don't need the support of a label anymore."

"So you're suggesting that she cut Honeysuckle Records loose?" Thomas asked, coming in on the tail end of the conversation.

"If they don't accept our next offer, I'm suggesting that your wife walks. The label deal was good when she was a single parent and just getting started. Now, she's established and she can do more for Honeysuckle than they can do for her."

"What do you think, baby?" Thomas asked.

"What do you think?" she returned to him. "We'll be completely dependent on you. You'll be the only one in the family with a regular paycheck."

"Go with your gut instincts. I've learned to trust your instincts, they're usually right," he advised.

"Do you know how much I pay in health insurance alone on a monthly basis?" she asked, calculating her expenses.

"I'll adopt Justin and add him to my group insurance at work. We were going to change his name anyway," Thomas offered. "Perhaps I should adopt him. Make him mine legally."

"The name change is one thing, but I'm not sure if his father will actually surrender his parental rights," she said hesitantly. "I think it would be good for you to adopt him for more reasons than the insurance. I wonder what would happen to him if I weren't around."

"Well, if he doesn't let me adopt him, he needs to

start sending some money across the big ocean," Thomas said caustically.

"I don't need his money. If he starts sending money, he may want to get involved in Justin's life. No, we'll leave him where he is. Let me just see where we stand, okay, baby?"

"If that's the way you want to handle it. You know that I'd do anything in the world for Justin. I love that little boy as much as I love Tres."

"I know," she said.

"I can draw up some papers for the father to sign to relinquish his parental rights," Andre suggested. "Regina, don't be yourself when you talk to him. May I suggest that you use a little tact? Tell him that since Justin lives with Thomas it is important that Thomas has the unquestioned legal authority to make decisions on Justin's behalf should you be unable to do so."

"I have tact. I can be diplomatic, can't I, Thomas?"

"If you say so, baby," he said dutifully.

"Oh, don't try to act like a henpecked husband in front of Andre. He knows you," she said, socking Thomas's hard biceps.

"So according to your projections, if the Shelby Rodgers CD goes platinum, Honeysuckle benefits under the terms of the old contract?"

"That's right. Although it won't be released until January, they still had you under contract when you wrote those songs."

"I wish I'd cut them loose long ago. That album is the best work that I've done so far. We'll easily sell two million copies. Let's go for it," she said decisively.

"Do you mean that you want me to present your counters?" Andre asked, seeking clarification.

"No, I mean, cut the dogs loose. I don't need them. I don't need anybody telling me that I don't need money because I can afford designer clothes. Cut 'em loose."

"Okay. I have my marching orders, ma'am. I'll do as you say," Andre said, stuffing his papers and other paraphernalia into his briefcase.

"Then you'll stay with me and handle my negotiations while I freelance?" she asked nervously.

"I'm in your corner, sister. You have a convert. Even after you pay my—what did you call them?—exorbitant fees, you'll still come out ahead."

"I'm counting on that," Regina said. "Go do your stuff."

"Wait, before you go," Thomas broke in as Andre was heading toward the door. "We're having the team over after church this Sunday. Would you like to come, meet the young bloods?"

"Yeah, I'd like that," Andre said, smiling. "Are we celebrating something?"

"Yes, we have a big scrimmage that's going to be open to the public on Friday night and I'm counting on them to put on a good show. We're trying to create a lot of excitement and team spirit to increase our ticket sales. To motivate them, I told them we'd feed them on Sunday. That's when the cafeteria food is the worst ever."

"I remember those Sunday dinners. None of the staff wanted to cook on the weekend and they served us the worst mess. It sounds like you're creating quite a buzz around town already. Everywhere I go, somebody's talking about Renaissance basketball coming back to our old glory," Andre related.

"You'd better believe we are. Two years before I came the record was two wins and twenty-six losses. Last year we won ten and lost eighteen. This year, we'll turn that around. Buy your season tickets while they're still affordable," Thomas boasted.

"I know one thing. You are a good salesman," Andre said, slapping Thomas's hand.

"We'll see you Sunday. And bring your lady. I know she'd like to relive your glory days with you as you tell it to this new generation," Thomas said jovially.

"I'm sure she's heard those stories enough to tell them in her sleep, but bring her anyway," Regina teased.

Sunday morning, the entire Renaissance basketball team joined the Simmons family at eleven o'clock service. Thomas had invited them, but wasn't sure if they would accept his invitation. He was surprised to see each and every one on the team, as well as the staff, march in together. He wondered if the coaches had gone to the residence hall and pulled them out of their beds.

Looking at the wave of tall, muscular bodies where the shortest person was six feet three inches tall reminded Regina of the parting of the Red Sea. She could not see over the hoard, nor could she see around them. Pastor Bender and the congregation warmly welcomed the team and invited them back.

Immediately after service the group caravanned to Coach Simmons's home. Regina originally thought they'd bought too much food for the cookout, but looking at her husband's energetic crew with their size-fourteen and -fifteen sneakers, she wondered if they had prepared enough.

Before leaving for church, Thomas had put ribs and steaks in a marinade. They were already on the grill and the three assistant coaches were tending them while Thomas rolled the ground beef in his hand and patted them flat for hamburgers.

Although she was not given to domestic chores, such as cooking, Regina did enjoy having good parties. Luckily she knew a caterer who prepared food just as good as home-cooked meals. The food was delivered when they returned from church. She had several young men help the caterers bring in the huge foil pans of baked beans, salad, corn-on-the-cob, turnip greens, macaroni and cheese, baked apples, and green beans. Next she directed two of the young men to set the coolers of soda out in the backyard.

When she was finished, she ran upstairs to change from the silk dress that she'd worn to church to a long wraparound skirt and a linen shirt. Thomas could do things his way and she would do things her way. He wanted to stand over a hot grill and cook the meat when it would have been much easier if she'd ordered it from Joe's when she ordered the side dishes. Of course, Thomas was convinced that he had the world's greatest barbecue recipe and Joe's couldn't touch his. *Well, let him sweat it out over the grill,* she thought. *I'll rest up here for a while.*

Resting was not in the plan for her that Sunday. By the time she'd changed clothes the doorbell rang. Realizing that Thomas may not hear the doorbell with the loud male voices and music in the backyard, she rushed down the steps.

"Andre, hi, I'm glad you could come," Regina said when she answered the door.

"This is my wife, Tiffany. Tiffany, this is *the client* I've been telling you about," he said, with mock horror in his voice.

"I hope you haven't been telling your wife stories about me," Regina said, laughing at the exaggerated tremor in his voice.

"It's all true, sweetheart," he said, following his wife into the house.

"How far along are you?" Regina couldn't wait to ask Tiffany when she saw her obviously protruding stomach.

"I'm in my eighth month and it feels like I've been pregnant three years already," she said, wobbling through the house.

"Well, we'll get you all set up in a nice comfortable chair. Come on out to the deck," Regina said.

As soon as they reached the deck, Regina was assaulted with questions from Thomas, his assistant coaches, and Tres and Justin. The boys were hungry and couldn't wait to eat. Thomas wanted to know where the serving spoons were.

"You would think that Thomas didn't live in this house before I moved in," she whispered when she returned to sit next to Tiffany. "Just because I have two X chromosomes, he thinks that I know more about the kitchen than he does."

Tiffany laughed a soft southern laugh. "I know. Why do men do that? I read in a book that if I start answering Andre's questions about the baby, he'll always rely on me and think that I'm the baby expert. The book advises that I let him discover answers about the baby on his own."

"I guess you'll have to decide if you're willing to take that risk," Regina joked, and they shared a good laugh.

"What are you two laughing about?" Thomas asked as he and Andre joined their wives.

"You know, sweetie, our favorite subject—men," Tiffany said.

The men looked quizzically at each other. "Man, I won't touch that," Andre said.

"Did you bring your game ball for show-and-tell with the other kids?" Regina teased Andre.

"No, but I have the pictures taken at the ceremony when it was presented to me," Andre said, pretending to reach into his shirt pocket.

Regina rolled her eyes and shook her head. "Let's

start feeding the masses. These boys are beginning to look weak," she suggested.

While the crew lined up to eat, Regina sent Tres out with a noncarbonated beverage for Tiffany and she sent Justin to find a footstool for Tiffany to rest her feet on. "Doesn't she look content?" Regina said to Thomas when they were in the kitchen together getting additional sauce and serving utensils.

"She's practically glowing," Thomas replied. "I wish I could have seen you pregnant," he said wistfully.

"I was fat and irritable. I thought I'd never lose all the weight I gained," she admitted.

"I don't believe that. I can't imagine you any way but beautiful. Are you sorry that we can't have more children?" he asked, leaning closer to look at her as she answered.

"No. Tres and Justin are more than enough for any one woman," she said lightly. He looked at her again to see if there was any regret in her face.

"Are you two smooching in here?" Isaac Mathews, the team's recruiter, asked as he stepped into the kitchen. "I can come back later," he said, backing out the way he'd come in.

"Come on in here. Don't be afraid of a little affection. This is what married folks do," Thomas told his assistant.

Isaac looked at Regina shyly, but entered the kitchen. Regina returned to the backyard to tend to the needs of their young guests. She flitted from one cluster of athletes to another, offering more food or drinks. Thomas watched her and his heart swelled with love. She was the best thing that had ever happened to him. He looked at her with adoration, taking in her glowing dark skin, stylish haircut, full breasts and hips, and wondered how he could be so lucky.

"Look at Coach, man, he's going to let the food

burn up while he's rubbernecking his wife," one of the players said.

"If I had a wife that fine, I'd do the same thing. She's F-I-N-E fine," the teammate answered.

"She's hot. No wonder Coach's been smiling so much lately," the third guy said.

All three jumped, when they realized that Coach was no longer looking at his wife, but had joined them. "Are you guys eyeballing my wife?" Coach Simmons asked.

"No, sir," they said in unison.

"If I catch you three gazing her way again, you'll have to do one hundred laps Monday, got that?" Thomas said in his sternest voice before returning to the grill.

"I'll show them, staring at a man's wife and talking about me for smiling," Thomas grumbled.

Andre laughed and slapped him on the back. "Man, you should be ashamed," he said when he finally stopped laughing. "Your wife is cute and you know these boys have hormone problems."

"I know, I just thought I'd scare them. Teach them a little respect. They've got to remember who they're messing with," Thomas said, laughing with Andre.

"There's one good thing in this," Thomas added, dumping a stack of the large foil pans into the thirty-gallon-size black trash bag that Andre held open for him.

"And what is that?" Andre asked.

"We don't have to put food away or worry about garbage. These pans have been wiped clean." Thomas laughed.

"It looks like someone took a slice of bread and wiped out the inside of this one," Andre said, pointing to a pan that was still on the table.

"Did you notice how everyone got busy when it was time to clean up?" Thomas asked.

"I sure did. Tiffany said that she and Regina were challenged to a game of bid whist by two of your student athletes."

"Those boys don't know what they're in for. Regina gets vicious when it comes to games. She hates to lose. Let's finish up so we can go watch the slaughter."

When they had finished cleaning up, Thomas checked on the young men clustered about the lawn and throughout the house to be sure that everything was still in order. Large, oversized bodies were everywhere. Outside they were playing basketball at the goal on the driveway or hitting the birdie over the badminton net. A few, who had gotten too full with dinner, had gone to the "men's room" to try watching a movie, but were having difficulty with all the noise from the train set, video games, and air hockey with which still others were entertaining themselves.

Tres and Justin were in their heaven. They knew the players well and there was no way that anyone could convince them that they were not as old as the college students. Justin was helping one of his young adult friends learn to play a new video game. Thomas looked around for Tres and found him playing Uno in the living room where Regina and Tiffany were at another table intimidating two young men who were trying to protect their reputation as bid whist pros.

"Well, eat this," Tiffany said, slamming a ten of spades on top of a two, three, and five of clubs. "When you call your trump, you've got to remember to count. You didn't know I had this one left, did you? My trump beats all your downtown cards," she said jubilantly.

"We just ran a Boston on you," Regina gloated, gathering the cards from the center of the table and beginning to shuffle them.

"Do you want to play another game to redeem yourselves?" Tiffany offered.

"No, no, I'll go outside and shoot a little ball," one of the young men said.

"Me too." The second one followed close on his heels.

"Next!" Regina yelled, still shuffling the cards.

"How about you two? You look like you can give us a challenge," Tiffany said, looking from Andre to Thomas.

Thomas sat down in one of the chairs just vacated. "You had Myron sweating. The seat of this chair is still wet," he accused the ladies.

"Well, excuse me. We can't help it if they couldn't back up their bluff. They were all talk and no game," Regina said. "Wanna try me?" she challenged Thomas.

"No, because I know that by now you and Tiffany can read each other like a book. Myron and Wes didn't know about your subtle signals the way I do," Thomas said. Looking at Tiffany, he asked, "Can I ask you a personal question?"

"Sure. I guess. I don't have to answer it if it's too personal, do I?"

"I just want to know what happens to that soft southern accent and those submissive mannerisms when you're slamming cards on the table."

Tiffany laughed so hard that she had to hold her large stomach. "You know how it is with a southern accent. They come and they go. Listen to Regina. Her home is just as far south as mine, but she talks faster than a New York street hustler when she's excited. I'm from Mississippi and she's from way down in Alabama."

"I thought you knew, Thomas, that we southern girls know what we're doing. When the situation calls for hospitality, we're hospitable. When the situation calls for lots of loving and good fun, well, count on us," Regina said, seductively.

"In other words," Tiffany interrupted, "we're the southern girls that Frankie Beverly and Maze sing about. We're so fine, he had trouble going back north of the Mason-Dixon line."

"Do you think you'll ever go back up North?" Regina asked innocently, winking at Thomas and making him get that flutter in his stomach again. He wondered why she enjoyed flirting with him in front of people.

"I don't think I'll ever leave the southern girl that I'm with," he answered, trying to keep his voice steady. Regina knew that he could never play her flirtatious games. He'd be filled with desire and too embarrassed to stand up while she was only playing.

"I'll tell you one thing about this southern girl. I don't think that I could drop a baby in the cotton field and keep working," Tiffany said, rubbing her stomach. "This boy had his foot tucked under my rib all day. He finally moved it and now he's playing basketball," she groaned.

"I see his foot. May I feel?" Regina asked, fascinated. "Wow, he's strong. He almost moved my hand."

"Are you ready to go, sweetheart?" Andre asked, concern in his voice.

"No, Andre. I might as well be miserable here as anywhere."

"Let's get out of these hard folding chairs and go sit on the love seat," Regina suggested. While the men helped Tiffany lower her body to the love seat, Regina slid a hassock over for her feet. As soon as she was settled in her seat, Andre sat on the hassock in front of her and held her feet in his lap.

The couples chatted about plans for the coming Thanksgiving holiday, the basketball season, and the state budget crisis. They found that they had a lot in common and Regina liked the couple mostly because they had not known Thomas when he was married to Paulette. She was a little tired of everyone either trying to avoid a reference to Paulette or telling her about how happy Thomas had been with her.

When the coaches came to announce that they would be taking the boys back to campus, Thomas was unaware that the fall sky had turned dusky gray and the warm fall day had given in to a chilly evening. The vans were loaded and headed back to north Nashville when Andre said, "I guess I'd better get my love home, she's looking rather wilted."

"I admit, I've had quite a day and I missed my afternoon nap," Tiffany agreed, wiggling to the end of the sofa so that she could stand.

"It was so good meeting you," Regina said at the door. "Call me if I can help. I know how it is having a baby with your family so far away."

"Don't make that offer if you don't mean it," Tiffany warned.

Two voices said in unison, "She wouldn't," just as Regina said, "I wouldn't."

They laughed and the men shook hands while Regina and Tiffany embraced. When all of their guests were gone, Regina and Thomas prepared the boys for bed. For once, they had no argument from the boys. It had been a long, full day.

On Wednesday Andre called to tell Regina that he'd received a response to the letter that he'd written to sever her relationship with Honeysuckle. "They're not taking you seriously, yet. However, they have added a few more concessions." He listed them for Regina and gave his advice. "You know, Regina, this sounds pretty good. This is better than what you told me was on the contract for either Jimmy Bob or Kent's contract."

"They still don't believe that I'm walking. They think

I'm bluffing when I say that I'll go out on my own. Are you still willing to represent me while I freelance?"

"So you won't consider the new offer?" Andre asked.

"No way. I've seen their true colors and I don't want to go through this again. I thought that I was just after more money, but now I realize what I want is respect. Let's see what happens on the open market," Regina instructed her business associate and friend.

"You're gutsy, Regina. You need to realize that you're giving up your security," the attorney felt compelled to remind his client.

"After all this, you still don't believe in me. You have no idea how good I am," Regina said boastfully.

"This is not a game of bid whist, and as your legal counsel I've got to warn you of the risk you're taking."

"You went over those risks quite thoroughly last week. The numbers may have changed, but their attitude hasn't," Regina said, cutting him off before he began going through the numbers again.

"Aren't you afraid of the risk you're taking? Aren't you afraid that you may never publish another song?" Andre asked in his friendship voice, no longer speaking as her attorney.

Regina sensed the difference and responded in a like manner, "This change could not have come at a better time. Somehow, the Lord always knows what we need even before we realize it."

"What do you mean?" Andre asked and paused, waiting for her to continue.

"Thomas is about to enter a very difficult basketball season and so much is at stake for him professionally that I don't mind putting my professional life on hold. I honestly don't know what to expect, but I've seen the schedule and it frightens me. He has two big exhibition games coming up before Thanksgiving and then during the month of December we'll be on the road more than we'll be at home. They play on Tuesday, Thursday, and Friday nights and Saturday afternoons and even sometimes on Sunday—" Regina said, without pausing for air.

Andre interrupted. "Hold on for a minute. Take a deep breath. It's not as bad as it sounds—" he began, but Regina interrupted him again. Having someone that partially understood the schedule had opened her up and released all the worry that she had suppressed. Words spilled out on their own volition.

"Yes, it is as bad as it sounds. In fact, it's worse," she continued. "We've got two children in the first grade and their school requires parental involvement. I'm completely overwhelmed because I know that Thomas wants me at his games and I want to be there for him. Now I know why he wanted to be sure that we were married before the season started. I'd never see him if we didn't sleep together," Regina went on breathlessly in her run-on fashion that Andre had learned could not be stopped until she wound down.

"Regina, you know I played ball at Renaissance," Andre tried to interrupt again.

"Oh, how well I know," Regina quipped. "The game ball and all."

"That's not my point this time. My point is, it's not as overwhelming as you might think. It works out. I played ball and maintained a 3.8 grade point average and managed to graduate in four years. People can do more than one thing at a time when they set their mind to it. You'll be there for Thomas and still get the children to school on time in the morning. I know you and Thomas, maybe not for very long, but I sense that your marriage is similar to ours. I know that you two are in love. Everything will work out. You'll work together and find your pace," Andre said soothingly.

"You're good, counselor," Regina said on a sigh. "I guess that's why you earn the big bucks."

"Why don't you take a break until *Sweet Romance* is released in January? Then you can capitalize on that success when we go to market again," Andre suggested.

"I don't like the idea of not producing. I need a steady income," Regina countered.

"Regina, your royalty checks and residuals should keep you in shoes and hats for quite a while. Your house across the street has already sold. You should be okay," Andre reminded her.

"I guess you're right. I can't do much more right now. When the boys get out of school Friday, I've got to have their things packed so that I can take them to stay with my friend Rosemary. Then I have to get on the plane with Audrey Morgan and the administrators so that we can be in Cincinnati before the game begins at seven-thirty. We'll board the plane again immediately after the game and return home that same night," Regina said, breathless at the thought of what lay ahead.

"It sounds difficult, Regina, but I guarantee you, you'll be so pumped up by the excitement of the game that you'll wonder where your energy came from. The adrenaline will keep you moving."

"Okay, Andre, I'm going to trust you for that. How is Tiffany doing today?"

"She's going crazy. I had to tie her sneakers for her so that we could go walking this morning. She doesn't mind having me wait on her when she can do for herself, but since she's rather helpless she's not enjoying it," he said with a smile in his voice.

"Of course not. Who wants to be helpless? Give her

my love. I'll stop by one day early next week and bring her some of my good home cooking from Joe's."

"I'll tell her. You enjoy yourself. I wish that I could go on the road with you guys. Maybe next year," Andre said before they disconnected.

Chapter 13

As Andre had predicted, the spirit of the crowds at the games gave Regina energy. It also helped that Regina had become acquainted with the players and had listened to Thomas discuss their strengths and weaknesses with the coaches, as well as with the players themselves. With that inside knowledge, she watched "her boys" from the perspective of an insider. However, she'd need the rest of the season to understand the referee signals.

True to her word, Audrey kept Regina surrounded by friendly faces at games both home and away. The Morgans became another set of parents for the young couple. When the boys were able to attend games with Regina, the attentive university family would care for the boys so that she could focus on the game.

She was amused and somewhat flattered when Audrey orchestrated the seating arrangements at the game. Regina sat between Audrey and Veronica with John on the other side of Audrey and Richard on the other side of Veronica. Then a rotating host of other administrators would be recruited to cover the rear and front positions. They made certain that she was buffered from the unflattering remarks and demands hurtled at Thomas.

She also learned that not all the remarks tossed at

Thomas were unflattering, nor were they related to the game of basketball. Many of the women thought that it was okay to make comments about the coach's good looks or physique, even with his family present. These remarks, too, the administrators tried to keep from Regina. However, it was totally impossible not to hear and see the women's attempts to get Thomas's attention. Although Thomas claimed that he never heard or saw anything other than the game.

She knew that he was being truthful about tuning out his admirers because he was totally focused on the game. In fact, this was a different side of Thomas that Regina was surprised to see. Her gentle-spirited, playful husband turned into a maniac on the sidelines. He paced, screamed, and fell to his knees—praying at times and cursing at other times. She'd seen him jerk his tie off and yank off the collar button on his shirt as if he were suffocating. Before she'd seen him in action, he had bragged that his game was completely intellectual and that his superior strategies would win. However, at game time he was pure emotion. By the time the contests were over he was hoarse, drenched with perspiration, and full of pent-up energy.

After the games, there was only one way that he wanted to release that energy. Regina was glad that she was free to attend his games, because by sharing his experience she vicariously shared his emotions and could respond to his physical needs.

As soon as they were able to get to their rooms, they stripped off their clothes and met each other's needs without any conversation or pause. Caught up in their heat and passion, he felt as if he was consumed by the need to be with Regina. Her scent, her warmth drove his greed. In turn, his greed heightened her hunger and they did not stop until they were temporarily satisfied.

One night after a victorious game and the first heat of their lovemaking was at a lull, Regina lay sprawled across Thomas's torso in their hotel suite. He idly stroked her cooling back, noting that the heat was slow to leave their bodies. Tonight she had been like a fever, spreading through his body and setting a fire to his soul, leaving him weak and dazed. Her breathing had slowed to a normal rate and he had thought she was asleep until she rolled away from him and sat up in bed.

"I have a question," she said out of the blue in her straightforward way.

"Go ahead," he answered, suddenly motionless, preparing for anything that she might ask.

"Were you always like this after a game?" she asked.

"No. Never. Not until I married you," he answered, when it slowly dawned on him to what she was referring.

"What did you do after your games last year?" she persisted.

"I usually came up to the room with Tres and we watched cartoons or played video games. That's how he got so good at the games," Thomas explained.

"Why do you think you are so passionate after your games now?"

"Are you fishing for a compliment about how sexy you are?" he asked, cupping her hip in the palm of his large hand.

"No, I want a serious answer," she said, stilling his hand.

"I don't know. Before I met you I was practically numb from the waist down. All of my desires and dreams had died with my—with—Tres's—with her."

He was having difficulty thinking of how to refer to Paulette, Regina noted. He could no longer say "my wife" because he had a new wife and he could no longer refer to her as Tres's mother because most people now referred to Regina as Tres's mother. For some reason, he still could not say Paulette's name in front of Regina. It was almost like a man cheating on his wife.

Thomas continued, hoping to make Regina understand what his life had been like and how different he was with her. "But even before, it was never like this. Regina, you bring out things in me that I didn't know existed. Things that I don't understand myself." He reached up and pulled her head closer to his. Straining on one elbow, he whisked her lips with a kiss.

At that point, she forgot all of the other questions she was about to ask. She slid down in bed and back into her love's arms. Still on one elbow, he pulled her closer and kissed her forehead, then her nose. As his lips hovered over a target between her neck and silky-smooth shoulder, he was frozen by the surprising thrills shooting through his bloodstream when she firmly gripped his rigid member and began massaging it. With each upward stroke, she let her thumb caress the thick seam on the cap. The pleasure was too much for one man to bear.

This woman was full of surprises; he never knew what to expect from her. So far, to his delight, all of her surprises were full of pleasure for him. Oh, Lord, if only life could always be this good.

When he thought that he was about to explode, she stopped suddenly and invited him in. With a slight smile on her lips, she wrapped her arms around his neck and pulled him to her. "I know, I'm being selfish, but I want you inside me. I don't want to waste any time when we could be together completely."

He hovered over his petite wife for just a moment; looking into her eyes and seeing his own feelings reflected there, he entered her. Moving with an unconscious rhythm that neither he had created, nor could he control, he gave her the pleasure that she sought. Matching him beat for beat, she flowed with his rhythm. She became breathless, moaning a song of sweet release, and he quickly followed her.

The pattern was set for them. This was their way after every game, until the Renaissance team narrowly defeated the University of Nevada in Las Vegas when Regina decided to do things differently.

That night she suffered with total emotional attachment to Thomas. Feeling what he felt, she had challenged the referee calls, cursed the missed three-point shots, and mourned the injury of one of his best players. She felt that they'd been put through the wringer that night.

When the game was over Tres and Justin rushed to their father and stayed at the gymnasium with him while he went to the locker room with his players and coaching staff. She figured he'd be there for at least a half hour, but not much more, because he either congratulated his team when they won or consoled them when they lost. He saved the analysis of the game until Monday when they reviewed tapes and went through drills.

She caught a ride back to their hotel with Audrey and Veronica, hoping that she could get to their room, shower, and stage her setting before Thomas got in.

Veronica noted, "You seem rather agitated tonight. Do you have big plans for the evening?"

"Sort of," Regina hedged. "I'm a little tense because I always have a lot of pent-up energy after games."

"What do you guys do after the game, anyway? We never see you in the lounge or any of the parties?" Veronica continued.

"We, uh, we . . ." Regina stammered and flashed her big, bright mischievous smile.

"You don't have to answer that," Audrey cautioned.

"Well, I'll give you a clue—we like to be alone. After all, we've only been married three months," Regina said with all the poise she could muster, trying to keep the memories of their hot nights of raw passion from showing on her face. She desperately hoped that neither woman could read her mind.

"Don't you remember being a newlywed?" Audrey asked Veronica.

"Only slightly. It's a dim memory, very dim," Veronica joked.

"You go on up to your room, honey," Audrey said gently. "Even if the coach did come down after the game, he wouldn't have any fun. He'd get more advice and criticism than he needs. You're doing the right thing."

Tonight, Regina had decided, she was going to make her husband say that he loved her. While she tried to reassure herself that she knew he loved her because she could see it in his eyes and in the way he treated her, a stubborn streak that she couldn't get rid of insisted that she had to hear the words.

How could he continue making love to her, without saying the words? Was it merely her role to help him release his pent-up energy after the games? Lust had its place, she had to admit, but tonight she wanted love.

In their suite, Regina quickly showered and put on the slinky, gold silk negligee that she'd bought but never worn for their wedding night. The soft, swirling pleats of the gown complemented her hips and made her look taller. She slipped her feet into gold satin bedroom slippers that had tiny bows near the toes. After a final inspection in the mirror, she brushed her hair back from her face and pulled a few stray hairs from her eyebrows. Just before room service knocked at the door to deliver their dinner, she sprayed a mist of cologne and walked through it.

Shortly afterward, Thomas walked in with the jubilant smile on his face that he usually wore after a major victory. He took one step toward her and she put up a hand to stop him. She could see the Adam's apple bob in his throat as he swallowed hard.

"What's wrong?" he asked.

"Slow down a little bit, baby. Hold your horses," she said, standing far enough away from him to look into his eyes. She saw the heat and lust simmering there.

"Baby, you really look good," he said, thinking that she wanted him to compliment her attire. "Your eyes are so beautiful. Are you using a new makeup?"

"No, silly, I combed my bangs back, that's all," she said, taking another step away from him. She tried to remain light and playful, despite the intense lust shining in his eyes.

He took another step toward her. "It smells so good in here and you look so damn good. I just want to feel you in my arms to see if you're real," he said, his voice raspy from all the yelling he'd been doing for the past couple of hours.

"Let's do something different tonight," she said, walking toward the table. "Why don't you eat first while your dinner is still hot? I've got prime rib, loaded baked potatoes, baby carrots, broccoli, and apple pie."

He watched the swirling gold float around her as she walked. A belt cinched the fabric at her narrow waist, and then it flowed gracefully across her round hips, and the movement of her legs created a flurry of gold near her feet. He looked at her with an ache inside him growing so strong that he could barely hear what she said.

She raised the silver dome from one of the plates. "Don't you want to eat?" she asked.

"You know what I'm hungry for, Gina. I'm too pumped up to eat. We just beat UNLV by twelve points. They beat us by ten last year. I want to celebrate. I need to release some energy," he said, feeling rather desperate to make her understand how he was feeling.

"After every game we tumble into bed like a couple of teenagers. Tonight I thought we'd talk, relax, and enjoy the ambience."

"What if I don't want to do that?" he asked stubbornly, like one of the children.

"Then you'll never see what's under this gown, she said, unbelting her robe and letting the soft fabric caress her shoulders as it slid to the floor. Her soft dark shoulders were silky in the glow of the candlelight and her heavy firm breasts stood high, straining the silken fabric across her chest.

He felt like he had to touch her or go crazy. How could anyone this beautiful be real? He walked toward her as if he were in a daze, and when he was close enough he kissed her shoulder. When she didn't move from him, he wrapped her in his embrace and kissed her lustfully as his big hands roamed her body.

"Don't you want to see your interview on television tonight?" she asked in between kisses.

"No, Sonia will record it," he said, walking her toward the bed.

"It was a good game tonight, baby," she said, trying to get him to slow his pace.

"Yeah, but not nearly as good as you are. You smell so good," he said, bending to nestle his lips at her neck.

She put both hands on his chest and gently pushed him away. "If you're not hungry, I am. Sit down and keep me company while I eat."

He was so surprised by her continued resistance to his advances that he simply stared at her as she took a seat at one of the two place settings and removed the silver dome from the food and set it aside. One of the thin straps of her gown slipped from her shoulder. She casually slid it back; then in a second, the other one slipped. She raised a hand to put it back in place, but he stilled her hand.

His hot hand sent fire straight to her soul. Totally unnerved by his touch, she wasn't sure if she could resist him much longer. She looked up at him and was puzzled by the mischievous smile she found there.

"Tell you what, Gina," he said seductively. "I'll do whatever you say if you'll do what I say."

"I don't know," she hesitated.

"This is your game tonight, but can't I make one rule? It's only fair," he cajoled.

"Okay. But I say when we go to bed. Deal?" she said after considering his offer.

He took a seat across from her and began eating slowly. "Before I continue eating, I'd like to improve the view."

She raised a questioning eyebrow, but said nothing.

"Could you please lower the straps on your gown?" he requested.

She looked at him quizzically, not quite understanding what he wanted.

"The gown. I want you to let the straps fall from your shoulders. You're having trouble keeping them up anyway," he clarified.

She was game for whatever he wanted to play. Boldly meeting his eyes without wavering, she shrugged one strap from her shoulder, then the other. Without moving her eyes from his, she lifted one arm, then the other from the confines of the straps and lowered the gown to her waist.

When she lowered her eyes, he lowered his and almost gasped when he saw her firm, beautiful breasts jutting out across the edge of the table. A combination of cold air and his lustful gaze immediately hardened her nipples. The dark nipples looked like firm, ripe berries. Now he was really hungry and had no appetite whatsoever for the food he'd tried to eat for her.

"Is this what you wanted?" she asked in her soft, sultry voice.

"Yes," he answered through the lump growing in his throat that was almost as constricting as the lump between his legs.

"Would you like champagne now?" she asked calmly, noting that whatever he'd planned for her had obviously backfired. He was the one suffering great discomfort.

"Yes, wine will be nice." Maybe the champagne would clear his throat so that he could swallow the prime rib he'd been chewing for a while.

She gracefully reached to her side where the champagne rested in a silver wine cooler. Just as calmly as if she were fully dressed, she lifted the bottle, poured a glass for him, then one for her. Her breasts jiggled and swayed with her movement. He was completely enthralled, unable to take his eyes off her. Without the least bit of embarrassment, she offered a stemmed goblet to him. Their fingers accidentally brushed, sending hot sparks between them. She smiled to acknowledge the feeling, but said nothing.

As if they were having dinner at their kitchen table with the children present, she asked him about the game. "Why did the referee give the UNLV coach a technical file?" she questioned him.

He actually could not remember. He barely remembered the game at all. Slowly his pulse and heartbeat returned to a more normal pace as she talked about everyday matters. His plan to turn the tables on her and to speed her to bed had backfired. She was still in control.

"Gina?"

"Yes, dear?" she answered in a sweet, everyday voice.

"I'd like to make my champagne sweeter," he said with that mischievous gleam in his eyes, warning her that he was up to something again.

"Here's the sugar," she said, passing him the silver-plated sugar bowl.

"I'd rather suck my champagne off your breasts," he said smoothly. "They'll make it sweet."

"Of course, that sounds nice," she replied evenly. He raised one eyebrow, but said nothing. He was surprised that she had not balked yet.

He walked around the table and turned her chair around with her still sitting in it. Getting on his knees before her, he watched her face as he slowly poured the bubbly gold liquid over one breast and then the other. Before her body had adjusted to the shock of the cold liquid, his hot tongue was licking it away. He followed the slope of her breasts with his tongue, taking away every trace of the recent libation. He removed the trail between her breasts and then eased her gown down to suck the liquid from her navel.

When she thought that she could stand no more, he stuck his fingers in the shallow remains still in the glass and used it to paint her nipples. After they'd been totally saturated in the champagne, he sucked one, then the other, making greedy noises like a nursing baby. She cradled his head in her hands and cried out from the erotic pleasure.

He lifted his head and gave her a satisfied smirk. "It looks like it's run lower. I need to pull your gown further down. Raise your hips, please," he instructed her. "Let's get rid of this wet gown." She obeyed with no argument.

"Just as I thought, there's champagne between your legs. I'll get it."

She gave up trying to resist. His hungry licking and sucking had her spinning out of control. Being with her husband felt entirely too good. When she'd finally returned to earth, her only desire was to make him feel as good as she did. "You have to say when we go to bed," he reminded her.

"Let's go to bed now," she said quickly.

When they were on the bed, she rolled him to his back. Sitting astride his pelvis, she slowly began to caress his body with hers. She stroked his chest with her fingertips and rubbed his nipples with the soft palm of her hands.

He tried to control her movements, but she took his hands from her hips and stretched them above his head. In order to do this, of course, she had to stretch out on him. When her breasts were near his mouth, he tried to catch them as if he were bobbing for apples.

"Tonight, Coach Simmons, I'm going to give you pleasure like you've never known before," she whispered in his ear.

"Every time I'm with you, I experience pleasure like I've never known," he answered, trying to get comfortable with the idea that he couldn't touch her. She was doing things to him that were driving him out of his mind.

"Relax and enjoy your flight, sir. You're about to fly Air Regina. Remember to keep your arms above your head and also remember I'm in charge."

Through the rest of the night, they took one another to ecstasy, each trying to give more pleasure than the other. Finally, their energy spent, they fell into an exhausted sleep.

The phone rang too early the next morning, but Regina was instantly alert. Tres and Justin had spent the night in the room with Conway Howard and his roommate. She had confidence in Conway because he had worked in youth summer programs at home and had a good rapport with the children.

Yet, Regina listened to Thomas's responses on the phone until she could determine that the call had nothing to do with their children. Something was wrong, but at least not with her children. She got out of bed and placed the uneaten food from the night before on a tray and set it outside the door to the suite.

Thomas was still on the phone when she returned, so she decided to take a quick shower. Because he had a seat on the president's plane for their return flight, she was sure he'd want to assemble the team in their suite before their departure.

By the time she came out of the shower, Thomas was dressed and ready to head out the door. "One of my players is missing. We've got to find him."

"How are you going to do that here? You don't even know your way around this town."

"Mathews and I are going together, while Davis and Smith get the rest of the team ready to go. Their flight leaves at one this afternoon."

"But Mathews knows Las Vegas as little as you do," Regina responded. Seeing the look on his face she quickly added, "I'll be here."

She spent the morning packing. She realized that she always traveled with too much, but she reasoned that with a tall and handsome husband she wouldn't get noticed walking beside him if she was some dowdy little housewife. Flashy was the only way to go, she reasoned, if she didn't want to get lost next to him.

The others in their party, more conservative faculty and administrators, indulged her because she was in the entertainment industry. It was okay for her to be flashy. They did not realize that her attire had nothing

292   *Christine Townsend*

to do with the entertainment industry, but everything to do with having a young gorgeous husband who was still being chased by unscrupulous women.

As she packed the gown from the night before, she reflected on their night of lovemaking. Well, her plan had certainly backfired last night. She had wanted to hold out on their lovemaking until Thomas said that he loved her. Not only did she not get any declarations of love from him, she had convinced herself that she was totally lost in him. He could absorb her soul and spirit so easily. She was one with him and she wasn't complaining. She knew that she was a strong woman, but with him she became molten iron.

No, she certainly wasn't complaining. Her husband was a wonderful lover and she couldn't get enough of being with him. She loved him so much that she could not imagine how she had ever lived without him. She would resign herself to never hearing the words *I love you* from his lips as long as he continued to adore her.

Count your blessings, silly girl. She heard her mother's voice in her head as she listed Thomas's virtues for her. *You've got a good-looking man, who has never once asked you to do anything that you don't want to do. He's ready to adopt Justin as soon as you receive the signed documents from Justin's natural father. He has his paycheck deposited to your joint account and in three months of marriage, he's never once asked how you've spent his money.*

Okay, Mom, you're right, she said silently. Just six months ago, she was envying Shelby's marriage and sweet romance. Now she had her very own. The Lord had indeed been good to her. But what was it that made Thomas hold back just a little of himself? Why was he still holding on to Paulette so fiercely? He would not say Paulette's name in front of Regina, almost as if he felt guilty. Perhaps all of this was just her imagination.

Toward noon the men gave up looking for Myron, the missing player, but when they returned to the hotel they found him in his bed. "Get up, Myron," Thomas said, barely able to control his anger.

"Hey, keep it down, man. I've got a headache," the athlete answered, turning his face to the wall.

Thomas went to the other side of the bed and lifted the mattress, dumping the player to the floor. "What's up with this?" Myron yelled.

"Where were you last night?" Thomas asked through clenched teeth with his fists at this sides, ready for whatever came up.

"Stop bugging me, man. I'm here on time. I didn't miss my flight," the player said, sitting on the floor, looking rather ridiculous.

"Hit the shower. We'll talk when you smell better," Thomas answered.

"Damn, this is Sunday. Don't you ever take a day off?"

"You're my responsibility. What you do reflects on me, your team, and the university. Now hit the showers and we'll finish this conversation when your head is clear. I want you to remember what I'm going to tell you."

When Myron came back, he was still arrogant and anxious to show Coach how irritated he was with his intrusion. "Coach, you may not know this, but I'm a man just the same as you. What makes you think you can tell me what to do?"

"The authority that makes me your coach is the same authority that allows me to tell you what to do," Thomas answered evenly. "Now where were you last night?"

"I was with some hoes. You know prostitution is legal in Nevada," Myron answered with a smirk.

"It's not legal for you. You had a curfew and your

curfew was midnight. At seven o'clock this morning, I was awakened from bed and had to ride around half the day looking for you," Thomas said, no longer able to contain his anger. His players knew that he did not tolerate derogatory terms for females, regardless of what the females had done or who they were.

"Yeah, you were up in bed with that fine little wife, but I'm supposed to go to bed with a bone on. What kind of mess is that?"

"I'll tell you what. Until you decide that you can follow my rules, you'll be playing on the bench."

"Hell, no. I'm not taking that. I'll go to the NBA," the boy-man said, jumping from his chair and standing over his coach. At six feet eight inches tall the athlete was several inches taller than Coach Simmons.

"I don't see anyone lined up to draft you," Thomas said in a neutral voice.

"You can't take me out of the game. If you do, I'll never get drafted. They won't see me playing," the young man said, sounding like a desperate child.

"Myron, you've broken my rules one time too many. You can ride the bench or turn in your uniform," Thomas said and stormed out the door.

Thomas returned to his suite in a foul mood. He didn't want to tell Regina about it, but he knew he owed her some explanation. He briefly told her as they hurried to meet with their group for the flight home.

Final exams started that week and the team had to slack up on practice. To Thomas, getting an education was still the number-one priority for his student athletes. Since he was home more that week, Regina was able to spend a little time with Tiffany. They had felt a real affinity for one another. Both had left a circle of friends at work, and now they were rather isolated. Tiffany had been a corporate attorney, but wasn't sure if she would return to work.

One day while Thomas stayed with the boys, Regina picked up two box lunches from the Cooker Restaurant and went to keep Tiffany company. They were sitting and talking after they'd eaten every morsel of cheese/potato soup and chicken salad sandwiches. "O-h-h-h. Another pain," Tiffany would moan from time to time during their conversation.

Regina became concerned. "You've been saying that about every fifteen minutes. Are you sure that they're not contractions?"

"I don't think so, but they could be," Tiffany answered.

Regina discreetly looked at her watch the next couple of times Tiffany moaned. "Girlfriend, they're getting real regular now. You'd better call Andre. I'll see if Thomas will pick up the children from school. I'll stay with you until Andre gets home."

Andre was in court until five o'clock and as far as his secretary knew, they would not have another recess. She promised to try to get a message to him. When the contractions were five minutes a part, Regina said, "Okay, it's time to call your obstetrician. Let's swing into action."

Regina calmly drove Tiffany to the hospital, discussing everything from the scenery to last week's game as they drove. At the emergency room, when a nurse put Tiffany in a wheelchair to prepare her for delivery, Regina went through Tiffany's wallet to find the insurance card and other information the hospital would require.

When she was finished with the admitting clerk, Regina discovered Tiffany had been moved to a delivery room. "Remember your Lamaze. You know what to do," Regina said, stroking Tiffany's forehead.

"Where is my husband? He'd better get in here and watch me suffer," the demure little southern belle roared so that the whole wing could hear her.

When Andre finally arrived, Regina felt as if her fingers had been welded together where the delicate Tiffany had squeezed her hand so tightly. "Here, you take over," Regina said, gladly relinquishing her role as labor coach.

"Get this thing out of me," Tiffany demanded through clenched teeth.

Regina backed toward the door. "Since you're here, I'll be leaving now."

"Don't you leave me with these men," Tiffany yelled. "They don't know what I'm going through. You're the only one who understands." Now she was crying pitifully.

Regina relented and told Tiffany that she would be back as soon as she found a place where she could call Thomas. She walked through the hospital, trying to find a safe place to use her cell phone. After explaining the situation to Thomas, he assured her that he would have things under control at home. The boys were at the gym with him, but he'd leave early enough to pick up dinner and have them in bed on time.

"By the way, Regina, there's a packet here from Nigeria," he said before they hung up.

"Do you think it's from Peter?" she asked.

"It looks like it might be, although there's only a return address with no name."

"Open it if you like. I'd better go up and take care of Tiffany."

She was entering the hospital room when she heard Andre say, "I see his head." She hurried to Tiffany's side.

"It's a damn big head, too," Tiffany said between grunts. "It must have a big basketball head like his father's."

Regina looked at Andre and laughed. "Don't you ever say anything about my being foul. Your princess has me beat any day."

Within the next few minutes, Andre and Tiffany became the proud parents of a little boy who weighed eleven pounds and fourteen ounces. Regina quietly left the room as the new parents inspected their little bundle.

When Regina returned home late that night, she tiredly walked into the master bedroom where Thomas was sitting in bed dosing. He awakened instantly when she entered the room and listened quietly as she described the miracle she'd just witnessed. When she told him about Tiffany saying Andre had a basketball head he laughed aloud.

She lay down next to him and rested her head on his chest. He stroked her back and said, "I know that you must be exhausted. You didn't plan on this today, did you?"

"Well, you know how babies are. They come when they decide and everything has to stop for them." She yawned loudly and sat up. "I'm going to get dressed for bed. I'm too tired to think."

"Oh, there's one more thing for you to think about. The packet from Nigeria is on the nightstand," he said. "I opened it and read the letter that Peter wrote to Justin."

"What did it say?"

"Read it. I think I like this guy. He sounds like he really wanted to put Justin's welfare first. I believe that Justin will be glad to have the letter now and it will be something to hold on to as he grows older."

Regina pulled the letter from between the legal papers and read:

Justin, my dear son,

You are my first son and will always have a special place in my heart. I have other children and perhaps your mother will, too. But you were our first. I want you to know that you were born of love. I loved your mother deeply when I knew her. She was a pretty, bright, and energetic college student and I found it impossible not to love her.

However, a commitment to my family forced me to return to my home country, leaving your mother behind at a bad time. But I did not know that she was pregnant when I left. I asked your mother to come with me, but being an American, she refused to give up her way of life to come live with me here, far from everyone and everything she knows. I understand because, given the choice, I would have stayed in America and become an American like you and your mother. But my obligations are greater than my personal wishes.

Although I have not spent much time with you, I know that you are a lot like your mother. With her influence in your life daily, I know that you too will be talented, intellectually gifted, and very blessed.

Your mother has asked that I let Thomas Simmons become your father. She says that he is good to you, is a positive influence in your life, and is also intelligent and patient. Those are the virtues that I want you to grow up surrounded by. Having this new father is better than having no father at all and since an ocean and continents separate us, for now, I am like no father at all. However, I also believe that it takes a man to raise a man. I am glad that you will have a man to raise you, to care for you, and to teach you the things a man should know.

Please know that I love you, Justin. You are my son born of a deep and passionate love. I relinquish my role and rights as your father only because I cannot be with you on a daily basis. I relinquish my rights only in a legal sense for the American judicial system. However, I will not relinquish my love for you. I will love you forever. I am still your father in every way, except legally.

Should you ever need me, just call. Yes, we do have

*phones in Nigeria. There is no ocean wide enough or
deep enough to keep me from coming to you. We also
have e-mail. Please use the enclosed address to contact
me via the Internet.*

With love, your father, Peter

Regina refolded the letter and put it back into the
envelope. "I'm glad he wrote this. I would hate to have
Justin grow up thinking that his father didn't want
him," she said.

"Now all we have to do is pass these signed documents
on to Andre and wait for a court date," Thomas sighed.

"Yes, I'll take them to him as soon as he returns to
his office," Regina agreed.

"I guess Andre will be out of the office for a few
days?" Thomas asked.

"I think so. His labor was pretty rough." Regina
laughed.

Chapter 14

At Christmastime, Thomas wanted to invite students who were unable to go home to come stay with the Simmonses for the holidays. They had made the same offer at Thanksgiving and had spent the long holiday weekend entertaining several students from a variety of the university's athletic programs. This time all of their takers were students from foreign countries who could not afford to travel home for a relatively short visit.

Thanksgiving weekend had been okay, but Regina was hesitant about inviting guests for an extended period of time into what she felt were already cramped quarters. However, Thomas and the director of international student affairs assured her that the students would be grateful to be with a family for the holidays. The accommodations would be quite adequate.

Thomas almost rescinded on his offer to host the students when Regina begged off attending his games shortly before Christmas so that she could entertain their houseguests. "Look, Thomas, I just can't go with you this time," she tried to explain. "We can't invite the young people to stay with us, then turn around and leave them."

Remembering that Julia Lovejoy was very upset that Regina was not bringing her family home to Alabama for Christmas, Thomas had a burst of inspiration.

"What if I get Madame Julia to come chaperone the household while we're away? Will you go with me then?"

"She'll never come. Let me tell you, our accommodations definitely will not be adequate for her," Regina warned.

"Remember those words, sweetheart, because in about five minutes you're going to have to eat them," Thomas bragged.

Getting Julia to agree to come to Nashville was more difficult than Thomas had thought it would be. At first Julia refused to travel away from home during the holidays, saying that the young couple did not need the additional burden of a mother-in-law. But Thomas was persistent. "Come on, Julia. We need you here. It's been a tough basketball season for Regina and we have a game a few days before Christmas and one three days after Christmas. On top of that we have students from all over the world who are staying at our house during the holidays. If anybody ever needed you, we need you here," Thomas pleaded.

"I don't know, Thomas," she said, "I just don't want to be in the way."

"In the way! Oh, no, Julia. We need someone here who can bring order out of this chaos," Thomas was now begging.

"You just want me to come up there and cook for you," Julia guessed, still trying to gauge his sincerity. "I told Regina that she needs to learn to cook. That's fundamental to managing a household."

"No, no. We don't need a cook. We have the cooking under control. Regina has made a schedule and each student is responsible for dinner on a specific night. They had a ball grocery shopping and educating everyone about their native recipes. We're eating the most interesting things. All we need from you is to keep an eye on things so that Regina can go to the games in Illinois and Kentucky with me. The house will be all yours. You'll be in charge and you can stay as long as you like. We really need you," Thomas pleaded, feeling her resolve melting.

That cinched it for Julia. "You've got a deal then," she said, eagerly accepting the invitation.

"My mother is actually coming, but it did take you thirty minutes to convince her," Regina said pointedly. "I guess I don't have to eat my words after all."

"No, it took me longer than expected, but I still got the desired results. Now congratulate me," Thomas said, trying to recover his deflated ego.

"Oh, no. Now I have to entertain Mama on top of everything else," Regina exclaimed, though surprised that Julia had agreed to come at all.

"You guys seem to be getting along so much better. I thought you would enjoy her company," Thomas said in answer to Regina's concern.

"We do get along better. I guess old habits are hard to break and I don't need her to come here making suggestions on how I could keep house better. I'm new at this," Regina complained.

"Your mother will be a big help. When we're not on the road, she'll give you a chance to visit with Tiffany and spoil the baby or anything else you want to do that you can't do with the children tagging along," Thomas suggested.

Julia came and immediately got caught up organizing the household for the holidays. She received no complaints from anyone when she started cooking big holiday meals. The students were ready to give up kitchen duty and Julia didn't want them "messing up" in the kitchen. That Regina had no plans to do any major holiday cooking was a no-brainer for anyone who knew her. She spent the day making a batch of fudge, becoming bored in the middle of the task, and finishing as quickly as possible with no plans to return to the kitchen any time soon.

Regina caught up on visits with Tiffany, Rosemary, and her other friends while Julia and their other visitors enjoyed taking care of the boys. One day, miraculously, Julia and Regina found themselves alone. The students had taken Tres and Justin to the ice rink. When Regina asked Julia what she wanted to do, she admitted that she was itching to see Tiffany and Andre's baby that she'd heard so much about. The new baby was an instant hit with Julia.

Julia eagerly picked up the round bundle and began to cuddle him in a nearby rocker. "I know I'm not supposed to hold the baby too much. But I just love rocking him," Tiffany confessed.

Julia advised, "Tiffany, there is no way that a newborn can be spoiled. Hold this baby as much as possible because one day he'll be all grown and will barely let you touch him."

"You're not talking about me are you, Mama?" Regina asked.

"You're my only baby, so everything I know is based on my experience with you. But as an elementary school teacher, I can definitely distinguish between the children who are in loving homes and those who are not. Let me tell you, some people don't know how to love their children."

Regina was surprised that she'd never noticed this softness in her mother before.

The two weeks of the activity-filled holiday season sped by and before Regina realized it, the students were moving back on campus and the boys were back in school to finish up their first grade year. The thought that her mother's two-week stay was over too soon caught Regina by surprise. She had actually enjoyed Julia's visit this time.

Regina was sitting on the guest room bed watching her mother pack when Julia stopped what she was doing to sit next to her. The mother took her daughter's hand in her own very similar hand and looked at them both. Regina's hand was still youthful and unlined. Julia's, though just as small, was beginning to show age around the knuckles.

"There's something on my mind that I must discuss with you before I leave. I feel a certain reserve in you when you're around Thomas that I didn't notice before. I don't know what it is, but you need to resolve it. I know that sometimes I would get upset with you because you have to talk through everything, but this time I think you *should* talk."

"There's nothing—well, maybe there is something, I can't talk about it because I can't exactly put my finger on it yet. I know I shouldn't complain. I know that you keep telling me that I have more than enough. You've also told me to count my blessings, and I do. I am thankful for what I have and I feel that I have no right to complain."

"But you do have a complaint?" Julia asked, raising one professionally sculpted eyebrow.

"No—Yes. We're just so busy right now that I can't figure it all out. I don't know what's wrong with me," Regina tried explaining to her mother.

"You will always be busy. You have to choose your time. By the way, how far along are you?" her mother surprised her by asking.

"What? What are you talking about?"

"I'm your mother and I know you inside and out. I'm the one who walked the floor with you through strep throat and pneumonia. I can see every change in your body. It's very early, but you have that same look in your eyes that you had when you were pregnant with Justin. I think you should get your iron checked. The whites of your eyes have a yellowish tinge," Julia said, looking directly into almond eyes so like her own.

"I just had my period two weeks ago, I can't be pregnant. If I am, it'll be a miracle," Regina said softly.

"Why do you say that? You're both young and healthy," Julia said.

"Thomas had a vasectomy when his first wife was ill. I knew before we married that we wouldn't have any more children, but I can accept that. We're blessed with two wonderful children. That's more than a lot of people get," Regina said seriously.

"Then you're in for a miracle. I'm fairly certain that you are pregnant. You need to resolve whatever problems you're having with your husband. Talk with him. He's a good man, he'll listen. You two can fix whatever it is," Julia encouraged.

"Thanks, Mama. I'll take your advice," Regina said, hugging her mother. She wondered how in the world she could talk with Thomas when he would barely let her mention Paulette. Her problem had something to do with Paulette, but she couldn't quite say what. Regina only knew that her husband should be able to say his first wife's name around her and he couldn't. She also knew that he should be able to tell her that he loved her and he couldn't.

"I see you have a lot to figure out. I'm just asking the questions. You don't have to answer them for me, but you need the answers so that you can be happy," Julia said and kissed her daughter on the cheek.

The ringing phone interrupted their mother-daughter talk. "Hey, girl, what's up?" a familiar voice greeted Regina.

"Jimmy Bob, how are you?"

"Missing you. At least after you got married to that dude, I could still see you from time to time. Now he doesn't even let you out of the house and you don't even bother to call us." Jimmy Bob laughed.

"I miss you too, Jimmy Bob. Now tell me why you're really calling," Regina said, joining his laughter.

"Just to tell you merry Christmas. I know I'm about a week late, but I was waiting for you to call me. I don't think your husband likes for me to call the house too much," her friend said, only half joking because in truth, Thomas did not care for Jimmy Bob's calls.

"I know you, Jimmy Bob, you have a big news break. I hear the excitement in your voice and I know that Santa wasn't that good to you. What else is going on?" Regina prodded.

Without further prompting, he said, "I know that you don't hang out on Music Row anymore. I hear you haven't even worked on the Tin Pan South Committee?" he questioned.

"That's right. I spent three years building the project up; now it's time for fresh ideas. What's the word, Jimmy Bob?" Regina asked again.

"So you probably haven't heard all the buzz."

"What's the buzz?"

"*Sweet Romance* will be nominated for album of the year. Shelby's been nominated for Best Female Artist and we are up for the Songwriters of the Year Nomination," Jimmy Bob said triumphantly.

"Congratulations," Regina said sincerely, but sedately.

"You don't have to go shout it from the rooftops or anything, but I did expect a little more excitement," he responded.

"I am excited, it just hasn't sunk in yet."

"Girl, do you know what this will do for your career—for our careers? You can write your own ticket."

"That's pretty much what I'm going to have to do anyway. I haven't written anything for a long time. I'll get back to it in the spring."

"Well, if you need any help, you know the drill," Jimmy Bob said before hanging up.

The day after Julia left, Paul and Sara Evans had a planned layover in their flight from Boca Raton. It was good seeing the older couple again. They'd not come to the wedding, explaining that it would be too difficult for them. Since the wedding, however, they had called frequently and were extremely kind to the young couple.

When Thomas explained that they were about to take the boys to a sitter so that they could get on the road for a game, Paul and Sara offered to stay longer. In fact, they were eager to have the boys to themselves.

Regina and Thomas were in Houston on January 3, then on to Salt Lake City on January 5, and by the end of the week they were in Dayton, Ohio, at Wright State University. Regina was exhausted by the time they returned home, but as usual she was glad that she'd been with Thomas.

The team had suffered a devastating defeat in Ohio and Thomas had needed Regina more than ever that night. Whereas victory was an aphrodisiac, the defeat called for something to soothe his aching spirit. What better balm for a battered ego than good hot sex with the woman he loved? As soon as he entered the hotel room, she melted into his arms and felt his fire, letting his ignite one within her. They could barely remove their clothes. They were driven by the urgency of the intense heat between them. She'd given up trying to slow him down because she was usually smoldering too. Win or lose, their passion was intense.

At the beginning of the new semester, the team record was twelve wins and two losses. The prognosticators moved the team from seventh in the conference to third. Thomas swore that before playoffs, they would be number one. People no longer doubted him.

To Regina's dismay, they had as many games left as they'd already played—not including the tournament games. What kind of sadist made this schedule? Then she remembered that the sadist was her wonderful, attentive, and ambitious husband.

After the Ohio defeat, Myron had gone in to see Coach Simmons. "How long am I supposed to be benched?" he asked.

"Until you tell me that you understand my rules and show me a change," Thomas said evenly.

"That's bogus, man. You know you need me on the team. With a few of my three-point shots outside the paint, we could have had Ohio," the young man boasted.

Unimpressed, the coach answered, "We'll never know what you could have done in Ohio because you were on the bench. You let your team down." He fixed Myron with his penetrating gaze. Noting no contrition whatsoever, he realized that the boy had not come to apologize but to force the coach to put him back on the team.

"No, Coach, you let the team down. It doesn't make any sense, replacing me with that freshman. Conway let them push him around the court. You won't have a chance at the championships without me." Myron was almost pleading, but his attitude was still defiant.

"Yes, we do. We have a real good chance. We have a lot of disciplined talent on the team. Winning championships is not my top priority, but discipline is. Without discipline we don't have a chance," Thomas reminded the student athlete. "This was the third time you broke curfew in one semester. Obviously you have no interest in following my rules. Why are you here?"

"Just waiting for the NBA, man. Just waiting for the NBA," Myron said, rubbing his stomach under his shirt.

"Then wait somewhere else. Until I see a change in you and get a commitment that you understand and respect my rules, the NBA will see you sitting on the bench," Thomas said, rising from his seat and walking Myron to the door.

"Screw this," the young man said, slamming the door against the wall on the way out.

Although the team's star, Myron, had sat out the last five games, the team's standing in the conference had improved. Excitement was high at Renaissance and throughout the community with the thought of having their team play in the NCAA Tournament. Thomas was contemplating this in his office in the Raven Center Complex one day in February when Veronica stormed into his office.

"Thomas, you've been accused of NCCA violations," she said without any greeting.

"Is it because of the money Regina gave to the program? I thought that they accepted our self-investigation and the issue was resolved."

"No, this is something new. I just got off the phone. They're going to fax the charges to me. They have received an anonymous call accusing you of academic fraud. At first they were going to dismiss it as a crank call, but today they received documentation that supports the accusations," Veronica said with agitation obvious in her voice.

"Against me? Why? Which students?" Thomas asked incredulously.

"They said that they have real solid proof that you

had final grades changed for Conway, Michael, and Timothy."

"Those students are academically well qualified. Conway scored a twenty-six on the ACT. Why would anyone think that I would have to change his grade?"

"Well, it was his first semester in college. One could suggest that he was having adjustment problems. Did you talk to Rosa about his English grade?"

"Yes, of course. One of her part-time instructors gave all the basketball players in his class an I, saying that their course work was incomplete. He was well aware that they would be away at a game before he scheduled an exam, but he held them accountable for it. After they returned, he gave the students the exam, but apparently he never went back to change the grade. When I talked to Dr. Johnson about it, she completed the forms to remove the I's and submitted the new grades. It's all on record," Thomas explained.

"So Dr. Johnson can corroborate your story?" Veronica asked.

"Certainly. It was just a few weeks ago, shortly before Christmas. She should have the documentation," he said earnestly.

"We'd better get the athletics committee together, especially our faculty representative. You know the faculty will get their drawers all in a knot if they think athletics is trying to shirk our duty to academics. We don't want them to think that we're trying to hide anything." Veronica stood to leave, then stopped at the door. "Is that all, Thomas?"

"Yes, Veronica, that's all," he said firmly. Walking with her to the corridor, he stopped as if the thought had just occurred to him and asked, "Do you think a faculty member planted this story?" He was trying to fight a sinking feeling of déjà vu.

"Who knows? You know as well as I do, it could have

come from an opposing team, the faculty, or anyone," Veronica said, looking squarely at Thomas. "Get ready for the meeting. It'll be at five o'clock."

The faculty senate stormed the meeting of the athletics committee. Rather than sitting on the sidelines as interested observers as was customary, the senate was quite vocal. Dr. Henry, a man who was enamored with his power as head of the faculty senate, pretty much told the athletics committee that he and his group believed the unknown accuser over any defense that Thomas might have.

In his intellectual arrogance, Dr. Henry admitted that he did not believe that it was possible for someone who dribbled a basketball for a living could favor academic excellence over winning games.

Ruled by emotions and his long-held belief that the athletic department received more than its fair share of the university's budget, Dr. Henry turned the meeting into a free-for-all. When the athletics committee chair reminded the group of their purpose and requested that the discussions stay focused, Dr. Henry turned the discussion to all of his pet peeves about athletics. He complained that the head basketball coach's salary was greater than that of any person holding a doctorate. Further, he complained that the university spent more for weights in the training room than for microscopes in biology.

Once Dr. Henry got the ball rolling, another professor suggested, "Scholarships for athletics far outnumber the scholarships allocated for academics." No one wanted to address the documentation that Thomas presented on retention rates, graduation rates, and grade point averages of the athletes. They did not want the aggregate numbers, but they did want it for individual athletes.

A third member of the faculty senate threw out, "I

believe that the athlete's major, grade point average, and academic advisor should be posted for all to see."

Thomas, who had tried to remain neutral during the confrontational meeting, could not restrain himself a moment longer. "No, that's not what we should do! These boys have rights that should be respected. That would be an invasion of their privacy."

"What are you trying to hide, Simmons?" Dr. Henry asked.

By this time the chairman had given up on keeping the group from getting tangential. The complaints grew, but none had anything to do with the allegations of academic fraud. Thomas felt as if he had become the whipping boy for all that was wrong between academics and athletics.

Things disintegrated to the point that those who supported athletics, who were in fact the majority of the faculty, actually left. Thomas and Veronica were left alone with the vitriolic minority. After meeting for nearly five hours without anything resembling a resolution, a subcommittee was appointed to work with the university's compliance officer. They would investigate the charges and present their findings within the next three days.

Satisfied that he'd had his opportunity to beat up on the athletic department, Dr. Henry was silent as the subcommittee was selected. He reminded the group that Dr. Morgan wanted this mess cleared up as quickly as possible.

Thomas headed home feeling depressed with a foreboding sense of gloom. After pressing the garage door opener, he sat at the mouth of the garage looking at all of Regina's boxes lining the walls on all sides. They were things that she felt they would need first in the new house. If he lost his job, there could be no new house.

In a flash, he decided that he wouldn't tell her about the violations yet. She was quick to worry at this point because they were living on one income and she had not published a song since their marriage. For some reason, she didn't feel that her royalty checks counted as income, although he was quite impressed by the sum they added to their joint account.

Something was up with Regina anyway. Over the past few days, his talkative, energetic wife had been quiet and lethargic. He had silently waited for her to tell him what was wrong for several days. It was so unlike her to suffer in silence.

Regina sat at the kitchen table waiting for Thomas to come in. She was certain that she'd heard the hum of the motor raising the garage door. Tonight they would talk. She was no longer going to hint or wait for him to think of the words on his own. For some insane reason, she needed to hear the words *I love you* from his lips. She needed to hear the words before she told him that she was pregnant. She wasn't sure if he'd say them then, because she wasn't quite sure how he would feel about the baby.

After taking the home pregnancy test three mornings in a row, she was now positive that she was pregnant—vasectomy or no vasectomy. She wondered if he'd had the vasectomy because he truly did not want any more children, or was it simply to protect his wife as he'd stated? What was the saying from that old TV show? "Don't do the crime if you can't do the time." He'd done the crime, and now he'd have to either enjoy or endure eighteen more years of child rearing. She gathered her resolve when she heard the car door slam.

Thomas walked into the kitchen and greeted her with an empty smile that she didn't notice because she was absorbed in her own resolution. She prepared his plate as usual and sat down to keep him company as he ate. Silence invaded their kitchen. When he set the fork down after his final bite, she said, "Thomas, do you love me?"

His startled eyes met hers and they sat in silence again. Making his decision he finally said, "Regina, girl, you know that I adore you. How can you even ask me that? You should know that I worship the ground you walk on. I've shown you a million times that you're my sun, my moon, and my everything."

She looked at him oddly, but asked again, "But do you love me?"

He reached across the table with the intent to cover her hands with his, but she jerked her hand away. "I have never once heard you say that you love me and my soul is starving for those words," she said slowly and distinctly. "I'm not trying to control you or anything; something inside me just needs to hear those words."

"I should not have to say those words for you to know how I feel. I care for you. I'm here for you and you can depend on my word. I'm concerned about you. Any idiot can say the words 'I love you.' Guys say that all the time just to get a piece. I'm sure Justin's dad must have said those words to you many times and look at where that got you," he said, realizing that he'd gone too far too late.

Feeling as if her heart would shatter, she slowly walked out of the room and up the stairs without saying another word. She held back the tears until she was in the shower and the water was running as hard as her tears were falling.

When he came upstairs to prepare for bed, she was still in the shower. He tried the door and was surprised to find she had locked it. He knew that he should have been able to tell her that he loved her. But his tongue became stuck when he tried to say the words. He felt ambushed, walking into her demands before he'd had a chance to recover from the attack at school. How could she have done him that way?

He put on his pajamas and climbed into bed. When she finally came out of the bathroom, she already had her gown on. She crawled into the king-sized bed and lay as far away from Thomas as she could get and still be on the same mattress with him. He rolled toward her and said, "Regina, baby, I—"

"Don't try to explain anything else to me. I understand perfectly how you feel," she said without turning to face him.

He hurt for her, but his head was full of his own ordeal. He was worried about something much more practical, such as keeping a roof over their heads.

By the end of the week, the internal investigation into the NCAA violations was complete, but unresolved. Dr. Morgan insisted that the compliance committee meet again and make a recommendation. They responded that they didn't have enough evidence to either clear or convict the school. The committee was too political and too torn to render a decision. Without a resolution, the NCAA would have to do an investigation.

For the first time in years, Renaissance was a contender for a championship. Yet, rather than riding high on their promised glory, the charges against the school's head coach cast a gloom over the entire institution. The report was submitted to the NCAA and they arranged a follow-up visit to conduct their own investigation.

Thomas and Regina had barely talked for more than a week. Her needing to hear the words *I love you* lay like a sword between them. In order to say those words to her, he would have to break his vow to his first love. How could he call himself a man of integrity if he did that?

Thomas sat in his office barely able to focus on the

contracts that lay scattered on his desk. Before she had told him what was on her mind, he had known that something was bothering her. She was not as spontaneously affectionate toward him outside the bedroom as she had been. And now he realized what he missed most. He had not heard her say the little *I love yous* that she would whisper in his ear before he left for work, before they made love, or when he called her from his office. Had her tender utterances merely been to get a response from him? Had she ever meant them? He pushed away from his desk and went to stare at the big maple and oak trees outside his windows.

When Regina went to the beauty shop for her regular appointment, Rosemary quietly shampooed her hair. After applying conditioner, she put her under the dryer for a deep-heat treatment. When the dryer cut off, Regina left the hood down and waited patiently for Rosemary to finish another customer.

She heard the soft hum of female voices, but did not focus on the words that they were saying until she heard them say her husband's name. "Coach Simmons probably changed those grades. Hmmph, I know I would have if my job depended on it," a female voice said.

"Well, the investigators were on campus today. I heard that they confiscated his computer hard drive and went through his and Dr. Johnson's e-mail."

"Girl, do you think he and Dr. Johnson really have something going on?"

"I don't know. But I know his wife. She's really cute. She sings country music. Can you believe that? A black woman doing country music."

"Maybe he got tired of listening to country music," the first voice said and then laughed loudly at her own humor.

By the time Rosemary had finished her first client and walked her to the door, she heard the same conversation. Lifting the hood on Regina's dryer she said, "I'm ready for you, Mrs. Simmons. I hope that I didn't keep you waiting too long. I know that you told me that you have to meet your husband, the coach, for dinner tonight." Rosemary talked loudly and distinctly for the two gossips to hear.

When they were back at the shampoo bowl and out of earshot, Regina asked, "Do you know why Thomas is being investigated?"

Rosemary put her hands on her hips and said, "Those gossips don't know when to stop."

"Do you know anything about what they were talking about?" Regina persisted.

Looking carefully at Regina's bewildered face, Rosemary said, "I guess Thomas hasn't told you anything?"

"No, he's told me nothing," Regina answered miserably.

"All I know is that Thomas is accused of changing grades for some of his players. No one knows where the accusation came from, but some members of the faculty believe it. They're spreading the rumors around," she whispered, watching the front of the shop to be sure they weren't overheard.

Regina felt bad that she'd been so needy that she'd been emotionally absent while Thomas needed her the most. She had been so wrapped up in herself she had no idea he'd been going through such a devastating ordeal. Sure, she knew he'd been working late, but she thought he was trying to avoid her. She had not realized that he had something so heavy to deal with.

That night, she called Keisha to stay with the boys while she went to visit Thomas on campus. Although she had not yet forced him to say that he loved her, she knew that all of that had to be put on hold for the time being.

After checking a final time on the sleeping boys and giving Keisha last-minute instructions, she tightened the belt on her long black trench coat and headed out the door. She parked in the lot adjacent to the Raven Center and noted with relief that the only remaining vehicle was Thomas's black Navigator. She knew the main entrances would be locked, so she pulled in at the door nearest his office. The noise of her heels tapping on the concrete hallway was the only sound she heard in the usually noisy building. All the students, athletic coaches, administrators, trainers, and equipment managers had vacated the building. It would be just Thomas and her tonight.

The door to Thomas's office stood open as usual. He seldom closed it unless he was counseling a student. He was sitting at his computer, completely engrossed in the blue and white figures on the screen. As he sensed a presence at the door, his first look was one of astonishment, which was quickly replaced by a joyful, dimpled smile.

"Hey, handsome. Do you know where I can find Coach Thomas Simmons?" she asked in a sultry voice. Leaning against the door frame with one hand on her hip, she looked seductive in a full-length black coat that was belted at the waist and the red five-inch stiletto heels with the T-straps that he had given her. Her dark black hair glistened, even in the weak, fluorescent lighting.

He quickly took in her appearance and said, "I might know him. Who wants to know?"

"His lonely wife who misses him desperately," Regina answered in a throaty whisper. She felt as miserable as he looked. He looked so tired and vulnerable that she wondered why she had not noticed that before.

"I could be the person you're looking for," he said, wanting to rush to her, but not certain what her plans might be.

"Do you notice anything different about me?" she asked.

He wasn't sure what the right answer was, but he knew that when he got it wrong it usually had something to do with a new outfit or new hairstyle. "Your hair looks real pretty," he guessed.

"Thank you. I went to the beauty shop today. Guess what I heard there," she prompted him, still speaking as if she might cry.

He turned his chair to face her fully. He wondered what this was about. His initial joy at seeing her was giving way to apprehension. "What did you hear?"

"I heard that Coach Simmons—that's you—is being investigated for academic fraud. Why didn't you tell me? Look at me, Thomas. Look at me carefully. I'm the same old Gina. I'm your friend. I could have been there for you."

"At first I didn't think they were serious. Then I thought it would go away since there's a logical explanation for all the allegations. I thought that it would all be over with an internal investigation. I figured I'd be telling you about the close call we'd barely escaped. I hoped that there would be no need to worry you," he explained.

She crossed the distance between them to sit on his desk next to where he was resting his elbows. "I'm here for you, Thomas. I told you that I didn't want marriage to ruin our friendship. It looks like our friendship is on fairly shaky ground."

He rolled his chair closer to her and wrapped his arms around her waist, resting his head on her bosom. "What happened to us, Gina?" he said tiredly.

She gently stroked the back of his head with her soft

fingers, soothing him with her gentle touch. He sighed deeply before raising his head. She stroked his thick, black glossy eyebrow with her fingertip as he spoke. "Gina, I—" He forgot what he was going to say because her coat had fallen open to the waist, giving him a glimpse of what wasn't beneath her coat.

"Wait a minute. What do you have on under that coat?" he asked anxiously.

She hopped off his desk immediately and when she was almost out the door she challenged, "You have to catch me to find out."

Before he could push the chair from the desk, she was down the hall. He heard the tapping of her heels, but didn't see her until she was going into the women's locker room. She knew that with his longer legs, he could catch her without breaking a sweat. She had to think smart. She hid behind the door until he was deep into the room; then she darted back out the door, letting it slam so that he would know to chase her. He followed close behind her and could hear her giggling as she ran toward his office. She was afraid to look back for fear of losing the lead she had, but she couldn't judge how close he was. He was wearing nearly silent sneakers.

She headed toward his office but at the last minute, she changed directions and darted into the men's locker room. Just as she crossed the threshold, he caught her around the waist, lifting her off the floor. Her feet were still in motion, making her feel like a cartoon character.

"Put me down. Put me down," she yelled, struggling against his strong hold on her.

"Why should I?"

"Because you want to see what's under my coat."

"How do I know you won't run again?"

"Because I want you to see what's under my coat. I have on your favorite color," she added enticingly.

"Okay," he said, leaning forward and whispering in her ear, the warmth of his breath sending delightful tremors through her body.

When her feet touched the floor, she was shaky for several seconds. With all the attitude she could muster, she strutted away from him, fully aware that he had a weakness for her full hips. When he began to follow her, she tossed over her shoulder, "Stay right there."

Mesmerized, he let his eyes follow the sway of her hips until she turned to face him. Slowly, she untied the belt at her waist and let the coat fall open. Through the opening, he confirmed that she was wearing a red garter belt, black hose, and nothing else. He swallowed deeply and in three long strides, he was standing near enough to touch her.

She opened the coat and pressed her nude body against his fully clothed body. At that moment, his greatest desire was to shed every article of clothing he was wearing, to have nothing between them.

He ran to lock the door to the locker room and shed his clothes along the way. She'd kept herself from him far too long. He was anxious to be with his bride and hoped that she wouldn't make him wait until they got home.

She didn't. The fire that was burning within Thomas had also consumed Regina. After being emotionally and physically estranged from him for more than a week, she could not wait for their reunion.

Spent and exhausted hours later, Thomas sat length-wise on the narrow bench in the locker room, his long legs resting on either side of Regina and his back against the concrete wall. For now, the coolness of the

concrete was a pleasant contrast to the heat still res-
onating through his body. His chest served as Regina's
cushion.

They sat idly for a few minutes, neither anxious to
prepare for their trip home. "Thomas, don't think that
I'm jealous or anything, but I was wondering about
something."

"What is that?" he asked, his hand gently stroking
her arms to be sure that she didn't become chilled.

"The women that I overheard in the beauty shop
implied that there is something between you and Dr.
Johnson. What has she to do with the investigation?"

"She is the only person who can corroborate my claim
that the players' grades were legitimate," he explained.
"She's been very cooperative and has put her reputation
on the line among her fellow academics for me."

"What's the problem then, if she can confirm your
claims?" Regina asked, puzzled.

"The allegations are based on just enough fact to
seem true. I had some players on the road during a time
that one of the professors in Rosa's—Dr. Johnson's—
department decided to give an exam. We had submitted
our travel dates at the beginning of the semester with
the hope that faculty would cooperate and not give
exams on the dates that our team had road games.
However, if they did schedule exams, the policy is that
the students can make up the test. It's counted as an excused absence," Thomas recited tiredly.

"And why didn't the plan work?" Regina asked.

"The students missed an exam and they were allowed to take a make-up. However, the instructor
never submitted the proper form to change the students' final grades in the computer. When I got the
grade sheet for my players, I knew that something was
wrong because the players involved were some of the
strongest students we have. I doubted that they would

have failed a class. I was especially certain that they did not fail because at midterm they were passing their English composition class. I called the instructor, but I was too late. He was an adjunct—"

"A what?" Regina interrupted.

"An adjunct, a temporary instructor," Thomas explained patiently. "He wasn't on the tenure track and worked on a contractual basis. At any rate, he had left for the holidays and wasn't under contract to return this semester. He was not up for rehire, Rosa confidentially told me, because of some other issues that she had with his work. So of course, we can't expect him to cooperate in any way. But he did tell Rosa that he'd left the test papers and his grade book. When Rosa saw where he'd changed the grade in his grade book, she changed the grades through her computer access."

"So what is the problem with that? Didn't you tell me that she's the head of the department?"

"You have a good memory. Yes, she's the one. And before you ask, she is also the woman that I took out to make you jealous," Thomas hurried to admit.

"I wasn't going to ask about that. You asked me to marry you after you went out with her, not before. So again, what's the problem?"

"The problem is, the test papers are now missing and the grade book was sent to the NCAA as evidence that the grades were changed. Well, hell, the grade would be erased and marked over. The instructor himself had changed the grade. However, Rosa and I are accused of changing the grades in the grade book. And of course, Rosa's password is in the computer for changing the grades. None of this looks good."

"That's ridiculous," Regina said angrily. "Don't they know what an honest person you are?"

"No, I'm afraid not. Many of the faculty believe that

those in athletics are ignorant and should not even be on campus. Recently, there has been a push to de-fund athletics completely."

"Do you think that will ever happen?"

"I'm not sure, but of one thing I am certain. If we are going to recruit athletes, we have to ensure that they get the best education that we can give them. I'm not going to use the boys athletically and then send them on their way without a degree," Thomas declared vehemently.

"I know that and anyone who knows you should know that by now. Obviously these are people who don't know you," Regina said, just as strongly.

"You, know, Regina, the most difficult part of all this is that I've been through all of this before. The only difference is that the last time I was emotion-ally exhausted. I was still recovering from my personal problems. I didn't want to fight. I resigned and when I got the call from Dr. Morgan, it was like someone had tossed me a lifeline. I love coaching and believe that I have had a positive impact on the young men I coach."

Thomas began to feel more energized as he dis-cussed his situation with Regina. "We have a home game tomorrow. Did you remember?"

"I haven't missed one of your games yet," she an-swered and reached for her coat, which was at the end of the long bench.

"You're getting goose bumps. Let's get out of here. Why don't you leave your car and ride over with me in the morning to get it?" Thomas suggested.

"That means that you'll have to take Tres and Justin to school," she reminded him.

"That'll work."

On the drive home, Thomas tried to wrap an arm around Regina. Afraid that he was making her uncomfortable, he settled for holding her hand. He'd missed her so much over the past week, that he had to keep touching her to be sure that she was still with him. This wife of his never ceased to amaze him. One never knew from day to day what to expect from her.

Chapter 15

When they arrived home, Regina soaked in the tub while Thomas hurried through the shower. Dressed in pajamas, he sat on the vanity bench to talk with her while she lounged in the oversized tub.

She rubbed suds over her outstretched arms carefully as she measured her words. "You know, Thomas, I don't think you should be passive in this investigation. I don't know anything about the NCAA, but I do know that you should fight to clear your name. You know that you're innocent of any stupid rules violations. You've got to get your energy back so that you can plan your strategy."

"Okay, Rocky. How do I fight this? So far it's a case of my word against some unknown accuser who stole a grade book," Thomas said, both amazed and amused by Regina's resilience.

"I'm not exactly sure. All I know is that you'll always have this aggravation as long as you have to deal with rules, violations, and consequences. There's nowhere else for you to go this time. You've got to hunker down and fight it out."

"I don't need this distraction in the middle of a successful basketball season," he said, still sounding skeptical, but a little more energized.

"You don't think that people up to no good will wait

until you have free time on your hands to stir up their devilment, do you?" she asked pointedly.

"I guess not," he answered.

"You said that Dr. Morgan went all out to support you during your previous investigation. What is he saying now?"

"He's supportive, but he can't get too involved without being accused of trying to orchestrate a cover-up. So far he's kept his distance. But since I have an advanced degree, he has said that I can have a teaching position if I'm removed from coaching for a while. I could get some pretty severe penalties since those previous charges are still unresolved."

"We need to resolve that, too. Do people hire someone to defend themselves in these cases?" Regina asked, beginning to feel an idea growing.

"Not usually."

"I think you should. The resolution of your case can affect the future of our whole family. I know that Andre is an entertainment lawyer, but surely he'd have some ideas of what we can do. He knows basketball better than any other attorney I know." Regina planned and Thomas listened. Her enthusiasm and unwavering support were heartening.

After dropping the boys off at school the next morning, Thomas and Regina met with Andre. "I haven't been by to see my godson for a while. How is he?" Regina asked.

"Getting fatter. The pediatrician is on Tiffany to feed him every four hours, but he's hungry every two hours so she feeds him anyway," Andre said, smiling.

"That means that it's time to give him cereal. The formula is not filling him up," Regina said knowingly. "Tell Tiffany that I'll call her later this week."

As Thomas filled Andre in on the details of the case

against him, Andre made notes and asked for more details in certain areas.

After about thirty minutes, Andre told Thomas that he would talk with someone who was more familiar with this aspect of the law and call him back.

"Oh, one more thing," Andre said as they were preparing to leave. "Quincy called. He really does want to use the *Sweet Romance* single for a movie that he's directing. What do you think?"

"What do I think? Ask him if he needs anything else. That's wonderful. Why didn't you call me?" Regina exclaimed, full of excitement. "Will it be Shelby's version or someone else singing?" she thought to ask.

"Well, you know how innovative Quincy is. From what I understand Sade and Maxwell will sing it as a duet," Andre said casually.

Regina's joy over the prospect of her song being used on a soundtrack was dampened somewhat by Thomas's present situation. However, she was inspired to return to her music, which had always been a salve for her.

When Thomas came home that evening, he heard the sweet sound of her violin coming from the living room. He stuck his head in the door to listen and she paused for a moment to greet him, but went back to her music as soon as he moved on.

During the following week, Thomas met with the NCAA officials and responded to their questions with complete honesty, emphasizing that his major concern was the welfare of his students. "I believe that athletics teaches character, cooperation, leadership, and a sense of responsibility," Thomas told those at the hearing. "However, those qualities should not exist in a vacuum. They have to be interwoven holistically. The physical and mental should be developed to create the kind of well-rounded citizens we all need in our world."

One of the committee members said to Thomas, "Quite frankly, I am a little disturbed by your prior relationship with Dr. Johnson. I understand that you know her socially as well as professionally."

"That's correct," Thomas answered succinctly, not offering any explanation as Andre had instructed.

"Did you use your personal relationship to persuade her to change the grades for you?"

"Of course not."

"Then why did you go to her?"

Thomas tried to maintain his composure and not let his disgust with the questions show in his voice. "Dr. Johnson is head of the English department and she supervised the instructor who gave my students 'incomplete' grades."

"The *alleged* 'incomplete' grades," the interrogator corrected Thomas. "We have contacted that instructor and he says that he had three hundred students last semester and without his grade book he has no idea of what those grades should have been. Perhaps Dr. Johnson was just trying to help you."

"Dr. Johnson is a consummate professional. I have a great deal of respect for her professional abilities. When I first became head coach here, I met with all of the department heads and asked for their cooperation with the basketball program, including Dr. Johnson. And for the most part, I've gotten that cooperation. I told them that I am well aware that our student athletes must be encouraged to be students first and that would be our focus in the basketball program. I believe that my relationship with Dr. Johnson is similar to the relationship that I have with all department heads."

"Do you expect special concessions for your basketball players?"

"No more than those made for the officers of the student government association or the reigning Miss Renaissance," Thomas answered succinctly.

When the grilling was over, he was thankful that he had met with Andre. Thanks to his friend's coaching, Thomas had learned the best way to handle the questions and had remained calm.

That night, Renaissance University won their division championship, securing a bid to the national championship playoffs. At the end of the game, Thomas scanned the area where he knew Regina would be sitting surrounded by her entourage. Right before his celebrating team blocked his vision, he spotted her as she gave him a thumbs-up and he flashed her a big one-dimpled smile in return.

He was anxious to get home for their private celebration, but first he had to face the media. Tonight his sons were not with him because he knew that most of the questions would center on the NCAA investigation and not their recent victory. He was not quite ready to discuss the investigation with Tres and Justin, but he knew that he'd have to start explaining things to them soon, especially if he was suspended from his position as the head basketball coach.

Regina walked into the kitchen the next morning, and without thought pressed the television on. The TV screen was filled with a reporter standing on the Renaissance campus with the Raven Center as a backdrop. He was telling viewers:

"Popular Renaissance basketball coach Thomas Simmons is being investigated for academic fraud. According to sources at the NCAA, there was sufficient evidence to formally charge the coach. If he is found guilty of the charges, he will be suspended from coaching for an unspecified period of time.

"Earlier this season, the university conducted a self-evaluation when the coach's wife, Nashville songwriter Regina Lovejoy, contributed ten thousand dollars to the athletic program. An internal committee determined that the donation was not in violation of any NCAA rules because she was not considered a booster. She had never attended a Renaissance game at that time. However, considering the current charges, that violation is also being reinvestigated.

"Thomas Simmons left St. Luke University, where he was an assistant coach, while NCAA violations were still being investigated. At that time, Simmons was accused of funneling money to players to pay for restaurant meals and other expenses.

"We have been unable to get a statement from the university," the report ended.

Regina sat before the television set stunned. She was not surprised that the lead news story was not about the team's successful championship bid, but the NCAA investigation. She knew that her husband was a man of integrity and he'd suffered severely under those original charges, although he never talked about the ordeal. How dare they rehash that old mess just to create interest in their news story? She prayed that Thomas could withstand the pressures of the investigation.

It was Saturday morning and she'd come downstairs to give Thomas a chance to sleep in. Lately she was awakened by morning sickness and could not sleep as late as was her habit. She didn't want to disturb Thomas because he did not have many opportunities to be at home on the weekend, and with the tournament starting, things would be more hectic than ever.

When the boys came into the room, she quickly switched to cartoons. She'd have to think of how to handle this with them. She and Thomas had talked about telling them about the investigation, but had continued to put them off. Now that the story had media interest, she knew that the time had come for them to do some explaining to the children.

When Regina went up to tell Thomas that the story had hit the media, he shared her concern about the boys and they decided to discuss it with them that afternoon following lunch.

"There are some things at Daddy's work that you may hear about in the news," Regina began. "People may say that your daddy did something wrong, but we know that he is honest and would not do anything wrong deliberately."

"Oh, you're talking about the NCAA investigation," Tres said.

"Don't worry, Mom, we know all about it," Justin said. "We didn't want you to worry, so we didn't tell you anything."

With that the boys raced each other back to their video game. Thomas shook his head in wonder. "Do we have babies around here anymore?"

Regina's mouth became dry and she blinked twice without answering. Thomas began removing their plates from the table and said, "They grew up way too fast."

She realized he was not referring to her pregnancy and the new baby. She felt awful that she had not told him the news yet, but she still had misgivings about telling him. She was getting tired of her mother's weekly reminders that pregnancy is a secret that one can't hide forever. But Regina was worried that telling him at the wrong time could make matters worse and once she told him she couldn't un-tell him. Things had to be right. For now, too much was still going on in their lives.

Andre called Thomas early on Tuesday morning. "I have a report from North Carolina that you may be interested in. Your booster who contributed the funds that you allegedly gave the players is in jail."

"Why is he in jail?" Thomas asked, surprised that the prominent business leader and diehard St. Luke booster would be in jail.

"He was coowner of an insurance company and I believe that they have him for embezzlement. We have his signature on an affidavit clearing you of all charges at St. Luke. He told my investigator that he wanted to come forward before, but you left without trying to clear your name, and before he could do anything to find you he was distracted by his own trial," Andre said in a jubilant rush.

"Do you think that people will believe him?" Thomas asked.

"He has canceled checks with the president of St. Luke University's signature on them. Sure enough, the fund that they gave you for your players' travel expenses was funded by the booster as the NCAA had been told, but you obviously were kept in the dark as to where the money had come from. Evidence shows that you had no way of knowing that it was not legitimate money," Andre explained.

"I knew that. That's what I told you," Thomas said, feeling a relief deeper than he'd expected.

"And I believed you. That's why we investigated that angle. You knew it, but nobody else in North Carolina believed you, except those who had set you up. And they weren't about to tell the truth. Now we have proof of your innocence," Andre summated.

Whispering a prayer of thanksgiving, Thomas only half listened to Andre. When he tuned in again, Andre was saying, "Being clear of those original charges may influence the decision made on your current case. You need to get this information to the media as quickly as possible. You may use your sports information people or hire a private firm."

"I'll go with our sports media people. Sonia has been behind me all the way and knows the background information. Thanks so much for taking me seriously and looking into those old charges," Thomas told his friend before ending their connection.

Thomas and Regina wanted to celebrate, but knew that there was still too much to do. The NCAA would come back with their decision within a week, which would be this Friday. They needed to do some damage control and Thomas agreed with Regina, he couldn't be passive this time. He would take matters into his own hands.

That evening the sports newscast covered the story of Thomas being cleared of the old charges in North Carolina, but continued to paint him in a questionable light with a summary of the current charges against him. Thomas decided to be content that they had at least run the story that he was clear of the charges in North Carolina.

Not only did Thomas launch a full-scale public relations campaign with the help of Sonia, his sports information director, he also began his own investigation into the charges against him at Renaissance. He had assumed that his anonymous accuser had been a faculty member, but perhaps he had been looking in the wrong direction. He decided that there was a possibility that a student could be behind his problems.

To investigate he would need to tap into the student grapevine. Under the guise of preparing them mentally for the tournament ahead, he called each member of his team into his office one by one. He discreetly probed to see if they knew anything about his accusers.

After two days of talking with his students, Thomas

had come up with nothing and the NCAA decision regarding his violation was due in the president's office in another twenty-four hours. That night, he and Regina were in bed talking about the upcoming tournament and what Thomas would do if he were removed from coaching during the tournament. He told Regina that Isaac Mathews was prepared to lead the coaching staff during the tournament if the NCAA ruled against the school. If Thomas went to the game, he would be there as a spectator.

Thursday night, they were startled when the doorbell rang and even more surprised to see Wes, one of Thomas's players, at the door. "Come on in," Thomas said, stepping back to let the young man walk through his door.

"No, Coach, I won't come in. These are for you," Wes said nervously and handed his coach a rubber-band-bound stack of papers. "Yesterday you asked if I knew anything about those NCAA violations and I lied. But when I saw you on television trying to clear your name—well, I knew I had to help you. Man, this whole thing is whack."

"Where did you get these from?" Thomas asked in disbelief.

"I found them in the apartment that I shared with Myron," the boy answered before loping off the porch.

"Wait, wait!" Thomas said, moving out the door into the frigid February air.

Wes turned and looked at him. "I'm sorry, Coach. I should have done something sooner. At first I didn't know what they meant. Then I heard Myron bragging that he'd gotten even with you. I didn't want to bust my friend, but you've been pretty decent to us. I can't let you and your family get all messed up over this thing. I'll see you at the gym," the student said as he backed away toward his car.

Thomas stood on his porch and watched the boy get into his Toyota and drive away. He looked at the stack of papers and wondered what was going on. He looked at first one, then another, and a third, and fourth, before he realized what they were. Each had a red letter grade in the upper right-hand corner and carried the December 8 date of the exam in question.

"What is it?" Regina asked from inside the house. "Is Wes in some kind of trouble?"

"No, baby, Wes just got me out of trouble," Thomas said bemusedly.

He took the papers inside and they looked at each one carefully. "I think that I should call Veronica and the compliance officer. I have no idea what will happen if I keep these overnight. I might be accused of tampering with the grades again," Thomas said after a while.

He called Sonia, who agreed to call Veronica and the Morgans. Sonia called him back immediately to let him know that they'd decided to call a news conference to announce the new information to all the media at once.

While Thomas called Andre and Tiffany to let them know of the latest development, Regina hurried upstairs to dress. It was only a matter of moments before their house was filled with unplanned guests.

Sonia arrived with Veronica and several reporters, photographers, and videographers in tow. The story of the reappearance of the missing exam papers, which verified the grades that the players had earned, would be the lead story on the morning drive-time radio news, in the early edition of the newspaper, and on all television stations.

"Greater than the damage done to my reputation, I am saddened by the damage done to the students in question. These were freshmen students, just beginning their college careers, and we have invaded their privacy by publishing very personal information about them such as their grades and ACT scores. They are living away from home for the first time and their parents trusted the adults on our campus and in this city to care for and protect their children. I believe that as a result of this episode, we failed to keep their trust. Sometimes the damage that we do cannot be repaired."

Dr. John Morgan loved the camera. He gave his personal, prepared statement. "I never had any doubt regarding Coach Simmons's innocence. Not only is he the best coach in the nation, as you'll see when we bring the NCAA Championship trophy back to Nashville, but I am also convinced that this man has the best interests of our students at heart. He has never made me doubt that our students' total welfare is his top priority and that's why we wanted him to lead the Renaissance team. With his ability to attract the best and brightest to Renaissance, we couldn't help having the victorious season that we've enjoyed. Audrey and I look forward to seeing you at the Sweet Sixteen Championship in New Orleans." He pulled Audrey closer to him and that close-up was the clip that ran to promote the news several times the next morning and during the day.

Around midnight most of their neighbors came over to see what all of the commotion was about. One of the women made the mistake of asking Regina if they needed anything. It was a mistake because Regina was well known for always having a specific response when someone offered to help.

Regina eyed the pound cake that Tiffany had brought with her and quickly said, "Yes, my friends brought over this pound cake and we need coffee to go with it. Do you know how to make coffee?"

"Certainly. Where is your coffeepot?"

"We don't have one," Regina answered.

"I'll go get mine," the woman volunteered.

Her husband added, "Yes, and we'll bring that big box of sweet rolls that we got at Sam's Wholesale House. We'll never eat four dozen sweet rolls."

Another couple spoke up. "We'll bring our ham. You all can eat that up for us."

By the time all the neighbors had returned with their offerings, enough food was available to feed an army. The commotion downstairs eventually awakened Tres and Justin.

"Are we having a party?" Tres asked, rubbing his eyes as he entered the large kitchen filled with friends and neighbors.

"Is it Christmas?" Justin asked, following closely behind Tres.

"We're celebrating our victory," Thomas said with a big smile that wouldn't seem to go away.

"Did we have a basketball game?" Tres asked.

"No, we're celebrating because everyone knows that I didn't cheat. They know that I'm honest," Thomas said jubilantly.

Regina wanted to celebrate, too. But her morning sickness wouldn't let her. When Thomas noticed that she wasn't in the kitchen, he began looking for her and found her in the little guest powder room behind the stairs.

"What's wrong?" he asked, concerned when he saw her red eyes.

"I'm sick," was all she could gasp.

"I'll get you a cold cloth," Thomas said, dashing from the room. He returned and applied the cloth to the back of her neck and held her head as she wretched and heaved.

After she had rinsed her mouth, he held her in his

arms and let her rest against his chest. "Regina, every morning you go through this. What's going on?"

"It's sinus drainage. It must be my allergies or something," she lied and instantly regretted having to do so. She just couldn't tell him about the pregnancy. Not now when they had a houseful of people. She was still unsure of what his reaction would be.

"Are you sure? I want you to make a doctor's appointment. This could be something serious," he said, his voice full of concern.

A soft knock on the door kept Regina from having to lie again. They heard Tiffany's voice. "Regina? Thomas? I hate to disturb you, but people are beginning to leave."

"We'll be right out," Thomas responded.

Thomas walked their guests to the door while Regina hurried upstairs to recomb her hair and brush her teeth. By the time she returned their only remaining guests were John, Audrey, Tiffany, and Andre, who were bagging trash and wiping off the countertops.

"This is getting too familiar," Andre teased Regina.

"What is that?" she asked.

"It seems that every time I come here I end up bagging the trash," he said.

"We all eventually rise to our level of competence," she quipped.

"Mommy, I don't feel so good," Tres said, coming to sit on her lap.

"You're probably just sleepy," she said mechanically until she had his hot little body in her arms. Then she exclaimed, "This child is burning up! Thomas, give me the thermometer."

At the loud beep of the digital thermometer, she removed it from the child's mouth and announced, "His temperature is 103.6. We'd better get you to Dr. Jackson first thing in the morning," she said, stroking the child's back and soothing him.

"Excuse us," Tiffany said, rising. "I'm going to get my baby out of here before we catch something."

"I'll call you later," Regina said, laughing at Tiffany's haste to leave. "We're glad you guys got out of bed to come over."

With the departure of the last of their guests, the family returned to bed. Regina put Tres in bed between Thomas and herself so that she could monitor his temperature. She and Tres were at the doctor's office as soon as it opened.

That afternoon Thomas called to check on Tres. "What did the doctor say?"

"His glands are swollen and he has an ear infection. She wrote a prescription for an antibiotic and told me to give him a pain reliever for the fever. He's been asleep since we got home."

"Does Justin have any symptoms yet?"

"No, but the doctor gave me a refill on the antibiotic in case Justin becomes ill. Right now Justin is driving me crazy because he missed school today. He wants me to go over all of his homework with him, to read to him, and then to check his journal," Regina said. She was not complaining, because she was actually pleased that the boys enjoyed school so much.

"I guess you won't be traveling with us tonight?" Thomas ventured.

"With Tres feeling so bad, I don't think I should leave him with anyone. When he wakes up he calls for me," she answered, feeling torn because she had not missed any games up to this point.

"Thank you, sweetheart. I'm grateful that you're there for him. I'll stop by the house before we leave this afternoon."

"Did you hear from the NCAA today?"

"Oh, I almost forgot about all of that. Yes, we were able to verify that the papers are authentic and the NCAA has closed their investigation. They will release a statement to the media that they have closed their investigation and they have found no evidence of wrongdoing," Thomas told her jubilantly.

"Praise God. I knew that you wouldn't be left holding the bag this time," Regina said.

"I don't know what I would have done without your faith in me. Thank you for believing in me," he said huskily.

"I didn't have a choice. You've never shown me anything else but your integrity," she replied sincerely.

"Regina?"

"Yes, Thomas?"

"Did you ask the doctor about your nausea? Do you think you caught something from Tres?" Thomas asked, disappointing her with his question.

"No. I didn't think to mention my nausea to the *pediatrician*," she answered dryly. "I have to go check on Justin. He's working in his workbook. Call me if you don't get to stop by the house before your flight out," she said before pressing the "off" button on the receiver. He stared at the receiver that he held in his hand, wondering at her sudden haste to end their conversation.

During the game that night, Thomas must have looked over his shoulder at the area where Regina usually sat at the half-court line a million times. Although he coached the game as intensely as ever, he missed her presence. After the game he returned to his empty hotel room and seriously thought about taking a quick flight home, but he remembered his obligation to his team.

By the time Thomas returned home, Tres had bounced back and was himself again—a wise, ener-

getic six-year-old. Sunday afternoon the boys were outside in the cold sun while Thomas and Regina sat in
the kitchen listening to the boys' laughter. Regina
thought this was the right time to tell Thomas about
the baby. They were getting along well and the NCAA
mess was behind them. When her mother had called
that morning, she had reminded Regina that she was
already about two months along and needed to get
things in order, such as going to an obstetrician and
telling her husband.

Regina took a deep breath, but before she could
speak Thomas said, "Just look at our boys. They're getting so tall and long-legged. They'll be grown and
gone in no time. We'll give them twelve more years,
and then it'll just be you and me here all alone.
Doesn't that sound great?"

"Don't you ever think about having more children?"
she asked tentatively.

With a pained look on his face, he said, "You know
that can't happen." For a fleeting moment, she
thought that her news would ease his pain, when he
added, "I have twenty other children over there on
campus. Our hands are full trying to take care of two
children with the schedule I have. I only regret that I
can't help you more. I feel bad that I've put so much
on you."

She felt cowardly and deceitful, but once again she
let the moment to tell him about the baby pass. She
tried to swallow the bitter taste of deceit, but it lingered on her tongue as she began to talk to him about
the upcoming weekend.

To change the subject she said, "Don't forget when
we get back from New Orleans next Sunday, we're supposed to take the kids to Chuck E. Cheese's."

"Why are we going there on a Sunday?"

"When Justin's new birth certificate came with his

last name changed to Simmons on it and showing you as his father, he wanted to celebrate. I told him to wait until you were at home. We promised him that before we knew that we'd make it this far in the championships."

"You know that we may not get home until Sunday afternoon," he cautioned her.

"Thomas, you're the head coach. Tell Veronica or whoever is in charge that we need to get home early Sunday morning or make arrangements for me on a commercial flight," she snapped impatiently. She rose from the table and put her glass in the sink.

"I'll see what I can do," he said, stunned by her tone.

"Andre just secured a contract for me to write songs for Alison McKenzie's new album. She says she's depending on me. It's been almost a year since she finished her last album and she's antsy to get going again. I'll be in the music room—the living room— working for a while. By the way, did you look at those plans that I left on your desk for you?" she asked, still in her strident tone.

"No, ma'am, I didn't get to it yet."

"We need to move out of this tight house. I need help finding a suitable plan," she said angrily.

"I was going to look at some game tapes, but I'll do that first," he said and stood and saluted her in jest.

Not smiling or giving him a second look, she hurried out of the room, leaving him wondering what he'd done this time. He sat at the table for several minutes more before going to the "men's room" and popping the video into the player.

Regina sat at the piano picking out a tune. She knew that Alison wanted something upbeat, but her mood was dismal. Every tune she played was mournful and pensive. The words came to her in a rush, of their own volition. She began playing and singing them.

Tears flowed from her eyes as she wrote the words to the song. For a moment, she hesitated putting them down. They were too true, too close to her heart.

Late in the afternoon, when she knew that the song was the one, she left a message for Alison and told her, "I have the first song for your album. Call me when you return so that we can arrange for you to come by and hear it."

Later in the week, Alison stopped by to hear the song. She was moved by its melancholy melody and bittersweet words. "That's perfect," she said. "It's not what I expected, but it's unique. It will be an instant attention grabber. I can just see the video for it now. What kind of mood were you in when you wrote it?"

"You know how it goes. I'm a temperamental artist," Regina said lightly. "Now let's sit down and see what else we can do."

By the time Alison left in the late afternoon, Regina had good ideas for the rest of the album. It would be recorded under the Honeysuckle label, but Andre had negotiated a lucrative contract for her for the project.

She picked up the boys as soon as Alison left and was headed home with them when one of their thought-provoking conversations started. "Mom, I'm glad that you're my real mama now, but I wish I remembered my first mommy," Tres said sadly.

"It would be hard for you to remember her because you were just a year old when she left you," Regina explained gently.

"Why did she leave me? Was she mad at me?" Tres asked.

"No. She was very sick and her body hurt so much that Jesus told her to come to heaven with Him. There is no pain in heaven," Regina answered.

"Tres was sick and he didn't feel good either. Why didn't he go to heaven?" Justin inquired.

Lord, will these questions never let up? Regina thought. *They use all of my creative energy when they start these "why" conversations.* She took a breath and tried to explain. "Tres had medicine that made him feel better. His first mother had many medicines, but they did not make her better. She couldn't get better," she said, gently.

"I heard my grandma say that she got sicker because I was born. She said her daughter was my mama and her daughter would have been well, but she wouldn't take medicine when I was in her stomach," Tres said, near tears.

"When did she tell you that?" Regina asked, becoming angry at the carelessness of adults. She knew that Sara Evans would not hurt Tres intentionally, but still she had hurt him. She pulled into a McDonald's and parked so that she could comfort the child. "We'll eat here. Is that okay?"

"Okay," Justin said. He obviously felt bad because Tres was crying. They pulled into the McDonald's and Regina moved to the passenger seat before pulling Tres from the backseat into her arms. She held him until his crying subsided.

While she rocked Tres, Justin asked, "Why do we have three grandmothers?"

"Name your grandmothers," Regina instructed.

"Grandma Sara, Grandma Nadine, and Gran Julia."

"And how many is that?"

"Three."

"Do you know whose mothers they are?"

"Yes," the boys answered and explained the relationships.

"Very good. Now you know why you have three grandmothers. Now, Tres, when did Grandma Sara tell you that your mother became sicker because you were born?" Regina asked again, trying to use the child's exact words. She did not want to use any other words that might plant other ideas in the child's fertile imagination. He was already wounded enough.

"She wasn't talking to me. Her friend came over and they were drinking coffee in the kitchen and I came to get water, but she kept talking to her friend when I came into the room and I heard her. But I left before she said anything to me," Tres recalled.

"Was that this summer while you were still five or was it the one when you were four?" Regina asked, wondering how long the child had been carrying his guilt.

"Just this summer. I was still five. It was before I went to stay with Grandma Nadine. Before we came home for our wedding." The boys referred to Thomas and Regina's wedding as if it had been the family's wedding, which indeed it had been.

"Tres, do I tell you what to do or do you tell me what to do most of the time?" Regina asked.

"I don't know," the small child answered.

"When it's time to go to bed, do I tell you to go or do you tell me?" she clarified with an example.

"You tell me to go to bed," he answered, proud to get the answer right.

"Ask me one," Justin pleaded.

"When it's time for vitamins, do I give them to you or do you give them to me?" she asked Justin.

"You give me the vitamin," he said, laughing as if they were playing a game.

"Do you know why I tell you what to do?"

"Because you're the mother?" the boys answered in unison. This was a frequent drill that Regina conducted to remind the boys of her authority.

"Exactly. I am responsible for you. I am in charge. If your mother stopped taking her medicine, it's because she was the mommy and knew the best thing to do. You could not tell her what to do. It was not your choice and it was not your fault. You are the child and she was your mommy. If she was sick, she had to make a decision about the best way to take care of herself. She was ill, but she loved you so much that she wanted to take care of you. She did what she thought was best for you," Regina explained, her heart aching for her son.

"For God so loved the world, He gave His only *forgotten* Son," Justin quoted. "We learned that in Sunday school. My teacher said that God thought that His Son was the best thing He could give us."

Regina smiled and decided to wait to tell the proud little boy that the scripture should say *begotten* Son, not *forgotten* Son. He'd need an explanation on what *begotten* meant and she didn't want to leave their present topic yet. So she answered simply, "That's right. God sent His Son to us so that we could have everlasting life. Tres's mother loved him so much that she wanted him to have a safe and healthy life. She didn't want to take medicine that would make him sick while he was in her stomach. Now we have handsome, wonderful Tres," Regina said with a smile on her face and a happy voice.

"You're beautiful, Mom. I wish I knew how my first Mommy looked. I don't even remember," Tres said, thoughtfully.

"When we get home let's try to find pictures of her."

Regina spent the rest of the afternoon going through boxes in the attic, trying to find pictures of Tres's mother. After a couple of hours, they found a box of photo albums and loose pictures. They must have belonged to Paulette.

"Here's your baby book, Tres," Regina said jubilantly, holding it over her head. She wanted to take the whole box down the ladder, but realized that she should be careful. She didn't want to risk a miscarriage. She ended up making several trips, taking a few photo albums down at a time.

They sat on the sofa and looked at picture after picture. "This is your mother holding you right after you were born," Regina told Tres. She had to fight back the personal pain she felt when she looked at Thomas's joyful face with his wife and newborn. She wondered if he would be so jubilant over the birth of their newest baby. This wasn't about her, she reminded herself. This was about a small boy who was seeking understanding.

"We need to put some of these pictures out. Would you like to go to the mall to get some picture frames?" Regina asked.

"Yes. I want a picture of my mother next to my bed like Justin has of his first dad," Tres decided.

Chapter 16

When Thomas walked into his home that evening, he felt as if he had been emotionally assaulted by his past. The first photograph startled him, leaving him feeling slightly dazed. He couldn't quite fit the photograph in with the environment, which left him with an odd feeling. His reasoning did not progress to the realization that the only way the photograph would be displayed was if Regina had put it there. He was later than usual getting home and she was soaking in her whirlpool tub when he went looking for her.

He returned to the kitchen to eat his dinner alone. As he ate dinner, Paulette's face stared at him from the frame on his kitchen counter in a house that Paulette had never inhabited. After dinner he walked out into the hallway leading to the stairs and saw that a picture of Paulette holding Tres as an infant had joined the grouping of family photos, next to the picture of Regina holding a newborn Justin. Passing the living room, he spotted a portrait of a young and healthy Paulette.

"Daddy, Daddy," Tres called. "Are you coming up to tuck us in? We're getting sleepy up here."

"I'm coming," Thomas replied, coming out of his past-induced stupor. He sat on Justin's bed and listened to the children pray.

"And thank you, God, for my first mommy and my new mommy," Tres said, ending his prayer.

Thomas leaned over and pulled the covers up on Justin first and then moved to Tres to do the same for him. That was when he spotted all of the snapshots of Paulette on Tres's bedside table.

He was feeling odd and couldn't quite sort out his emotions. Was it anger? Grief? Fear? A name for what he was feeling escaped him. It had been too long since he'd spent any time analyzing his feelings about Paulette's death. A constant guilt hounded him for sure, but he'd never confronted it, he just did what he could to shut it out. Now that he was face-to-face with his memories, he was forced into a confrontation for which he was ill prepared. He was not ready to analyze the guilt that he felt whenever he thought of Paulette. Since he married Regina, the guilt had increased significantly. Now it seemed that things were about to come to a head.

He descended the stairs feeling as if he had been sucker punched. He entered Regina's music room and there on the mantel was an eight-by-ten photo of a young, beautiful Paulette in a new silver frame. This house had been his refuge. It had been his opportunity to get away from the memories that haunted him in North Carolina. Paulette had never been in this house and now her presence was everywhere. It was bad enough that he felt guilty for caring and needing Regina so much after he'd sworn to Paulette that she'd always be in his heart. Now he was remembering how he had let Paulette down when she was alive.

"That's a beautiful portrait," Regina said, coming up behind him. "Was it taken for a special occasion?"

"It was the engagement portrait that her mother sent to the local papers. She had it taken right before we graduated from college as a gift to her parents and me," he reminisced.

"It's lovely. The children and I spent the better part of the afternoon looking for these pictures; then we went to the mall to get frames. That was our project for the day," Regina said, feeling pleased with her efforts.

"You had no right to go through her things," Thomas said quietly, still sorting through his feelings.

"Tres couldn't remember his mother," Regina tried to explain.

"You should have talked to me first. You don't need to spread the pictures all over the house. You'll have Tres getting upset and missing his mother again. It took me a long time to get him to stop asking for her," Thomas said, becoming more and more aggravated with Regina's audacity.

"I don't think it'll upset him now. He needs a connection to his mother like any other child."

"You're his mother now. You don't need to confuse him. I wish you hadn't done this. I'll put them away."

"Don't you dare. Leave them out for a while and after Tres gets used to seeing her pictures again we'll put them away a few at a time."

"Regina, damn it, you don't know everything! I said I don't want the pictures out, and who told you to go prowling around in her things in the first place? I had put them away so that no one would bother them."

"Well, excuse me, Mr. Nasty," Regina said, trying to tease him to better humor.

He ignored her playful remark and continued. "Now I know that you think you know what's best for everyone here, but sometimes you should stop and consult me."

"I'll remember that," she said icily and turned to walk away.

He grabbed her arm. "Gina, wait a minute. Don't walk away from me this time. Let's finish this now."

"You'd better let go of my arm. You don't want to hear what I'll say if I stay," she said through her teeth.

He didn't let go of her. "You can't keep walking away from me. You need to stop and hear what I have to say sometimes. We're going to finish this here and now," he said, full of righteous anger.

She turned and looked into the round, black eyes that she loved so much. They were filled with anger and desperation. "Don't *Gina* me," she hissed. "You may not call me *Gina*. I am *Regina* to you. I used to think that *Gina* was a term of endearment, but there is nothing dear between us."

"Gina, you are dear to me," he said, still holding her arm and trying to pull her toward him. "Don't be so sure of yourself. You're not right all the time. You don't understand what you're doing. You don't have all the answers for all of us all the time."

She jerked away. "I will if you'll let me in on your love affair with your dead wife. I'm not the other woman, Thomas. I'm your wife. In this state, it is illegal to have more than one wife at a time. I don't know what I am to you. I married you because I was in love with you, but now I'm left to wonder why you married me. It used to be so easy for me to tell you that I love you. Now the words stick in my throat because I know that you can't even echo them. Our marriage could have been so good. I figured that I had enough love in me for both of us, but now I know I was wrong. My loving you is about the same as one hand clapping. I can't do this alone. People thought that my competition would be other women. I know I can stand up against any woman alive. That doesn't scare me. What scares me is trying to compete with a dead woman. Well, I can't. When I'm old and fat, she'll still be young and beautiful." Tears threatened to spill from Regina's eyes and she rushed away. No man had ever brought her to tears and seen them. She certainly wasn't going to start crying and getting wimpy now.

Thomas stood stunned, letting her words sink in. When he could finally move again, he was numb. For the rest of the evening they were back to barely speaking. It would not have been so bad if she thought that he loved her, but the truth was she was certain he could never love her. He was still in love with a dead woman. There was no way that she could compete with the impossible perfection of a woman who only existed in his memory.

The next morning she endured her bout of nausea before staggering back to bed. "Something is seriously wrong with you, Regina. Tres is better and you're still throwing up every morning," Thomas said, concerned.

"Really?" she answered sarcastically before turning her back to him.

"I know you're angry, but you need to listen to me. Stay in bed and I'll get the boys ready for school. After I drop them off, I'll be back. We need to talk."

"I've said all I'm going to say," she mumbled. This was not the marriage she expected with Thomas. She'd liked him so much as a friend and had fallen deeply in love with him because of his playfulness and concern and kindness. Now all she wanted was his love. If he were in love with her, she was certain he would not have been so emotional over seeing pictures of Paulette. He should be able to say Paulette's name if he didn't have such an emotional attachment to her still. *This is the last time I'll marry a widower,* she vowed, not recognizing the humor in her thought.

When Thomas returned from taking the boys to school, he walked into the bedroom to talk with her. She was too bone-tired to be bothered. Her muscles ached from her many trips up and down the attic stairs the previous day. She lay with her face to the wall and ignored him, pretending to be in a deep sleep. Before he left the house, she really had fallen asleep.

He decided to let her sleep because she was obviously ill. He was gripped with an ominous fear that it was something terminal because she had been sick for so long. Hadn't Paulette tried to hide her illness from him in the beginning? He decided that he'd go to the office and adjust his schedule so that he could take her to the doctor later. He wondered if she would be able to fly out with him that evening. They had moved on to the semifinals of the championship and the game would be played in New Orleans on Saturday night. This time the team would travel a day early so that they would have time to rest before playing.

When Regina finally awakened, she sank into her big tub and let the warm water rushing from the jets soothe her aching muscles. She'd probably done too much the previous day, climbing the steps to the attic and moving those heavy boxes of books and clothes around. He had even kept all of Paulette's clothes. *This man has it bad and that's not good for me,* she thought.

Maybe she should try to look at things from Thomas's perspective. Usually she made decisions regarding the children without consulting him because she was there and he wasn't. Perhaps she could pick up the phone and check with him from time to time.

As she thought about it, she could imagine his shock at coming home and finding his dead wife's image all over the house. Perhaps she should have prepared him for that. She wasn't sure where he was in the grieving process—somewhere between denial and acceptance was the best that she could guess.

Although they were not on the best of terms, she didn't even consider not going to the game with him.

Dressing carefully in the suit that she would wear on the road that evening, she decided to go have lunch on campus with Thomas. They really did need to sort things out. Things weren't perfect in their marriage, but what marriage was?

If he wanted to hold back part of himself, then he'd surely never know all the joys of what their marriage could have been. But even without a full commitment, their marriage was still better than many she heard about.

It had been ages since she'd surprised him by showing up in his office with lunch. She decided to get two hot lunch platters at Joe's and eat with Thomas in his office. On a travel day, he was always too busy to get away for lunch and he hated campus food. Maybe that would relax him and let him know that she was willing to extend an olive branch.

She took a final look in the mirror and decided that her appearance was decent enough to make Thomas proud that she'd stopped by. Pulling the car out of the garage, she noticed the dark clouds for the first time. She ran back into the house and got an umbrella before heading on her way.

Thomas wasn't able to focus on travel vouchers or anything else that morning. Too much was out of order at home. Regina was angry with him and worse yet, she was ill. Luckily during the NCAA investigation he'd prepared his staff to operate without him in case he was suspended before they went to the tournament. Today he decided to turn the job over to his staff. He needed some time with Regina. She was greatly perturbed with him this time, but that seemed to be a constant with her lately. He couldn't do anything right.

Seeing those pictures of Paulette all over the house last night had been like a step back in time—a very bad time. At first he wondered if it had been someone's macabre joke until he realized Regina thought she'd done something good. She had no idea how those pictures of the young beautiful Paulette contrasted with the young woman who'd become skin and bones, ravaged with pain and crying desperately to be released from this life.

In the beginning Paulette had worried about the change in her appearance—her hair loss and the rash that appeared suddenly on her nose and cheeks. Later, after she suffered kidney failure and dialysis, she no longer worried about her appearance. Her biggest regret was that she could not care for her baby. In her last days, he had sat at her bedside and tried to soothe her. Each breath that she took was filled with pain until she welcomed the relief of death. And he was glad to see her relaxed face when she had finally succumbed to death.

He allowed himself to think about Paulette's last few months and was overcome with grief. Without a second thought, he decided to go home and talk with Regina. He didn't know why he'd put it off so long. He did not question his certainty that his best friend would understand when he told her everything.

His drive home became rough with the winds getting higher and debris blowing toward his windshield. A couple of times he thought about turning around, but he was very concerned because Regina had been so ill that morning. He didn't want her alone in this storm. What if she needed to get out to go to the hospital or something?

All across campus the tornado-warning signal had alerted students and employees to move to areas of safety. By the time Regina arrived, the Raven Center Complex had been evacuated. Cars were still on the parking lot, but she did not see Thomas's. He was probably out running last-minute errands to get the team ready to travel. When she walked into the building she was surprised to find it empty at that time of day, especially on a game day.

Surely Thomas was in there somewhere. As she stood in his office, trying to figure out what was going on, loud claps of thunder and bright flashes of lightning drew her attention to the window. It had suddenly become as dark as midnight outside.

Regina's eyes became as big as silver dollar pancakes when she saw a funnel cloud and two trees that were over one hundred years old fly by the window with their roots dangling in the air. They were tossed aside like stalks of broccoli. Suddenly the windows shattered throughout the building. A million pieces of glass filled the air and the sound of glass breaking echoed throughout the building.

Reality set in and Regina realized that she needed to find a safe place. Her first thought was to head to a lower level. However, the fire doors had been released, sealing off the hallways and preventing her from reaching the stairs to the basement. As she raced across the gleaming hardwood floor of the gym, loosened concrete and plaster was swirling around, filling the air.

She raced into the men's locker room, but still felt unsafe because of the outside wall. Somewhere in the back of her mind, she recalled the weather reporters advising to stay away from outside walls. Although they were masonry, she felt certain that a vicious tornado could move them. She instantly recalled the image of those gigantic trees being tossed about. Looking around she spotted the janitors' closet, which had four inside walls, and decided to crouch in there until the storm was over.

The wind whipped around his Navigator and rocked the big, solid SUV as if it were a toy. As the garage door rose, revealing an empty garage, Thomas was shocked that the Volvo was not in its space. Regina had not mentioned going anywhere. She should have been in the house packing. Maybe she had run some last-minute errands.

When he entered the kitchen, he rushed to the cordless phone on the kitchen counter to call the boys' school to see if Regina had gone there to put in some volunteer hours. At any rate, he wanted to check on the boys' safety. A recording told him that the children had been moved to the basement for safety and parents should pay attention to the media for advice on when to pick up their children.

The phone rang as soon as he ended his call to the school. "Hello," he answered anxiously.

"Hi, Thomas, this is Tiffany. Is Regina there?"

"No. I was just about to call you. I thought maybe she wanted to spend some time with the baby before we go away for the weekend."

"I haven't seen her. She left a message for me to call her with my obstetrician's phone number and the correct spelling of her name. Here it is," Tiffany said and rattled off the name and number.

"Okay, I've got it. This is your OB-GYN, right?" Thomas said, poised to write.

"No. He's not a GYN. Just an OB. He only does babies. Didn't Regina tell you that she didn't like the OB that her GYN had referred her to?"

"I—uh—"

"Sorry, Thomas. I've got to run. This storm is really beginning to kick up out here. I don't like to talk on the phone during storms."

She was gone before Thomas's head had stopped spinning. Regina pregnant? How could that be? A vasectomy was 99 percent effective. What was going on here? He flipped on the counter television and sat at the kitchen table to wait for Regina.

He was stunned for the second time in a very few minutes. This time the images on the small television gripped him with apprehension as cameras scanned the storm damage. He had no idea that it had been that bad while he was out.

He went into the game room to monitor the storm on the big TV, feeling helpless that there was nothing he could do to ensure his family members' safety. A camera focused on the Red Cross building where the windows had been blown out. Another camera showed how all of the patrol cars on the police department parking lot had been tossed around like so many Matchbox cars. The odd thing was, only the rear windows were blown out of the cars.

Veronica called during a lull in the storm. "I guess you know that our flight out has been canceled. Let's plan to leave at about eight o'clock in the morning."

Thomas hesitated before saying, "Veronica, I'm looking for Regina. Have you seen or heard from her today?"

"No, I had my secretary call yesterday to confirm our departure time. But we haven't heard from her today. You know that we can't go back to the Raven Center. The roof's been taken off. I'm using an office in the presidential suite to reorganize our trip."

At that point the line went dead and power in the house was lost. Thomas went back to the kitchen for the battery-powered television. The hyperexcited weather forecaster was talking enthusiastically, telling viewers the storms were gaining in intensity and power. He said, "Hail, high winds, and rain are pounding the midstate area. Nine dark, fast-moving funnel clouds have been spotted in eight different counties. One cut a half-mile path across the Renaissance campus, taking the roof off of the Raven Center. No injuries were reported."

Thomas sat mesmerized before the TV for more than an hour. As the time neared for area schools to be dismissed, an emergency bulletin advised parents to refrain from going to or calling the schools. According to the report, it was safer for the children to be in their secure school buildings than to be in transit. The reporter assured listeners that his channel would notify parents when it was deemed safe for children to travel. For now they were safe, the announcer concluded.

Another newsperson interrupted the continuous weather broadcast to report that one of the tallest buildings in downtown Nashville had collapsed, damaging a whole parking lot of cars. Fortunately, there were no casualties. At five o'clock a report alerted parents that children could finally be released from their schools.

Concerned that he'd miss Regina's call, Thomas tried her cell phone number for the hundredth time. Getting no answer, he double-checked the power in his phone before heading to pick up the boys from school. Traffic was horrendous. Low electrical wires blocked several streets and Thomas had to back away and try alternative routes.

When he finally reached the major thoroughfares, signals were out, causing more traffic jams. The torrential rains continued and the sky remained dark. Thomas watched the funnel clouds as he drove toward the school. In the snarled traffic, he was only able to inch toward the school.

Finally at six o'clock he had his boys in the car with him. Both tried to tell him what they'd seen at the same time. The fright in their eyes was unmistakable. "Where's Mommy?" Tres asked after he'd calmed down.

"I don't know," Thomas replied honestly.

"Is she still sick?" Tres asked.

"Did she go out of town without saying good-bye to us? Did she leave already since we're late getting home?" Justin asked, trying to reason about his missing mother.

"No. She hasn't left town. She wasn't at home when I got home. Maybe she went to the mall and is waiting until it's safe to drive. It's really not safe yet," Thomas said. "I wanted to see you guys so badly that I came to get you."

By the time Thomas got the kids home, he understood what Regina endured every day with their double-teaming relentless questions. As soon as you answered a question from one of the boys, the other hit you with one from another direction.

After he'd fed the boys and gotten them settled, he was nearly paralyzed with fear. He heard a report that the roof had blown off the mall closest to their home. However, there was no guarantee that Regina would have gone to that mall. She had no loyalty to any particular one.

He paced the game room while the boys played. Their power had been restored and the appliances were humming again. Thomas went to the bedroom and found her phone book. He felt ridiculous calling her friends and acquaintances, but he couldn't let his ego endanger Regina. He had to ask.

He called Jimmy Bob, Kent, Alison, Rosemary, Shelby, the Morgans, everyone that she knew locally. Then he called the Drummonds again. Tiffany answered the phone and told Thomas that she had not heard anything from Regina. Then she covered the phone and asked Andre if she'd stopped by his office or called him. His answer was also negative.

In desperation Thomas called the area hospitals. Nothing. No unidentified patients had been brought in. He was reassured with the information that although the storm was severe, it was without casualties or injuries at this point.

Sitting on the side of their bed, he decided to call Julia. "We've had tornadoes here all day, Julia, and I can't find Regina. I don't want to worry you, but I wondered if you'd talked to her today. Perhaps she mentioned her plans for the day," he said tentatively.

"No, I haven't talked to her since Sunday. You'd better find my baby. Do you need for me to come up there?" Julia asked nervously.

"No, ma'am. Maybe she told me something and I just don't remember," he hedged.

"I know you better than that, Thomas Simmons. If she told you something, you'd remember. I know how much you love my daughter even if she doesn't," Julia said.

"She doesn't know how much I love her?"

"Have you ever told her that you love her?" Julia asked in a straightforward manner reminiscent of Regina's.

When he did not answer right away, Julia continued, "You won't talk to me about very personal things and you don't have to either. But you two have to talk with each other. Now you go find my baby and tell her to call me," Julia said. "And, Thomas, there's one other thing that you may need to know in case—in case there's been an accident."

"About the baby?" he asked.

"Yes—oh, thank God, she finally told you. I was so worried that she was waiting too long. I'll let you go now. Be sure to call me back."

Taking a quick look at the clock on the dresser, Thomas headed downstairs to get the boys. It was way past their bedtime. This was totally unlike Regina. Even when she was angry with him, she did not stay away from home. She liked for him to see how angry she was.

After the boys had showered he went up and listened to them pray before tucking them in. "I'm very worried about Mommy," Tres said. "Do you think she left because I asked about my other mommy?"

"No, son. She was happy to talk with you about your other mommy. I had a hard time talking about your other mommy because I didn't understand why she had to leave us. But Mommy understood that you needed to talk with someone and she tried to help you understand."

"Yeah. She told us about heaven. She told us that heaven is a good place," Justin said.

"Maybe she went to heaven with my other mommy," Tres said.

"No, I don't think so. She would say good-bye to you first," Thomas said.

"Did my first mommy say good-bye first?"

"Yes, she said she loved you very much and told you that she would always love you," Thomas said without the usual pain he felt when Tres asked him questions.

The phone rang as he left the boys' bedroom. He dashed to his bedside table to answer it.

"Hello, Coach, this is Mark Greer. Dr. Morgan told me to call you to see if I can help you locate your wife," the chief of the campus police department told Thomas briskly.

"I appreciate your help."

"What kind of car was she driving and what is her license plate number?" the captain asked succinctly.

Thomas provided the information and the captain said, "I'll phone this in to the Metro police department in case she's stranded. You know how the flash flooding is around here."

"Thanks, Captain, I owe you," Thomas said, feeling a little relief.

"By the way, do you think that she may have been on campus?"

"I don't think so. But again, I don't know. I actually

thought that she was at home packing for a flight out for the game," Thomas replied.

"Well, you know how women are. Sometimes they get it in their heads to do something and they just do it."

That's right, Thomas thought when the conversation ended. Regina was used to being independent and doing whatever it was in her mind to do. *Now what is it that she wanted to do today?* He thought back over the morning and the strain between them.

In the tiny closet in the Raven Center, Regina was straining to see her watch. She couldn't see the time, but knew that she'd been in the closet for hours. She tried with all of her strength to push the door open, but it would not budge. She was sealed in. Her feet and clothes were wet because water had seeped in under the door. At first the howling wind had sounded as if it were in the building with her. Then she'd heard several loud crashes. Now she heard absolutely nothing.

She climbed up on boxes of toilet paper and wished that she'd at least brought the food in with her. Instead she had left it sitting on Thomas's desk when she'd fled to safety. Her purse with the cell phone and mints was sitting right next to the plates of food. Her intense hunger was greater than the discomfort of being soaked to the skin from the waist down was. Usually she tried to eat something for breakfast, but this morning after her bout of nausea had passed, it had been too close to lunchtime. Then she'd put off eating because she'd wanted to have lunch with Thomas.

To entertain herself she sang songs and tried to recite as many scriptures as she knew. In between singing and talking to herself she prayed. "God, thank you for all you've given me. I have a wonderful, adorable husband whom I love. Please let me be able to go home

and love him again. I won't ask for anything more
from him, dear Lord. Please let my sons be safe wherever they are. Lord, please let me get out of here so
that I can take care of my children. Please let the baby
that's still in my womb be okay."

After each prayer she felt a bit calmer. She knew that
straining on the door too hard would not move the
door and could cause injury to the baby. So she made
a resolution to wait. Someone would find her before
she starved to death.

She closed her eyes and composed a song for Alison's new album:

> *"There's a dark cloud a-comin', Mr. Death Angel.*
> *Please don't stop me from running.*
>
> *The lightning strike not far away, Mr. Death Angel.*
> *Please let me make it one more day.*
>
> *Rain's fallin' on my face, Mr. Death Angel.*
> *Please stay away from this place.*
>
> *Have mercy on me please, please have mercy on me."*

Thomas looked around their bedroom after talking
with Captain Greer. She had not even started packing
for their trip. He wondered if there was any significance
in that. She'd felt so bad that morning that maybe she'd
decided not to go. Or maybe she'd decided not to go because she didn't want to be with him.

Looking in the walk-in closets that were stuffed with
her clothes, he hadn't a clue as to what she might have
been wearing. A quick glance in her jewelry box told
him that she was wearing her wedding ring. He wondered why his mind had gone in that direction.

Surveying their bedroom a final time, he turned off the lights and headed back downstairs. He stopped in the living room, her music room, and looked at the portrait of Paulette. "You would have really liked Regina," he told the photograph. "She's a real energetic, outgoing person. She'll help Tres keep your memory." He smiled at the photo with a new kind of ache in his heart before turning away.

The scored music sheets on the piano caught his attention. He knew that Regina had been writing again, but he'd not paid much attention. He picked the sheets up and read the words to "What Am I Supposed to Do?"

What am I supposed to do when you hold me and she's in between me and you?

When I can never touch the part of your mind I need so much?

When in your heart you hold in special reserve for her the truly sacred part?

When her voice is not a memory but a song so loud that you can't hear me?

When so strong is her fragrance it's intoxicating to you even when we dance?

When her touch is the one lightly, gently, tenderly constantly stirring you?

When the one you hold so dear, so good, so special, so sweet is the one who's no longer here?

He looked at the words and tears formed in his eyes as a gut-wrenching pain swept through him. His pain was quickly compounded by feelings of deep remorse. He'd been so busy trying to keep his word to Paulette that he'd almost destroyed the love that he had here and now. Almost like a breeze sweeping over him, he instantly knew what Regina had been experiencing. He had a keen awareness of what she'd been asking for and he'd denied her.

Filled with a desire to find Regina immediately, he called their neighbor, apologizing for calling at such a late hour. After explaining that Regina was missing he asked if their daughter, Keisha, could stay at the house with the boys while he looked for Regina.

At ten o'clock the rain stopped completely, but tree limbs, wires, and other debris still littered the streets. He drove to the nearest mall and looked to see if her car was on any of the surrounding lots. Nothing. Driving around a second mall and still not seeing the Volvo, he decided to go farther north, almost to Goodlettsville to the mall out there. Nothing ventured, nothing gained, he thought as he drove the nearly deserted Interstate 65.

Why would she leave and not tell him where she was going? Maybe she'd left a message for him on his office voice mail. Checking it on his cell phone, he learned she hadn't. Surely she would have called if she was doing something outside her normal routine. She had been angry with him, but they always told each other their plans out of concern for the boys. The only reason that she would not leave a message for him was that she was going to see him.

Perhaps she'd gone to his office. She would have left him a note there. As he neared the campus, he was shocked by the devastation there. Trees had been uprooted and bricks lay in the middle of the road where some buildings had been nearly destroyed. He was driving slowly toward his office when his cell phone rang.

"Coach, meet me at the baseball field near the Raven Center. One of our officers has spotted your wife's car out near left field," Captain Greer's brisk voice instructed him.

"I'm already on campus. I'll be there in five minutes," Thomas replied.

He saw the blue flashing lights first; then he saw the Volvo. The field and everything was completely dark. Apparently, electricity had not been completely restored to the campus. Behind him stood the Raven Center, which was usually illuminated at night, but now was completely dark. A large blue tarp had already been secured to the roof to prevent further damage to the interior of the building.

The car was as battered as if it had been in a head-on collision. The officers confirmed that no one was in it. They'd already searched the field to see if her body had been thrown from the car. Captain Greer pulled up and ordered several of the officers to search the woods surrounding the athletics complex.

Then Captain Greer and Thomas decided to search the building. They entered the battered building, followed by three other officers. Thomas went to his office first and was flooded with relief when he saw Regina's purse sitting on his desk next to a big white bag that contained their lunch.

After his initial relief, Thomas was filled with dread. Something had to have happened to her to keep her from calling or coming to her family. Certain that she was not in his office, they began an office-by-office search of the building. It looked as if it had been turned upside down and shaken. Nothing was in order. Chairs were in the middle of the gymnasium floor. Glass from broken windows was everywhere. Concrete and plaster coated the hardwood floors and walls.

* * *

Regina had been nodding, but she was sure she'd heard the door to the locker room open and close. She sat up and listened. Nothing. Had she missed her chance? She took off one shoe and hopped down from her perch on the toilet paper boxes and beat on the door as hard as she could.

Thomas turned around in the hallway and listened. He'd glanced in the locker room and noted that all of the lockers were lying on the floor, but he'd been positive that no one was in there. He listened again. He heard the steady banging.

"Hey, Mark, get your officers over here. Someone's in the men's locker room," he yelled as he headed back into the room.

Inside the tiny mop closet, Regina could hear movement. "Help me. I'm in the closet!" she yelled.

"I'm here, baby. I'll get you!" Thomas yelled back.

They couldn't get to the door without moving several rows of lockers that had been tossed against it. Darkness filled the room with very little light coming through the starless night sky that was now easily viewed through the decimated roof. Captain Greer ordered the men to go back to their vehicles and bring all of the flashlights.

With flashlights illuminating the room, they stood the lockers upright and dragged them into the hallway. Doing whatever gave them quickest access to the door, they worked steadily, pushing and shoving the heavy metal lockers. An inch of water coated the floor, making the men lose their footing at times. They slipped and sometimes lost their grip on the large metal storage units. After a look at the determined expression on Thomas's face, none of them even considered stopping until his wife was freed.

After more than two hours of work, with steady reassurances to Regina, the door was finally clear. The men stood behind Thomas when he threw it open and was almost knocked over when she sprang into his arms, knocking him backward.

He held her tightly in his arms and said over and over, "Regina, I love you so much. I love you. I love you. I love you."

"Thomas, I'm so sorry for my attitude. I love you, too."

While the couple hugged and kissed, Captain Mark Greer motioned for his men to leave. "It looks like our work here is finished," he said in a loud superhero voice.

Regina looked around Thomas and yelled, "Thank you!"

Without taking his eyes off his precious wife, Thomas yelled, "Thank you, fellas. Thanks for every thing."

He led her to "their bench" where they'd last spent time in the men's locker room. "I know you're tired, baby. Let me look at you for a moment." Then he took her in his arms and covered her with kisses. She felt something different in his kisses. They were more poignant in their sweetness and tenderness. He was totally lost in loving her and she was so glad to be in his arms again that she accepted all of the loving that he had to give her.

"We'd better head for home. Keisha is staying with the kids and it's after midnight," Thomas suggested.

"Why aren't you in New Orleans for your game?" Regina asked. "I figured you might not miss me if you thought that I was going to meet you in New Orleans."

"I was on my way home to talk with you when the first tornado hit and I guess you were on your way to my office," Thomas explained. "At any rate, the team didn't fly out tonight."

After he'd helped Regina got into the Navigator, Thomas took a blanket from the back and wrapped it around her. "Maybe you should take off those wet clothes before you get chilled," he suggested.

"You'll try anything to get me out of my clothes," she teased through chattering teeth and trembling lips.

"No, Regina, it's not like that. I love you so much that I want to be with you any way I can," he answered sincerely. "You and our baby."

Chapter 17

"The baby?" Regina repeated. "How do you know about the baby?"

"First I took a message for you from Tiffany, who left an obstetrician's number for you. I was still pretty unconvinced after I talked with Tiffany. You know, the vasectomy and all. But then I got a call from Julia. With Julia, there is no misunderstanding. She told me that I'd better get out and find you and her grandbaby," Thomas explained.

"Well, what do you think?" she asked nervously.

Thomas pulled the SUV to the side of the road and stopped. "I think it's wonderful, baby," he said, pulling tighter around her the blanket that he'd wrapped her in. "I guess I can understand why you hadn't told me, but I feel awful that you didn't feel that you could."

"Did you admit to yourself that you loved me before you knew about the baby?" she asked.

He asked her, "Why do you need to know that?"

"Because I wasn't sure if you wanted the baby. I didn't want the baby to influence how you felt about me. If you were going to love me, I wanted you to love me and not just say it because of the baby. But if you didn't love me, I wanted to know before I told you about the baby."

"Did you think that I would leave you if you were pregnant?" Thomas asked, horrified.

"I didn't think so. But I haven't been sure of anything these past few weeks," Regina answered honestly.

"Regina, baby, I'd never leave you. There is certainly no way that I would walk away from an unborn child and I can't let you take my sons from me. So I guess we have to plan on staying together forever."

"Thomas, I—" Regina began.

"Baby, we have all night to talk. Let's get you home before you get chilled," he said, pulling back on to the road.

At home he tenderly removed her soiled clothing before helping her into a tub of warm water. That night they spent hours talking and shaking the glass and debris from her hair. He was so tender with her, trembling with the thought of almost losing her. Yet he couldn't wait to begin talking—the thing that they'd needed to do for so long, but neither knew how to begin.

"Regina, things are so much clearer to me now," Thomas said, anxious to start their conversation as he used tweezers to pick the larger pieces of glass from her hair. They were afraid that her scalp would be cut if he washed her hair or rubbed her scalp in any way.

"What is it that you understand?" Regina asked.

"Why you needed to hear me say that I love you. I didn't realize how important those words could be. Now I know that you were asking me if I am totally committed to you and you alone, forsaking all others. That's what love is to you, isn't it?" he asked earnestly, hoping he'd finally learned the lesson.

"Yes, Thomas, that's part of it. I love you so much, but I need to know that you are just as deeply invested in this relationship as I am. I had to give up my independence, and to a certain extent my way of life, when we married.

I'd do it all again in a minute, but I need to know that you love me. With your love, I can keep on giving and giving, like that big pink bunny. Without your love, I will wither away to nothing," she said, finally finding a voice to explain her needs and emotions.

"Baby, I didn't know," he said, shaking his head sadly. "I thought our marriage was just fine. I couldn't understand how you could want more."

"I felt guilty for wanting more," she admitted. "But I was going through a lot of changes. I had become a full-time mother, I was writing very little music, and everyone in town knew me as the coach's wife. All of those things took some adjustment. And I didn't know how committed you were to the whole thing. I knew that you wanted to be married. I didn't doubt that. But I needed to know that you were willing to work to make the marriage gratifying for both of us. Do you understand what I mean?"

"I think I do, but it took forever for me to figure it out. I thought that since you knew how much I needed you and depended on you, that was good enough. I figured that all a man had to do was be good to his wife and she should be happy. When I realized that you didn't need me to take care of you financially, I was somewhat apprehensive."

"I'll say." Regina laughed. "You were more than a little apprehensive. You freaked out. I had no idea that your male ego was so fragile."

"Well, now you know it. The male ego is fragile, so handle it with care. But you have to admit, I was good to you and we enjoyed being together. Everything between us was all right, as far as I was concerned. The money thing didn't seem to bother you, so I decided not to let it bother me."

"Money comes and goes," Regina said nonchalantly. "I believe I can always get more money if I work hard enough. It's the people in my life who are important to me."

"And you made me feel important. Everything was going so well that when you started changing, I couldn't believe that you wanted more than romance or sex. In fact, I couldn't believe that I wanted more than romance and sex until I had to live without hearing you tell me that you love me every day," Thomas explained.

"I just couldn't say it anymore. The words stuck in my throat. I needed something to respond to. I needed to be able to say, *I love you too,* for a change. I felt that you cared for me, but I couldn't get you to that other level of commitment. The one that's unconditional, forsaking all others and surpassing all thought. That oneness that I thought we should have. When I entered our marriage, I thought that since we were already good friends, liked one another, and desired one another, marriage would be a breeze. I was surprised that wasn't enough. I tried not to complain, but you know I'm not used to playing second fiddle," Regina said.

"I shouldn't have let Paulette come between us. I was caught up in guilt and misguided devotion. I felt guilty because Paulette didn't want to go to Japan and I'd forced her to go. She wanted me to play in the NBA, but I knew that I would never be a starting player here. The offer in Japan was great. There I was a star. I received premium pay because I was one of only two Americans on the team. The crowds loved me and everywhere I went, people asked for my autograph. When Paulette became ill, it was a while before I realized that it was something serious. She was misdiagnosed several times and by the time they figured out what it was, she was pregnant. I felt like a real dog," Thomas said, looking embarrassed.

"It must have been hard carrying guilt all of this time," Regina said, hoping to alleviate his embarrassment. She stilled his hand working in her hair and looked at him with compassion in her eyes.

"That's not the half of it," Thomas continued, anxious to get his story out. He turned her head again so that he could continue his careful ministrations in her hair. "When she was finally diagnosed with lupus, the treatment made her afraid that she'd miscarry so she refused treatment until after Tres was born. Her doctor suggested an abortion, but she was in her second trimester by that time. After Tres was born, her illness had advanced to the point that she couldn't even take care of him. That's when I matured a little and made the decision to return to the States."

"That seems like a smart move," she assured him. "What happened when you moved back?"

"My plan was to play for the NBA. I had been such a big star in Japan that several NBA teams were looking at me. But by the time we were settled, Paulette was frequently bedridden. I hired someone to take care of Tres, and our parents would come stay with Paulette, but I realized that taking care of them was my job. So I heard about the position at St. Luke's, got the interview, and was hired on the spot. I thought I was being noble, but it seems that everything I did was too little too late," he related regretfully. He shook his head and paused for several minutes.

Regina felt that he needed to tell the whole story in order to purge his guilt. She raised her head from his lap and looked at him, taking his hand to comfort him, and asked, "What else could you have done? Did you know that her illness was terminal then?"

"No, I didn't. Most people live very long lives with lupus. It's seldom terminal anymore. We still thought with treatment and rest she would get better. But her condition worsened in stages. Her final stage was when her kidneys failed. When the doctors told Paulette that her kidneys were no longer functioning, she was so brave. She went through dialysis three times a week, six hours a day, until her veins collapsed and her body resisted the tubes. Even in her weakened condition, she'd hold Tres and tell him how much she loved him."

"You need to tell Tres about that. He needs to hear it. Thomas, I think you should share your memories with Tres. I won't feel left out if that's what bothers you. Not saying Paulette's name bothers me more," Regina said through tears.

"Some of the memories are too painful to share. Every day she would dress and comb her hair until her clothes began to hang on her and she lost her hair. She had a big patch across her face and she worried that I no longer found her attractive. She was worried about what I thought and she was fighting a battle for her life. I admired her courage and determination. She suffered so much, Regina. While she was dying, I promised her that I'd love her forever. I promised her that no other woman would ever take her place," Thomas said, his voice now husky with unshed tears.

"Thomas, I never wanted to take Paulette's place," Regina whispered.

"I know, baby, but you are more mature than I am. You understand that people can love more than one person in a lifetime. It took me a while to figure that out. But Paulette knew it too. I am so blessed to have been married to two such smart women. Paulette knew she was dying and had become reconciled to the inevitable. I insisted that I would never love anyone again and she shook her head and whispered that I shouldn't make promises that I couldn't keep. But I constantly swore that I would never love anyone else."

"You were trying to comfort her in the only way you knew how," Regina reasoned. "You'd made a vow to her and you wanted to assure her that that wouldn't change although everything around you was changing."

"That may be true, but at the time I meant it. I loved Paulette so much. I never imagined that I could love like that again. Nor did I ever again want to experience the excruciating pain of losing someone whom I loved so much."

"Then we met?" she supplied.

"Yes. And then I met you and you turned my world upside down. I was totally confused because my rational mind said, *No way*, but my heart wouldn't let you go. You were glowing with good health and sparkling personality. I felt so guilty that I kept denying I had feelings for you, but I fell in love with you anyway. I fell in love with you so hard and fast that I didn't recognize what happened. So I kept denying that it was love. You said that we were just friends so I thought that we had a very good friendship."

"Yes, *very* good friends." Regina laughed. "I thought that we could pull off that friendship plan, too."

"Yesterday, while I was looking for you during the tornado, I realized that my love for you is much different than the love I had for Paulette. It's a mature, unselfish, complete love. I thought that I had a choice in marrying you. I never had a choice. You, Regina, are a woman to be loved. And I love you. There's no way that I could have lived the rest of my life without you," Thomas said. His hands had long ago stopped picking debris out of her hair. He pulled her into his arms and looked intently at his almond-eyed beauty.

"Did you think that by not saying the words, you would not be in love with me?" Regina asked.

"I don't know what I thought," Thomas said. "I was

trying to keep an old promise, but I couldn't stop loving you."

"Thomas, I love you so much!" she exclaimed, wrapping her arms around his neck.

"I have one more question," he said after she had loosened her grip around his neck. "If I had never said that I love you, when were you going to tell me about the baby?"

"On the way to the delivery room," she said, laughing.

"I noticed your breasts are getting bigger," he said, reaching into her robe and stroking one.

"I wondered when you were going to put two and two together. You know, the morning sickness and my breasts bubbling out of my bras."

"The vasectomy had me too confident. It fooled me," he explained.

"I'm glad you don't have to live with a decision you made under such stressful conditions," Regina said with a sigh.

"Our child is going to be so beautiful," Thomas said, looking at Regina lustfully. "If it's a girl, I hope she looks just like her mother." He kissed her upraised lips gently.

Epilogue

Julia Nadine Simmons was a considerate baby. She made her entrance into the world in early October so that her mother would be able to travel with her father when baskertball season began again. The family learned to travel with disposable bottles and a baby-sitter. The sitter was necessary so that the parents could indulge in their postgame activities. By the time the season was over, the baby already had her father wrapped around her chubby little finger.

Her brothers were a different story. At first they were afraid to touch her. Next they decided that she was an exciting new live-action toy or a wonderful, round bas-ketball. Finally, Julia Nadine took matters in hand and taught the boys that she responded best if they played finger games with her, sang to her, or let her watch them in their antics. To show them that they were on the right track, she would gurgle and laugh, delighting them when they did as she expected.

Though she wasn't exactly thrilled with the name Julia Nadine, she accepted it. Especially after her mother told her that her father had wanted to name her Miracle. He reasoned that it was a miracle she was conceived, given his vasectomy. Further, it was a mira-cle that she was born after her mother's tornado ordeal. And it was an even greater miracle that she survived the couple's trials during the early months of her gestation. However, Regina had prevailed and Thomas had finally compromised, accepting the name Julia Nadine.

Thomas accepted her name, but the little girl never developed a fondness for it. She accepted the Julia because it could easily be shortened to J or Dr. J, as everyone called her as soon as she was old enough to walk and dribble.

During the spring before Julia Nadine was born, the family moved into a big five-bedroom house, with a music room for Regina and another dedicated to playing for all the other Simmonses. However, it was no longer called the "men's room" because it was a part of Julia Nadine's territory, too.

In the new house, Justin proudly displayed his framed birth certificate on his bedroom wall. He was glad to be a member of the Simmons family, sharing the same surname as all the other family members.

In the new season, Thomas did bring the NCAA trophy to Nashville.

Dear Readers:

I hope that you found Regina and Thomas's story as entertaining as I did. It was fun setting the story in Nashville, my hometown, and exposing some of our popular locations. I wanted to use this novel as an opportunity to tell about the role of blacks in country music. For too long, the contributions that African-Americans have made to that musical style have been hidden.

If you have never thought about country music as a genre that you would enjoy listening to, you may wonder if my story line is purely fictional or if blacks are actually interested in country music. A recent survey showed that nearly 25 percent of African-American adults in major markets listen to country radio. Not only are we listeners, but there are many black performers. Emily Harris taught me that talent has many tunes.

It is my sincere wish that *Sweet Desire* entertained you and perhaps enlightened you in some way. Please let me know what you thought of my writing debut. You may e-mail me: ChristineTownsend6l5@yahoo.com. If you prefer snail mail the address is P.O. Box 330555, Nashville, TN 37203. Please visit my Web site: www.ChristineTownsend.com.

Warmest regards,
Christine Townsend

ABOUT THE AUTHOR

Christine Townsend lives in Tennessee with her wonderfully supportive husband and two creative children. She grew up in a family of storytellers who enjoyed entertaining one another with dramatic and comical stories. As an adult, Christine enjoys weaving compelling tales of how couples meet and sustain their love. She invites you to visit her Web site: www.ChristineTownsend.com.